Awakening

Rejected Mate

L.T.MARSHALL

Pict Publishing
Empowered Voices

Just Rose

The Carrero Series

Jake & Emma

The Carrero Effect ˜ The Promotion

The Carrero Influence ˜ Redefining Rules

The Carrero Solution ˜ Starting Over

Arrick & Sophie

The Carrero Heart ˜ Beginning

The Carrero Heart ˜ The Journey

The Carrero Heart ˜ Happy Ever Afters

Alexi & Camilla

The Carrero Contract ˜ Selling Your Soul

The Carrero Contract ˜ Amending Agreements

The Carrero Contract ˜ Finding Freedom

Bonus Books

Jake's View

Arrick's View

You challenged me to something different, so here it is.
To the fan group and all my Weirdos and Warriors, enduring
lockdown together has been memorable.

ALORA

You know those stories about unwanted rejects whose loved ones either died or abandoned them to drift aimlessly through the world? A worthless no one,
almost invisible to other people. There is nothing spectacular about them, no grand rise from nothing to something as they dawn into adulthood.

Yeah, well, that's kind of my story.

My name is Alora Dennison, and I am literally hours away from my Awakening Ceremony at the ripe old age of eighteen, with absolutely no one who gives a crap about me to be there; no support, no family, and definitely no friends. I'm a late bloomer, I guess. Not that it's unusual in my bloodline, as almost every female in my family didn't 'come out' until they hit their late teens, from what I can remember. Much like the others in the orphanage, stuck here with me. Another reason we are snubbed and left to our own devices in this hellhole they call a home.

My ceremony has me churned up inside and restlessly pacing the room I share with Vanka. She's like me, although in all the years we've bunked together, I can't say we have ever become friends of any kind. She makes it clear she doesn't like me and, much like everyone around me, they all keep their distance. We tolerate one another, but none of us has ever bonded.

1

I'm an orphaned no-one whose parents died in the war ten years ago against the vampires. So is she, but it didn't warm her to me in any way. I guess because she's from a leg of the Santo pack, and they have hated the Whyte pack since long before the war. We were feuding before the vampires united every one of us, and old scars and grudges are not something that wolves let go of quickly.

We were two small girls left with no immediate blood link guardians, put in this place for unwanted cubs to live out our days in unexceptional ways. It would have been kinder to end our misery back then than leave us to live as outcasts among our people, our own kind. Shunned because we are the shameful proof that their packs failed them. I don't think they knew what else to do with us. So many young with no one left to care for them and raise them in our ways and seen as cursed. They were ashamed of the failings of our families, and we are the ones to carry that burden like an eternal black mark painted on our faces.

I'm amazed that kids like us even get to go through with the ceremony. I mean, it's kind of a big deal, and we are kind of not. We're a bit like the lost boys in Neverland, except ... none of us wants to stay here, and growing up is the only way out.

Your Awakening is a bit like graduation, in a sense. A passing from child to adult and usually where you would find your place, rank, in the pack, and get a mate. I have no delusions that it means anything of the sort for any of us turning tonight. There are four from the unwanted home, and I hear maybe three from the packs around. Just a handful of kids trying to break free, find their path, and all in the fabulous presence of the entire 'Packdom.'

The Packdom being the dozen or so wolf tribes from the state. They all have to convene on Shadow Rock to watch you transform fully for the first time under the first full moon of your birth month. It's not hard to figure out when you're ready. In the weeks running up to your birthday, you start to change in small ways, and, goddamn, it hurts like having your insides snapped and stretched in fits of severe twisting pain and zero control over it happening.

The signs are pretty clear to all. Kind of like puberty for werewolves, I guess. Maturing, physical improvements, and a

2

massive rise in appetite and aggression. Little moments where you start to transform painfully, and then it dissipates as quickly, so you never really reach the first transition, but it's reported, and no one can hide it. The pain you know will come with the first time; it's saved for the full moon after your birthday.

Some don't go through it until later in life, and some earlier. Usually, it is a sign of where you stand in the hierarchy when you turn. According to the Santo elders, the longer it takes, the weaker your DNA, but my parents never mentioned it when I was young. So, being eighteen puts me way down on the pecking order and confirms my bloodline was not that of warriors or strong enough to be anything of importance. Vanka is sixteen, and she too is turning tonight, but with Santo's blood somewhere in her veins, she should have turned far earlier. I guess whatever mix is in her is why they reject her as one of their own.

I mean, look at the Santos. They are the reigning pack in the state, and everyone in their bloodline turned before ten. Colton, the next heir as Alpha, is nineteen years old, lords over all in our kingdom, and he has been running with the pack since he was a mere eight years old.

Every single one of his family returned from the wars, which speaks volumes about the purity of their genes, strength, and abilities in battle. He's destined to take over from his father as Alpha one day, and the way things are heading, he won't just be Alpha of the Santo pack, but all of us. Something that has never happened in our lifetime but will begin a new dawn in how the packs live.

Santo is not a nice guy. None of them are. He walks around surrounded by his sub pack, looks down at the likes of us, and never makes eye contact or responds to anyone below his station. That's how it works here. Dominance and strength are everything to wolves. He has his father's arrogance, and he knows that every female hitting puberty is craving to become his mate. He hasn't officially paired or marked yet, and despite having the same girl always by his side, he's fair game until he does.

Faultlessly good-looking in that dark Latino, pretty boy way with far too handsome a face. He's over six feet of muscle and radiates aggression without trying, and is a rare black-furred wolf on turning, one of the largest among us. I think the one time he acknowledged my existence was the day he pushed me out of his way in passing. I tripped in front of him in the hallway to the great hall, and he didn't bat an eye or miss a step in shoving me back aggressively like I was a lightweight piece of trash. All the girls laughed at me when I landed on my ass and skidded back into the trashcan, and I've made sure to never get in his way again.

Not that we have much time in the same place. I live in the orphanage and go to the school built purely for our kind, away from 'normal' people. He was ahead of me by one year, so we didn't often cross paths in all that time, and since he lives with his pack on the south side of the mountain, only coming to the shadowy north when required, I never see him or any of his subordinates. Like all the rest of the people who avoid the 'Rejects.'

After the Great War, our people moved from all surrounding areas and convened nearer the mountain. Keeping close to stay protected and no one ever left again. His father is the unofficial Dominant Alpha and likes to check in with all on the mountain when he sees fit. Since Colton graduated from school, we only see him for official visits at his father's side. Lording over their newfound kingdom of obedient and submissive packs, keeping law and order.

Rumor has it the vampires have been brewing and gathering for several months, maybe even years, to regain numbers and launch a new war on our kind. We always knew they would. I mean, we won the battle, but we didn't defeat them in the way we wanted. Many survived and fled and have been out there for almost ten years, recovering from it and licking their wounds. It's been quiet for so long, eerily so, but there is so much unease and unrest in the air that the packs called together a meeting a month back to decide the fate of our future. Trouble stirring, and we could all feel it, our senses on high alert and that vibe that something huge was coming. They think coming together to create one pack and one unity is the answer to a brewing war. Not that it changes much, as we have been living almost that way for a decade.

4

We were never united before under one Alpha, though. We fought as separate packs, and it almost wiped us out. There was no leadership, and it meant packs like mine, known for peaceful living and farming, were virtually annihilated. Many of our kin never returned, and it forever changed those who did. Those like me, who lost everyone, my parents, grandparents, uncles, and my brother, are shunned by people who like to pretend it never happened. My family was lost, none of them came back, and therefore, in the eyes of the pack hierarchy ... my bloodline is weak. They don't want to claim us as their kind anymore, and they sure as hell don't want us procreating and spreading our genes to future wolves.

Warriors came home. The weak did not.

We were never ready for it.

They were farmers; they were peaceful and had never had to fight in their lives. Like human legends and stories dictate, not all wolves are savage killing machines or feral beasts. Some are quiet, land-loving people who never want to experience the thrill of a hunt or the warm blood of another being in raw savagery. In a whirlwind of months, we were dragged into a battle to the death, and children were left in the care of the old and frail or the pregnant.

We waited endlessly to find out who of our loved ones would come home to us until one lone night. When the people who cared for me in their absence, the last of the Whytes who were too vulnerable to follow them, were slaughtered by invading vampires in our own homes. On the far edge of the farmlands, I was a lone survivor who was then shunted to the orphanage. The events of that night are so foggy and hazy. I don't really remember it or why I was even spared. I was just a child.

I still remember the agony of the day I watched others return en masse, the battle truly over with the vampires in retreat, and no one, not a single person from my bloodline, came home. An entire pack of over forty people I called my own was all gone, everything I knew ... every single last one of them. I was all alone.

There is no pain compared to an eight-year-old child learning that everyone she ever loved and was protected by was never coming home for her. My security was shattered and my future dead, and all I have known since was the isolation and solitude of being one of the many who were thrown here to rot.

So now here we are, a house full of teens who bear the only living connection to our past loved ones. A mixed bunch of leftovers, but no one in the packs will bond to us for fear of producing weaker offspring. It's all about dominance in our world and power, standing, and ability. DNA is everything. They call us the Reject Pack, which sums up exactly why we are overlooked.

We don't belong to anyone anymore, even though by rights we should be part of the united wolf community, this new singular pack location bonds us after all. We're not, though; they see us as cursed children and deny our mere existence, throwing us to the dark-shaded side of the mountain, so they don't have to see us. This house is the only home we know now, and the people who care for us do so out of duty but not love. They're afraid we curse them by proximity.

It's forbidden to abandon a pack child, even if they come from a shamed bloodline. The Fates and traditions have laws and rules from old that we have to abide by, and abandoning the vulnerable is abhorrent. So, we are given a home, shelter, food, and education. Basic care on the understanding that we get to leave upon our awakening. Severed like a rotting limb.

We can go out, find our path, and fend for ourselves. Turning gives us gifts and abilities to go it alone. Find a pack who wants us, if that is even possible. Solves their problem and shirks off any responsibility they have for us, which sucks if you happen to turn at a young age while caught here with us.

So, that's where I am now. Just a mere four hours before we have to climb to Shadow Rock for the full moon, and I'll transform for the first time in my life. Changing from child to woman and my gifts will manifest along with the first emerging of my entire wolf self and whatever that will look like. Not that I have any clue what those will be if any at all. Not all of us have a special gift, and it's unlikely I will. My parents never talked of theirs.

I've watched this ceremony once a month for many years, and it still terrifies me to know I will be one of them. Finally, standing in the center, terrified of what the new light will bring. It's a blood moon tonight, meant to be symbolic or biblical or some nonsense. Signaling the end of times. Not that I paid attention to our lunar studies, as they held little importance to me.

With a first transformation comes pain and a lot of it. It's inevitable. You hear the cracking of bones, the tearing of flesh, and the howling of those going through it, haunting you for eternity. It's awful to see, it traumatized me the first time as I was still so young, but they tell us it only hurts that way the first time. After, we'll be different, and the pain will be far less clawing because we can heal and withstand it so much more as a stronger breed.

I've seen it. Physical improvement, they call it. It's the leaving of childlike features behind, firming up, muscling over as though somehow you get an injection of superhuman enhancement. All who have turned become superior in every way, even in terms of attractiveness, which explains why most females consider 'Lord' Colton, a god. His genes are strong.

Not that I want to change. I'm already tall, slim, and athletic, and I wouldn't say I was ugly. I'm on the pretty side of plain, with full lips, mousy brown hair, and abnormally green eyes. I take after my mother, and when I look in the mirror, I'm haunted by her memory in the most bittersweet way. Proud to carry her face with me but broken that it reminds me of what I've lost.

I guess I am what one would call a 'girl next door,' but it's another flaw in my genetic makeup.

The Alphas are all handsome or beautiful and physically perfect. You can't deny good genes when it's shown in every single little way. Compared to humans, they are like gods among men.

Now all I can do is wait.

Shower, dress, brush my hair, and pace like a maniac as I watch the clock and count down the minutes to the first moon of my new future.

This could be the first step in changing everything.

I can leave after tonight; I can walk away from this mountain and the people who treat us like we are nothing. I'll be free to run far away, with no bond to anyone or anything. No one to care if I never return.

I need to get through it first, and then it's the start of a whole new existence for me.

THE AWAKENING

My blood is rushing through my head to the point I have a headache, palms sweaty, and adrenaline
spiking as I follow the path to the top of the cliff on Jell-O legs. Walking in behind the others, like me, who are to go through the ceremony at the highest point of the full moon. I'm breathless, fighting nausea and internal shaking of fear, body trembling, as I watch where I step a little too closely and almost collide with the girl in front of me. Staggering sideways and kicking stones in my path, accidentally, to avoid her.

"Watch where you're going, reject!" The growl of one of our accompanying mentors hits me in the side of the face with an open palm as he leans in close and shoves me back in line harshly. Hard enough to send me crashing into the rock face we are brushing up against, and I almost hit the ground with the force, coughing out a whimper of pain. I catch myself, right my body quickly, ignoring the burning pain of abrasions, and skip two steps to catch up and get back in line while rubbing my bruised arm and shoulder from the collision. Trying not to look his way, knowing if I do, he will probably smack me in the face for showing zero respect to a superior.

One of the Alpha's prominent pack leaders of the subs, one of the Santos. He's called Raymond, and he's around twenty-four. He hates anything to do with us. Another superior wolf from a pure bloodline who sees us as an inconvenience and unworthy to breathe his air.

This is the reality of my life and how little value I have in this hierarchy. Reject is the name for all of us like we don't have separate identities anymore, and I can't wait to be free of these people and this life.

"Halt!" A booming low, and gravelly voice ahead of us stops us all in our tracks as we come to the level top of the cliff known as 'Shadow Rock.' It's more of a large plateau than a rock, but the sun never seems to lay its light and warmth in this nook of the mountain, and yet it gives us a direct and uninterrupted view of the moon every night. It's been the point of this ceremony for hundreds of years, and we're finally here.

I pull myself past the girl in front of me and come to her side to gaze at the familiar scene before us. My stomach churning with the knowledge it's happening. The ceremonial set up of flares and burning fires at points near the ledge are already there and glowing bright, all the way around the curve of this giant platform. Creating a red and amber glow that illuminates the space in what will soon be the wall-to-wall darkness of this still night. The center of the clearing is marked out with symbols in chalk, and a large set of circles surrounds them, one for each of those who are to awaken. I shudder inside as reality hits home that this is it, and I have nowhere to hide. You can't outrun it; there's no way to stop it from happening.

"Clothes off here and put these on." Scratchy gray blankets are thrust into our arms by a tall, muscular Santo, looking down at us with almost black eyes as he snarls his contempt. Walking past as he dishes them out, I am aware that many have gathered around the ledges and above us on the cliffs' edges to watch this. Probably annoyed that they even allow my kind to go through this as everyone else does.

All the packs are here already, and right in the middle stands Juan Santo and his immediates. His second in command, his third, and his son, Colton. The ceremonial Shaman, in full dress, is standing with his staff, awaiting the start of his duties. Something he could do with his eyes closed, I expect, as he has been here for so many years.

I don't wait to question the order, eyes down, nerves frayed, but get to it. I know the drill. I throw it around my shoulders to conceal my body as best I can, the same as the others, and we quickly strip down inside our coverings with haste. Discarding our things into neat piles that we'll return to later.

Transforming rips your clothes to shreds, so being naked is the best way to deal with it. Afterward, we'll be able to get dressed again, but this itchy old blanket is all I have to cover my modesty for now. Not that anyone cares. Nudity among wolves is common and not something they stare at or find abnormal. So many turn in the blink of an eye and come walking back in human form with no covering at all. It's another sign of weakness to be body shy and hide if you have to go home without clothes.

The Alpha types walk around in the nude without worrying, seeing they are physically perfect. The only time it's an issue is if a mate is being ogled by someone who isn't hers. Males are territorial, jealous, and aggressively unpredictable when mated up, so it's typical for regular testosterone fights over looking at each other's women.

It's kind of basic and primal and another reason I won't miss being part of a pack. We're animals by nature, and humans would be disturbed by what is standard among us. I mean, aggression, physical hostility, and even beating each other are not viewed in the same way humans would between married people. Mates fight, sometimes in wolf form, and bites and scratches are usually the best way to resolve disputes.

I undress fast and leave my clothes and shoes in a neat pile between my ankles to stand up, pulling my blanket around me snugly to await the following orders and shield myself from the cool air. Visibly shaking with nerves, I glance around me quickly to see the others' similar fear, pale skin, and solemn faces. I'm not the only one who is terrified. We've all seen how bad this gets, and before the night is out, we will have felt pain incomparable to anything we've been through in our lives.

"Move!" Raymond shoves the male to my left to make him lead the way, and we dutifully follow silently, in a line, to the open clearing and head towards the chalk circles awaiting us. I close my eyes for a second and try to swallow the clawing fear spreading through my veins like ice, my throat dry and itchy with the effort. Holding myself together, I quickly move to the first circle I see as the line in front of me dissipates. Hundreds of eyes are on us as they watch and wait. Silence eery in the oncoming night, and I look up to the sky to find some sort of eternal calm. The moon will be upon us soon enough. Soon it will be dark and dotted with twinkling stars, but for now, it's daylight, and we have to begin.

After everyone shuffles quickly into place and settles, the booming voice of the Shaman breaks the hush as he gestures for us all to sit while he raises his staff. I do as I am told, slide down quickly, and sit cross-legged within my blanket on the cold, hard, gritty ground beneath me. Trying to get enough of the covering underneath me to make it less uncomfortable. I'm aware of the penetrating stares from all around, and I try to blot them all out.

"Drink." Something hard shunts me in my ribs from behind, and I strangle a yelp, sitting upright sharply, and spin my head around to see a wooden cup held out to me. Another Santo shoves it into my hand as I unravel it out to take it.

"What's it for?" I ask innocently, always wondering when we watched from a distance and stupidly naïve to think I'll get any sense from one of them.

"Drink it and find out," he smirks, walking away with no actual answer. I sigh, internally irritated at his attitude, before staring down at the dark amber liquid contained within, its heavy scent of herbs and perfumes wafting up into my face. I spot the others drinking it down fast, without question, and I follow suit.

It tastes like thick gloopy honey, laced with chemicals that burn my throat as I take it down and almost choke on its thicker consistency. I gag but manage to claw myself into staying still and swallowing hard with multiple gulps. Closing my eyes as the taste turns bitter, spreading down my throat and into my stomach, immediately warming them both. I can feel it disperse into my veins and limbs, knocking the cold of the rocks away from anywhere my skin touches, and almost immediately, I get a little dizzy. The

12

ground around me moving and swaying softly, like the sea coming in on the tide.

I shake my head, but it's completely pointless. Hunching forward so I don't fall over, I now understand why every time I watched this, the newest to awaken would sit the whole ceremony slumped down and immobile until they turned. Seemingly oblivious to all the tradition and its stages, the light faded to dark. They have drugged us for the pain, and I start to lose track of everything around me as a veil of surreal sweeps up like a warm fluffy fog and devours me whole.

I don't know how long we are this way or what's happening, as all I can hear is the chant of the Shaman as he dances around, shaking things, singing, and clapping. Vision blurry and coming in waves, my body heavy yet detached, and I no longer feel like I am here or even conscious. Time passes, but I have no clue how fast or slow, and all I know is it gets dark so quickly around me, and I can't seem to stop myself from drifting into space or losing track and fading away. Cocooning me into the little bubble of black space around me, where the smell of fire and incense makes me giddy and sleepy. It's peaceful, yet somehow it's not, and there's a stirring of awareness and fear almost out of reach.

Lulling into a weird semi-sleep state, I can no longer open my eyes or understand what is going on around me. There are warm hands on me, maybe, but I'm not sure. The sudden breeze, although it does nothing to cool my eternal warmth.

Cold liquid and wrinkled hands, as something is smeared across my forehead, making me cringe with a second of reality, and I grasp to focus on the dancing form in front of me. Rattling, blowing smoke, chanting a song as it runs down the bridge of my nose, and I pull from memory that the new turns are marked with a fresh blood kill to prepare for their turn. My face will bear the mark of a wolf from an animal our Alpha will have slaughtered.

The roughness of something pulling across my skin startles me slightly, and then suddenly, I'm levitating out flat or floating, or maybe lying down. No clue anymore. I've never felt anything close to this, not even being drunk for the first time a few months ago when we found some alcohol in the orphanage storage cupboard. I'm too wasted to know what my body is doing, and the heavy, loud tones of the wolf song echo across the mountain as the packs sing to welcome our moon.

The memory of witnessing this many times reminds me they take them and pull the blankets free for the turning, laying them down to be blessed by the full moon, and logically, a part of my brain is telling me this is what is happening. It's almost like I'm no longer attached to my limbs as warm sensation trails firmly across my cheek. A raspy voice comes through the fog at me.

"It's going to hurt ... I can't wait to watch it, Reject. Or maybe I might take advantage of you like this. Finally, get my way." I barely recognize the voice, but gut instinct tells me it's Damon, a boy from the Conran pack who tried to kiss me a year ago. He cornered me in the school hallway, pushed me against the wall, and tried to force me to kiss him while shoving his hand up my dress. I fought him off, leaving him with a nice scratch down his smarmy face, and he has been gunning for me ever since. Not that I marked him badly, we heal fast, but I left a dent in his pride and ego.

I can't react, and as a hot invasive sensation moves down my shoulder, I can only squirm, wanting so badly to get his hands off me. He's not that dumb, though, and with all eyes on us, he leaves me alone to my fate as I try to fight to come back to a sense of now. Suddenly afraid that he will be the one to tend to me like this after this is done. Responsible for ushering me back to my clothes and the concealed shadow of the cliff edge. Who knows what he will do? I don't recall if the turning takes you out of the drug-induced stupor when it's done or not.

I can't dwell on it any longer as a burning light hits me hard over my entire body surface, almost like a blowtorch was turned on, and I spasm instinctively into an arched position on the floor. Every inch of my skin bubbling and blistering to searing levels of torture as though I have been set alight and I strain and claw the ground beneath me, gasping with effort. Breaking nails on rough terrain as I scramble for relief and yet can do nothing but scream.

Crying out in pain, writhing in agony, as an intense sensation rips my skin from my bones and engulfs me. My voice deepens, scraping and hoarse like I'm swallowing splinters, and cries become growls, my throat almost bursting into flames with the effort. For a second, it's like I'm being strangled. I'm under attack. My body is being ravaged, twisted, snapped, and slain, but this isn't another wolf ... this is the turning. It's so much worse than I ever imagined it could be.

Cracking, convulsing, and devastating agony rip through me hellishly. Sending me rolling around to relieve the pain as grime, rocks, and dust scrape at my flesh and burn as I graze across them. I whimper and moan, but it eases nothing of the torture of my body crunching and shredding itself apart. I cry out, beg for my mother to save me, wail for the Fates to stop this, and claw at the rocks, breaking fingers with the sheer force of my fight and gouging what's left of my skin on sharp edges underneath me.

No one could prepare me for what this feels like, and I'm being turned inside out while slow-roasted over an open bed of hot coals. I can't breathe, I can't scream anymore, and silently, I writhe and jerk and twist and turn as I am consumed by hell.

Our noises are drowned out by the stamping, chanting, and clapping of the packs, thundering through the ground and reverberating through my broken, smashed body, giving way to howls as the moon reaches its peak. They encourage us to make the final transition to become like them. Combining to howl, under strict orders that none are to transform tonight and break the ceremony. Only the new shall change tonight. Only our blood will spill as our human form is destroyed to build something better.

I want to die.

The pain is unbearable, driving me to the brink of insanity, and it truly feels like my human self is being tortured to nonexistence. Every bone in my body snaps and reforms as though it's being done manually, one at a time. My flesh tears free and pulls away from the muscle. I'm wet, a hot pouring out as blood drains from the hellish self-inflicted wounds that seem to last forever, covering me in sticky warm heat, smothering me, and leaving a vile metallic scent. I can't tell what's sweat, blood, or maybe other kinds of fluid. I howl and strain with all my might, so I extend my face up into the air and gasp with relief as my lungs inhale and I finally take a breath. Barely holding on, reaching a pinnacle where my mind is on the verge of collapse, and the dregs of sanity teeter on a cliff edge.

And then ... everything is still.

It all stops. Like having a cold drink poured over scorched sunburn, instant soothing hits hard and intensely as my noise becomes silent, my burns become cool, and my breaks become one.

I stop fighting my body. I am aware of the immediate cease of all of it and the eerie quiet that surrounds me so suddenly. The unnatural silence. Hazy and blurry as my head spins, and I grasp for some sense of reality. Catching my breath, gulping in cool air, and calming ambiance as the fog clears, my vision returns only slightly.

I try to get up, right myself, although it feels different and stumble sideways with a disorientated sense of uprightness. I'm on my hands and knees even though I don't know how I got this way. I can't stand or push myself up as I would because it all feels strange, and I blink and shake my head to clear my eyes enough to see which way up I'm facing. I blink, my eyes watering, as finally, dry is restored to moist, and I see forms and shapes and shadows which then define details and more. Confused, yet there is a calm taking over me, a sense of serene with heightened senses in every way.

I gaze down, and I see paws that startle me at first. Gasping at the closeness and realizing they are mine, where my hands should be, flat on the ground. Large, clawed but strong paws, bigger than I thought they would be. I lift one and shake it, almost as if I need to convince myself that I can use and control this limb. It's genuinely connected to my body. My legs are solid, with thick silver-gray fur up my muscular chest. I have a streak of purest snow white that travels as far as I can see. I stare at it, lean back, and pull my chin in tight to follow it until I can't strain any further to see.

I have very little memory of my mother in her true form, but I know this is from her. She was a white and my father a silver, yet it's rare to combine both in such a way. Most wolves are brown or gray

... white is a mutation that's almost unheard of, and my mother used to try to hide because it brought only stares.

Staggering on strange legs and fall flat, splaying out and bumping my undercarriage as I collide with stone. I shake my head, the unfamiliar weight of a different form pulling me from side to side, not entirely in control of my limbs or movements yet, but aware it's so much bigger than my human skull. Aware, suddenly, of the scene around me coming back into focus and realizing we are still being watched. Sobering fast as my new metabolism pushes the last drugs out of my system and cleanses my blood.

The atmosphere is charged, and I'm surrounded by newly changed wolves of all shades of gray and brown, although I'm the only one with white in my coat. Turning as the Shaman's chants draw my eyes back to him, I trip over my uncoordinated self as I try to right myself and get up. It's hard to use my hands as front legs, and I instinctively rear backward too far onto my haunches, lose my balance, and reel forward again to correct it before tumbling face on. I slump to the ground once more and meet the dust with a lower jaw clunk.

"It gets easier. Try to stay on your feet. All four of them." The voice above me pulls my head to tilt towards it, and I recoil as I realize Colton Santo is standing right by me, watching as I make a spectacle of myself falling flat out on new legs. I don't know if I'm shocked that he spoke to me or wary that he did.

I've never trusted anything about him or any of his motives and wonder when he got so close here. Avoiding looking directly at him, keeping my eyes averted from his, attempting to get to grips with this weird body and focusing on learning to use it. All I can do is whimper back, realizing I can't form words this way, and go into my head link instinctively.

We don't have the vocal cords for human talking. Wolves in the same pack have a connection mentally, so they can communicate without talking, which, admittedly, is impossible for a wolf. It's also possible when close enough to speak to one, not from your pack, if they are willing to hear you.

It feels strange.

17

I attempt to link with him, weirded out by this new, almost natural ability I didn't have before. I am overwhelmed by all of this and not sure if I am still heavily drugged when in this form or if this surreal new way to experience everything is wolf's sense. Things affect us differently as humans, and this disorientation might be something I have to adjust to.

Yeah, well, walk it off. Learn fast.

He links me back, a husky familiarity to his voice inside my head that does strange things to my stomach. It's hardly a polite response, and the tone tells me he doesn't want to communicate with me, especially not in a head link.

I'm not one of his pack, and I'm not even on the same level as him. It's disrespectful to try. He walks off towards his father to further demonstrate the point, and I flop down to get to grips with everything I got hit with. I'm heavy, unsure how to navigate my dog's body when I've spent my life walking on two legs. I must weigh four times my average weight for sure, although the size of my paws suggests maybe even more.

"The turning will not last ... only fleeting moments for your first time. You will be awoken when you come out, and your path will lead you to your destiny. Pay attention, be alert. You are now on the other side." The Shaman states it loudly, and his voice echoes around the mountain like a prophetic song. I have heard it so many times, yet it finally means something to me this time.

I get up on unsure legs, slowly, like Bambi on newborn limbs, and lift my head as I know I'm meant to. In unison with all around me, we stretch our necks out, lift our noses to the heavens, and howl at the moon for the first time in our lives as one united pack; no matter who we are, where we are from, whatever our bloodline or our past, long and soulful with meaning. United in one song that completes our transformation. A sound that echoes around us, through us, is joined by the hundreds who watch until we fill the night sky with a low, eerie hum that will reverberate around the mountains and put the fear of God into the wildlife.

It feels strange at first. My throat vibrates; it aches and rasps my vocal cords, but as my belly empties, my air departs, and the longest yowl comes cascading out of me until it scratches my throat and leaves me breathless. I feel alive. Like I have been holding my breath and waiting for this my whole life. I guess I have. This is what I was born to be, and with the awakening comes freedom.

I can leave.

I can run.

I can live off the land and hunt to survive. The confines of humans no longer bind me to get by. Wolves can live anywhere as long as they can hunt, and although we have a pack mentality, I've heard stories of isolated wolves doing fine on their own. That is what I have planned, longed for, waited for, and I know where I'm heading. I can finally realize my dream of leaving all of this behind me and finding my solitary peace somewhere out there. As far away from these mountains and people as I can, and never looking back.

As soon as I relax, our call stops, and my energy fades fast. Overcome with fatigue, I slump back down and flake out on my belly, sighing as my body tingles and itches with a thousand tiny tremors. Glancing down in time to watch as everything changes back faster than I thought it would.

Fur that was keeping me warm, on paws instead of hands ... it all begins to recede, and unlike my transformation to the beast, the reversal is not painful at all. It's fast, almost instant, and before I can blink or even get to grips with what is happening, I am nakedly human. Smeared in my blood and flat out in a huddled heap on the floor, saving me some of my dignity by shielding my body.

I scramble to pull my body into a ball, aware I am entirely uncovered and exposed to the hundreds of eyes around me. I jump when my blanket is tossed towards me by the nearby Damon, smirking as his eyes devour my nudity, and I recoil. Embarrassed, ashamed at being naked in front of everyone, and mad as hell that he made sure I would have to cross eight feet to get the blanket. I glare at him, forgetting myself for a moment, then ponder not going to get it and huddle up to cover myself instead.

Others had theirs tossed directly at them, and looking around, I realize I am the only one who has to go crawling for hers, like an animal. He is trying to humiliate me, and I move fast to catch it.

Shocked when the slightest movement sends me shooting towards him at lightning speed, I end up almost at his feet in the blink of an eye.

"Wow," I blurt out loud and get laughed at by someone nearby as they realize how naïve I am about the speed and power we all inherited. Another change in me I have to get used to. I grab the blanket and try to crawl backward while pulling it over me and fall onto my back as it's jerked tight and yanked back taut, sending my head crashing on the smooth stone below me and bouncing my skull painfully.

Damon sniggers, his foot on the edge, as he looks down at me with complete disdain. My face reddening with heat, aware of many more muffled sniggers and laughs at my expense, and I can't conceal the shame washing over me. Laughing at how much he enjoys making a show of me, I have no choice but to try to pull the blanket from him once more.

I know others are watching; my senses are heightened, and my body is goose bumping in response. I can feel them on me from all over, and I want to sink into the ground and disappear. I yank, but the blanket tears from the pressure nearer my end, and I have no choice but to stop or be left with a scrap that will cover nothing.

"For God's sake, Damon. This isn't the time or place. My father is staring at you. Pack it in." Colton snarls his way, pushes him from behind, and comes into view, shoving him off the blanket, and swoops down to pick it up with speed. He walks forward in two confident strides and hands it straight to me, bending slightly as he does so to make sure I get it with no more interference. I know he's only doing it to save face, exert his dominance in front of his father and save Damon from punishment later. Either way, I am thankful for him and relieved he is an Alpha in the making for the first time.

I reach out and take it gratefully, quickly pulling it around me and hiding what's on show, afraid to look at him. It's almost impulsive as his hand, still attached to the corner, briefly touches my shoulder in passing because of how speedy I am. A hot searing flash runs through my body alarmingly, igniting something tingly inside me I can't identify. Like being zapped by a low-strength taser,

I gasp at the contact, glancing up at him as he attempts to rise to stand, seemingly also recoiling for what was maybe just an electric shock. For one brief millisecond of synchronized surprise, our eyes lock.

It's all it takes.

One second of direct focus, a meeting of eyes I have never dared to look into before, and the worst thing in the world happens to me. We connect: visions, images, and projections flow through my mind at a neck-breaking speed that fries my brain, and I cannot break his gaze or look away. Startled into silence, locked in, and unable to fight what happens. My body is rigid and paralyzed, controlled by this higher force as we're forcefully held, trapped in an intense stare down, and his dark, almost black eyes eat into my soul.

His memories, my memories, his fears, my fears. They become a jumbling mass of zooming information, flooding, invading my mind, and overtaking me as I'm body-slammed with an overwhelming amount of emotions, in literal seconds, that could potentially zap your brain to death.

My body, heart, and soul are pulled into this flash of breath, which completely spins my world on tilt and instantly changes everything. Neither of us can do anything in our paralyzed state but let it happen until the wild ride of transferring all we are, all we know, all we feel, is done and leaves us shell-shocked from the fallout. Rooted to the spot, aware only of the darkest chocolate eyes on mine, unable to break free yet marooned like I suddenly found a home, and his gaze goes from sworn enemy to lifeline in my darkness.

Breathless, reeling from the invasion of his life, memories, and history pouring into my memory banks, I finally snap out and fall backward into a slump. Released from whatever the hell that was and momentarily dazed. I am entirely incapable of any kind of movement as I lie on the ground, startled into silence and lightheaded from what felt like a physical assault.

"Holy shit!" Colton's voice waves my way, sounding equally shocked and as breathless as me, and I strain up to see him also on the ground. On his knees, though, looking like someone sucker-punched him in the stomach, he falls forward to drop his palms on the floor to hold him steady. Eyes wide, skin pale, unusually for his usual, tanned hue. He looks like someone told him the worst news he ever wanted to hear in his life, and he's reeling in the aftermath. Complete silence surrounds us. A pin drop could be heard, and I have no idea what to think.

"They just imprinted," one solo voice squeaks out and echoes around us like someone announcing a death sentence.

"No, that can't have happened," another, moments later, and then another, and another. The mutterings of one or two become many, deafening as they all verbalize their questions about what they saw. The voices blend and blur as my fingers find my skull, and I scrub my head to get my brain to function. To figure out what just happened to me.

Me? I did what? ... No. It can't be.

I lie here dumbfounded and try to pull my thoughts together, unsure why I now know how he likes his coffee or his favorite song or why I suddenly can't get the strong scent of him out of my nostrils or the need to get up and hug him, out of my brain. The crazy primal urge to get up and sit on him and do things I never wanted to do before, or even a few seconds ago. It's like every part of my soul is suddenly attuned to him, even though he's feet away. Deep heavy longings tingle in my body, and every urge is to have Santo all around me.

I lie back down and try to breathe through the oncoming panic, try to rationalize what this was as I draw in the air with shallow breaths, and let my body recover from the colossal zap he gave me.

"Silence!" Juan Santo demands with a vicious bark, echoing around the mountain, and like a sudden clap of thunder, his voice halts the rest of the chaotic noise, giving me some relief before my brain explodes.

He storms towards us and physically drags his son up by the shoulder from his slumped position. Gripping and hauling him like a madman and angrily turning to face him once on his feet, raw anger erupting.

"Tell me you didn't!" He demands at him in a harsh tone, but Colton seems as spangled as me. His usually confident stance is loose, and he seems unsteady on his legs. Knocked sideways and unsure what the hell happened to us.

"I don't know what that was ... I've never ... I don't know!" His cocky, dominant tone is lacking too, and I can feel his eyes back on me as I struggle to sit up, pulling myself into a sitting ball and finally have the courage to stare at them.

As soon as I meet Colton's eyes again, that same jolt hits me in my heart and stomach like a massive thud, and I know this isn't anything else. Heard enough about it to understand what it is. Saw it happen to others. He stares at me with the same instinctual longing I throw his way, the unspoken need to walk towards him and touch each other. The need to go over and wrap myself in his arms, the longing way we stop and gaze at each other as urge blots out sense and beast overtakes human reasoning.

We imprinted, and the Fates gave me my mate.

Colton Santo is my destined Alpha, the wolf I'm supposed to spend eternity with and follow wherever he goes. He's my path set in stone, my lover, my life, the father to my future offspring, until the end of time.

And I can't imagine anything worse.

The Fallout

Everything happens so fast that my head spins, and I can barely catch my breath. Our imprinting sends the ceremony into quick dispersal, and I'm dragged away by Santo's pack and ushered into an awaiting car, my clothes thrown in my face and ordered to go to the packhouse and be quiet.

Everything is in uproar as though I committed the crime of the century, and it rippled through everyone present. Juan is exploding magnificently at the possibility that our future Alpha got betrothed to one of the lowliest of the packs, and I'm not exactly happy about it either.

I've kept my head down for ten years, stayed out of sight, in the shadows, and away from the drama the way others like me have not. Became almost invisible and made no real friends, all with my eye on the one goal of escaping this place with no noise. Only to be put on show on the most important night of my life, in front of the entire mountain, and have everything come crashing down on top of me.

This can't be happening! Imprinting is for life; there is only one way out—and that's death! I can barely breathe as the panic sets in that this is not goddamn reversible and not a tiny thing that can get brushed aside and me sent on my merry way.

That is NOT an option for me. We can choose to walk away and ignore it, but the bond won't break, and the urge to bind us together will only grow stronger if we fight it. That's how this works; everyone knows that. If I leave, I'll crave for him for the rest of my life until it pushes me to insanity or even death from a broken soul.

If I stay, I'll never be able to fight the need to be with him, and Juan made that excruciatingly clear that it will never happen.

I'm bustled from car to dark alley and given only seconds to pull my clothes on under my blanket before I am forcibly pushed in a side door and almost fall flat on my face into a bright hallway. The men charged with bringing me here are being less than hospitable, shoving me around and shoving me cruelly. I feel covered in bruises, and I still have blood residue over my body and face. I 'ooft' at the impact of meeting hard floor, body already tired and weak from what I endured tonight.

I'm still reeling from the drugs and the first transformation of my life, on edge, hackles rising, and dealing with this new semi kidnapping trauma. I feel trapped in some sort of daymare and want to wake up before I have an all-out freakout.

A tall, familiar, attractive blonde meets us in the hall as she stalks towards me. Without missing a beat, she slaps me hard across the face and sends me flying off my feet and skidding into the wall. Burning pain engulfs my cheek and eye socket as I groan it out and spreads across my head and down my neck, rendering me senseless for a second. I am slightly dazed with the force of that bitch's assault as I try to pick myself back up but fail when a foot stomps on my spine to force me back down.

"How dare you! How goddamn dare you, you whore! He's mine! We have dated for two years, and you think you can sweep in and take him! You are a goddamn nothing, and you have no rights to him!" She's livid. Puce with rage and comes bearing down on me, climbing on top of me while winding her fingers around my throat like a crazed psycho. I lash back to defend myself in my panic, but she's bigger and stronger, and the glow of amber in her eyes tells me she's on the verge of turning.

She's another of the pack which turned young and has her gifts well under control, while I haven't even begun to explore mine yet. "I'll kill you before I see you take him from me." Her grasp tightens, and I try to claw at her face, struggling for breath, panicking, momentarily blacking out before she is hauled from on top of me by two strong arms and lifted high into the air.

25

"Enough! She didn't do this any more than I did!" Colton's voice cuts through her hysterical squealing, and he drops her on her feet away from me. Standing between her and me as he turns to her and tries to reason and shut her up. His whole body is taut and alert as though he's ready to take her on, and I'm not sure it won't go that way. Females, when angry, tend to turn and attack even people they love. It's how disputes are resolved most of the time among wolves. Physical fights are the norm, even between mates. "Go home, Carmen; let us deal with this. The elders and the Shaman are coming with my father. Just go and let us figure this out." He sounds pissed, with a deep, commanding tone like his father's, only with a boyish edge.

"Why can't they kill her and be done with it? She's nothing to the pack," she wails at him desperately, the noise prickling at my ears, so I wince in reaction with an 'ahh' and grasp to cover them and wonder if this is a new thing with my senses ... hearing things more painfully.

"Are you dense? Killing her will kill me. Hurting her hurts me! Even a slap! We are imprinted; we are one. Her soul, my soul ... did you never pay attention in class?" He sounds as mad as her now, and he throws a look at me crouching on the floor, dazed and in shock about the turn of events. Not mentally ready for any of this.

"Here." He turns, a softness changing his handsome face slightly, making him more appealing, less cold, and he extends a hand to help me up. It's the first time I ever saw any real humanity in this guy, and it renders me mute as I let him pull me to my feet. That heat and transference of sparks at his touch makes me jump, and that familiar urge and need for more of him, his touch, makes me pull my hand away quickly. Internally bristling and inhaling fast to cool the sudden heat that rides up my neck and face. Blushing, I look away to break contact.

He frowns at the sensation too and backs off as soon as he lets me go, obviously uneasy at how much chemistry is stirring up from something so simple. It's not a secret he and Carmen have been a steady thing for a long time, so I guess he feels like this is somehow cheating on her. She watches like a hawk; I can feel her hatred burning through my soul and wishing harm on me. The sting on my face tells me she probably left a handprint, and I try not to glare her way and provoke another outburst.

"I swear to God, Cole ..." Her voice breaks, and tears spring from her eyes, instantly dampening her cheeks. "If you leave me for this little reject ...." For a second, the pure heartbreak in her tone gets at me, cutting me in the chest, and I'm a little sorry for her. Not knowing what love feels like or what this would do to my heart if it were me. I guess a slap isn't comparable to a devastated soul and the thought of losing someone you thought was your mate.

That stupid part of me that cares has me staring at the floor guiltily, as though somehow accepting I've done something wrong here. I feel ashamed.

"Be quiet. Go home, and I'll talk to you later. Right now, we are nothing until this gets rectified. I can't have two mates. You know the laws." The edge in his tone signals him executing his dominance, and she recoils quickly, knowing when not to question or argue, even if her face gives away the pain in what he said. Alphas have a tone reserved for times when pack animals won't obey. It renders us mute and makes us do what is asked of us, which is one of those times. Even I tremble at its effect on everyone present and have to stop myself from slinking back into the shadows. Not every male has the gift, only those born to lead.

"Alora? That's your name, right?" Colton turns to me, surprising me with the change, those chocolate eyes melting me when we connect, and I have to look away again, too, pulled towards him for my liking and nod shyly. I have no control over his effect on me, and I don't like this one bit. Freedom was calling to me, and now this annoying, undesirable need to be wrapped around the one guy I never wanted to know.

"Or Lorey ... I get called both." It's a feeble quiet mumble, and I inwardly curse myself for sounding as weak as his pack always labeled me. I'm no match for an Alpha. It's no wonder they cast my bloodline into the reject pile.

Relax, I'm not going to hurt you.

27

It's his voice in my head, and I flicker up, startled that he spoke to me inside my mind and not verbally. We're not supposed to do that when both in human form and especially not when we're not from the same pack.

How can you ....?

I start to ask, replying in the same way without thinking, and then inhale sharply as I realize I did the same thing. I've no idea if that breaks the rules, considering who he is.

We imprinted. We have a link. We can hear each other even from miles away. No distance is too far. No one else can tap into this. It's like our own personal telephone line with dampeners.

He isn't looking at me. He's watching Carmen walk down the hall crying into her own hands and creating a bleak picture. I can sense his pain from watching her go, and it pains me, too. Feeling what he feels is another downside to being connected to this guy. I don't want to feel heartbreak or pain or any of this crap.

I'm sorry. I didn't mean for any of this.

The honesty and ache in my response bring his eyes to mine, and we do that weird thing where we lock eyes, get a tremor of something we can't deny, and both look away again. Neither of us wants this; that much is clear.

You didn't do this. Fate did. Now we have to figure out how to undo it, if that's even possible.

The hesitation in his tone catches me off guard, and I look at him properly despite myself. His side profile of chiseled square jawline. Sallow skin and dark hair to match those dark eyes and brows. Colton is tall, muscular, and fit, which is only enhanced by being among the giant wolves in the pack, even at his age. His family originated from Colombia, and you can see his heritage, in the best way, despite his mother being Caucasian. Me, I'm a good old country white. Dull hair, plain girl, and nothing unique or beautiful that I know of. Carmen is a goddess compared to me.

The atmosphere turns cold as a troop of men come marching in from the same door we did, and I'm pushed out of the way ungraciously by one of them. I get knocked sideways, unable to stop myself, and spiral down as I lose footing. Still on unsure legs after tonight's ceremony and unable to stop myself.

Colton's low growl and quick reflexes as he jolts in beside me and catches me sends my head spinning. His arms lasso me and stop my body from colliding with the concrete wall, hitting his chest instead as I grasp on impulsively. His eyes glow amber over my head as he death glares his displeasure at the men, unconcealed as that flash of warning oozes from him. That fierce mate protection is coming out instinctively, and I honestly don't know how to react.

Becoming someone's mate is as much about instinct as anything else. It changes you and makes you feel and do things you didn't before. Even if he hated me before this, that need to protect me and look after me will become his mission in life and vice versa. It's completely crazy, and I can't believe it's happening to me.

His father, however, almost takes his head off with the rage-filled bellow he aims his way. I realize that's who shoved me out of the way so forcefully right then.

"Did you just growl at me?" He snarls our way, and Colton firmly curls his fingers around my waist and arm. Juan lowers his brows severely and glares at his son furiously, moving into his head link to continue his chastisement; the way Colton stiffens around me tells me so.

Locked eye to eye, an intense standoff as the air thickens and his energy bristles. Captured in a tight embrace, I know I shouldn't try to break free from it, although my body responds quite happily to the contact. Feeling his anger radiating from him and the anxious, uptight bubbling inside me as I sense what he's feeling.

I was never good with aggression and rage. And now the overwhelming amount he can spit out, as my mood takes on his, has me recoiling. Colton has a sea of dominant fury inside him, and his hostility knows no bounds. I try to blot out the projections I'm getting and close my eyes to focus on my breathing instead. Combatting growing heat and pulsing need from his touch and fear and faintness from all the negative emotions flying between these two terrifying men. I feel like a piece of raw meat hung between two ferocious beasts. It's like I don't have complete control of my mind or feelings anymore, and try as I might; Colton now lives in my body as much as I do.

They argue inwardly, silent on the surface, but all in the hallway remain still and patient as they are meant to when their Alpha demands. Juan is one of the most intimidating pack leaders, and I guess it's why he moved so quickly to the prime position.

Colton's father finally spins on his heel, signaling they are done, and marches into a nearby doorway, clicking his fingers and gesturing for us to follow. It's so hostile and terrifying that I cringe, my heart erupting into hammering thuds.

"If people could keep their hands to themselves and off my mate, that would be great! Thanks." Colton mumbles it under his breath, not meaning for me to hear, and I throw him an awkward glance. My heart flipping over, and my stomach churning uneasily at his words.

He called me his mate.

I can hear you, and it's what you are for the time being. We imprinted. We don't exactly have a choice.

Colton throws me a look that translates to 'relax and follow me,' I mutely do so, cheeks burning from stupidly letting him read my thoughts. I'm embarrassed that I'm stupid enough not to remember that thirty seconds after figuring it out. He lets me go, and my body cools a little, somehow suddenly cold from his loss, and a weird emptiness fills me instead.

I follow behind him quickly into a large room that looks like a study with extra couches. The men all file in and sit down in random places, and Colton ushers me to a nearby chair, padded and semi shadowed in the corner, out of the direct line of the men. He stands close by and waits as his father circles a bookcase and comes to perch in the chair at the desk, looking out at all of us in his position as leader.

"I need solutions. This ..." He points at Colton and me. "Happens over my dead body. My son is destined to be Alpha one day, and I will be damned if a mongrel with bad breeding dilutes his lineage. She will not be our Luna. Fix this. Find a way! I don't care what the history books say. There has to be a way to break the bond and sever the connection, so he is free to mate up with a chosen female." The stern tone of a man who doesn't want to hear excuses, yet a tiny ounce of hope fills my chest. That there might still be a chance I can get out of this and here and follow my plan to get the hell away from Radstone once and for all. It's even weirder that, at the same time, though, a desolate pain cuts me in the heart at the thought of leaving him. Winding me, blindsiding me for a second.

"You cannot fight fate. There are consequences if you ignore destiny. Imprinting does not happen to us all, and when it does ... you do not question it." The Shaman is quick to verbalize, but Juan slamming his hand on his desk, sending a loud thud through all of us, brings silence once more. I stare at my feet and will the ground to open up and take me. Crushing pressure on my chest as anxiety envelops me.

"Did you not hear me when I said, THIS is NOT happening! She will NOT be my son's mate. I will kill her before I let that happen."

Silence befalls the room as his biting tone echoes in the air, although I swear I hear the subtlest of growls come from Colton's way, so close beside me, and make sure I don't look at him. Instead, I stare at my hands in my lap and pray for this to be over. Shaking internally and genuinely fearful for my life. Never have I wanted to be left to go back to the orphanage to spend time in my room with Vanka, but now it's so calling to me.

I don't want anything as much as I want that right now. Well, except maybe this weird primal urge for the guy at my left to calm down a bit and stop plaguing me. I can feel him, overly so. Way too in tune and aware of him, even if he is three feet away. My body and mind are doing weird things concerning him, and as terrified as I should be right now, I don't feel it when he moves closer and somehow calms me without even looking my way. One backward step of maybe a foot, and he soothes my nerves back into warm gooey submission, that inner heat spreading as he gets close enough that his scent sparks some internal fire in me.

"Then your son will die too, and we lose our future leader. You cannot break the bond without severe consequences. The choice has been made. Fate has chosen for him, and you must obey." The Shaman comes back, undeterred by Juan's anger, and stands as though to press the point. He's low-toned and confident in his wisdom and does not seem intimidated in any way. "He can choose to sever the bond if he wishes, but history has shown us that mates who do ... both die! The only other option is denial to consummate. They choose to walk away; no mark is made, no union at all, and they deny the bond completely. It will never die, and they will live lives craving what the other can give them, no matter who they end up with. Is that what you want for your son?"

All eyes turn on Juan. So much tension in this room as the elders talk internally, so I cannot hear them. Colton paces, and I can tell he is privy to what is being said. They are his pack, after all, and two are his blood. Father and Uncle. He doesn't seem happy, and the waves of his anger are all lapping over me and affecting my sanity. Dampening the heat, replacing it with his rage.

I can't take it anymore. As the minutes' tick by and my nerves fray, I feel like I may scream, an internal burst of nervous crazy whooshes out.

"I'll leave. I don't want this either." I blurt it out into the deathly silence as hysteria gets the better of me, and every single face turns to me in shocked response, like they suddenly remembered I was here in this corner.

I know I just spoke out of turn and disrespected everyone in this room, but I'm sitting here, wearing my own dried blood, shredded emotions, and exhaustion pushing through. My head is a mess, and in the space of thirty minutes, I discovered that being a virgin doesn't mean you cannot get crazy urges to strip naked and jump someone's bones, even if you previously avoided that someone like the plague. I've pictured him naked at least twice, without even meaning to, since he gave me every one of his intimate memories, and some of those are him showering. *What?*

"What?"

Both Colton in my head and his dad verbally, in unison, and I panic that I spat this out loud.

"It was the plan, my intentions. I mean, after my ... the umm ... tonight. My turning. I was leaving. Going away, and it doesn't have to change." I sound insane. Babbling like a fool with verbal diarrhea and aware of the way all eyes are eating up my weak presentation of my crap contribution. I should have run when I had the chance and screwed the running ceremony.

"That won't break the bond. We'll still be connected, still linked. It will make us miserable. Don't you see? What happened tonight changed everything for both of us." Colton sounds deflated, and I get the visual of him and Carmen kissing. Right from his head to mine and have to shake it away as insane jealously claws at my insides from out of nowhere, proving his point. Irrational, illogical, but there it is, and he didn't even mean to project his sad thoughts about her my way.

"Then what? Because all I am hearing is hopeless submission or death!" My anger snaps, and out of somewhere deep inside, my bravado increases and pushes me to my feet, voice firm and frustration seeping through. An inner surge of tingling electricity as my emotions flare up, and Colton looks at me oddly. Suddenly stopping and staring insanely into my eyes while furrowing his brow dramatically, screwing up that cute face.

"They're not amber." He comes out with the most random reply, and I blanch at him like he has two heads and no idea what he's talking about.

"What?" I stammer as he paces towards me.

"Your eyes ... when your inner wolf peaks. They're not amber. They're red. No one has red ... we all have amber." He stalks towards me, grabbing my hand and spinning me to him to inspect me closely. "Show me," he urges, and I gawp at him in bewilderment. Confused at the side-tracking of this conversation and feeling like I fell through a reality hole.

If I knew how to do it on command, I would, but as I only transformed for the first time tonight and have no idea how to call my inner wolf into my eyes again, I stare at him, completely dumbfounded with the importance of color.

"Why does that matter?" I know that despite the more urgent topic at hand, the Shaman has moved towards me also, and so has one of the silent elders. A formidable tall, and muscular elder whose gray-white hair is unsuccessful in lowering his intimidation levels, and he snarls my way.

"Because you are part white, and now Cole sees red in your eyes. It matters. Now show us, or I will make you fully turn on my command, and you won't enjoy it." He seethes my way, full-on hostility in his tone, and I wither back, scalded and instantly fearful. Colton reacts instinctively at the veiled threat, and chaos ensues. In the blink of an eye, he's between the elder and me, growling, eyes glowing wildly, body larger and bristling with tension as he turns to him and huskily warns him off.

"My mate ... mine! You touch her ... I will exert my right to maim or kill to protect her. I don't care who you are in this pack!" His tone drops to satanic levels, and I recoil behind him, seeing the ripple of spines up his back as he begins to transform aggressively. My stomach hits my knees, making me weak, unsure of what else to do as the Shaman intervenes as fear paralyzes me to the spot.

"See. This is what happens when you delay the bond. The urge gets insane the longer you deny it. The need to protect, the need to be joined. It creates madness. Colton, be still. No one will touch your mate without your say, and we will look at her eyes in time. Breathe and come back to us." He places a hand on his shoulder and gently brings Colton back to my side, lifting my hand and gently placing it on Colton's before patting both and setting us down. The instant spark and warmth generated between us give me all kinds of safe and familiar vibes I've not known in almost ten years. Not since I last saw my parents alive and home. It seems to do the same to him as his eyes fade back to brown, and he inhales slowly, bringing peace to the aura between us. "His mate holds the key to bringing him calm. Be that now. We need to talk without you both here. Go, the room through there."

The Shaman points us towards an adjoining door, and Colton grasps my fingers tightly, his energy pulsing through mine, and it seems to bring him back from turning. I can't explain it but here, holding his hand, it's the first time I feel a connection of love for anyone in a long time. That sense of belonging that I lost the day my family left me.

I barely knew him this morning, and yet, here and now, my instincts are that I would die for him if I had to, and the longer this plays out, the stronger this need to be near him gets. While being physically joined causes all sorts of inner sparks and sizzles as tension builds between us, and I move obediently as he pulls me with him. It's insanity, and I don't understand how this can be, but it is what it is. Colton is part of me now, and I can't do anything about it.

We are ushered to the door, hands still entwined, and I follow him closely, the heady need to wrap myself around him worse when we have prolonged contact, and as much as my head tells me to let go, I can't seem to. The growing ache in my stomach and pelvis is getting irritatingly intense, and I am more than aware of how good his skin feels against mine. Our hands are slotted together, warm on warm, weirdly sensual.

Colton leads me to the other room and shuts the door firmly behind us. He is still holding my hand and keeping me by his side as he turns to me. He gazes down at our entangled fingers for a long second. Seems like he, too, is telling himself to let go, but he doesn't.

We stand stiffly, pulsating energy growing between us as the air thickens, and I find it harder to breathe the longer he's this close. Fully aware of him towering over me in all his beautiful muscular glory, hot body, and he's way too good-looking. Even his voice does crazy tingly things to me, and standing, absorbing his heat, inhaling his unique scent, I get clammy in really embarrassing places. My eyes keep straying to his face, mouth, and beautiful face, and I edge closer absentmindedly, biting on my lip as crazy thoughts about leaning up and biting his course through my brain alarmingly.

I need to cool down and pull this back in. Hormones are well and truly kicking in with his proximity, and I need to breathe a little.

"How can I want to kiss someone so badly that a few hours ago, I never even knew? I have a girlfriend. Did have one. My head's a mess." He seems instantly distraught and squeezes my hand in his a little forcefully before reluctantly releasing me and stepping back. Calming my jets as guilt punches me in the stomach, I realize maybe he's not getting as hot and bothered as I am standing here. "This is ... insane. I don't know you. How can we ....?" He paces away from me, seemingly in turmoil, then past me twice, back and forth, and then turns to me again.

I shrug at him, unsure what else to say. If I knew the answers, I guess we wouldn't be here like this. I'm a little out of my depth and struggling to get this raging fire under control in my pelvis as what I assume is my libido finally introduces herself to me, and I have to stop checking out his ass as he keeps waving it past me. It's making me all squirmy and uneasy and so sure he can probably tell with a look that I am about three seconds away from launching at him. Shuffling from foot to foot and swallowing hard, blowing out heavily to release this growing pressure in my stomach.

"Please tell me you are feeling this, too. That this is not just me?" He stops and frowns at me, his eyes looking a little hazy and intense as he stares at my mouth and almost electrocutes me with the connection. I glance away, face flushing with his effects on me, and try to focus on the floor, the table, a wall, and cool off in this vast, suddenly suffocating room around us. I can feel him without touching him, his presence seeping into me and stirring up all kinds of longings and sensations.

"I think that's how it's meant to work. We're supposed to want to, you know ... mate." I blush as I say it and look away again, overwhelmed with sudden shyness. Uneasy with this admission, he wants to kiss me while I'm all kinds of flustered, hot, tingly, and itching to slide my hands over that full and broad chest and ...

Oh, God, stop. I want him to kiss me so badly I can almost taste it. I mean, I do too, want to kiss him, that is. I have done since after the whole imprinting thing, but I don't think we should admit those things, especially when neither of us wanted this. And I'm finding it hard to breathe as my lungs constrict and my heart flakes out with him being close enough to inhale, lick, grope ... I need to get a grip. I pull the neckline of my T-shirt to release the heat coming off me in droves and fan my face to push these insane urges and mental images of him naked out of my head.

I don't get a chance to give any verbal response or encouragement. I don't even get a chance to look up or think, and his sudden sweep into me, his fingers yanking my chin up as his lips crash into mine, knocking me for six.

I'm shocked, frozen for a second by the instant lip to lip assault, but as soon as his warm mouth molds to mine, I lose all control. I kiss him back, hormones let loose, and that craving hunger finding what it wanted after all, with a fever incomparable to anything, and get lost in the sweetest tasting pastime ever invented. Now I know what an urge taking over feels like, and my inner wolf pushes beyond any control I have.

His lips open mine, tongues meet for the first time, and I experience my first French kiss with a much-practiced mouth. I groan, succumb to his expertise as he yanks me into him and crashes our bodies together intimately. Our teeth clash with sheer ferocity in the devouring way we go at each other, and his hand rakes my body, grinding me to him like he can't get enough as I ultimately succumb.

Lust fuels the animals in us, and he picks me up under the thighs, his grip bruising my tender skin as he wedges his body between my legs, pulling them around his waist and walking me back so he can jam me up against the wall, to push himself against me fully. He kisses me harder, with a passion that sets us on fire, and I grasp and claw at his shoulders and neck in utter abandonment, scratching, biting, kissing, and finding my rhythm and confidence in what he's doing to my mouth. His tongue caresses mine, and mentally I blurt insanely ...

I want you inside me. I'm going to self-combust if you don't.

I'm not even sure if I mind-linked or where this thought came from, given I'm a virgin and never had a sexual urge in my life, but it only seems to make him kiss me all the more passionately. We lose all sense as this bond engulfs us, and he grinds into me until my urges reach a fever pitch of heightened horniness, and I pant with the effort as my body vibrates and craves his desperately.

I wrap my arms around his neck tightly, almost choking him with how I latch on. Devouring him with equal enthusiasm and find my motion, rubbing my pelvis up against what is evidently an erection. A substantial bulge in his pants as we meet in every way. It doesn't even shame or shock me; instead, it fuels my need to strip him naked and get on top of him to complete this union.

He feels like the best thing in the world, smells, tastes, touches in a way that drives me insane with need, and I now realize this bond is more powerful than even I gave it credit for. I want him so badly I might lose my mind if we don't do this.

Grinding into each other, my crotch fitted to his and breathing labored, I experience the real first moments of a building climax, even though we haven't done anything properly. Just the motion of his rough jeans between my thighs, over my panties, his kiss, his hands on me, and the feel of him has me unraveling insanely. I never knew much about sex before today, and now, I cannot contain the need to have it with him and might even get my first orgasm without losing my virginity.

Colton catches my hand roughly and pulls it above my head, pinning me against the wall hard, crazily sexy, exposing my neck to him while my arm pulls my long hair back out of his way. I instinctively turn my face, knowing what he wants, heart hammering through my labored breathing and tightening my grip around him to keep him close. Sliding away from my mouth to my neck, he licks from the base of my throat and up to my jawline, igniting a wave of tingles and goosebumps that makes me clench my thighs together around him. He groans at the pressure, which shoves his hard-on against me firmly. My core is pulsing with need as he focuses on something else entirely.

Mark me ... take me. I'm yours. Finalize the union.

The wanton voice of a girl that I don't recognize is begging for release, and he responds with a low growl that stirs everything deep inside me.

I want nothing more. God, I need you so badly.

The primal urge is no match for common sense, and as his teeth elongate and graze the soft skin of my neck, holding me taut against the wall, fully submissive, angling me in readiness to leave his mate mark on my neck, I moan in pleasure and squeeze my eyes closed at his touch. Holding my breath as I wait for the one thing that will calm the insanity in this need between us.

A transference of blood and sex will unite us for life. Bearing marks that tie us together will show everyone we're bonded.

I tense and exhale as his hot breath, and soft mouth nestle on the naked skin near my jugular, and a sharp graze presses against the pulsing spot of my throat. A tiny inkling of piercing points pricking into the first thin layers, fully ready for the stinging pain I know will probably come, but so close to self-combustion that I think it might make me climax. I dig my nails of my one free hand into his shoulder, clamping onto him brutally in sheer ecstasy and swell with the transference of the pleasure he feels as it consumes me too. Seems he likes a bit of pain.

An almighty high-pitched screech assaults my senses and shatters glass in the room around us in dramatic mini-explosions. It combusts inside my head so crazily painfully that I snap my eyes open and scramble to claw my palms over my ears, yanking them from him.

Colton's body tenses, and he releases me clumsily in reaction. Dropping me to my feet in alarm, that has us scrambling to shield our ears in unison, brains shuddering with the excruciating squealing whine on our elevated senses. Colton bristles into half-turning teeth, claws, and face changing as his protective instincts make him ready to fight and poised to protect me. Turning on the source as he tries to stay upright, I crumble behind him to the floor in a useless heap. Clutching at my head to drown it out before my brain pops.

"How could you?" Carmen wails, so insanely tonal it's like a dog whistle, and things on the shelves in the room vibrate as she keeps that infernal noise going.

It dawns on me that this is one of her gifts. She can shatter with high-pitch frequency, and I clutch my ears in alarm as she howls louder. Colton somehow seems to be more able to battle it and attempts to tackle her into the hall to stop the ear-piercing noise. It's insanely painful.

"You said you loved me!" She screams at him, pushing back to get at me, losing her sanity and going for the kill. He changes from pushing her out to dragging her away from me and wrestling a mid-transforming she-wolf. Her eyes glow the brightest orange as she loses all self-control as her nails elongate to full-on wolf claws and her teeth peek.

"I did ... I mean, I do. I don't know what I'm saying. Calm down, Carmen." He picks her up from behind, covering her mouth with one hand harshly, pressing until she relents on a gasp of air, and turns her around before pinning her to the wall to restrain her and get control. The tone that dominates, the one none of us can fight, comes out of him ruthlessly and reminds me why all should be afraid of the Santo Alphas.

"Stop it now! And stop screaming!" He growls at her devilishly, and even though I'm not saying a word, I instantly slam my mouth shut. Instant feeble submission because he Alphatoned us, and there's not much you can do about it.

She quiets instantly, falling into utter silence, relief immediate, but my ears are ringing in the aftermath, and I am so dazed I can't immediately get up. As I finally scramble to my knees to try, the door bursts open, and Juan storms forward, half-man, half-beast, semi-transformed in a ripped shirt and jacket, ready to take on the intruder, and stops dead in his tracks. The elders and Shaman are hot on his tail in a similar state of urgency, and they all gawp at the scene before them.

"What's going on? What happened?" he commands snappily, enraged, and I sink into the corner once more, huddling into a ball and wishing myself a million miles away from all of this. This can't get any worse.

"Your son was in the middle of marking that ... that reject! MY mate has betrayed me!" She wails again in desolation, and I feel every single glare turn from her to me and then Colton as silence deafens us all.

REJECTION

I pace my room for the hundredth time, sighing, frustrated, and mentally working through the war
going off inside me and end up 'arghhing' out loud in frustration. So over this crap already and tired of feeling this strung out. I feel like the last few days' events have changed me in subtle ways, and I wish I could go back to before.

Things have not been going well since that day in the packhouse. That day changed everything in my life, and I'm a prisoner in the orphanage until further notice. Under lock and key, metaphorically, through the pain of death, should I disobey.

Colton's father erupted when he realized that being left alone for mere minutes was enough to send his son spiraling into hormonal lust for his new mate, throwing all sense aside and almost marking me. So now we're forbidden from being near each other, indefinitely. His father thinks he can control fate by refusing to let things run their course. Despite everything, the Shaman warned and tried to preach.

Juan is adamant I'll be the downfall of the Packdom should Colton honor our bond, and I goddamn hate him for interfering and thinking he can control me in this way. I'm not one of his pack. He has no claim to me or my bloodline, and since I turned, I'm free to leave this stupid mountain, but he won't let me!

Nothing like this has ever happened before in the history of imprinting, and the Shaman warned of terrible foreboding should we anger the Fates and deny something as substantial as imprinting.

41

Juan didn't care. He only cares about what Juan wants, what Santos need, and I'm an annoying little fly in his soup. Not worthy of his son's attention or his seed.

My running away plan is pointless because mine and Colton's souls are now linked in every way, meaning I'm not allowed to leave Radstone at all. To go off on my own, for fear I endanger the life of their future Alpha in my unworthy, incapable way in case some terrible mishap befalls me. If I die out there in the big bad world, then so does he.

I mean, the Fates made your mate inseparable from you for a reason; beyond lust and procreation, the desire to never be parted is as much about survival. The Alpha should protect his femme at all costs, and she shadows her dominant for life. Always by his side, watch his back, and become an unbeatable unit. If one falls, they both fall. They become one.

So basically, after being screamed at by Carmen until my ears bled, literally, and they still hurt, bullied into a corner by Juan, who threatened to tear me apart, and Colton almost took his head off. Then dragged home to house arrest by some of the overly aggressive Santo pack, I'm confined to live inside these walls, with no contact from the person fate decided would be the other half to my soul for eternity. Everything sucks. Just goddamn, all the way to hell and back, sucks!

Happy sucky eighteenth birthday, Alora.

It's going well so far.

We're forbidden from linking, talking, or seeing each other, and I doubt that will ever change. Bonding is for life, and distance won't do much about it. You cannot sever a bond. You can choose to deny it, ignore it if you can, but Colton has to be the one to reject me, or I will be, and currently still am, his mate. He said the words; he verbalized the choice and started to mark me. Juan cannot make that choice for him. He has to say the words to me. I have to hear it from him before it breaks the union we started. Not that it does much in terms of our link, but for his pack, for the code, he can't have me as his mate and then go back to Carmen without doing this first. One mate ... there's no leeway in that.

It's been agony, though, and the Shaman was correct in that denying the bond only makes it worse.

I swear, I've been dreaming, obsessing about him since they pulled us apart, and I can't sleep or eat for pining for the mate I will never have as long as his father has any say even if he made it clear that he wants me, too. It's so crazy, given that I didn't know him at all, and now I know everything about him, can feel him, see him in my mind's eye, and even hear that sexy, subtly accented Columbian voice of his whenever I want. He's ingrained in me now.

He's in my head, creating dark, unhealable holes in my heart, and my entire being feels empty and lost without the other half of me to complete it. His kiss has ruined me in so many ways, and I replay those moments until I scream in agony and try to push the taste and feel of him out. I never knew this kind of pain could exist, and now I curse the Fates for doing this to me. Why they would inflict this kind of incurable disease is beyond me. It's a form of insanity, and I am powerless to cure myself, no matter how strong I think I am.

I'm desperate to reach out and link to him for one second to appease my eternal cravings. Still, as I have heard nothing from him, I'm assuming he too agrees with his father that we should have no contact for the pack's future, considering he closed down the head link, and I can't get to him at all. Dreaming about him smelling his scent in the wind when it blows from the south is driving me crazy, and I have no idea how to fix myself while I don't even know what we are. Held captive, still his mate, yet denied all that goes with it.

The only upside to my turning and finally becoming my true self in all of this is the physical difference, which shocked me when I finally got home to wash the grime and blood caking every inch of me. Catching sight in the bathroom mirror held me still with disbelief as I took myself in slowly and digested the image staring back at me.

The woman before me in the mirror, where a girl once stood, is almost like a stranger to me, yet not. Still Alora, in a way, I recognize myself as me, yet I'm angular, fuller-lipped, with clearer skin. My features are somehow better without changing too much, so I can't put my finger on the why. My hair's thicker, fuller, lighter, so it's a highlighted caramel with hints of honey and gorgeous waves instead of mousy brown. My eyes are greener, almost dazzling, and my body is toned in places I don't think I could ever improve on. It enhanced, tweaked, and brought me up to par with the already turned walking around this kingdom. No longer plain; I'm desirable, which brings its own problems.

Males in heat circle me whenever I venture down to the kitchen or into the courtyard for air. The orphanage still has many who live under this roof, even after turning, who have no desire to leave. I may have imprinted on a mate, but I bear no mark to solidify a union; therefore, I'm mateless in their eyes and available, and I need to watch my back. Pack rules bind not all in this new era.

Generally, males treat femmes with respect after turning, but not all. Hormones, lack of a mate, and sometimes undirected testosterone levels contribute to rogue males with little consideration of punishment when fueled by a need to have sex. We are primal animals, and sex is in our basic everyday makeup once we turn for the first time. I know I'm already suffering for the cravings to be fulfilled. My body is yearning for my mate to join me until I feel I may turn inside out with the painful internal pangs for his body. The annoying part is that no one else will do, and I have zero interest in any kind of instant relief with any other male, or any form of self-pleasure, not that I would know how. It's not been high on my list of priorities in life.

I've become aware, more than ever now, that I am no longer safe in this home when surrounded by unmated males. The lack of an actual pack means a lack of protection and any kind of consequences from a male who brutally takes what he wants. We live in a cruel world, and, like an unwanted, no one cares about the rejects. Especially not if one reject attacks and violates another. We have no backup.

It doesn't matter if every one of them saw me imprint on Colton; it's public knowledge Juan is denying the bond, and he has sent me to dwell here to stay away from his son. They know not to kill or maim me, but messing me up a little, doing unspeakable things ... his son would recover the pain quickly and not carry the emotional scarring that I would - I'm not safe.

I stop my daily ritual pacing and slump down on my bed. Vanka came in, grabbed some belongings, and left again. She is also keeping her distance since the turning. It seems my public shaming with Colton put me on some kind of social outcast list, even among my fellow unwanteds.

Not one of them has looked my way or talked to me in days. No one wants to know me or be seen associating with the girl who had the audacity to bond to someone way above her station. Especially not Prince Santo himself. Like I somehow orchestrated all this, and it wasn't fated at all. Committed some kind of heinous sin that marks me as the lowest of the low, even in this crappy home.

The only thing keeping me from being killed is that Colton will die if anyone touches me. I mean, I'm sure if I were cornered and attacked by someone, it would affect him too, but it doesn't seem to matter to the circling predators in this house. Most hate the Santos, any of the Alphas for that matter, because they know they will never be them or match up to them, and jealousy and ego are a lethal combination. They won't be hunted for inflicting pain on him, only if he dies.

I lie down on my bed, my stomach growling with hunger while tying my insides in knots, but I can't seem to face eating. I try; I go down for allocated mealtimes, but I pick at my food, and it all tastes like cardboard when I put it in my mouth. Nothing shifts this feeling, this deep emptiness creating a cavern inside me, and it's bottomless and cold. The longer this goes on, the worse it gets. The only thing my body craves and wants, it can't have. I hate that he can mess me up like this when we were strangers only days ago. It's not fair!

I close my eyes and will myself to picture anything but him. Push the thoughts of him aside and try to bring forward an image of my parents instead, something I do when I need to self-calm or get a happy memory into the depression of my daily life. I try to conjure an image of my mother's face to bring me some comfort, but they are all becoming blurry, faded pictures in the dark recesses of my mind so that seeing them properly is no longer easy at all. Time is taking them from me, and I have nothing left of them in any form after the elders destroyed all links to our past dead.

I need to see you.

The familiar voice comes out of nowhere, inside my head, and I jump at the intrusion, having a minor heart attack as its beat elevates crazily. Sitting up fast and spinning my head around to scan my room as if he will be standing right here. I know his voice well enough; I hear it in my dreams whenever I sleep, and my body tingles in response to the contact, goose bumping all over instantly. Insides tingling with anticipation of seeing my mate again. I miss him beyond words, even if it's insane to do so.

Where are you?

I reply desperately, unable to contain the surge of adrenaline that hearing him inside my head gives me. Just a tiny ounce of contact, restoring some of this desolate emptiness I've been feeling since that night.

I'm in the packhouse, and we have to be discreet. Meet me in the West forest, deep down by the old cavern, within the hour. Don't let anyone see you leave. I'm being watched like a hawk, but I know how to get there unseen.... We have to talk face to face.

I almost sob with both the sheer happiness at hearing his voice and the fact I will get to see him for real, not just an image in my head. To share physical air and lay eyes on what my soul craves the most. The only thing dampening my crazy instant joy is the solemn, almost monotone hint in his voice and the lack of excitement I'm experiencing as I pick up emotions through the link.

Can't we talk like this first? I don't know if I can get out right away, and it feels so good hearing you inside my head again. Don't go. Talk to me now.

I sound as desperate as I feel, and I don't want him to close the link once more. I've waited endlessly to have him link me like this.

No. It's harder like this. It only strengthens our bond when we link this way, and I have a lot to say. I told you, this needs to be face to face. There's something we have to do correctly.

My heart plummets into my stomach as his Alpha tone sees through, and I know I'm being commanded and not asked. That doesn't sit well, and the sense of foreboding that sentence gives me rips my soul in two. Whatever he wants to say will not be about finding a way to make this work without his father's blessing. He wouldn't worry about our bond strengthening if that were true. I try to ignore the suspicions, but I can't.

Just meet me, please.

This time the tone is gone, and it's a request with a little underlying plea. I hold in the urge to beg him to talk more now and push the tears aside, clinging onto hope that maybe face to face it will be something good, not what I fear, and nod into my empty room. Heaviness consuming me as heartache gnaws at my stomach and chest.

I'll be there.

I sound deflated, sad. Close to breaking, with a raw huskiness in my tone that I can't conceal, I wait for him to close the link between us. Like waiting for something painful to happen, and I hold my breath.

Alora? I'm ... I wish it didn't have to be this way. I'm sorry that it was me.

Before I have time to reply to that strained, husky reply, he closes off, and I physically feel the link between us go dead. My mind is quieting back to solitary, and I know he's gone. Even with a bond, a mate can choose to close the communication channel at will, and he did like he has been doing for days. I stare at the wall numbly, lost in the moment and how empty everything feels once more. Knowing that my prison will be eternal and I can't see any other way out.

I know I'm getting to see him, finally, but everything about that interaction breaks me open, and I roll over into my cushions to sob it all out. Crying in pain that's not too dissimilar to mourning my entire family ten years ago. I feel worse now I've spoken to him briefly. This feels as much of a loss as then, even if it seems crazy and not a comparison. Like something awful is coming, and when I see him, it will only cause me more devastation.

A nagging voice of logic and haste in the back of my head pulls me out of my dark depressive state and reminds me that if I want to get to the forest within the hour, I need to get up and motivate myself. In human form, it's a trek and a half, and I need time to get ready. I've been living in my nightwear for days.

In wolf form, I'll get there in minutes but completely naked, and I haven't yet tried to turn of my own accord. Too preoccupied to even attempt it and wouldn't know how to start without a bit of practice. I need to shower, change, make myself look half-human at least, and hide the dark circles and shadows from pining my days away. I don't want him to see me at my worst.

I am desperate to find relief in the meeting, even if the outcome won't be what my heart hopes. My body is weighed down with lethargy when I drag myself up, and it takes all my willpower to haul ass to the bathroom moments later. Torn in two, though, with a little shining light of delusional hope telling me that maybe what he needs, and wants to do face to face, is mark me as his mate. Perhaps we can do this in secret and find a way to be together—or maybe not.

I still cannot seem to get to grips with how this can be. How imprinting on a relative stranger can completely derail everything you knew before and make you so insanely in need of them you would tie your life up in theirs just to breathe. Pushing that person into the center of everything and craving them with the intensity of severe addiction.

I know more about him than anyone in my life, and I have barely spoken to him. My mind is a chaotic tangle of his life and mine, which once ran separately yet now coincides, and memories blur into one another. I have mental images of him at every age and random knowledge about things most people never know of their mate. I know everything he does about himself, his life, his family, and I'm guessing the same goes for him, too. You truly merge when imprinting, and now I see why it's so rare and potent when it happens. You lose control of everything, and the only thing which matters from there on in is your mate.

We are one in every way possible.

I wash quickly, dress, dry my hair at speed, and attempt to fix my face to hide the blotchiness of my tears. Makeup was never my thing, but this sudden obsessive adoration for Colton makes me want to look my best for him, even if our meeting has a tone that doesn't spell happily ever after for me. I need to have hope.

I clock watch as I apply the bare minimum enhancements and tousle my hair out with my fingers as it forms natural light waves. For a moment, my reflection reminds me of my mother, and I swallow a lump in my throat as the shooting pain of remembered heartbreak hits me like a sucker punch and almost buckles my knees under the weight. Bruising my heart in that unique way that only their loss can.

"I miss you, Mom. I miss all of you."

I stare at the resemblance while biting back tears and then shake her out of my head as I have come accustomed to doing over the years, to bear the ache, and turn to ready myself for getting out of here unseen. The only way I dealt with their loss was to never dwell too long on it. I never really learned any other way.

I turn my attention back to what I need to do. I've never snuck out of the orphanage before, nor ever needed to, but I have a route plan, and I think I know how to get by unseen, where no one will miss me for an hour or two. It's not like this place was ever set up as a prison, and we don't have any guards watching us.

I scribble a hurried note for Vanka, should she care, which is doubtful, telling her I'm taking a book to a secluded part of the garden to hide and read and know she won't bother checking. She doesn't care if I live or die most days, so she sure as hell won't care if I'm not in my room now I no longer have classes to attend.

School ended for me on the day of my turning, as coincidence has it, and I should have been on my merry way to a new life, much like Vanka is planning before the month is out. She's been making arrangements to head off, and soon, this room will be mine alone. That will be the only upside to being stuck here for eternity.

It's not like any new orphans will be heading in here or have done for the last decade. Newborns have families, and unless another war wipes out a lot more of us, I doubt the orphanage will have any new rejects coming in.

I yank on my sneakers, my blue hoody over my tight T-shirt and jeans, and slide out of my room into the deserted hall. It's during class time, so most of the kids are in the rooms of the left-wing right now, learning all about our traditions and history with some academia thrown in. For the most part, they raise us to live among humans, to fit in and exist in their world, so we learn all the same crap they do and how to conceal what we are.

I guess I was lucky that the war confined us here, in our school, and I haven't had to interact with non-wolves since then. Those of us left with no family got pulled out of our human schools amid rumors of a deadly virus plaguing families on the mountain skirts, which meant no officials came knocking. Some of the Alphas, like the Santos, too, for their protection and lineage, but the general population were allowed to keep their places in the real world as though nothing happened. I don't plan to go back there anytime soon either. Now that my change has drastically altered the course of my path.

I sprint to the end of the hall and down the servant stairs to the kitchen, not that we have any, but this house used to belong to the Alpha of the Romaine pack, none of whom returned at all from the great wars, and the place was repurposed for our use. Their wealth is committed to the cause of repairing our society. Probably because they were the smallest of the packs, living on the edge of solitude and far from the rest of the villages, it was a prime location. The house and its lands are secluded enough to confine unwanteds in one corner, to forget us and leave us to our own devices. I guess it's why Colton picked the West forest. It's easy to access from here and close enough for me to get to without effort.

It'll take him longer to get there from where he is, though, as his pack lives on the south side of the mountain, almost seven miles from here. If he can't be seen leaving, he will have to go on foot, not use his truck, and the only option is to turn and wolf it this way. We can cover ground faster as our true selves, and I wonder if I should take him some sort of clothing. Not that seeing him naked is a bad thing, but it might take my focus away from what he wants to say.

I shake my head at my stupidity and realize he probably thought of this and will carry some sort of bag and attire for changing back, that's if he intends to. Maybe he will stay in form and talk to me that way.

No stupid, he said face to face, as using our mind-link will make this worse!

I chastise myself, blaming the lack of sleep for my dumbing down lately, as I slide through the kitchen unseen and get to the back porch door in record time. Getting used to my new speed and zipping around when you don't want to be seen is the perfect practice. I've stopped bumping into things and tripping over my own feet in hyper-speed mode, but I haven't yet mastered how not to get breathless. It takes it out of me after a short sprint.

The garden is empty, but most of the classrooms look into the courtyard, so I make sure I stay in the shadows against the wall and slide along to the concealed part of the garden behind the outhouses. Up and over the eight-foot brick wall with an easy leap, I'm free to run for the woods with no one seeing my escape. It's easier than I thought. Then again, no one expects me to defy rules and go chasing after Colton Santo. I was never this girl before him, and yet now, he has to say the word, and I go ... blindly following my Alpha; another annoying trait of being mated. He commands, and I do. It's kind of pathetic.

My senses are firing on all cylinders of their highest ability, and it's making me a paranoid wreck as I try to forge a path without a trace through the dense forest that leads to where I want to go. I run in the direction I need to go, stopping and dropping behind trees anytime I catch sight of movement or pick up a sound or scent. Heart pounding so hard through my chest, I'm sure anyone nearby will hear it. I try to calm down but to no avail. I've never been a risk-taker or had the bravery to do anything wild, like defy Juan Santo. I must be insane.

I know if I get caught, they'll drag me in front of Juan for breaking the rules set for me. He might worry about killing his son, but he won't worry about putting him through a bit of pain, and I'm not one for a public flogging if I can help it. Colton is stronger than me, and even if he feels my pain, Juan will use it to teach us a lesson.

I don't doubt that cold-hearted bastard would do it for that reason. I've never liked him.

I feel like I've run at least five miles before I stop for much-needed breath, gasping crazily with crushing agony, my limbs beginning to ache and burn from overuse, and the unfamiliarity of running at speed like this. Much like unfit people, we have to build our stamina so the human side can catch up, and I have not been good at building up to this kind of sprint. My legs and muscles are throbbing, and I feel like my tendons are being torn apart. I collapse behind an overgrown ridge to regain some equilibrium so my lungs don't cave in and give myself a few moments before dragging myself up and walking the rest of the way at human speed now that I've made up good time.

Deep in the woods, following the worn animal path to the cavern that I know well, I feel a little lighter and less depressed. Every kid has been here at least once in their life, long before the vampire attacks. This used to be the go-to spot to hang out, play, and swim in the lake nearby, and the path made it impossible to get lost. Animals walking the link to their watering hole left a helpful guide once you reach the shadowy depth of a forest so dense that it's permanently in the dark, even on the brightest of days.

I know this is why he chose this place. As a child, in my memories, he would have seen I frequented it a lot with my brother, Jasper. He knows I know it well. No one comes here now; they're too afraid, yet every kid knows the way and knows exactly how to get here. The fear of vampires still haunts us even now with all the years of quiet living. They are still out there somewhere, and shaded, gloomy, secluded areas like this would be ideal for them to hunt.

A twig snapping off to my left makes me jump a foot high, head snapping to follow its source and eyes burning to see what is coming. I dart inside a large hollow log to conceal myself and glance around, heart elevated and breath laboring quickly. Senses are kicking into red alert.

It's me ... don't be afraid.

The much-longed-for voice in my head, smothering me with calmness like thick honey, and I exhale with both relief and something else. That joy at being close to him again, but I wonder why I haven't picked up on his scent or his proximity yet. We're supposed to feel our mates when they're close.

Where are you?

I mutter awkwardly as I crawl back out, peeking cautiously, picking the dried moss from my hair, and straighten up to scan the woods around me.

"Keeping my distance, downwind of you, over here." He calls back verbally, drawing me to him by voice alone. That explains why I didn't feel or smell him approaching. He's close enough to make me jump, and I spin in the direction his voice came from. I catch sight of him, jumping down from a rock overhanging the clearing to one lower as he pulls on a T-shirt over those sculpted, tanned abs and throws a backpack to the side of him. He must have carried clothes with him, and I have to admit, I'm a little disappointed but eye him appreciatively. My body is heating up with the insane lust I feel for this man because he got within fifty feet. My crazy hormones have had me dreaming of doing all kinds of naked things with him that a virgin shouldn't know how to do.

I move towards him, but he raises his palm and throws me a serious frown that stops me in my tracks. That dominant warning I have to heed.

"Stay there. Don't come closer. It's better for both of us if we keep our distance." He seems exceptionally wary. His voice is a little husky and unsure.

"Why? What do you think I'm going to do to you?" I retort, hurt stupidly, and react as if he offended me on every level. It's an insane disappointment, eating me up inside because all I want to do is run into his arms and continue what was interrupted days ago. I need to feel his skin on mine and hate that he clearly doesn't.

"It's not you. It's me. I'm finding things hard, and after what happened at the packhouse, it's safer to keep you at least thirty feet away from me at all times." He shrugs, rounding those large shoulders and drawing my eye, making it obvious he doesn't trust himself.

I guess he means the kiss and the urge to mark me that followed seconds after. I guess I'm wrong, and he does have the same insane need I do. I have to agree; proximity makes me want to touch him all the more, but thirty feet is a little extreme.

"So why bring me here if you have no intention of coming anywhere near me?" I spin on my heel and head to the log once more to stomp some of this sudden aggression out, only this time I climb on top of the rickety old wood and slump my butt down, dropping my legs over the side to sit comfortably. I am sulking inwardly, like a chastised toddler, and focusing my eyes on the snowdrops pushing through the only crack of sunlight to hit the ground rather than look at him. My pride is wounded, and as stupid as it is, I'm mad at him for it. This hunger is only cured with contact.

"I owed you some sort of explanation for cutting off our link. For staying away after we ... I needed to do this properly."

Colton's voice makes me all kinds of crazy. That deep male sexiness laced with a raw, husky, almost commanding edge. He has always had a lovely voice, that underlying hint of a Colombian accent in its depths, and now, more than ever, it does insane things to my insides and dampens my irritability a little. Not quite all, though.

"Your father made it pretty clear, all the whys and whatnots. I don't need you to repeat it." I snap a little too tetchily and instantly get hit with a wave of sadness, maybe regret, as it moves over me, and I pick up on his feelings. I glance up and see he is marginally closer, and I guess that's why I can now feel what he does. In our separation, I couldn't feel much except my misery. I think that's the only positive about being apart. Now I'm carrying both of our emotions.

"I need to explain *my* reasons. I don't blindly do what he says ... I have my own mind. Please don't be like this. I'm trying to move us forward." He also slumps down on top of a rock not far from me and mirrors my pose, dropping his legs over the edge as we sit facing each other across the clearing in what seems like a vast gulf between us. All my hopes of reuniting with passion and lust, dying a hefty death, and depressing me even more.

"So explain and let me go back to my exciting solitude and imprisonment. I'm totally missing out on the adventures of the day meeting you here." It's sarcastic and drenched in bitterness that even shocks me, and I flinch at how nasty and cold I sound, but it's the pure frustration at the predicament we find ourselves in. Realizing my hurt feelings are getting the better of me, I try to swallow it back and throw him a wary look fleetingly. I catch him out of the corner of my eye frowning and then looking down at his swaying feet, regret all over his face that pains me all the more for my hostility.

"I'm doing what's best for the future of the pack ... all of them. You included. I care what happens to all of us. My father was right, and my mate needs to be worthy to lead by my side one day. We need a strong Luna with pure blood. A warrior who can rise in battle if needed, and we both know that's not you. The vampires won't stay down forever. They'll rise in my reign, if not before. I need to think of our kind and not what my soul craves. Distance is best, and in time, maybe we'll learn to live without it consuming us the way it is now. We have to be practical and think of my responsibility with who I am. It's a heavy weight I've carried my whole life ... it's not yours to share. I need someone like Carmen, with strong gifts and a thirst for blood when the time comes. She's a warrior ... you're a land child. Your family was growers, gatherers ... not hunters, not killers. It is what it is." His whole manner and tone are low and apologetic, a slight rasp to his voice, and he can't seem to look me in the eye. I can't speak as his words choke my throat almost closed. My eyes fill with warm tears that blur everything in front of me. Wounded by something I already know as factual, at being weak blooded and nothing close to a leader, but it still stings to hear him say it so directly.

I've never been more ashamed of my bloodline than at this moment. My heart aching painfully with stabbing throbs, and my insides clench with the sharpest of pangs as he verbalizes exactly what I have known was coming, deep down inside, but too afraid actually to believe.

"You're rejecting me as your mate." I point out croakily, fighting myself to get the words out through the shards of broken glass caught in my throat and dying a little inside. It's almost unheard of for your mate to reject you after imprinting. I don't think it's ever happened. No one challenges the Fates in this way. I should have known it would happen to me, though. I mean, not even a regular wolf wants to shackle himself to a reject as a mate. That kind of shame tars a family for generations. And he's hardly regular.

I knew this was how it was if I stopped and looked at the bigger picture, but somehow, it's different having him say it instead of Alpha Juan. I guess I held a small candle of hope that Colton would feel as strongly as me within our bond and deny his father's commands. As stupid as I know that is, I wanted to believe I was worthy of someone, and maybe the Fates were telling me that. I've always known the importance of his position among us. It's why he has spent his life acting like royalty among us and avoiding my kind altogether. This shouldn't be a shock.

"I have no choice, Lorey."

I instantly break and sob at his use of the pet name used by my family so long ago. Turning away from him and slide off the log to move so he can't see my tears stinging my face with their invasive appearance. Another sign of my weakness and flawed lineage—I cry when everything goes wrong.

Then why bring me here for this? Why not tell me this back in my room and avoid this agony?

It's sent mentally, defying him on his stance of linking anymore, unable to say what I need verbally as I stagger away from him and break into a run. Knowing leaving is a knee-jerk reaction, but I have no space in me for this kind of pain right now, and I don't want to stay and drag it out for what is next to come. I can't handle it; I need to go back to my room and never let him close enough to feel ever again. He wanted me here for one reason only; he has to declare my rejection to make it final. Screw him.

Lorey, wait. Don't go. Please.

I ignore his mental pleas coming at me desperately, struggling to breathe as I break into a super run and try to put distance between us. Sprinting and then hitting full stride, I quickly skim over the landscape and clear fallen trees. Caught in my need to flee and focused on nothing else. Reverting to all fours as my body aches to transform and set me free, I rein it in and shake it out of my head. I don't want to be in wolf form when this distraught. That kind of loss of control can be devastating and forbidden.

I run with blurry vision, washed almost blind with my tears, and gasp when I'm suddenly yanked back, mid-jump, and hauled backward to tumble into a mossy patch in the forest floor with a thud, to roll and land on all fours and instantly bristle defensively. Breathing heavily as I square up to my pursuer aggressively, a new feral kind of instinct I've never felt before, full-on fierce triggered. I calm instantly when faced with Colton, his eyes glowing amber and equally poised for battle. We stay separated, panting, staring each other down, mere feet apart, closer than we should be, and fueled by pure, painful emotion.

"You think this isn't just as hard for me? That doing this is going to cure me of everything?" Colton's desperate plea shines through his own broken words, breaking down my anger and shattering me into tiny pieces. "I had my life mapped out. Chose a mate I loved and thought I knew what the future held. I didn't think this could ever happen, and now, I spend my every waking second wanting you, needing you, and thinking about you until it drives me insane. The love I had for Carmen died the second I imprinted on you, and I can't get my head around any of this either. This isn't a cure ... it's a necessity. For the good of our existence, our pack. No one will follow an Alpha or respect one who shackles a shamed wolf to his side."

Anger overtakes me as jealousy twists my heart around at the mention of her name, the words coming from his mouth, making me irrationally furious at him once more. Heartbreak and sheer hatred for this situation are coming out of every pore.

"Just let me go. This is pointless, and you telling me these things don't help. Just go away and leave me alone. I don't want you near me ever again. I get it ... reject me, say it, and be done with it. Save your precious pack and your honor and go to hell. I was never one of you, anyway!" I snarl at him and wipe the soggy mess from my face with the back of my hand aggressively, full-on faux bravado, and put on the tough girl act as best I can.

Swallowing my tears and gagging on the acid rising in my throat, I stand up to tower over him in his crouched position, adopting an air of 'I don't care anymore' and will him to be done already.

"I didn't want this either. I was leaving. I had a plan, and it was thousands of miles away from all of you. Especially your kind. Santo! You've despised us for a decade, treated us with disdain, and shunned us to the shadows of that damn orphanage. I spit on your family and all they are. You're the last person in this world I would ever want to imprint on, so go ... go mark your mate and follow your destiny because it sure isn't me. Be with your chosen one and leave me to find one of my own. My heart will heal from whatever this was, faster than you can imagine, and you can stop pretending you don't want her. I don't want you either!"

It's said in anger and heartbreak, and I can't conceal how much pain is ripping through me anymore. All my energy is going into pulling on this hard outer shell and showing him I don't give a crap anymore. I turn, this time to walk away slowly, too exhausted for anything else and unable to maintain a run as fatigue overtakes me.

"I love you. No matter what I do to try to break it, I can't stop, and the thought of you being with another kills me. There is no her anymore, Lorey. There's just us. We imprinted and got to know each other in a split second, the way a lifetime of being together would. I feel like I've loved you that long, no matter how insane that sounds." His words stop me in my tracks, and I inhale sharply. Stunned that he came out and said it, but saddened that he verbalized what the agony I have been suffering is called— Love! And why it feels like he's been in my heart since the day I was born. Imprinting royally messes you up.

It made me love my mate as soon as it happened because it makes you relive every second that came before, in your head, within your memories, with that person's entwined even though they don't belong to you. I have his life in my head; therefore, I've known him intimately for that long. It's insane, and he's right. We

58

can't break it because we were never in control of it. Fate did this, dealt us a hand and a cruel joke, and fate doesn't like defiance. Knowing he feels as I do doesn't make it any, though. It doesn't change a thing.

"It doesn't mean anything. Your father was right when he told us to stay away and break the link. I can't ever be what your father and the pack need, and you can't ever be the mate I need. So, we shouldn't do this again; it's only torturing us more than we are already. Just say the damn words already. I don't care." I don't know where this is coming from, this detached, cold bitch, as words spill out of my mouth. It's the exact opposite to what my heart craves, and I turn to face him to drive it further home that I'm not playing. Wiping my expression as clean as I can to show him nothing of how this is killing me. My words die on my lips when our eyes meet, and Colton looks as openly broken and disheveled as I am.

"You can't lie to your mate, Lorey. I can feel you, even if what you're saying sounds honest. I am what you need, and you're what I need. Fate made it so. When you strip everything else away, and it's just us, here and now, with no one else to think about ... we need each other to feel sane. To stop this eternal agony and emptiness, we're both harboring. We don't need to pretend it's any other way. There should never be lies between us." We both stand in hopeless silence as he gets up to stand too, towering over me by at least a foot, yet we're still at least three apart. He doesn't hesitate and closes the gap, pulls me to him by the waist, gently, his touch searing my skin through my clothes, and I can't deny that I do need him. I can't fight it.

Bringing his forehead to mine, he places us together, so his breath fans my face impulsively. I close my eyes and inhale his scent. Our connection only drives home that we are meant to be like this. It's familiar, safe, and home. Where skin touches, amazing things happen, and the energy which sizzles between us is incomparable. Lighting my body on fire, and I burn to be joined entirely to him, aching with a need that makes my legs turn weak. For the first time since this began, I'm at peace instantly, and every pain and torment, all the confusion I've been through, quiets to absolutely nothing.

Just him and me, and a sharing of every feeling. Highlighting the peace we can find in touch.

We both let go of our held breath and exhale in unison, as though finally finding where we need to be for a moment of serene. A second of calm in the stormy sea that has been thrashing us around since I awakened.

Colton lifts his hand slowly and strokes a single finger across my cheek, brushing away my hair, and tucks it behind my ear. Leaving a hot, tingling path where he connects with me. The heat draws down deep inside my soul to bring warmth to the coldness dwelling within.

"I want nothing more right now than to unify our bond and mark you. Believe me when I tell you that if I were anyone else's son, you would already bear my mark and know what it feels like to have me inside you. The union would be complete. I love you, Lorey, in ways I didn't know I could love anyone. I thought I knew what it was to commit my soul to my mate, but I was wrong. I need you to know this isn't what I want ... that I'm sorry ... but I have no other choice. I have to reject ..." Colton falters, his raw croaking tone breaking, then he swallows hard, bringing back all the anguish from before, and a solitary tear rolls down his cheek and drips onto mine to continue its painful journey. Wounding me with its searing burn. His pain is evident, and for a second, his anguish and confusion flow through my soul, too, telling me he can't do it alone. My heart is already turning to ash as he destroys me with his words, but we have to be stronger.

I know what he has to say, that it has to be done. Know why. It's how it is. We can't change, fight, or do this any other way; hearing it may kill me, but I have to let him do it. There's no alternative, and as much as I want to scream and stop this, I understand. I can't hate him for it.

I'm no Luna. I'm a Whyte wolf from the family Dennison. A shamed bloodline who all fell in battle, and we don't have a right to stand up by an Alpha's side to tar his name. I don't have it in me to lead, and I'll be nothing but a weight of shame hanging around his neck, his weakness in battle, and the demise of his bloodline. I can't be the reason he loses the respect of the packs and upturns his entire life.

I say nothing, stay deathly still, silent tears escaping from my closed eyes as they begin to pour down my face. Warm, bitter, stinging rivulets of despair. He can feel me and hear my thoughts, so he knows my acceptance is in my silence. My pain is his; my distraught agony in knowing this is over before it began is all around and in between us. He knows what to do. His breathing gets heavier, labored, as he struggles to compose himself and push the last of the words out in a voice I barely recognize—low and strained. Ravaged and hoarse. He clears his throat and swallows loudly as though to pull himself together.

"I ... Colton Juan Santo, son of the Alpha of the reigning Santo pack, and future Alpha of Mount Radstone ... I'm sorry, baby, don't hate me for this ... reject you as my chosen mate and deny the bond of imprinting. I set you free ... to ..." He swallows hard again, voice wavering, choking on his tears, pulling me into his embrace, crushing me with strong arms to find the will to carry on. Wrapping me up in his body as though he wants to shield me from what he is doing and memorize the feel of me for eternity. I can feel everything, know his emotions as if they are my own, and it kills me. His regret, anguish, and overwhelm at the pain of being the one who delivers the wounding blow to my heart.

"... find a chosen mate as you see fit, as will I, with no interference, even if it causes pain. My word cannot and will not be broken, and I will not intervene should you find your path. This cannot be undone. I set you free, for now, and for all eternity. May the Fates be kind and give you a pass to a better future." His words are barely audible, his voice so much lower, breathless, as he binds me against him almost cruelly, with the force of his passion. The sound of blood rushing through my ears blots the world out as I spiral into a complete emotional breakdown, tearing my mind to shreds.

Finish it!

I blurt through the head link, knowing he has to. I can't stand this any longer. I need the words to stop, for it to be over, and this to be done. His touch is my torture, and his voice my final blow. Colton shudders in my arms, his face wet too, and he buries a hand in the back of my hair as he cradles me against him tightly. Almost like he can stop it hurting me if he crushes me to him and melts our bodies to one form.

"After today, the link will be closed, our bond ignored, and we should never cross paths again. That is my command. It's done. We're done. Forgive me, Lorey. I'm sorry. I love you, and I wish this could be different." The final words deliver the crushing blow I knew they would, and I feel like my heart is giving out and refusing to beat. My mind blanks, my tears still with shocked numbness, too much heartbreak for my mind to deal with anymore.

The Fates will pay no heed to his request, but I'm no longer his mate or bound to be by wolf law. His father will rejoice when he tells him. He's set me free, and we've chosen to live with the pain of severance against the imprinting. No matter how much it hurts.

We stand for what feels like the longest minute, holding each other, broken inside, and crying silently in our own, and combined, personal hell. My face buried against his shoulder and his face in my hair, arms entangled and fully fitted frontally, so every curve and line meet, right down to our ankles. We inhale, we cast each other's scent to memory, and when I don't think I have the strength to let go, he finally leans back and lifts my chin to his, pushing me to open my tear flooded eyes, so I fall into those chocolate browns for the last time.

"I love you." He utters hopelessly, anguish in his stare, the tensing of that square jawline, and yet all I hear is goodbye. A raspy farewell, one I can never erase from my memories or how he looks while saying it to me. He's too beautiful for words.

"I love you too," I mutter, so quietly, it's not even a whisper, but it's impulsive and raw and honest. He leans in and gently kisses me on my lips, so softly it's feather-light, but it ignites that all-consuming agony that only he can cause. It's so perfect it hurts. A brushing of warm damp softness, grazing that destroys what little is left of me, and tears unleash with enthusiasm once again.

As though casting my face to memory, he stares at me long and hard, pain etched on his face and his own eyes wet with the evidence of his regret. He kisses me one last time, on my forehead, tenderly, holding there a moment and fighting all the need and desire inside of us. The fire is burning despite the fact we deny it.

He lets me go, backs up several steps, and then turns on his heel and runs. No looking back for a second time, no torturing himself with one last lingering look, leaving the heavy air of sorrow floating between us.

He makes it only a few feet before he jumps a log turns in mid-air, his clothes disintegrating into wispy pieces of fabric floating down to earth, so silently destroyed. That flash of midnight black wolf, so beautiful and strong, and a sight to behold.

He's gone at the speed of light. Leaving me standing alone in the forest, abandoned and lonely, unwanted. I break down and crumble into a pit of despair and wracking sobs into the moss under my feet, no longer wary of my surroundings as a broken heart consumes me.

The sounds of a distant, painful wolf howling, pulling me to stare up into the emptiness of where he was, fills the forest air with the wails of his misery and despair. It's the worst noise in the world.

THE BEGINNING

It's been thirteen days since Colton left me in the forest, and I don't think I have the will to keep trying anymore. I'm tired of life, and everything has become so mundane. Everything I thought I experienced before that day is nothing compared to how I've been since. It's like my family has died all over again, and I am bereft and inconsolable. I've no more tears because I've cried so many. I'm nothing but a numb, hollow shell, and the sunlight has withdrawn from my world to leave me in eternal cold shadow.

I tried to stop the spiraling depression; I fought hard to beat this feeling of being sucked free of all life, but the Fates don't play when you deny them. I'm not even living anymore. Such is my empty continuous state of nothing.

I robotically move from my room to kitchen, kitchen to chores, and chores to my room, day after day. I've nothing to say, nothing to add to the conversations around me, and nothing to do or think about beyond focusing on this eternal emptiness that I drag around day after day. It's like a sack of boulders chained to my back, and I can't free myself to outrun them.

I was never this girl. I survived the loss of so much more, yet I don't know how to fight this. I've read books in the library that blame the severance for my worsened state and mental decline. Cast free; set afloat by a rejection of this level messes with you more than the rejection of a regular union ever could.

Wolves can pick mates; it's not always fated. And usually, both parties get a choice, so you have to be pretty sure to shackle your heart to someone if you're going to ask them to be mated for life.

Scenting happens. That's when the mate you are most likely to bond with can smell out your scent among the many and identify you quickly. It's usually how we figure out who we want before seeing them. Mates should, and can, smell each other, no matter the distance or the crowds. So, rejecting someone who syncs with your scent can be crushing as it is. Rejecting someone who imprints at the hands of the Fates; there is no recorded outcome. No one has ever defied it because, quite simply, no one fights the union.

Imprinting is soul mate lore. It's magical. Unbreakable, pure, and potent, defying logic, sense, or reason. It's all-encompassing 'insta-love' and a need and hunger more powerful than any bond in the land. No one wants to deny that kind of obsessive connection and walk away to find another mate—until us.

I can confirm rejecting that kind of bond is like dying, only not letting the body fade out to black when the soul leaves you. I'm a walking shell. Zombified and unable to do anything about it, and death right now is looking a hell of a lot rosier than this. I'm in purgatory, only it looks exactly like my life before, yet a whole lot suckier.

I don't even know if this is how Colton feels because sometimes the rejector has minimal backlash in the way the rejected does. They choose to end things, and, for some reason, the Fates let them get away with crushing another's soul. I guess that's why selecting a mate is not an impulse thing, and marking someone you have been dating can sometimes be a choice for many years.

I mean, look at Carmen and Colton. Two years and he still hasn't marked her, even though he told me he chose to mate up with her. Even he wasn't ready to commit in case she turned him down, and everybody knows how much she loves him.

I've tried not to wonder over the past two weeks if they have rekindled their love affair, but I guess I would know. We're bonded, so I would feel it if he had sex with anyone else, whether I want to or not. Hell, I'll feel it if he even kisses anyone. From what

I have read, even a verbal renouncement should make no difference to me being able to know when he betrays the Fates and procreates with another. The only balance to that is he'll feel it if I do, too. Whoever ordained this bullshit needs therapy because someone up there has a twisted sense of what's right.

I jump out of my skin when the door slams behind me and brings me back to reality with a bump. Daydreaming again while folding my laundry and flinch when Vanka strolls in, smoking a cigarette, and fills our room with the putrid choking smell of her bad habit. We're supposed to have a house rule against smoking, but it's not like Vanka ever does anything she's ever told.

"Do you mind?" I snap at her bitchily, wafting my hand in the air as the smoke curls towards me. Trying to stop it from invading my newly heightened senses and stifle a cough as it hits the back of my throat.

"No, not really." She blows a fresh wave right at me as she strolls past, sashaying her hips, and hits me with a sneer as she goes. I bite on my lower lip and ignore her before this turns nasty. She's always been quick to aggression and left me with some pretty bad bruises and scrapes over the years. I know better than to start another fight with her.

I sigh heavily and go back to what I'm doing, folding clothes on my bed, wanting to have this done before lights-out in a few minutes. There aren't many house rules for us, but our guardians have very strict lights out and locked doors rule as soon as the moon comes up. It goes back to the wars and that vampires can only come out when the sun goes down. The only time we have an exception is the full moon, every cycle, for the ceremony on Shadow Rock. We don't have packs to protect us here, so we don't get any leeway in our freedom living in the orphanage.

Vanka's eyes bear down on me, and, reluctantly, I look up and penetrate her with a questioning stare. She wants something that's obvious, but it won't come as a polite request. It never does.

"I'm going out after the guardians go home ... if you snitch, I'll mess you up." The amber glow in her eyes adds weight to the promise, and I eye-roll, no longer intimidated since my power to heal and fight back improved dramatically with my turning.

"Why would I snitch? I don't care what you do." I go back to staring at the endless pile of laundry, mostly PJs, and try hard to ignore her. No energy for this at all.

"Good. I have a hot date with one of the boys from the Ryleigh pack. It's nothing serious, totally slumming it, and wants to try it on with a shameful reject. He's a weird one with some serious kinks." She laughs dirtily, looking for a reaction, igniting an instant unease down deep in my stomach.

Most she-wolves save themselves for the one-day mate, but I guess girls like us don't have any reason to. Even when we get a chance, they reject us based on who we are.

"Use protection. An unwanted kid would end up right back here, and you'd have no choice but to stay." I warn, more for my benefit than hers. I've been counting down the days when she leaves me in peace, and I can fumigate her rank scent from this room. I've nothing else in life to look forward to anymore, so I may as well have that. Room to myself, space to call my own.

"Whatevs. Maybe you should try it and fuck up that pretty little Santo head a little for throwing you in the trash. It's bound to sting." She sneers and laughs at her devious plan, but I ignore it. As much as he's broken me, I still love him and wouldn't want to inflict that kind of pain. Hell, I wouldn't want to do it to myself; I've no desire to have sex with anyone that's not him, as stupid as that sounds.

"Tell me ... is it true you two were mid-screw and ready to mark when Daddy walked in and threw your ass out?" It's the snide, catty tone that riles my temper, and I throw her a pointed snarl, pinning her eyes with mine as she hits a nerve. Erupting furiously, without restraint, as it comes out so fast, I can't counteract.

"It's got nothing to do with you, so shut the hell up." The insane instant deep rumble and scathing tone I elicit scares even me, and as her eyes widen in shock, she drops her cigarette right out of her gawping mouth. I recoil, wondering what the hell that was. I didn't sound like me at all, and that hostility came from nowhere. My blood riled and heated up in a split second and forced out what I assume was my wolf growl. I guess she hit a nerve.

"What the fu ... your eyes ... they're red." She stutters, visibly shaken, and backs away from me a little before realizing her lap is burning and starts madly grabbing for her dropped fire stick like a mental person. Soon as she retrieves it, she backs up and slides by me, near the wall, before escaping out of our bedroom door with a wary backward glance, a look of unadulterated fear, and takes off at speed.

I'm left dumbfounded at both my guttural, aggressive response and this goddamn red crap. I push off from where I am, stepping to the mirror in three strides across the room, and stare at my reflection before the rage in me calms back to numb. I have to see this. It's a stirring memory of Colton's words, and I blanch when I see the evidence for myself and gasp in horror.

She's right.

Colton was right.

There before me, seeing for the first time how I look when my eyes flash with a warning that I am on the verge of turning, I face two glowing orbs of the darkest blood red in place of where amber should be. They are almost satanic in their fire and sparkle, making me look insane or demonic.

The shock and instant fear that cascades through my veins icily mute them back to natural green instantly. I fall back, eliciting a yelp as I'm gripped with a sense that something is really wrong with that.

Red? What the hell?

They're not red. They can't be. No one has red, never in all the times, notes, books, packs, clans, and history, of our kind. I've never heard of it, and I realize that the elders have forgotten about Colton pointing it out that day. It was never mentioned again. Maybe they thought he was mistaken, or they were so preoccupied with the fact he almost marked me right under their noses that was a far more pressing issue. I mean, it's ludicrous.

It's not a thing; this is not a thing! Our eyes are amber. They can't be any other color.

I start panicking, pulling myself back to the mirror and trying to force myself to bring them back, but that ingrained terror running through me stops it from happening. I don't know what to do or what it means.

Am I sick? Is there something wrong with me? I don't know what to think, and I pace insanely, flustered and freaking out, heart close to popping an artery as it thunders insanely in my chest. My brain is spinning nauseatingly that maybe there is something really, really wrong with me. I thought nothing of it when Colton said it, and to be frank, I thought he was tripping and not seeing clearly. Somehow with all the chaos, the drama, the heavy emotions swirling around, he saw red because of his own rage and mood at the time.

I should go to the medic, right? I should call the Shaman. Maybe he will know?

My breathing's shallow as my lungs burn with the effort to get oxygen, wringing my hands and running my fingers through my hair as I try to self-regulate the insane pounding of my heart. My blood pressure is hiking, and I start to feel woozy, nauseous, skin bristling with searing temperature as I lose control. I mean, I feel like I've found out I have cancer or a deadly virus that's incurable, or that Armageddon is on its way, and we have nowhere to run.

I need to calm down. If I don't, I might turn and do something stupid in a blind haze. We're not supposed to turn if we feel like we can't control it. That's when bad things happen; wolves do terrible, awful things to the humans nearby. Frenzied, bloodlust-driven, murderous things and then have no memory after.

I have to breathe and slow it down. Except I can't. I'm spiraling, and I flop down on the ground pathetically, crumpling as my legs give out from shaking crazily. I clutch my head to force myself to focus on my breathing. Face planking the floorboards to get a grip on reality.

What's wrong, Lorey. What is it? Talk to me. I can feel your panic and your fear. What's happening, baby. What's going on?

His voice renders me momentarily stunned, and I snap up, spinning around on my ass, looking for the intruder before sense tells me he is inside my head.

Colton? Why're you in my head?

I blanch and press my hands to the sides of my skull, and slump back down to put my face between my knees. To continue trying to regulate my breathing once more, confused that he linked after the two-week silence of rejection I've endured and still caught up in my meltdown.

I told you. I can feel you freaking out. You're afraid. What is it? What's happening? Tell me. If you need me, need my help, I need to know where you are.

The sob that bursts from my throat as he says the words I've been longing to hear since I last saw him breaks me all over again. That care and need to protect me because, despite rejection, he still has the urges of a mate. I blurt out my worry and break into over-emotional terrified tears, fueled by knowing I'm a freak with blood-colored eyeballs.

My EYES are RED!! I think there is something seriously wrong with me.

I snort and wail into the emptiness of my room, gripped by actual devastation. Really not too focused on the fact that he's actually talking to me because this is bigger, scarier, and overwhelming.

Jesus Christ, Lorey. I thought something was happening to you. Don't do that to me! Stop crying!

The sharp Alpha tone of dominance winds me, and I instinctively obey. I choke and then cough on a tear that had been midflow when he hit me with that crap. Instantly enraged, as the pain of my body shutting off my emotional response momentarily winds me, forced out of a real heartfelt need to cry by a bossy asshole abusing his gift.

Don't use that tone on me! Don't tell me what to do!

I snap back, bristled in a fury, forgetting myself as anger bursts forth, stunning me into immediate silence as I clasp a hand over my mouth, despite saying nothing verbally.

He's not my mate anymore, but a dominant in our lands, and talking back like that could get me seriously messed up if he saw fit.

It's disrespectful on so many levels. No one of my standing would ever, should ever, snark back at an Alpha.

I'm sorry. I didn't mean that.

I backtrack like a total coward and start to whimper as fresh tears begin to fall all over again. A combination of my previous panic setting in and the sheer devastation of talking to him like this once more now that my faux pas has shaken sense into me. It hurts more than I can bear.

It doesn't matter. Calm down, I'm sorry. I just needed you to stop ... listen to me, Lorey. I knew about your eyes, remember. There's nothing wrong with you. The Shaman has been researching all this time. Just try not to let anyone see in the meantime until I know what it means. There've been others, but none you will find in the history books. The Shaman doesn't know why, but you have to keep it under wraps and stop freaking out. Do you hear me? You almost gave me epic heart failure coming through like that.

I wipe my face and try to pull myself together, exhaling heavily to steady myself and sitting upright forcefully. A little soothed by what he said, enough to rationalize and stop acting like a complete idiot. Bringing my attention to the fact that things feel less harmful when he's in my head. My pain subsides enough to function with even this kind of connection to him.

I didn't mean to project on you. I wasn't trying to reach you; I know how things are between us. I swear.

I sound like a pathetic whiny child, and it drives home how non-Luna I am.

This wasn't you. We're bonded. When you're afraid to that extent, hurt, anything like that, I'll still feel it, no matter what we do. Just try to be rational. Hold it together.

I guess it works both ways. Not that big tough Colton Santo probably ever gets freaked out or scared. I doubt I'll ever feel any extremes from him on my end, he's way too mature and battle seasoned for any kind of hysterics.

What if I'm sick?

I pout petulantly. Not all that settled with his explanations and still mulling. Shaking now the shock is settling in and sniffing my mess away.

You're not sick. I would know.

He almost chastises me as a paternal tone takes over, and I try not to picture his face as his voice surrounds me. It already hurts enough to hear him; I don't need a visual reminder on top of that.

Then what if I'm cursed, and this is how you know. Maybe I'm a walking hex! Red's the color of danger.

I point out. There's a real possibility in that. I mean, it's me, after all.

According to our kind, all of you in that home is cursed ... are their eyes red too?

I swear that was a hint of sarcasm, warming his tone to suggest humor, but I let it slide.

Okay then, what if I'm not a werewolf and I'm something else?

The silence that stretches out between us makes me shudder, and the panic once again soars.

OH, my God, that's it, isn't it?!?!

I squeak, unleashing a god-awful noise in the process, and jerk upright, eyes widening as that fear hits me low in the belly once more, and I lurch to my feet to pace erratically.

NO! No ... okay. I was considering it, but that's dumb. There are no others like us, so it's not that. Besides, I saw you turn! You're a wolf, a pretty one at that.

Colton soothes, if somewhat bossily, yet it seems to work, and I exhale heavily and stop walking around in manic circles. I blush at the wolf remark, even if I know he's probably trying to be nice to pull my head out of hysteria.

Hmm. How do you know there aren't other wolfy-type beings?

I push, voice strained and fear still lingering now my brain is on this path to self-analysis. My heart rate is climbing higher, and my feet itch to start walking again.

We imprinted. I'm pretty sure two different species can't do that. Fate wouldn't allow that. It's insane. You're the same as me, Lorey, trust me. We'll figure this out.

I hate that despite everything, his deep soothing tone and sexy voice have a commanding ability that makes me feel like he can make everything okay. That he's in control and there to catch me.

It's not your job to figure this out. There is no we.

I remind him sullenly, and that familiar pang I've been carrying for weeks comes back to nestle in my chest. My fear subsides, overpowered by my longtime companion and shadow —heartbreak.

Lorey ...

It's a soft regretful whisper and tears my heartstrings. He doesn't get to finish whatever he was going to say, as a deafening painful scream, so insanely loud, high pitched, ad blood-curdling in its reverberation, tremors through the house and vibrates everything around me. My head, my body, my brain, and the surrounding forests shake and stutter in such a way that my whole body spasms aggressively. It turns my blood to ice instantly, frozen still in fear, and catapults me out of my head like a vicious eject button that sends me crashing to the floor heavily.

It's the loudest, most painful noise I've ever felt in my life. In a crumpled heap and gasping in terror, it feels like something physically swept through the walls, like an invisible wall of power and chaos, and rendered me completely useless. The overwhelming nausea and agony it inflicts on me at that moment send me reeling across the floorboards, scrambling nails on the slippery surface, to fight the penetrative pain of my brain nearly exploding.

What the fuck? What the hell was that? Lorey? Lorey ... answer me?

Colton's panic-stricken tone dances through my mind, but I'm still reeling from the internal vibrations consuming my every nerve ending, from that god-awful noise that seems to pulse around me as my senses fade in and out. My body is twitching, and I don't feel right at all.

It's done something to me. I'm weak and unable to move, barely able to breathe as though all my organs are struggling to fight the pulse and function. Dragging myself to lie flat on my stomach, I try to haul myself to the door. Head pulsating with the aftereffects of whatever that was, brain bruised and throbbing, and although it's no longer blasting, I can feel something in the air around me. Like invisible thick smog holding me down, swiping my ability to get up as though it's sucking all the oxygen and energy away.

Colton ... something's wrong ... I can't get up.

I gasp for air, head swimming with stars and darkness invading my vision, trying so hard to pull myself up. I'm wracked with pain and have no strength to fight it. I'm powerless, and as the effects of whatever that was have rendered me completely useless, I lose the ability to link to Colton, too. Feeling him drop out of my head on my end as though my gift ceases to be before blankness fully smacks me in the face, and I pass out.

Vanka

I wake up groaning, spitting blood and phlegm, and scramble to get off the floor in the pitch black of my room. The hot fluid running down the sides of my face tells me my ears are bleeding, my head's aching like it got stomped on repeatedly, and I'm so dizzy I can't seem to focus on anything. The air is deathly cold, and I scrape my hands around the dusty wooden floor to get my bearings. I've no idea what's happened, why there's no light anymore, or why I'm so messed up, dazed and confused, and my body aches badly.

The air is filled with noises so terrifying I freeze in utter fear as they filter through, and I pick them apart, stilled as I listen and try to make sense of what they are. My heart gripped in icy terror.

Screaming, howling. Wails of despair and sobbing. Something else, too, a weird, almost chatter-like taunting noise that I swear is precisely how I would imagine the devil would sound laughing. It sends the fear of God through me, and I shudder violently, pulling myself up to huddle on my ass, aware I can move again, even if a little slow and with great effort. My limbs are insanely heavy, and I'm hazy and not all the way here.

There's a metallic stench in the air so intense it makes me gag, completely vile in its density, and although I don't know what's going on, my internal instincts are warning me to be very, very afraid. I shiver and curl up into a ball, trying to be small as childhood instincts take over, swallowing down the urge to cry and struggle not to gasp as much because it's making me lightheaded. I screw up my eyes to get them to adjust to the pitch blackness faster

75

and try to make out all the forms and shapes of my room. My sight adjusts quickly and lets me see some of my surroundings.

There's a sudden thud, thud, thud, which piques my attention like a sixth sense and echoes my way softly, my stomach turning with fear-induced nausea as I zone into it. I hold my breath and freeze, as still as a statue, as I tune in, trying to focus all my effort on what it is. It's less imposing than the rest of the noises, sort of dull, heavy, and foreboding, but it's slicing through and pulling my painful hearing toward it, demanding attention. I can feel it getting closer, almost like each thud syncs with my heartbeat, and my pain drops to my stomach with every bang of its harsh noise. I tremble inside with extreme terror, knowing that it's coming my way.

The overwhelming stench of something familiar wafts my way as I focus my energy, and it distracts me from listening. I know the smell. It's not metallic; it's a scent. A wolf scent, familiar ... someone I know.

Instinct makes me push back, despite the world tilting and swaying around me, and I slide backward under the nearest bed. Scrambling flat again and using my palms and all the strength I can muster to force myself into the shadows of my only protection. I inhale sharply, and that scent forms a picture in my mind of the face it belongs to, so clear now it's almost upon me.

It's Vanka's. It's her smell, her scent. Strong as though she's afraid or in wolf form. I don't know.

I claw and pull myself under, breaking nails painfully in the process as I scramble in panic. Something's telling me to hide. Until the sheets conceal me, she leaves hanging over with her refusal to make her bed, and, for once, I'm glad of her untidiness. Thankfully, her bed is always a mess, leaving chaos around it, which now conceals me, and I curl into my own body to fit in one corner. I peer out, gut telling me I should be quiet and stay hidden. I hold my breath and cover my mouth with my hand as tears roll silently down my cheeks. Fear trying to consume me, making me shake so badly I'm sure it'll give me away.

My door is still open, and as I become accustomed to the dark, my nocturnal eyes coming out to play for the first time since my turning, I make out something passing the open space and inhale quickly to quiet myself into stillness. Heart bursting through my chest, pounding my ribs erratically as tears drench my hand and wrist.

Something tall and dark swaggers in the space out there, imposing and blurry as I adjust, but it pauses and stops, right outside. Almost like it senses me, and I recoil some more, trying to make myself as small as I can. I'm so scared. It turns slowly to peer my way, and everything in me turns to ice as a terrified feint drains me of all blood. I close my eyes, screw them shut tight, and clench my fists, trying to become completely cut off and invisible as best I can. Praying to the Fates that they don't see me. Whatever it is, I know it's not a friend. It's not one of us.

"Here puppy, puppy ... where are you hiding? I know there's at least one more up here ...." The bloodcurdling words make me scrunch my face up to combat hysterical tears, the voice alien to me, almost satanic, low, and husky, with a heavy accent in its depths. Foreign, yet I don't know what. I don't know this voice.

The scent is nothing I've ever encountered before and dampens over the one I vaguely recognize. It's not Vanka, but I can smell her close, which only confuses my fear-addled brain. The sadistic laugh that follows his bold verbal turns my insides to mush, and I physically weaken with an icy wave as whatever, or whoever, it steps inside the room with me.

"I can hear your heart beating, little one ... Bumpity, bumpity, bump, bump, bump. You're scared. Why don't you come out and play like your friends are doing? I want to play with you, too." He laughs again, a sound that curls my toes and sends shivers across my scalp and down my spine so that I shudder uncontrollably. The sound of someone truly deranged and evil, and I almost lose control and freak out. Tightening myself stiff and holding my breath to keep myself together.

I cover my mouth again, tighter, as the urge to break into a sobbing cry hits me harder, and I shake, holding my breath and praying to God he leaves me alone. I don't know who he is. I'm so disoriented, and the smell overpowering my senses has me trying hard not to gag while keeping my focus on this stranger. I can taste something foul in the air, hitting my tongue, invading my lungs, awful and cloying. So metallic and potent that it makes my eyes sting and water with its toxicity.

He's not one of us. I don't know what he is, but his intentions aren't good. I can almost taste his desire for blood, and it renders me completely useless. Frozen and terrified. He ventures in further from the doorway, dragging something heavy along behind him that identifies the thud, thud I heard coming my way.

I choke on instant bile as it rises in my throat and almost suffocates me in the process. My heart is near imploding as my body convulses at the sight of the lifeless and headless body he's dragging behind him. Gagging on my vomit, I can't block out her scent.

Panic, hysteria, and the crumbling of my mental state as I identify what and who, he has with him. There is no mistaking who has fallen foul to whatever this is. I can't unsee or blot it out no matter how much I try to turn away, wash it out of my eyes and mind with snotty tears.

It's Vanka. She's dead! She's right there, feet in front of me, dragged by this monster and used as a toy for his sick, twisted game.

"I know where you are, puppy. Why don't you come out and do me a favor? I don't want to have to drag you out from under there. It's no fun if I have to do that." There's a sneer of venomous hatred in his voice, and I imagine the way his face curls into a sadistic grin, glaring my way through the darkness. Enjoying every moment of this.

He drops her lifeless form on the floor with a dull thud, her body splaying her arms out in a star shape, and I recoil, tears blurring my vision as I try to make myself as small as I can back here. Whimpering internally.

I don't know what to do. I'm petrified, and if Vanka was no match for this thing, then I'm not either. I don't know how to fight; I've never had to. I'm not a warrior or even aggressive. I'm nothing, a reject from a farmer's family who is worth nothing to no one.

I bite on my lip, fear paralyzing me when suddenly, the entire bed is ripped from above me, the gust of the action throwing my hair around my face, and he sends it crashing into the other wall effortlessly, displaying strength much like ours. I gasp and react with a shuddering splaying of arms over my head defensively as it flies and lands over on top of mine dramatically. The crashing, splintering noise of a wooden bed crumbling and shattering into chaos. I'm left exposed, fully accessible prey huddled in the smallest of corners. He comes at me with a flash of speed that I see coming as if in slow motion, and I gasp in horror, choking up and immobile for a second.

Move, Alora ... move!

Some strong inner voice hits me as I chant to myself, trying so hard to make my body work with me, to command it somehow, but nothing is happening. It's like my brain is in slow motion and my limbs in hibernation. I shake my head, try to dislodge this overwhelming dizziness, and focus on doing something. Anything ...

It's dark, it's eerily still, and it's like time has slowed, so his movements are almost paused. Instinct takes over, finally. Blood rushing and pumping at speed as he scrapes a step closer to me.

In a flash equal to his speed, if not more, I bolt from my flat-out position with a renewed lease of energy from God knows where and aims for the door. Adrenaline spiking, survival instinct kicking in, and praying I turn without even knowing how to. Even though I'm stronger and faster in human form since turning, our wolves are way more so. I need to turn, to survive and to heal, to fight. We only heal fast when in form. We only have abilities of extreme strength, ferocious aggression, and razor-sharp claws and teeth when we turn.

I don't get far because he catches me by the back of my hair effortlessly, snares and tugs it, and throws me backward as though I'm a limp rag. Smashing me into the vanity with force, sending me crashing through the mirror and splintering wood, and into a heap on the floor as heavy objects tumble on top of me. Pain slicing at my body as I convulse at the assault and am rendered mute with the wind being knocked out of me. Completely defenseless, weak, and no match.

I submit to the pain as I feel every single one of those slicing shards pierce my skin, writhing in agony and bleeding out. I scream out loud. A blood-curdling wail of hell as I'm inflicted with a thousand tears and cuts and the bone-crunching, splintering of my body snapping.

Adrenaline takes over despite my body vibrating with the sheer effort, and I get up, grinding my teeth against the crunching of broken bone and dull burning ache, clawing the walls to get purchase. My hands start changing before me, and relief washes over my mind at the evidence I'm turning. This is what I need, but it's not fast enough or not progressing, and he has me from behind, around my throat in an effortless maneuver before it takes effect. He throws me and sends me flying forward with a thrust, straight through the window of our third-floor bedroom with another flinching of unavoidable, stabbing agony.

If I thought hitting furniture was painful, then the slicing assault of a thousand glass shards breaking on your already torn and bleeding skin as you fly through at speed is so much worse.

There's a moment of silence as I hit the air, and my body changes direction, weightless for a second. A moment of ease before realization sinks in that I'm three floors up, and my stomach lurches as gravity takes hold and yanks me downwards.

I hit the ground below with a stomach-churning thud at a crazy speed that reverberates through every cell and pore and knocks the life out of me as it shatters any unbroken pieces I may have left. It's so beyond painful, it almost doesn't hurt at all for a second, stunned, until my lungs try to stir, to recover, and I start choking on my blood and bile. Gasping for breath, body convulsing as I try to move, but I'm bleeding out profusely, and the ground beneath me is turning dark with the evidence.

Slashed all over, from breaking through the glass, and shattered from my fall. I'm hurt all over and can feel my life ebbing away from me as I become dizzy and useless. More so than I was. I'm dying. I know it, I can feel it, and try as I might to cling on, I can't.

I lie here like a useless piece of discarded nothing, unable to move in any way, as my body fights for dregs of energy and consciousness.

The kind of pain my turning inflicted is the only way to describe how this feels, and I don't know how to finish transforming. If I don't, I'll die for sure ... we can't heal the way we can as wolves, and I'm critical. Something's keeping me weak enough that turning isn't happening. No matter how desperate my instincts are, the self-preservation function of my kind seems absent. We're meant to turn without thought when we're seriously messed up. To save ourselves. It's so typical that I can't even get that right.

I can feel my human body giving up on me. I'm losing so much blood the grass around me is soaking parts of my clothes that weren't wet before, and the metallic stench of my essence is dowsing out everything else. I claw the grass around my hands, which are splayed out as I'm on my stomach, and pull myself forward painfully. Refusing to give up altogether. Trying so hard to fight this and sobbing out loud with each wincing attempt.

The impending fate is falling over me like a heavy dark cloud, and I know this is futile. So slowly, painfully so, that I make little progress, only to shudder when a ground-shaking thud beside each side of my head signals the landing of two feet. He jumped from the window above and landed perfectly next to me, in human form. This is no wolf. This is one of them ... coming back to avenge what they lost so many years ago.

Standing over me, bearing down, he grabs me by the back of my neck and digs nails into my skin. Long piercing claw-like talons that bite with scorching pain, and he drags me partially upright to snarl in my ear. My body is cringing with the agony of being moved. I reach back pathetically to grip his hands on my flesh. The cold, icy, and clammy skin that's alien to anything I've ever felt before. I know what this is for sure—we heard stories —the ice-cold, vile touch of the skin of the undead. This lifeless, cold monster is a vampire.

They've returned.

"Too easy. Call yourselves warriors. You're all dropping like putrid flies, and one snap, it's all over for you, puppy. I'm rather enjoying dragging it out, though ... why don't you go on and beg as your little friends did. Whine and cry some, make it worth my while." His icy cold stinking breath fans my cheek and chokes me to quiet submission, and I wretch, losing consciousness despite my fight. I have nothing. My powers fail me, my words dead on my lips as I gasp for air that my lungs can't seem to take in, and I choke on my bodily fluids.

I can't turn, and I've no idea why. I'm as weak and powerless as Juan said I was. I failed to keep my mate safe by failing to save myself, and I don't deserve his love, his bond. Because of me, Colton will perish tonight, too. He'll feel this pain, he'll know I'm suffering, and as soon as my heart stops, his will too.

I'm sorry, my love. You were right. I'm no warrior.

I doubt he'll even hear me, as along with my ability to turn; my mind-link is silent and has been since I lost him upstairs. I close my eyes, trying hard to connect to him, to feel him inside my head one last time, but there is only deathly silence in the recess of my brain as fingers encircle my throat, and I wait for the inevitable squeeze to end it all.

My blurry vision focuses in front of me, straining across the lawn in a last-ditch attempt to see the world I'm leaving behind. He begins to choke the air out of my body, slowly enjoying the power, savoring it, smug about the lack of my fight because I have nothing left. Truly sick.

My eyes settle on the chaos lying before me, and my heart implodes with what I see, the devastation too much for me to compute. Tears roll down my face as sadness numbs out everything else. A quiet peace fills my senses as shock and reality hit to shield me from the horror of what I'm witnessing.

There are bodies everywhere. The unwanteds, the guardians, side by side. No care whether one was essential or not. There's blood, debris, and the lifeless souls of my reject pack, strewn wherever the eye strays. Headless, maimed. Some were torn to pieces, some bleeding out from wounds across their throats and already dead. Dark fluid taints it all. Blood in the shadows stains everything as far as I can see. Chaos everywhere. It's a massacre we never saw coming, and they hit the weakest in our kingdom, the ones who had no defenses. Most of us were children or teenagers, and we never stood a chance.

This is it for us. My story is finally over.

I close my eyes and accept fate, choking slowly, no longer panicking but accepting, as blood sours my sense of taste, and I gag and fumble at the grass, hot and sticky with the essence of my life beneath my palms. I'm struggling to breathe, my heart giving in, unable to fight while my body is broken and shattered. Paused and waiting for the final snap to end this agony and suffering.

The sudden wrenching of the hands around my neck makes me spasm in response, so in tune with the final blow, but instead of relief from this plane to the next, I'm set free. Dropped hastily, so my face collides with the damp, stinking grass, and the taste of my blood is rammed backward as I inhale forcefully. My throat is released, and the flash of air that whooshes by me turns my gaze to follow, weakly, the path of whatever just flew by me.

I slump my head down on my cheek to watch him, as I can't do much else. A flash of snarling fur, a massive beast in utter rage, taking down the form of the man that held me captive, and I can tell it's Colton as his scent follows on the wind. That instant inner completion only his presence can bring me, and a tiny ounce of my heart is restored.

He's ruthless, a true warrior, and one of the biggest of the pack as he towers at three times the size of my attacker on his hind legs. Within seconds, without any apparent effort or fight, he tears the man limb from limb, with no hesitation, as though merely pulling apart a piece of damp paper towel. Scattering him across the back wall in a vile dark red spray of body parts with an almost explosion-like drama.

Snarling, seething, so his teeth glint in the moonlight devilishly, he turns viciously before throwing its head across the courtyard with enough force that it clears the wall completely. It's an act of rage and fury, and he throws his massive head back, letting the most terrifying, stomach-churning howl erupt from deep within his body, alerting his kindred that they should come.

The noise fills the air, echoes insanely, and overtakes the silence and chaos as more of my brethren clear the walls effortlessly, like water over rocks, scaling and flowing smoothly in from all directions to land in the courtyard. Pouring from every avenue into the small space. Flooding my view with the forms of wolves of all sizes and shades and packs from every corner of the mountain. Uniting for a common enemy.

I try to get up, relief overwhelming me that they've come to our aid. Our saviors are here, but I can't move. Try as I might ... I can't move. My hands are bloody and ripped up, my body is weak, smashed internally, and I can't feel my legs anymore. So drained of my life force that I'm ebbing away into nothingness.

Lorey? Baby ... Lorey ... nooo!

The black beast is over me now, turning me gently with massive clawed paws, so I face those glowing amber eyes to fall into his safety and care. He calms from snarling teeth to human form instantly. In a blink, from ferocious to handsome and familiar. Suddenly smaller, naked before me, in the night sky and a look of utter despair washing over that furrowed brow and tear-filled eyes.

"I'm sorry." It's all I can splutter as I cough up blood and shudder with the effort, too consumed with fatigue to do anything else. Colton stifles a sob, scrunching his face up, and cradles me close. Picking me up as carefully as he can and pulling me against him gently, his pain at me being like this filtering back to me and weighing upon me tenfold. Sharing our agony, I can feel his heart shredding for me. The devastation is tearing through him at what he sees. I know he must feel my physical pain, too, but his emotions are overpowering that for both of us.

"You have to turn, please. It's the only way you can survive these wounds. Turn for me. Don't give up. Don't leave me, baby." The desperation in his voice ravages my heart, but I'm too weak, and I've lost too much blood. I'm so cold, so numb that even his touch can't warm me as it should, and I cry softly with desperation because I know, as soon as I slip away, his own heart will cease to beat. I can't let him die at my hands; I have to save myself to save him. He doesn't deserve this. He did nothing wrong. He came for me; he came to save me.

I have to try just one more time to give everything I have into healing myself, but it's futile. I don't even know how to turn, let alone if I can. It's like there is a disconnection and my abilities fail me. I muster any willpower I can, but it's like that veil of power is still weighing down, oppressing me, and I can't fight it.

"I can't. I don't know how." Tears roll down my sodden face as I let out a useless breathy whisper. So ashamed of my own inability to be a match for his strength and power. Colton stares at me, his face suddenly straightening as he sobers instantly. He looks to his own hand, curled around my shoulder, an instant twinge of his cheek muscle, and then a frown that I can't read.

Colton doesn't wait, something registering on his face, and he furrows his brow with determination, pushing the softness aside. He picks me up, even though I cry out in renewed agony of this new torture, and holds me tight. Pain slices through my wounds as I cry out at what he's doing, writhing and shuddering with the sheer pain it inflicts upon me. I push my hands to his chest to beg him to let go because it's too much, and my body can't take more. Glass stuck in my wounds, penetrating deeper with the pressure of his embrace, and I howl out in despair because he's only hurting me more.

"I'm sorry, baby. I have to." Pulling us to stand, he runs towards the nearest entrance to the courtyard. His focus is intent as he scans the wall and moves us as fast as possible to the nearest gate. It's a human run, not hyper-speed, and he hauls ass to get me outside the perimeter of the enclosed garden and building. I don't understand, and all I can do is cling on and stiffen and sob at the movements that bring me no end of agony.

His mind syncs with mine as soon as we are free from the confines of the courtyard; I feel it. Shocked by the sudden presence of him inside my head, even though he doesn't say anything at all. A change to the weight on my chest and the dull fog of my brain as he skids down to his knees, scraping across the tarmac, taking me down with him as soon as he feels the bond return so effortlessly.

"Try now. Trust me. You have to try. Focus on me; think of yourself as you were the night of your turning. The pain, the thrill of your new form, will it, baby, will it! Turn!" He begs, commands, and Alpha tones me all at the same time. Desperation in his plea, and I'm powerless to disobey him.

Something about taking me away from the house makes me feel different, as though the constraints have lifted from my soul and my head clears just enough. That internal foggy pain that held me weak moves aside, like lifting a foot from my chest, and with a bit of effort, my body starts to tingle.

"That's it ... your eyes ... keep going. You can do this ... it's not hard. Fight for me." He catches my hand and holds it in his loosely, waiting, watching, silently pushing me on with a look of fear in his eye that maybe it's too late. It causes chaos in my heart to see him so afraid.

I focus all my effort on pushing, some deep inner need in me to unite with my wolf again, and as soon as I open my mouth to utter the words 'I think it's working,' I arch in his arms and convulse as my body transforms me into the one thing that can save me. Right on the stroke of my human heart giving out and sucker punches me back into the land of the living in the most painful kind of way.

I gasp as I inhale loudly, coughing out, splaying my limbs, and shuddering viciously as he catches me in his arms and then immediately lets me go to twist and turn onto my belly. I wretch and gag at the same time before vomiting a ton of blood and mucus right over the top of Colton's naked thighs, as I've no control over my aim. My wolf body ejects all that internal damage as though somehow healing is just the process of getting rid of the broken bits I no longer need, and I'm covered in my own mess. Matting my leg fur and clinging disgustingly around me.

I scramble away from him so as not to make this worse, and find myself on all fours, suddenly rejuvenated as the pain diminishes, and I gasp. The transformation heals me as fast as is possible—from head to foot. Cuts close up, bones crack and re-form, and my lungs expand fully, allowing me to breathe again. Shaken, sore all over as it fades away properly, but completely healed. Within minutes, I stand up as though I didn't just go through hell and was near death in the bloody mess I left back there.

I slump down on the ground and almost immediately revert to human form, as I don't have the energy or the skill to sustain my wolf form yet. Exhaling with a strangled cry of relief and emotion as everything hits me hard. Like being in a train wreck, only it's all mental now the physical has been brushed away. That took so much out of me to save my life, and I'm spent.

Colton scurries over to me and hauls me into his arms without hesitation, a look of relief on his face, and yanks me close to his chest. Wrapping me up and smooths his hands over my naked body to check for any sign of unhealed marks. There are none. Wolf healing is incomparable and almost always entirely effective. There are only a few things in this world that wolves can't heal from, and none are present tonight. He tugs my face to his throat and hugs me with less panic in his touch, exhaling heavily as he allows himself a moment of relief that warms me to my core and brings me some calm.

"The pack have them in retreat. I need to get you to safety and follow them. There are survivors, and we have to stop them before we lose them." He nuzzles his face against my hair before shifting me, making it clear we can't stay here. He helps me up, pulling me to my feet, and, holding me close to his body, leads me to one of the abandoned trucks scattered in every street surrounding the school. I recognize them as belonging to the Santo family. They must have flooded in from every part of the mountain at a moment's notice.

"How did you know to come?" I ask weakly as he slides me into the nearest vehicle, pulling a blanket from the rear and draping it over my naked body as I begin to shiver insanely. I may be healed, but my body and mind are going into shock from all that has just happened, and I suddenly feel as though I'm in some sort of dream. Fully aware that him taking control is a necessity, as I don't have the presence of mind to do anything for myself.

"Your link was broken, and I couldn't reach you. I knew something was wrong. I could feel your confusion and then your fear. Your pain almost ended me, and I didn't think I would get here in time. They did something to the house. Soon as I got near it, my wolf form struggled to stay. There's some sort of noise or frequency around it. It stops us. I could feel it in the garden, but I couldn't hear it." He closes my door, jumps in the front of the truck, and scrambles around for keys, finding them still in the ignition, thankfully. Wasting no time in putting it in gear, reversing us at a screeching speed as though we're in pursuit of something and hightailing us towards the south road out of this part of the mountain valley. Getting me away from here, even if the threat is being chased off in the other direction.

"Where are we going? Why aren't you saving anyone else? There are more of us; it's not only me in that home! You can't leave them behind!" I sit up, panic-stricken and sudden concern for the others left behind hits me in the chest like a freight train as my tears return with a passion, and I half sob, half choke the words out. My reject pack is back there, they're the only family I know, whether I liked them or not, and there are so many innocents among them.

Colton catches my eyes in the rear-view mirror and looks away quickly, a sadness hitting me right in the heart as his emotion silences me with a swift shunt of my stomach. I immediately know the pain and sorrow in what he doesn't say. He avoids my eye as I stare at the back of his head, feeling him, reading him as he overcomes my senses. Tasting his hesitation and sorrow.

"There is no one else, is there?" I state blankly, numb shock weaving through me and hitting me with the gravity of this situation. He's in constant link with his pack so that they would know about survivors, and I'm guessing the fact they're chasing down the vampires who ran, and no one but Colton is shepherding one of us away means they already checked. The weight of reality settling on my shoulders to drag me back down to numbed calm.

He shakes his head, unable to look at me, and I catch his furrowed brow and the gleam of moisture glazing his eyes in the mirror over his head. He ups a gear, pushing the truck to dangerous speeds as we head out of the valley and up onto the main road that takes us around the perimeter and out to the south.

"We weren't fast enough. I almost didn't get to *you* in time. We just weren't ready for something like this. I wasted time assembling the pack when I knew you needed me." He sounds almost ashamed, but without the pack, he wouldn't have been able to fight all of them himself and save me at all. They would have taken him down as soon as he lost his wolf form in the gardens.

"All of them ... the unwanteds ... the guardians. They're all gone?" It's not a question, but more of a dazed reaction as my mind pushes me into shock at what's happened. Verbalizing the truth, I slump down across the back seat as silent tears fall down my face, diagonally across my cheek like cold, sobering smears, and soak the cold leather of the truck.

"I'm sorry, Lorey. I know they were all you had. We never knew this was coming." Colton's voice is shaky and low. Shame and regret tainting his usually sexy huskiness. We share the agony, but it doesn't lighten the load. Insides twist in cruel heartache as it sinks in fully.

In the blink of an eye, they're all gone, just like ten years ago.

The sad thing was, until this moment, I hadn't thought they were what I had at all. We were never a pack, or a family, in my mind before, but now, those others, they matter more than I ever gave them credit for. Even Vanka, my roommate for ten lonely years, and I would give anything right now to have her get in this truck and blow smoke in my face.

My heart crashes inside my chest as the most painful, debilitating heaviness hits me hard, and I let out a mournful sob that turns to a howl as my body turns without me trying. I lie on the back seat, breaking inside once again. My body is reverting to my wolf form to heal me from the agony my heart is in. A defense mechanism because my instincts think I'm dying all over again—how ironic.

The most heart-wrenching howl I've ever heard leaves my body, fills my ears and echoes into the eeriest silence of the dark world around us.

First my blood family, then my pack, and now my unwanteds.

Is there nowhere to run where fate won't deliver me the worst kind of blow and take everyone from me?

I tremble in front of the massive roaring fire in a state of a surreal daydream in the room that Colton left me in when he brought me into his packhouse. A blanket draped around my shoulders, covering my modesty as he went and got clothes.

I'm tucked into the armchair in the corner, out of the way, while some of his pack pace around in the clearing directly in front of the flames, inwardly thrashing something out. They're wired, agitated, the air thick with the stench of testosterone, blood, and fury, and more are returning by the minute to convene here in this house. The pack is returning from chasing off those vile murderous intruders.

It's all in their actions, their mannerisms, but, as I'm not privy to Santo Pack linking, all I can do is watch the animated expressions and occasional outbursts of a word here and there.

They know I'm here, but they're completely ignoring my presence, much as they have done for years. It's not like I care. My head aches, and emotions are fragile, barely keeping it together, and I can't stop replaying the horrific scene in my head of what I saw laid out in front of me in my courtyard. Vanka's scent burns my nose even still, and I shudder at every thud they make while pacing around so erratically. Unable to wipe that noise from memory.

"Here." I jump when Colton touches my shoulder, so preoccupied in my mind I didn't even notice he'd come back. I'm too nervy, coiled tight, and antsy. He drops a pile of clothes on my lap, a simple gray hoody, a pair of sweats, and a T-shirt that I guess is all his.

"I'll show you where you can dress in private," he motions for me to follow, his face softening and his manner following. I think he can sense how not myself I am right now and reverts to gentle handling. He waits for me to get up, pulling the dark gray covering around myself a little more snugly, before leading the way out of the room with me close on his heel, cradling my new bundle against me. My head stuck in surreality and detached from a whole lot of feelings at this moment.

"Cole? We need you in this!" A voice echoes his way, and he throws the male a silent look, eyes glinting as his wolf connects with his packmate. An exchange of nods, and he turns his attention back to me to hold the door open out into the large, spacious hallway.

"What the fuck is she doing here?" A nasty biting tone is spat our way as Carmen comes marching across from the open doorway in the main hall, which is sitting wide open for returning wolves, and squares up in front of me, accusingly, shoving Colton hard in the shoulder as she does so. It looks like she's just returned from the hunt, robed in a blanket like mine, and visibly grimy from being out as her wolf self. Most of the pack have gone straight to their rooms for fresh clothes on entry, but I guess she thinks yelling at us is more important.

Something inside me lets out a tiny murmur of a growl in outrage that she would physically shove him, come at us angrily after the night we have all had, and I quickly swallow it down and drop my eyes to the floor as she spins on me hatefully. Bravado waning fast as I sigh at my impulsive reaction with immediate regret.

"Did you just growl at me, Reject?" Anger swirling warmly in my belly as she pokes some deep internal beast. She bites it at my face, getting close enough to make me flinch. Snarling, scathing anger makes my body bristle, and, for a second, I swear my claws begin to peak involuntarily.

"Leave her alone. Go into the main room. I'll be there in a minute." Colton pushes in front of me to make her step back, intent on still guiding me away, but his need to protect takes over. She doesn't like it one bit, and the change in her manner is evident. She gets even madder. Spinning to face him down instead of me.

"I'm not going anywhere until you tell me what the hell she's doing here!" She spits a little more venomously this time, eyes glowing bright amber and throat eliciting a snarling, growling undertone in her words. She's on the verge of turning, and her wolf is already riled and ready to fight. I shiver, not sure I can take any more violence tonight. I may have healed, but I'm in no state to have a femme go at it with me over a mate who doesn't even want me.

"Trying not to die so I can also carry on breathing. Do you mind?" He snaps right back and extends a hand as if to say, 'can we get by.' Ignoring her hostility, exerting his dominance, but even I can tell it's not the right way to handle Carmen right now. She's running on extreme female possessiveness and green-eyed rage. Colton should be soothing her as gently as he is handling me, but he seems oblivious to that fact.

Carmen turns almost feral at his response, hackles rising, and her fingernails extend to claws as her anger leaches out of every pore. Turning and ready to thrash it out with her so-called mate because, quite frankly, he's being insensitive to what she's feeling about me being here. If I were her, it would probably be my reaction too.

"Over my dead body, you go anywhere with that mongrel! I forbid it. She shouldn't even be here!" She can't conceal her hatred and jealousy, barking an order that even I know she has no right to make to an Alpha, even if he is her mate now. I sink inside my wrap of an itchy blanket and try not to make eye contact in the hope she runs out of steam.

Submissive, nervous, beyond exhausted, both mentally and physically, and too tired for this. Doing anything with Colton is not high on my list of priorities when I just had the worst night of my life. I have more significant problems than teen drama and broken hearts.

"It's called trust. She's here for protection, and I'm showing her to a room so she can pull herself together ... nothing else. Don't assume you can tell me what to do, Carmen. That's not how this works." There's an edge to his tone, but as yet, his dominant vibe is playing cool and humoring her a little. He's aware he could shut her down with that one tone, but he's not trying to. I think it's dawning on him she's mad because she's insecure, and I'm the very good reason to be so. I can't imagine what it's like to have the love of your life suddenly start loving another.

"Trust!! Don't make me laugh. Where was that trust when you were inches from marking this little tramp? I wouldn't trust you with her any day of the week. I meant nothing at that moment," she spits, thrusting words like knives at his face.

"Well, it's just as well we aren't dating right now then, isn't it? Might be an issue otherwise." Colton snaps back in an icy tone, surprising me with that little statement. He shoves her aside aggressively before turning to catch my hand firmly and yanks me with him. I yelp at the sudden motion and almost drop the clothes I'm holding to my chest, anchoring the blanket in place. Distracted by his warm touch in my cool hand and by the absolute hatred being thrown at me from poisonous glares.

"I swear. You get one shot, Cole. You fuck up a second time, and we won't ever be mates. I won't even try to forgive you again. I mean it. Don't fucking touch her!" She yells it after us, a stifled sob mixed with bitterness, and I can smell the stench of the betrayal which fuels her. He bristles slightly but keeps pulling me across the hall without looking back, his mood taking a turn, and I can taste his aggression flaring up.

"Like you have in the first place." He snarls under his breath, out of her earshot, and I stare at his muscular back and shoulders and try not to react in any way. I never thought I would ever see the Packdom's dream couple talking to each other like this or for Colton to be so cold towards her.

I'm supposed to be fixing things with her and rebuilding trust. Fat chance when she throws it at me, every second of every hour of every fucking day.

He sounds pissed, and he's giving me the vibes as I feed on his emotions. It's said in the link, and I dart a glance back at the seething bitch watching us go before hurrying to close the gap and pull my hand out of his with irritation. Something rises from inside me, but I try to ignore it.

I'm sorry that I ruined things between you.

Even though it hurts me, for the obvious reason, that there is a Carmen and they're trying to work it out, I'm sorry I screwed it up for him. His life was fine before my cursed blood latched onto it and sucked all the goodness right out. I feel like I should apologize for something, anyway.

"Just remember who you chose as your mate, Colton Santo. Remember, you made a choice. A commitment. Remember you chose ME over HER!" She screeches as we reach a door diagonally from the one we came out of, and he throws her a stiff look back. Carmen is full-on shaking with a mix of anger and hysteria, obviously torn about her mate dragging his bond to some secluded room to dress. I can almost taste her mistrust and panic and can't help but pick up on her projections of seeing him kissing me that night. She's completely absorbed in misery.

"Yeah, I made a choice, but that doesn't seem to register with you, does it. I denied the Fates and stuck with you, yet it doesn't seem to weigh up much. I'm still dealing with this shit every day." Oozing with sarcasm and simmering anger, he opens the door, ushering me inside with a gentle push as he slides a hand behind me, but he stays out there glaring at her in a war of angry snarls. I duck under his arm and turn to grip the bathroom door handle to shut it, but he still has his hand on the edge up top, holding it open. I sigh inwardly, wanting to be free of this little battle and not stuck witnessing it.

"That's because I'm the mate you were meant for ... not that reject. Just remember that it's me you loved first and me that's made for you in all of this. You betrayed me, and I have every right to be mad about that." Her tone is more pained sadness than rage now, but he misses it entirely. I stand here, mutely uncomfortable, trying not to feel anything at all.

"Actually, I think if anyone should be mad, then it's Lorey. I denied the Fates and abandoned her to take my place with a chick the Fates didn't pick. How about you go be mad at them for not agreeing that you were *made for me*." He spits it at her, emphasizing her own words mockingly, and her instant gawping, shock, and sharp inhale make me wince.

That had to sting. I mean, it made me cringe, and it wasn't even about me.

Colton is pissed. Majorly so. I mean, to say something as hurtful as that to the girl he's supposedly repairing his bond with. I clock on to the fact my mouth is sagging open, and I quickly shut it and turn inside, trying to yank the door with me, sighing with relief when he realizes he is still jamming it open and lets it go.

"Screw you, Colton." She screams it at him, that piercing, high-pitched sound that sends me into a slumping cringe as I grab my ears and attempt to keep the pain out. I sync with Colton's pain, crumbling in the same kind of agony, and know she's just used her gift as an effective weapon against us once more. She likes to throw that around the way a toddler throws tantrums.

It stops as quickly as it starts, and then an eerie silence. I pick myself up from the floor, push the bathroom door to click fully closed with my foot, and hurry to pull his clothes on. Shaking from that assault and hoping to God she's run off to carry on her hysterics where her screams can't rupture my eardrums.

You okay? Carmen needs to control her gift when she's mad. That girl gives me major headaches.

He links me from the other side of the door, and I nod, stupidly forgetting he can't see me. Not that it matters; his voice is tense, and I pick up on the frustration and turmoil in his emotions, wondering if it's why I feel so tetchy too.

There's a profound irritation rising in me, I assume, is what he's feeling, and I'm absorbing. There's a burning ember of 'grrr' growing in my belly, and I can't pinpoint why. Maybe it's fallout from my trauma, and the anger and aggression coursing slowly through my veins is some kind of temporary PTSD. I push it aside and focus on getting these sweats on and tying them tight enough, so they don't slide down. He's so much bigger than me, and they swamp me.

I shouldn't have said that to her. She just makes me crazy lately. It's like I have no patience for her and no real guilt over what we did. I know that makes me shitty, but we are bonded, and she has no idea how hard fighting that is. In my head, we did nothing wrong, even though I know, technically, I cheated on my girlfriend. But she wasn't anymore. I mean ... we imprinted! And that pretty much

*meant you were my mate from that second on, and it blanked out
all other feelings for her. What we did was what we were meant to
do.*

He stops, and I inhale heavily. Guilt instantly thudding down
on top of me from my own heart and not his, pushing my irritation
button all the more, and I answer abruptly. Not sure I want to be
the one he pours all his Carmen issues out on. I mean, this alone is
making me feel sick with the stabbing pain it's inflicting on my heart.
I still feel the same way about him, so I don't know why he's trying
to talk to me about her.

You don't need to explain this to me.

In other words, I don't want to hear this.

*I know. It's just this whole thing sucks. It's a mess, and despite
her being the one I'm supposed to be working things out with, I
never stop thinking about you.*

I inhale sharply, and tears instantly sting my eyes that I try to
shake away. We went through this already, and it's futile talking
about it again. I know what we are and that there is nothing we can
do about it. This is pointless and only drags out the agony of
knowing so. He walked away and left me alone for these past weeks
to let that hit home. This, now, it's all just fallout from something
more significant than this mess. The attack brought him to me and
nothing else. His survival rests on mine, too.

Please don't.

I try to shake him out of my head, but I'm too tired to close the
link when he is this close.

*I know. I made my bed, right? I chose. And it's not like this
could ever work. My father would never allow it. I just don't get why
the Fates would throw us together like this if we can't ever be
together. They're meant to be the all-seeing power, and every choice
has a reason. What reason did they have to do this to us?*

His angst is evident, and I agree, but the way he's rambling
makes me lose all patience with him. Burned with my pain,
frustrated with all this Carmen bullshit he's throwing at me and now
this, what sounds like regret and wishful thinking, and questioning
our entire belief system as though he had no hand in this at all.

Wolves are superstitious as hell, and condemning the Fates is like breaking a mirror, crossing the path of a black cat, or worse! They always taught us never to question the powers that be, and this kind of crap could have all sorts of consequences for him. Not to mention, he's getting me mad. It's like he isn't listening to the words coming out of his mouth and his utter Prince Santo privilege just plain pisses me off. He has no idea.

You know better than to question the Fates, Colton. Don't tempt a curse. We shouldn't question.

I try a diplomatic, please shut up in a stern tone, but he misses it entirely.

Why the fuck not? They gave me you and an inability to do anything about it. They made us love each other in a way that nothing will ever be able to kill, and then they made sure we couldn't ever act on it. This is a curse! I can't even be around you without someone busting my ass, let alone touch you.

I fall silent as I pull on the last item from the pile, gritting my teeth at his pigheaded denseness as that ember erupts into a little flame, pushing my nerves taut. A small candle-sized one that hits in the dark recess instantly glows and grows to epic proportions of a full flame that moves me to dress faster with a hostile last tug to secure my pants. My blood is boiling as it overtakes me, and I sweep my hair back with sass and angrily grab the door handle.

Yanking the door open, surprised to come face to face with him as he's leaning his forehead against the door, and I almost headbutt him full on. His eyes glow with the turmoil of his emotions, but it does little to dampen mine. It only clicks my inner fury up another notch. They meet mine and lock on in that unique way we have whenever our eyes connect, the sizzle, the connection, but he isn't expecting me to respond. Nor the rage. That little burning flame of crazy that explodes at the sight of him.

"You didn't even like me before that night! You didn't know me! This, us, it's not real. It's something implanted inside of us by something up there." I point skyward, aggressively glaring at him. "We would never have fallen for each other, never have crossed paths, in any kind of way, if it wasn't for the Fates. I wasn't on your radar, and to be honest, I didn't like you either." I shove him back out of my space with a push to his abs, so he clears the doorway, and he just gawps at me like I've lost my mind.

Maybe I have!

"You don't even remember me do you, before that night? I didn't think so! You need to pull your head out of your ass and remember that. Carmen was the woman you loved and planned a life with, and you chose her—loud and painfully clear! You said the words to me, and this is done. The Fates didn't stop us, Colton. *You did,* and your family, and everyone else in this hellhole that confined my kind to a dark hole on the outskirts and left us there to die. So don't you dare tell me how awful this is for you because you have no fucking idea what awful is until you've walked in my shoes for the last ten years. You have Carmen, and you have a pack, a home, and a fucking choice in all of this. I never did! The Fates didn't punish you with this. They probably expected you to man up and do what they told you to do; for whatever reason, they decided on us! *You* did this to *us!* *You* did *this* to *me!* Suck it up and shut the fuck up!" I have no idea where this angry outburst comes from, but I deliver it in a raspy, accusatory tone, right in his face.

There is no fear or withering wallflower cowering in front of an Alpha of the pack. Just an angry girl, faced with a stupid boy who bruised her heart and is pissing her off by denying his part in it. A powerful frustration-fueled lecture with snarls and throaty growls included. I lock a penetrating gaze on him, pinning him where he stands as though I could impale him with looks alone.

It's true, though. He can stand making speeches and regretful apologies from now until eternity, but the simple fact is, Colton had a choice, and this is what he chose. He doesn't get to whine like some spoiled pup about it now. He's an Alpha, for God's sake, and he needs to own it. Not act like some overdramatic teen whose parents are being lame and stopping him from doing something superficial.

He stares back at me in utter shock, rendered mute at my outburst and unsure how to respond. Even his mind-link is silent. I don't think any wolf this far below his station has ever talked to him like that, and he doesn't seem like he knows quite how to respond. If I were anyone else, he probably would have me pinned to the floor by the throat and remind me who the Alpha is. Instead, he's silently shocked that I even had it in me.

I 'arghh' at him and shove him back abruptly, marching past, simmering with this sudden newfound rage, and I know it can only be some sort of delayed reaction to what happened tonight.

I'm angry, seething, bubbling away inside at him, at them, at life, at the goddamn Fates. Most of all, I'm mad at myself for being this weak, stupid girl who wasn't good enough to keep and too useless and vulnerable to save her friends her family. I'm not myself, I don't feel like I'm really here, and to be honest, this whole Carmen-Colton-Vampires bullshit and being brought to the home of the people who made my last decade worthless is all a little too much for me right now.

I lost everything and almost died. Terrified inside, deep down, like a churning pit of foreboding that shadows me, of the monsters I knew only from stories. The ones who jumped out of the fables and threw me out of my bedroom window.

Knowing they are out there and close enough to devastate our kind is enough to make me cower for the rest of my life. They had a weapon, a sound that, much like Carmen's, could hurt us and render us unable to turn. That means we're no longer the stronger in this newfound war, and we can all be killed. I have bigger things in my head right now than love confessions and pining assholes trying to mess with my head while arguing with his mate.

"I'm not going to spend my days whining about this crap, and I need you just to stop, okay. The words you said in the forest were the end of this. There's nothing to say or drag out and talk through." I turn on him aggressively, lifting my palms in a show of 'what now?', meaning, where the hell am I meant to be going in this damned house because I have never been here before, and I'm fucking lost. He nods back at the door behind me with very little to say. His expression ashen, temporarily without words, and not tackling my mood in the slightest.

To be honest, he looks a little shell-shocked right now, but I don't care. I have more significant headaches than him. I have weeks of pent-up heartbreak at this guy's hands, and I'm done being a pushover. My life, in one night, went from awful to completely rock bottom, end of the line, apocalypse kind of bad.

My emotions start shredding and unraveling now that I've let all of that out. Chest hit with a heavy shunt, and suddenly I don't feel so pent up and hostile anymore. Instead, I feel like I might cry. From rage and frustration to a sudden need to lie down and sob. Energy burned out from venting, and reality coming back full circle to remind me I've lost everything.

I spin away from him, then stop and shudder involuntarily as the overwhelming wave hits me at full speed and the tidal wave of tears comes out of nowhere. I don't even have a chance to try to combat it before it hits full throttle. Breaking and flinching as I lose control, and they start to fall. Coughing on the woeful sound that escapes me and smothering my face with both hands to try to catch the waterfall as it pours from my eyes.

"Lorey, baby, don't." Colton catches me by the arm tries to pull me towards him, but I throw him off, putting too much force into shoving him away from me and sending him back about three feet. Startling him with my show of force as he raises his palms to show he won't retaliate. Even breaking down like a feeble femme, there's an internal burning rage that just isn't ready to die.

"Don't. I don't need you touching me, consoling me. I just need you to leave me alone. All of you. I was fine on my own before, and I'll be fine on my own again." Not so accurate, but irrational and hormonal are not states to be argued with, and all I know is I need to get out of here and run. I need space. From him, from them, from this, my whole muddled head of pain, at knowing from tonight onwards, nothing is going to be the same ever again.

I turn and head for the front door impulsively, not caring about anything else but getting solitude, the darkness invading the open space as I reach it, sending an internal shiver of terror down into my stomach. I peer out into the unknown, from a doorway I've never known, and knowing that creatures out there worse than us mean us harm. They could be anywhere, and I have no place to return to now, either.

"No!" Colton yanks me back with force, and I spin on him tearfully. "I'll leave you alone, but you're not leaving this house. It's dangerous out there for all of us now, and I won't let you go." He pins me with a commanding look and a hostile tone, veiling a sliver of fear for my safety, but I throw it aside and cast off his emotions that are flooding me once more. I open my mouth to bark a refusal, but he hits me with a mental link and that dominant tone that instantly disables me.

You are not to leave this packhouse without my say so, and you won't argue! Stop it, now!

My head buzzes, both with rage and sheer frustration, as words catch in my throat and almost choke me. I can't get them out, his gift being misused to confine me to his home and stop my need to tell him what I think of his 'commands.' Rendered mute because he forbade me to argue and the only words poised tell him where to go. I instead throw my hands in the air, glaring furiously at him, and then sucker punch him in the abs out of intense frustration. He flinches, half-smiling with a shocked response and total disbelief that I'm being this aggressive and a little apprehensive about how to react. Hating on him for being such a bossy asshole and exerting his powers over me when he has no goddamn right. I storm left, heading for the bathroom I just came from.

Colton catches me by the elbow instantly and yanks me to the right instead, heading for the stairs at a fast pace that signals he's in no mode to argue about it. I fight him every inch of the way by tugging, squirming, and pushing him off, stabbing him with scathing pointed glares, refusing to relent. Forced by his strength. Not even letting me choose where I get to be alone, and it riles me, that simmering fire in my belly returns in a flash to push all tame aside, and my inner demon shows face. I pull his hand from my arm, getting madder when he grabs me by the other instead, a tighter, biting grip that is meant to bring me back to heel. I twist it away, but to no avail, as he shunts me from behind, then slides his arms around my body and continues to guide and push me forcefully where he wants me to go. It becomes a juvenile game of slapping, grabbing, shoving, tugging, and he gets me around the waist and lifts me from my feet before I ram an elbow straight in his face, crunching on the bridge of his nose and bruising my bone in the process.

"Fuck's sake, Lorey!" he snaps at me, losing his shit entirely, and stops as we hit the foot of the stairs. He turns me on snappily, hauls me towards him by the waist, bends, and hoists me over his shoulder like a sack of potatoes. Seriously emanating all kinds of rage at my refusal to be controlled and glares at me, hitting me with a full-on furious frown and sneer.

He is not playing anymore; his anger radiates hotter than the sun, but it only heightens my own. Carrying me as I squirm and wriggle and kick out, using my nails on his back to make him drop me. He grips me tight and does the worst thing he can do at this moment. He uses his gift again to get me to do as he wants, against my will.

Be still. Be quiet. Obey me!

I freeze, motionless, voiceless, all without choice and downright furious that he renders me immobile. My internal bubbling pot of 'how the fuck dare you' intensified to volcanic levels in the blink of an eye. Internally seething that twice, in the space of a minute, he's exerted his Alpha tone over me and put me in my place like an obedient little lowlife. My body is obeying him, my throat muting, and I honestly don't think I have ever felt this much venom for anyone in my whole life.

It almost explodes inside me, with the power to rip down these damned four walls. Like a kettle letting off steam after boiling to excessive popping abilities, and it fills every pore and vein with molten lava, straight from the depths of hell.

I loathe him more than I ever thought I could hate anyone, and despite being bonded and imprinted to this arrogant asshole, I want to rip his goddamn fucking, stupid, dumbass, shitty head off his shoulders and kick it down the stairs like a soccer ball.

That internal rage heats me like a volcano from inside out, my blood reaching boiling point, my temper shooting through the roof, and despite being utterly paralyzed and slumped over him as we climb the stairs, my mind and insides churn up a tornado that would scare the Fates. It feels like I emit a solar flare when I boom out via our mental link.

I FUCKING DESPISE YOU!!

It's a psychic scream, but as we pass two other Santos on the stairs, the very second it erupts from my mind to his, those two males cower and fall to the ground, grabbing their heads and yelping in agony. Colton also crumbles, dropping me clumsily with an ungraceful thud on top of him as we collapse in a heap on the steps.

Like a tremor of an earthquake erupting from my soul, every vase, glass, ceramic, and piece of pottery in the near vicinity explodes instantly, windows blow out all around us, and the chandelier of the main hall hanging to the left of the stairway shatters into a thousand specks of self-combusted dust, as though it just exploded. Scattering microscopic glitter into the air that comes to settle on everything around it.

It's a second of utter chaos, as though a bomb just went off in the center of the packhouse, and hard, brittle objects in every direction break under strain with a dramatic 'whoosh.'

People come down like tenpins around us, caving and crumbling while covering their ears, every single Santo in the downstairs hall who just walked in. I can see them from my viewpoint. All are gripping their skulls and screwing their eyes shut as it reverberates through and causes them all to collapse where they stand, in a ripple effect. I'm the only one not clawing at myself to keep out what seems to be overwhelming pain.

"What the f...?" Colton is breathless as he tries to regain composure, sliding his arms away from me quickly and skirting back to give me space, leaving me suddenly free to pull myself together. A hint of fear darts across his usually emotionless face as he flashes a glance at me and then on the carnage and debris all around us. I can sense his panic and confusion, and, for the moment, I can feel he doesn't want to get any closer, that he's wary of what I just did if that was even me.

104

I'm dazed and bruised from being dropped on a hardwood staircase and wholly bewildered about what the hell just happened. I feel like there was some sort of implosion around me, yet I'm entirely unscathed. And now, my internal thoughts, body, and soul are calm. All that fire and rage, just gone.

"Was that voice hers?" One male on the stairs crawls to his knees and attempts to pull himself up by the railing, staring at me warily. He, too, looks afraid and keeps his distance, getting further from me as he moves out of range.

"You heard her?" Colton spins on him, and I pale as both men nod. Eyes darting to me, then him, and they slide down the steps until they get on their own feet and scale it quickly to get away from me. Shaking legs and rubbing their heads, I can feel all eyes turning my way as others pick themselves up from the floor. The hall looks like Armageddon just rolled through, and there's smashed glass, china, and all sorts of carnage on every surface.

I know I did it in the headspace that only Colton should hear. No one else can access our bonded link. I didn't say it out loud, and as I move to sit up and gather my wits, I realize I'm no longer bound by his command either. I cough and croak out a shocked reply, weirded out that I can both move and speak. Shouldn't be able to until he undoes what he told me to do.

"I didn't do that." I implore him, turning with nervousness, wounded when he moves even further away, mistrusting eyes on me. I can sense his apprehension, and it cuts deep like he's rejecting me all over again.

"What the hell was that?!?!" Juan Santo bursts into the open space of the front door of the packhouse, surrounded by his entourage of men, all are dragging on blankets to conceal their nudity and looking utterly feral. All are casting an accusatory eye, first at those who have come out into the hallway to see what's going on, dazed and confused, to join those picking themselves out of the mess, but then his eyes scan up to where we are and lock a hateful glare right on me.

I can almost taste his disdain for me and the pointed way his eyes flicker to Colton in a 'why is *she* here?' furious unspoken question.

"I think that was Alora. I mean, it was Alora." Colton sounds sheepish, and even through all this chaos going off inside me, I can feel he's afraid to come near me. There's genuine confusion and fear inside him, and he's keeping his distance by several feet now. Bonded or not, right now, he is scared of me. He doesn't understand what I just did any more than I do.

"It couldn't have been. She can't have the power to inflict that kind of pain in the link state. Or break everything as far as the eye can see. No wolf can." A voice in the crowd echoes my way, and I'm aware of every set of eyes locked on me now and shrinking down into a huddled heap of shame. Heat rises on my face as I try to become invisible.

I immediately think of Carmen's gift, wondering if maybe it's coincidental, and this was her from somewhere else in the house, going catatonic in her misery, but I know it can't be. She can smash glass only in the near vicinity when sustaining a high-pitched scream for long seconds. It hurts our hearing, not our mental link, and she's never demolished everything around her the way I just did. Nor immobilized the entire pack with one pulsating psychic yell.

"Alora can." Colton's voice drops in the air like a heavy thud, and the deathly silence, wave of shock, fear, and utter confusion that meets his response send the fear of God right to the pit of my soul.

A War is Coming

I sit quietly in the bedroom I was frogmarched into a few hours ago. The food tray some random Santo dumped in here for me is untouched, as I've no appetite, and I'm lying on the bed staring at the endless white ceiling of a room that probably cost more to decorate than they spent on the orphanage the whole time I was there. Bored out of my mind, nothing in the house has been working since my explosion. Nothing electronic, no lights at all, and they are working on rectifying it. I'm still not convinced I did this, but it all seems to point that way.

Apart from the boarded-up window and the now décor free shelves after they swept through, removing the carnage of smashed items, it's pretty nice. Gold and cream with brown leather and opulent fabrics. It's like a hotel boudoir in a five-star establishment and bigger than the entire lounge and kitchen at the rejects' home.

The Santos always were one of the wealthiest packs in Radstone, and it shows. Their packhouse is a mansion with endless hallways and rooms, and they have stuck me in their west wing, far from everyone else in the building, until they figure out what I can do. I could scream and erupt in here, and no one would hear me.

Shunned to an unused part of their building, nothing changed there from being one of the black marks they left to rot on the darker side of the mountain. The house is now echoing with distant banging, drilling, and all sorts of construction sounds, as they try to secure their abode once more, and I can't say I feel any kind of remorse. I mean, at first, I was in shock, kept questioning if I did that, if I was capable, and now I'm numb again. I'm exhausted, in need of sleep, but empty of all other emotions.

A light tap on the door draws my attention from counting cracks that aren't there, and I know who it is before they open it. I can feel him. Felt him making his way down the hall towards me moments ago, and I really don't want to see him, or anyone for that matter.

That intense excitement at his presence that was there before is waning with everything that's happened since. The bond isn't weakening, but my emotions are overpowering everything else right now. Grieving a family I never knew was mine and replaying the horrors while also trying to push them deep down in the recess of my brain.

"How are you holding up in here?" Colton's voice drifts my way as he slides in, that sultry sexiness that still elicits tingles on my skin, and closes the door behind him quickly; I catch sight of him checking the hall before he does. Obviously, by his swift maneuver, he shouldn't be in here with me and is defying some rule, probably from his father or maybe Carmen. Checking no one followed him to the empty side of their palace. I sigh, look back at the ceiling, and ignore him. I'm annoyed that he is a part of all this and just another pack member that's shunned me for years.

"Still pissed, huh?" There's a defensive quality in his tone, not his usual commanding strength, and I roll away to face the wall and turn my back on him. Said all I needed to downstairs, and I don't know why he couldn't just leave me alone. He told me how it was going to be that day in the forest, and yet he's the one who keeps breaking his word and reaching out to me. He's pretty useless at staying away, and it doesn't help.

Every contact, every conversation, just makes us bond all the more and feel like I do know him. It doesn't matter if our interactions to date have been sporadic and brief. I know him inside and out in ways that only imprinting can give you.

"I don't blame you. What you said before ... it's true. I made a choice, but you know why, Lorey. Don't hate me for that. Not that right now, any of that holds significance with the new current events. The elders are in lockdown in the grand hall. I couldn't stand being in there anymore. I had to come to make things right with you and to talk." I hate that he has a pleasant voice, unique, sensually melodic and that alone is enough to affect me.

I close my eyes to blot him out, wondering if the topic of the day is vampires or the freak wolf who just busted their house up. Not that I care enough to ask. I remain still, don't react, open my eyes again, and stare at the shadowy, uninteresting cream-painted wall. My body is betraying me in small ways at his nearness, but I clamp down on the sensations winding through my limbs and stiffen to stop his effect on me.

"Say something, please." Colton appears closer in a flash, and I jump when the bed dips behind me, his warm body sliding up close against me as he lies down and slides an arm around my waist to turn me. I don't resist but let him roll me onto my back, pulling my face to him until we are almost nose to nose, leaning over me, and scooping down to bridge the gap. An intimacy he shouldn't be encouraging.

The room isn't brightly lit, only glowing from candles in the far corner, seeing as I smashed every bulb in the house, so he casts a shadow over the both of us, making it near impossible to make him out. I shiver involuntarily at our close contact, instant goosebumps from his touch and his general effect on my body and soul. Cursing the Fates for making me crave his touch, even when I'm seething inside.

"Something," I mumble with lackluster and catch a slight hint of a cute-boy smile from him, making him more handsome. Amused at me for giving him an attitude, it serves the purpose of softening me a minuscule amount. I can't deny the way contact with him always calms me, brings me instant peace when he's not being a jerk, and sends my body and senses on high alert, even when I feel like this. Pushing my bitterness aside and let his warmer mood seep in.

"You asked me a question downstairs. You asked me if I remembered you." It's softly spoken, the way a lover would whisper to you while held in their arms. He lifts his hands to trace my cheek with his finger, removing a strand of hair that I couldn't even feel,

109

and leans down closer towards me, so his breath fans my face, and for a moment, I wonder if he might kiss me again. I shake it away mentally, knowing how stupid I'm being. He already made it clear we would never be that.

He raises a brow as though expecting me to at least say something to that, but I stare at him blankly and give him nothing. My head is busy with ludicrous thoughts, and I try to empty my mind before he picks up on it.

"It's like that, huh?" He sighs, adjusting his position so he is propped up on his arm, a hand fisted against the edge of his jaw, and gives me a little breathing space. Moving back a few inches but still pressed against the entire length of my body and still touching my face. "Two summers ago, before Carmen and I started dating. You were wearing a green dress, serving candy floss at the meadow festival. You served me, wouldn't look me in the eye, and when you passed me my change, you dropped it on the ledge rather than hand it to me. You had a yellow flower in your hair." His voice is soft and husky, and I try hard to lock on his gaze as my memory dashes backward, trying to pinpoint what he's remembering. It's vague, but I remember the festival and how his pack spent the entire day lording over the rest of us and causing mayhem. It was an ordinary day, and nothing sticks out as memorable about it.

"You have my memories, so how do I know you're not just tapping into one of mine," I blurt out, a little stubborn indignation in the mix because I know he's trying to get me to be a little less mad at him. Colton smiles, shaking his head softly with a frown, lifts his fingers to my temple, and gently presses, projecting his memory to me among the many we share. It wouldn't be hard for him to look back and see me when he has all of mine in there to choose from.

An instant mental visual of that sunny day, and there I am, standing at that cart, making floss, and looking like maybe the day wasn't as bad as I remembered. I have a strappy dress in a delicate shade of mint green that brings out a golden color in my hair. My tousled waves blow free in the wind, and I look almost carefree for a second. Maybe even pretty. I can see myself, so these aren't my memories. They're his.

I watch myself at a distance, turn and spot the group of Santos heading my way, looking towards the person of the head I'm inside, and instantly put my nose down and go into total submission. You can almost taste the change in my disposition as I realize they're coming to my stall, and I'm not happy about it. I pull his fingers away sharply, cutting the visual and seeing enough, not wanting to watch any more of how feeble and unworthy I always was in their presence.

"Doesn't prove anything." I shrug and turn my face away from him. I do not want to revisit memories of those men making me feel like trash anytime they talked to me.

"The memory is from my eyes, not yours. It proves plenty. Do you want another?" The cocky hint, and I can feel the smirk as his hand comes back to rest on the flat of my stomach, a little too comfortable for my liking. It annoys me how easily he slides into a touchy-feely mode when he's the one who severed our ties. He has a woman somewhere in this house, pining for him, yet he is again touching me like I'm still his property. For once, I actually feel like Carmen deserves better, that he may have lost his affection for her, but she didn't for him, and he should still care about her feelings. This would hurt her if she saw us like this.

"Okay, so you remember me. Whatever. It doesn't mean much, except we interacted before. A few times actually, so of course, I'd be there, in the memory banks. That wasn't the point of what I was saying. All that memory shows is you saw me and remember it, not that it served any importance to you." I roll away, pushing his hand off me fully, hinting to give me space and return to my previous position, bristling internally with the war going off inside my head and returning to irritation. Hating the fact that all the usual little tells are starting to go off inside me at his proximity, and my body is yearning for him again.

"You don't remember *me*, do you?" Colton pushes me lightly in the back of my shoulder, almost teasingly, and I shrug him off. Not impressed with him trying to turn this around, I roll my eyes.

He's being a little too flippant for a guy who spent tonight ripping apart vampires.

His focus should be on our impending doom and our life from here on in, not on whatever this is—reminiscing the 'good old days' and adding weight to why he will never rebuild trust with his 'chosen' mate. He's not exactly acting like he cares about doing it, from what I've seen.

"Don't be stupid. How could I not remember the Alpha son of Lord Santo? I've known who you were since birth." I answer with dripping sarcasm. He's grating on me now. I mean, we share every single memory each of us has, so it's pretty dumb to tell me I wouldn't know something that he does. Or that I didn't remember him. How could I forget the guy who walked around for ten of them like our Lord and King? How could I not know the son of the man who ordered my kind into exile?

I don't get a chance to hit him with any kind of comeback, as his hand comes at me from behind, and he feels out my temple once more, projecting from the many hours of mental movies, a single one that shoots to the forefront in the blink of an eye and renders me mute. I inhale sharply as the vision of my mother comes into view, winding me instantly and pushing me to complete submission.

The place near where he asked me to meet him that day in the forest. My beautiful angelic mother, holding my hand as we walk around the edge of the lake near the cavern, and I'm young, really young. I'm a kid, maybe seven or eight, but I recognize myself. She's laughing, fixing the bow in the back of my hair that's keeping it all off my face, yet I'm seeing it from the eyes of someone in the water. I remember her too, my breathtaking mom and that dazzling smile, those blue eyes that are missing from my life, and it tears at my soul. The pain cuts into me and slices away some of my armor.

She walks me to the edge and lets me go so I can play and go swim. I run forward and splash into the water with no sign of hesitation. I clumsily gallop, splash in cannonball style, and dive under as soon as I get waist-deep, her calling encouragement from the edge as she watches me. A brave little girl who thought she was capable of anything when sheltered in the shadow of her family. I can't pull my mental sight from my mom's face, her laugh, the way her voice echoes in the air around us, and it surrounds me with unique warmth like she's hugging me now.

If I'm Colton in this memory, he watches me the child for a minute. It drags my eyes back to me, and mom fades off out of the scene. I have no control over where he looks because this is his memory. He follows my progress as I swim across the lake, and then he's pulled sideways, and I suddenly see water. Submerged in bubbles and blurry sight, hands in front, waving as I swim back to the surface, coughing and spluttering as another boy blocks my view. I recognize him as one of his closest Santo pack. A boy called Mateo who's usually in Colton's shadow wherever he goes. He was in the study earlier today.

"Do you like her or something? Why are you always staring at her, Cole? Is she why you made me come here? I feel like she's wherever we go nowadays." He teases, pushing me back, and all I hear in response is ...

"Shut up. She has a name. Get out of my face and stop being dumb." It's Colton's voice. Undeniable, even at such a young age, that smooth undertone of immaturity grew into how he sounds now. The entirely defensive edge and embarrassment hint that his friend is right, and I know from learning so much about him lately that he gets bristly and hostile when he gets caught out. It dawns on me what he's showing me as he lets go and breaks the projection.

I turn on him at speed, eyes wide and gawping, not sure I just interpreted that the right way, but what other way could I.

"You liked me?" I blurt out accusingly. I don't understand. That memory was long before the wars catapulted into our lives and changed everything. A time I can barely remember, and I don't recall that day either, of us having any kind of memorable interaction. He stayed with his friends, and I stayed with mine, and then I went home with my mom before the sun went down. I would have to claw through the memories to be sure, but there was nothing to suggest he even noticed me.

"I had a crush on you like you wouldn't believe. I don't know how many times I tried to talk to you and got completely blanked or lost my nerve. I used to hang out where I knew you would be, but then the war happened, and you became ...." His voice trails off, eyes averting, shame washing over his expression, and I know what he means without him finishing.

I became a black sheep—one of the shamed.

My family died, and our people scraped up the remains and shunned my kind to the darkest corner. One of the rejects, and much like everyone else, he would have been told we were cursed and to keep his distance. Colton was a kid, and I guess his father drummed it into his head that I was unworthy. His crush died, he forgot me, and he moved on with his life, onto Carmen.

"Why are you telling me this? I don't remember you ever trying to talk to me. I don't recall times when you were there in my childhood." Not that it means anything. Now it's just hurting me all over again, knowing that, even then, he bowed to his father's will and rejected me long before that day in the woods. If we were destined, then he failed me twice.

Colton sighs, pulls me close by the waist, and brings my face back to his so that he can move in and rest his forehead on mine. I don't relax into his touch but stay like cardboard and refuse to melt into him or succumb to his power over me. The kind of intimacy you would expect from a mate, and I have to remind myself that we're not anything close.

"I was shy, and you were this fearless, confident girl who walked around with her friends, oblivious to any of us. Boys were dumb, and you all liked to make a point of avoiding us at all costs." He points out with a smile, reminding me a little of memories gone by, so well buried to save my heart from the pain of losing my family that I almost blocked them out completely. A time when the packs lived in proximity but kept to their own. A time when the Santo boys were just 'that bunch of idiots from the south side' and had no authority over the rest of us.

It feels like a million years ago when life was normal, and I had a real home—my own warm bed in my little pink room on our farm.

I had parents, a brother, and grandparents. Happy and carefree and had no idea there was a storm coming that was big enough to take it all away from me. There was a time when I was just another wolf child, and Colton and his friends were not our superiors but a rival pack, and we had no real animosity. Not between kids anyway. The fights were for the grown-ups.

I smile at the possibility that Colton was once shy. I mean, I don't believe it now with who and how he is, but raking through memories stored in my brain that belong to him, daring to push back to the before, where all my visions pain me still, I guess I can pinpoint a few that show a much quieter boy. He turned young, and at first, he wasn't the fearless, aggressive wolf we all know now.

He was sweet at some point in his life until, I guess, the responsibilities his father laid on his head hardened him. He was nine when the wars happened, and as a boy who already ran with the pack, he would have lost so many years of childhood by taking over in his father's absence while protecting his family.

We had attacks here too, and many young boys had to fight for our survival. I don't doubt he was one. I can almost pinpoint the moment when he turned away from anyone who wasn't Santo, pushed people out, and stayed in his little bubble, snarling at others who dared to come too close. Colton, the shy, sweet boy, and me, the fearless, bossy girl who didn't let others push her around.

Oh, how the tables turned.

"So you knew me. It doesn't matter." I sigh finally, realizing he has worn me down enough to get me talking to him, and I'm no longer sulking in silence and staring listlessly at the ceiling. Instead, I'm lost in a million thoughts and feeling all kinds of sad and depressing things. This is why I never walk down memory lane to see who I used to be. I'm also betraying my willpower and have, at some point, curled up against his chest and pushed one foot between his ankles snugly, cuddling up so easily that I didn't even know I was doing it. I reverse, moving back a little, screwing my face up at how powerful this bond can be.

Colton narrows his eyes and stares at me for the most prolonged moment, knowing the direction of this conversation is futile and changes nothing. He can't undo what is done, nor who I am now. Even if he remembers me, liked me, we are where we are, and it's not important anymore.

"Anyway, why are you here? I thought you were scared of me now." It's a half-joke, half-real question because it's been playing on my mind since the first couple of hours they locked me in this lifeless room to listen to the house being mended and boarded up. It's also my attempt to bring us back from the intimacy that makes me uncomfortable as I push a little more space between us. I don't even have a cell phone to keep me occupied as I have no friends, and the orphanage wouldn't pay for them.

"Hmm. Haha. It's sort of about that. Why I'm here, I mean. About earlier and your moment of whatever the hell that was." Colton's face turns serious, those pretty eyes under black eyebrows that are way too nice turning back to mine, and I can almost hear the gear switch off his brain as he focuses his mind on that topic. All tenderness fades away.

"What about it? You came to tell me they all think I'm a freak and a threat, and I'm getting moved to an isolation tank." I say it so blankly like there's no feeling behind it, but honestly, I've had this worry in the pit of my stomach on and off for hours.

Isolation tanks dampen gifts and make you unable to do anything much about them. If they think I'm some kind of freak of nature, I can see Juan using that as an excuse to contain me. It would solve the whole imprinting issue and his son being in danger. I would live in a steel box, forgotten in some basement below one of the Santo houses. I could live and rot until I die of old age in there. Problem solved.

"They're all too busy figuring out what we do about our lands before we're hit with another attack. This shit is just the beginning, Lorey. All these years were wasted when we should have been preparing and building an army once more. Now they're calling on packs from the far reaches to consider uniting and mounting an offensive. No, you're low on the list of things that worry them today. Whereas, I have a theory." He smiles a little at that, a lightness hitting his expression, the look of smug knowledge spreading into those bottomless, darkest chocolate eyes, and that annoyingly sexy smile widening enough to bring out dimples and showcase lovely teeth.

"Which is?" I sound as unconvinced as I feel, and he smiles all the more, making butterflies erupt low down in my body, and I have to squirm to get them under control. I don't like the smug, twinkling something in his eye. My instincts start to shift, and suddenly, I feel wariness creeping in at the aura he's giving off.

"You have an absorption gift. And that's what you did. You absorbed the power of the weapon they used in the orphanage, and, for a short time, you can throw it out there as your own. It's not a common gift, and, usually, they don't come across devices like the one the vampire hit you with. It makes sense. You haven't learned to contain your power, and you were overwhelmed." He sounds so convinced, actually pleased at how smart he is for figuring it all out in a logical and almost believable way. I've heard of this type of gift among wolves. Well, I heard stories and legends, and, as he said, it's not common. They absorb and can use other wolves' gifts, and some they even retain for more than a few days. They turn any enemy's power back on them, making them almost invincible.

"Except—that weapon you're talking about—it didn't break anything. I didn't turn it to protect me, and it didn't do any kind of anything outside the house and courtyard. Your father said I sent shock waves for miles." I raise a brow and then sigh at the fact I just disproved something that could have potentially made me feel better about what happened.

"Maybe you can amplify it, make it more potent. Maybe that's part of your gift. We could test that out. The weapon dampened your gifts because you haven't mastered them, and you didn't even know you could. Don't you see? If you have a powerful gift, it could change things for us. My father might reconsider your place in our pack. We try to see what you can do." Colton shifts so he's no longer as close, but half sits and turns to tower over me, letting the candlelight illuminate his face once more so I can see him fully. He seems almost pleased, but the doubt and uneasiness inside me only grow stronger. I'm picking up on his weird, antsy signals, and my inner red alert is starting to peak, even though I don't know why. I push it aside and try to ignore it as nothing more than anxiety because of what he's saying.

"How? If I don't know how to harness it, what to do, or even how to use it." I query. Not sure I'm into this, but he looks pretty keen. My head is spinning with what he's saying, and trying not to dig too deeply into his father changing his mind on anything. Colton's being stupid, and we both know me having a gift that's above average isn't going to change the fact I'm one of the shamed and will never be good enough for an Alpha.

"I can trigger you. Absorb mine, and see how much you can amplify it back at me. If you can, then this is huge, Lorey. It means you have superior power, and we might ... Don't you see? You might be a Santo yet if you have it in you to become something amazing, a warrior for her people. If my father sees promise in you, then he might reconsider you enough to let you become one of my pack, and then ..." He trails off, but I can see where his mind is heading, and it now makes sense why Carmen is not high on his priority list. Colton is looking for a way to claim me as his mate, even after everything he said in the forest. I guess the bond for the past weeks has made him as miserable as I've been, and that's why he can't stay away from me.

Bittersweet pain riles up in my stomach. It hurts at the same time as making me stupidly emotional. Adoring him for looking for a way for us, not giving up on our bond, but being the realist and shoving hope out like trash.

It sounds ludicrously simple, except for one minor problem. Colton is an Alpha with all the gifts that go with that. He's aggressive, dominant, strong, fast, and ruthless when he needs to be. Can command with a mental link and get no resistance, can jump at insanely high levels. Colton can scale a house of many floors in just a leap. I can't even make it over a brick wall without catching on. I've no idea how he will expose me to any of that and then make me somehow use it on him. Triggering me might do nothing, or he might maim me in the process without meaning to. I don't want to do that. I could never hold my own in a battle with him. He would annihilate me even without wanting to or meaning to.

"I wouldn't even know how to, and you're making no sense. Your father isn't going to do a U-turn because I have a rare gift. My name and bloodline are what he despises, not my abilities." I sit up, pushing myself against the headboard, sliding my butt back until I'm entirely nestled, and gaze down at him.

"Abilities are everything! Don't be so sure. I'm guessing I have to do something near you or to you, using one of my gifts so that you instinctively defend yourself. That's how it should work, in theory. Instinct taking over and no room to think." Colton looks away from me, a small muscle in his jawline clenching that reveals his rarely seen dimples again, and I get a tiny surge of uncertainty. He's thinking about something, analyzing, worrying, doubting his own decisions, and I blink at him a little apprehensively. I don't like the vibes he's giving off. They have all my senses tingling, and now I'm wondering in what way he might make me want to defend myself.

"So, you're saying that you don't have any idea either how to do this, right?" I point out, rolling my eyes and playfully shoving him in the shoulder, trying to kill the tension and to get him to drop this stupid direction his thoughts are taking. He's making me nervous, and I don't like it.

"Hey, don't question the man with the brains. Of course, I know what I'm doing, and I have a foolproof, well, almost foolproof, plan. You just need to not hate me after this or kill me because that would be counterproductive." He may sound like he's joking with me, but there's a U-turn in his mood and a seriousness clouding over it that doesn't reach his smile. A severe tingle of apprehension hits me in the gut as I pick up on an undertone between us. An inkling of something hitting out at me that's subtly under the surface of his jokey manner and fast smirks. I can't put my finger on it, but catching him looking me over with a slightly vacant gaze, the tiniest of wrinkles between those brows of his, and the hint of muscle twinge in his jaw, my stomach sinks, and nerves seem to overwhelm me instantly. I tense, and I feel like I shouldn't trust him for the first time since we bonded.

"Don't hold back." He breathes it out and doesn't give me a chance to respond to that weird command. I frown, mouth opening to say 'What?' but he grabs me by my hips, yanks me down the bed, and jumps on top of me in under a second, using hyper-speed and insane reflexes, so I haven't even time for a breath, or a blink. I yelp with the surprise of the maneuver, winded with his sudden weight on top of me, aggressively heavy, his body fitting snugly against mine in every way, so he's nose to nose with me, and I can't move an inch. He's pinned my hands to the pillows beside my head with his, and my ankles shoved apart by his feet viciously. Stunned and suddenly feeling all kinds of things that conflict and collide, I gawp at him, heart rate pounding up to insane levels, and start to squirm in his harsh grip.

"What are you doing? Colton, get off of me." I whisper huskily against him, panic flashing that this doesn't feel right, or like that first time we started to mark, but he has me completely immobile. I'm instantly a little too hot for my liking and pulsing internally, as the bond need for sex boils up inside me instinctively, misinterpreting our body contact. Still, it's not the same, and it dies when I realize it's not radiating back at me. He hasn't even attempted to kiss me, and he's avoiding looking me in the eye. This isn't lust-driven and consensual. This isn't seduction and a willingness to mate with me to seal our bond.

Colton turns off all of his emotions and our link to completely shut me out internally, and I feel it go black almost the second he does, bringing my frenzied fear further to the surface. His face is somber, a wall coming up between us as his eyes glow amber, but not how they should between mates. For a second, I catch a fleeting moment where he seems like he isn't sure, and I swear there's a sweep of regret. My internal self-preservation mode tries to reach out and warn me to get out of this now, but it's too late. I can't move.

"Forcing your hand. I'm sorry in advance, but we have to try. Don't hate me for this. I won't hold back either." It's barely above a whisper, and I blanch at him.

"Wha ...?" I don't get the question out because Colton is all over me in a flash. His touch from tight to harsh, his eyes are glowing amber at ridiculous levels of fire and brightness and illuminating between us terrifyingly. Pinning me down, forcing my wrists over my head with one hand, his feet kick my legs apart, and he pulls at my clothes with his free hand. Using his speed and strength to lasso me within his body, he flips me onto my stomach, so I'm almost smothered by the pillows on the bed and lose sight of everything.

He is dominating me horribly, in a way that mates don't. He's yanking my clothes down and up to expose my naked body and follows with cruel grabbing and nipping of my skin with his semi elongated teeth. It all happens so fast that, at first, I'm caught frozen, unable to catch a breath and absorb what he's doing until the overwhelming terror wallops me in the stomach.

I gasp in shock as I try to fight him off, wriggling, bucking, squirming as much as I can, internal panic consuming me as he exposes enough of my body to make it clear what he's going to do to me. My ass upwards, his groin in behind me as he ultimately uncovers my lower body and gives himself access to take me from behind.

Stop it! What are you doing? Let me go. Colton, you're hurting me. You're scaring me. Please don't, not like this! Colton, please!!

I wail and beg, sobs and tears adding to the suffocation as I turn my head from side to side to be able to breathe. I can't get loose at all. My mind is manic, but it's like bouncing words off a brick wall because he's closed the link and is trying his hardest to keep me shut out. He pushes a hand on the back of my head and forces my face down, back into the pillows to quieten me and keep me submissive as he yanks his clothes off, binding me still with sheer strength and keeping me imprisoned in the position he wants as he gets naked. He's gone inside himself, locking down with determination, and suddenly I don't feel like I know him. Our bond is momentarily meaningless, and what he intends to do will forever change what we are.

Colton turns increasingly hostile, as though sensing my fear goads him on, using aggression and brute force to apply pressure and pain on me like he wants to push me into turning more than he's doing already. Somewhere in the back of my brain, sense and logic are trying to claw something back to the forefront, but I'm too lost in hysteria to think straight.

His commanding strength, which is easily overpowering me, is enough to keep me this way. His entire mood and manner are changing, his body bristles as he half turns to beast, and I feel it oozing from him as smooth skin furs up around me. Stupidly, I wonder if it's even allowed to rape a femme in human form while turned into a wolf. Surely that kind of damage will kill me. I don't think sex between the two is allowed even consensually, given wolves are four times a human in size, and I'm sure that goes for genitals, too. His lack of concern for how much he's hurting me tells me I'm his prey, and he isn't going to stop for anything and doesn't seem to care that I'm human and not willing at all.

I struggle again, sobbing crazily, gasping painfully, heart pounding erratically, hating how useless I am against this. Still, he rips my top open and sinks his head instantly, letting his teeth extend as he brutally drags them across my spine, leaving extreme pain and blood in his wake. I wail in agony, writhing under him as I try to close my legs, but he wedges a knee between them to force me to stay open.

My skin stings and burns as fabric rips across my shoulders, and he drags what's left of my coverings off, burning and marking me with the assault of their removal. His claws rake over my body as they make their way over my ass, my thigh, roughly scraping my skin as he circles under and heads for my core with undeniable intent.

"No, no, NOOO!!!" I scream so loud, my voice cracks, and my throat burns in searing agony. He has me held taut, stretched out, and fully accessible to do whatever he wants to do to me. Imprinted or not—destined mates or not—it always has to be consensual, and no matter how hot you are for your chosen, force is never an option.

It's a cardinal sin to take your mate without her saying so or her willingness. Femmes are treasured by their dominant. Respected and cared for. Rape is a crime in our lands that could get him hung. Only the scum and outcasts would do such an awful thing, even to my kind.

I can't believe Colton would rape me. I can't believe I'm bonded to someone who could do this to me. Or why? This isn't him; this isn't who I felt him to be when we imprinted. My head is trying to make sense of this, something nagging in the depths, but terror takes over, and logic dies a death.

I buck and close my eyes as his claws inch between my legs, getting closer to defiling me and taking what is no longer his to take from me. Twisting and turning my body in useless defense and trying to push him from between my thighs, to no avail. Trying to bite, even though my face is crushed to the soft plushness of the pillows, aware my teeth are extending, he has my head all but wedged between my arms, unable to get free.

His voice ricochets inside my head painfully, making my brain shudder as he reopens the link suddenly. Instantly assaulting my senses with the extreme loudness of his booming tone, his dominant gift, to control me further, I know I'm completely powerless against him.

STOP FIGHTING ME, AND LET ME TAKE YOU. I WANT WHAT'S MINE!

Like before, I momentarily lose my body and voice, outraged, hating him with every ounce of my soul, clawing back with a need to save myself from what he intends to do, but it sparks something inside me. That sudden surge of anger, rage, and power, fighting him with everything I have, to break free and defy him for thinking he could do this to me.

I'm not a possession or an object. I'm not trash to be used as he pleases and commanded with his will. I'm a heart and soul and a body that deserves to be treated as any other. I am NOT nothing! I'm a Whyte, and once upon a time, our kind was respected, loved, and accepted. He can't reject me then think I'm his to abuse or ruin for any other mate. I'm worthy, and *HE* is *NOT!*

HOW DARE HE THINK HE CAN BRUTALISE ME THIS WAY!

I combust, like an inner mind implosion all over again, but everything goes black this time, as my brain gives out completely.

I'M SORRY

I wake up face down on the floor in a heap. Arm draped awkwardly over my head, and limbs splayed out on the hardwood, disorientated, choking on my own blood, and gagging on bile. Gathering my wits and trying to get my bearings, I struggle to move, dazed for a moment, and then I remember where I am and what he's doing to me. It's like a rush of water flowing back to a dry riverbed when the dam is broken.

That surge of furious self-preservation, instant awareness as the room comes back into focus, and I jump up, heart tearing through my chest with pounding thuds, claws appearing, mind a burning mess of anger. Ready to take him on in a battle to the death and fueled by something inside me I never knew I possessed.

I feel like my hatred could melt steel with the heat radiating from my fiery depths, and I spin hysterically, ready to demolish my attacker. Body mid-turn in furious speed when I realize he is on the other side of the room from me and looking at me like I have two heads. At least a good twelve feet away and crouching down, panting heavily, as though he too is recovering.

"Woah, Woah. Lorey, calm down. I didn't do anything. Stop and breathe. Take a moment before you start again!" He jumps to his feet, aware of my sudden rise. His palms up, facing me, flat out, and he is entirely naked, as am I, which only pushes me to heights of venomous hatred.

Claws fully extend, as do my teeth, and my body shudders as it begins to transform around me, ready to fight him and maim him

125

until this pain inside my heart ebbs away. I'm crushed inside, as though my soul is ripped to shreds and hanging around my organs like unwanted trash on the wind. I've never felt this much aggression or bloodlust, and I have him fully in my sights. My body is tingling all over even though I have no memory of what he has put me through, but enough to know what he intended.

"What did you do to me? Why would you do that to me?" I scream at him, my voice pitched in raw, raspy hysteria, but he raises his hands higher and pleads with me mentally. His eyes soften, with no attempt to turn, as he watches me from a distance.

Please stop and listen. Let me explain. I haven't, and wouldn't, do that to you.

He coaxes gently.

You raped me!

I mentally scream back at him, not seeing anything around me anymore, just the pulsing beat of the vein in his throat as I home in and know where I'll be aiming with my takedown bite; I don't care if it ends us both. I'll kill him for defiling me, destroying my trust in him, ravaging my heart and soul this way.

He shakes his head, looking wholly devastated and disheveled. Radiating so many emotions my way, but I battle them back, like bouncing tennis balls off a glass wall.

NO, I didn't! I never intended to either. Lorey, please, sit. I'll stay here, you stay there, and just let me talk. I need you to calm down and listen. Think. Remember.

I'm breathing so heavily my chest is heaving, and I can't calm down. Especially not when he's telling me to. He has no right. He can't be serious with this shit after what he just did. He broke the trust, hurt us, ruined the bond, and nothing will fix that.

My body is on fire, my blood like molten lava in my veins, and I can already tell I've turned enough to heal the marks he made on my body because there is no pain and only dried blood. My complete lack of injury or any sort of niggling physical hurt tell me I already turned, but I don't know how if I was unconscious, or if that's even possible if you're not lucid. I shake it away and glare hatefully, focusing all my rage on his face.

126

I hate him so much I can almost taste it. I'll never let him touch me again or come near me. I'll rip his throat out if he tries. He's vile to me now and not who I thought he was. An abuser is an unworthy leader; he's not worthy as a mate, an Alpha, and not a Lycanthrope.

"What did you do? Stop lying." It's a hiss through a sob, a heartbreaking wail of betrayal, a howl from my wounded wolf, and I'm utterly desolate. I don't believe what he says he didn't do because I don't know. He said it. He commanded me. I blacked out while he was on top of me, doing things; he had no intention of stopping. He tried to immobilize me so he could finish the deed.

"I had to make you snap. I told you it's what I intended. And you did—it worked. You're amazing. Your gift, baby, it's fucking perfect." A frown follows a moment of joy as he realizes I am not sharing in his celebrations or relaxing from my stance. Instead, I stare at him in stunned silence. My brain is having a moment, and I think he might be some kind of sociopath, in denial about what he just did to me ... or tried to ... or ... I don't even know anymore.

"What are you talking about? I blacked out! How would I fucking do anything except lie there and succumb?" Another sobbing wail and Colton's face completely drops, apparent regret written all over him and the overpowering sense of pain waving my way. I can feel him telling me this isn't how it seems by using his emotion instead of words. I'm weakening as adrenaline wanes, but I won't relent and try hard to brick up my wall once more to keep him out.

"The human in you zoned out, not the wolf. You lost control, and you turned. You disabled me completely. You threw me across the room with a strength I couldn't match. You came at me; I swear, you had me running around this room just to stop you tearing me limb from limb. Complete direct focus and not taking out the house in the aftermath, so you're learning to channel it... Lorey, you had me, and I honestly don't think I'd still be here if your energy levels hadn't gone down before I did."

Again, with that hint of pride and joy, but my death glare and crouch to pounce stance has him rushing the words out, realizing he isn't calming me one ounce, and I'm ready for a battle or a second one.

I can smell a slight hint of fear coming my way, and it only fuels my desire to make him pay. "You pushed all your rage on my body, and if I weren't half-turned and healing fast, you would have killed me. Do you understand? Blindsided and feral, you would have ended us both—easily. You got in my head in ways I don't think any wolf has ever been capable of, and you commanded me to stay down and stop. I couldn't move. You Alpha toned me. You took my strength, my command, and you turned it around and made it a weapon. Baby, don't you see? You've barely grazed the surface of what you can do, and yet you have so much power and potential already. There's a sea of something inside you, and your eyes ... we still need to figure out why they're red. You're not a reject; you're not even a regular pack wolf. You're special, and now we know for sure we can harness it, nurture it, bring it out so you can control it, and show all of them who you really are. There's a Luna inside you, and the Fates ... they must know and gave you to me for that reason. My father can't deny you if he can see this kind of power in you." Colton moves slightly forward, breathless from talking fast and still wary, his hands still up and eyes locked on mine, but the trust is wounded, and I back away.

Snarling at him, baring my teeth as I flicker from human to wolf again slowly, panting with shallow breaths as my heart pounds faster and rage and fear claws me apart. I'm afraid, and I don't believe anything he's saying to me, even if a logical pull is tugging from the recess of my mind. He stops, looks utterly hopeless, and drops his eyes to the floor.

"I know how it looks. I had to make you fight back, and I knew that was a surefire way. I had to see. This changes things, Lorey, don't you understand? Our packs are verging on a war where more than ever, my mate has to be able to stand by my side and fight worse than us. You can absorb my gifts, which means you can absorb any you come up against, turn them into something more powerful, and use them with control. You were right when you said I made a choice, and I did, but this is how we change it. My father has to see that you're not a black mark on our people if the Fates gave you a gift like this. There's hope that I can have them accept you into the pack and lay claim to what the Fates ordained. You as my mate, as we always should have been." The muscle spasm in his jaw, the flicker of his eyes on mine as he begs me to believe, has me spiraling.

I shake my head at him, so consumed with mistrust, my mind a flurry of conflicting emotions, backing into a corner until I hit the edge of the bed. It startles me, and I seem to snap out of my intense focus on him and look around for the first time, really seeing the room.

There has been an epic battle in this room. It's complete devastation. Worse than the carnage at the orphanage, I gasp as my eyes follow the gouges and claw marks running not just across the floor and walls but ceilings too.

Furniture splayed or tipped over, trashed, or just balancing precariously. The pictures on the wall either smashed to the floor or hanging lopsided. Some clawed through where they hang. All the bedsheets are strewn across the floor, most ripped and slashed, and feathers float in the air from pillows that no longer exist. Destruction everywhere. I crouch quickly to grab the nearest sheet to wrap it around myself and conceal my body fast.

"There's one problem with that little 'hope.' I don't want you to touch me ever again," I snarl out, penetrating him with my glare, the second wave of anger, even though I'm beginning to see that maybe, partially, he isn't lying to me. He still made me believe he would; he scared me. I can't be sure he would have stopped, and for that few seconds of panic, before I blacked out, I was utterly afraid of him. You never do that to your bond.

"You're upset and angry with me. Baby, I would never do that. I swear on the bloodline of my pack. It was killing me to push you that far, and I almost gave in because I couldn't stomach hurting you like that. I had to see, I had to force your hand, and now look at you standing there, poised for a second-round like a seasoned warrior. You weren't that girl yesterday. You're changing. Coming into your true form and adapting as you do." He looks almost proud, but it tears through me, igniting the wrong bomb.

"Changing? I'm FUCKING furious with you! I'm REACTING because you're a sick, twisted bastard who laid his goddamn hands on me in the worst kind of way. I can't ever know for sure if you stopped. I only have your word. And nothing you say means shit to me now!" I scream it at him, not caring if everyone in this house hears me blow a fuse and go nuclear. What he's done is unforgivable. If we weren't so far on this side of the house, I'm sure a dozen Santos would have been in here already to see what the chaos and noise from this prominent battle zone were all about it.

"You can trust me. I would never do anything to hurt you that way." Colton goes for endearing and submissively calm. It's the wrong thing to say entirely, as I'm already volcanic. He just makes me erupt.

"TRUST?!?!?! Like I trusted the Santos to take care of their own when our people didn't come home! Like I trusted you to stand for me and honor our bond when we were imprinted. Like I trusted you to be alone with me in a fucking bedroom and not try to defile my fucking body! .... Trust, Colton? You've denied me; let me down more than once in our lifetime. You fall at every hurdle the second Daddy says NO. Maybe Carmen has the right idea, and you're not someone I should ever trust. Look at how you discard women and pick them up as you fancy. You're weak. You're no Alpha. Always in your father's shadow. *You* are the last wolf I would ever trust or choose to bond myself to. Not after this!" My words hit him hard, and his face closes up, the muscles in his jaw tensing as his eyes dart to the floor, trying to conceal the wounds I just inflicted upon his heart, but I don't care.

He has done nothing to prove I can trust him, and imprinting stupidly made me think I could. You don't insult a male's pride and ego, definitely not his strength. Especially not an Alpha, but Colton has not been a man for me. He's been a boy doing what he's told and denying what the Fates asked of him.

"Carmen slept with someone else, one of my brothers of Santo. She said it was in heartbreak and anger to make me feel the pain I inflicted on her. So no, I didn't just discard her. I had to swallow all of that and stick to my commitment. I made my choice, but she kept using us as a reason to punish me while conveniently forgetting her sins. Her jealousy and mistrust are her guilt. The imprinting didn't make me indifferent to her—she did. She wasn't fighting the bond or the lure of the Fates as I was; she was trying to wound me, and that, Lorey, is something you never do to a mate. That's why I can't feel anything for her anymore. It's why we're not dating. I found out after the forest, and since then, I haven't been able to feel anything but disdain for her." His pained, low-toned words momentarily silence me and my anger, not expecting that mouthful or the knowledge a femme would betray a mate with his pack brother.

That's all kinds of messed up, and I can't believe he is only telling me now, even if his heart was no longer invested. It would crush an Alpha's pride and ego to have been played like that. It could dent his respect in the pack, especially if he never took out any act of revenge on his pack brother to balance the scales. By Lycanthrope law, he should have publicly shamed her punished her and his pack brother. Instead, he was still trying to fix everything.

With my rage fizzing out and my logical brain easing in to calm my impulse to wreak havoc on him, I slump down onto the floor, completely exhausted, and pull my ripped sheets around me to self-console. My head is a blur of what he just said, some weird sympathy for him, even if I should still hate his very bones.

"Show me. Prove it ... that you never ..." I can't look at him. The storm has blown out of my sails, and I'm tired, but he knows what I'm asking, and he cautiously walks to me. Slowly and surely, keeping his eyes on me as though he expects me to turn and go for him at any second. I can sense his apprehension, which gives me a hint that maybe some of what he said was true. Something made him afraid, something happened between us, and he is still wary and ready to defend himself if needed.

He reaches out when he gets close enough and touches his fingers to my temple, so gently I barely feel it as he slides down to his knees, bringing his mind to mine, and projects the memory I am missing. I close my eyes and let it flood my mind.

It's as he says. After I blacked out, there was a moment of pause when he stopped, pulled my face to him from the pillows, and looked me over, aware I was no longer responding. His voice laced with concern, asking if I was okay and trying to rouse me. Genuinely afraid he'd hurt me or pushed me too far and that maybe he had stopped me from being able to get air. He turned me over carefully, checked my breathing, leaned in, and tried to stroke my face to wake me, saying my name softly.

It's like I stopped and became vacant, and there were long seconds of no response from me. He released his hold on me, panic rising inside him. Afraid he had done something to me, he checked my pulse, stroked my face again, and tried to shake me, whispering my name softly. He didn't do anything more to hurt me, just wanted to bring me round. When it looked like he started moving to pull me up to sit, drenched in concern, I exploded, transforming in a blink, like he'd woken the dormant beast.

My wolf form seemed to combust out of nowhere; my eyes snapped open, burning red with the rage of Lucifer, and then all hell broke loose. Just like he said, it did. I was out for his blood, relentless, and I don't recognize myself in the memory.

I cringe as the pictures and images show me wounding him in ways an average wolf would never have healed from. I was on him, after him, rolling around as he tried to battle me off without actually trying to hurt me. Bit him, clawed him, and savagely ripped at him, over and over. I wouldn't stop, and he was right—his power was no match for mine. He had to heal as fast as I was inflicting savagery, to stay breathing, and I was a tornado of hatred which was not willing to give in. Delivering a thundering blow, eliciting a yelp from him, so high pitched it hurts even in memory; my ears wincing at the sound.

My claws sank into his chest, an inch from his heart, which I guess is where I was aiming before my wolf gave up. Unable to stay in form when it's still so new for me and takes so much stamina, I slumped onto the floor, all ability zapped out as I transformed back to human form, passing out in a useless huddle.

Colton crawled from under me, sliding his torn body out while yanking my talons from his chest. Bleeding out and groaning, he struggled to the wall to turn and save himself. I awoke to find him, back as a man, recovering. That's where my memory rejoins to what I woke up to.

I have no words, and when he lets me go and sits back on his haunches, I can feel the relief swarming my way that he knows I can't deny what I saw. We can't twist the memories or alter them; he didn't lie to me at all. I saw for myself that what he said was true; I can't deny it in any way. I sit in stunned silence and let it sink in. So hyper-aware of his presence, sensitive, but emotionally all over the place and unsure how to feel.

"Imagine what you could do when you harness it and train to fight." His words are hushed, his hand coming up to touch my cheek gently, but I cringe away from him. Still on high alert and wary, but also submerged in shame at what I saw myself do. I didn't recognize that wolf as any connection to me. She was feral and relentless and insanely wild. This is why they never allow us to turn if we can't control ourselves.

"I could have killed you. I tried to kill you." It's uttered in broken shame, my voice shaking and raspy as it all filters through. Steeped in feelings of severe guilt. I can't look at him, but he leans in, sliding his hand under my face softly, tilts my chin up, and meets my eyes with his, a smile on that handsome face that shows no anger at what I did.

"The Fates wouldn't give me a mate I can't handle. Besides, if I died, you would have too, and we could have been together in the afterlife to carry on without all this drama." That cheeky smirk hits his face, mixed with relief that I'm finally calming down, and a little too cocky that he's winning me over. I can't help the tiny ghost of a smile that twinges on my lips, a little annoyed that he always seems to be able to draw me out like this. I have no words, and as I'm about to say something more, his face falls, and that serious tone kicks in, cutting into our conversation hastily.

133

"They've called all wolves to the great hall immediately." He drops his hand from my jaw and jumps to his feet in naked glory, and I avert my eyes, suddenly aware of this and instantly shy. He has your typical Alpha package going on, and it's not exactly easy to not look at. Generally, the males have something to be proud of, and Colton is no exception. My face reddens, heat rising on my cheeks, and I huddle myself in, still recovering from this shitstorm we just put ourselves through, and now blushing to my core because I ogled him and realized he's well endowed.

I wait for him to leave, hoping to pull myself together with a bit of headspace and also try not to check out his ass, but he pauses when he sees I make no effort to follow.

"That means you too. My goal is to have you initiated into this pack, Lorey. No matter what it takes. My father can't keep denying us if you're accepted. We need to have a plan ... steps to being together. I don't want to keep going through the emptiness of the last weeks and denying this between us. What I said in the forest— I was wrong." He shrugs as if he's reciting some bland speech and not altering everything I thought was happening in the last weeks of agonizing life.

My eyes dart to him, shocked, yet not. Deep down, I guess I knew this was his motive and his feelings on where we should end up. I'm just not so sure anymore. The words I said in anger still ring true, and my heart tells me that a bond should be stronger than his father's command. I can't shift that disappointment in him because I feel like he was too quick to give me up.

I'm a whirlwind of emotions, and so much has happened in the last twelve hours that I need some time to let my brain catch up. I've been through trauma, changes, a whirlwind, and I need to process it all. I can't tell which way is up, and I'm no longer in control of a single tiny thing in my own life. Not even where I'll sleep tonight, let alone live tomorrow.

"Come. Please. You can't say here in this mess, and we need to get you some clothes." He stretches his hand to me, extending his palm outwards, and I brush it away.

"Why can't you let me leave to figure this out on my own? This is the last place on earth I want to be." Tears begin to fall as self-pity hits hard, and I guess it's because I'm physically and mentally exhausted, too. This is not how I thought my life would go, and from the day I turned, it's been hell and heartache all rolled into one.

He exhales heavily, frustrated with me, and yanks me to my feet with a forceful lunge at my arms instead. Pulling me up despite my refusal. Taking charge and not in the mood for arguments.

"Listen to me. I don't want you to go. I need you to comply for a little while, and we'll figure this out together. When this settles, I'll go to the orphanage and pack up all your stuff, and we can talk about where we go from there; right now, I need you to come with me and do as I say." He has that edge to his voice I usually hear when he's leading his pack around. It's the 'don't argue with me' commanding tone of Prince Santo.

What else can I do? I'm technically a prisoner here with nowhere else to go. I'm on my feet, with persistent pain in my ass bossing me around, in a house full of people who hate me. I only have him on my side to depend on, and only because the Fates forced it. I have nowhere else, and if I'm being honest with myself, everything is too messy, my gifts too new, and my mental state a little too on the fragile side to be thinking about going anywhere alone. So, I nod reluctantly.

"Come on then. Stay close to me." Colton turns and leads the way, sensing I don't want or need him touching me, and I do as he says. Staying right behind him, clutching my sheet and waiting while he grabs one, wrapping it on like a toga, and heading towards the door. If Carmen saw us now, naked with ripped bedsheets to cover our modesty, she would only assume the worst, and I can't imagine that going down well at all. I shudder at the possibility she might see us.

Within seconds we're in the hall moving along the wide passage in semi-darkness due to all the boarded-up windows and lack of lighting, and he leads onwards, following some turns and a flight of stairs until we get to the floor below. They put me on the top floor at the far end of the house, away from everyone, and now we seem to be on the third floor in a brighter hallway with doors all bearing names and keypads on each.

Colton stops me with an arm, pushes me back around the corner we rounded, and hushes me with a finger to my lips as two Santo pack members appear from a door opening. Both walk out and head away from us, completely unaware of our presence. He makes us wait a second before leading us halfway down the hall to the third door on the right and turns, places his hand on the pad to scan his palm, and it clicks open. His name's on the door, so I guess this is his room.

"Why are we hiding if you're taking me downstairs, anyway?" I ask blatantly, composing myself since leaving that room. He slides an arm around me and shuffles me into the darkened space, pulling me in and closing the door behind us with a last outward check of the hall. He walks off across the bedroom towards a set of wooden doors in front of me, slides them open to reveal wardrobes, and starts pulling out clothes in multiples of two. Thanks to the boarded-up windows, it's dull in here, but the light is shining through the cracks brightly, illuminating enough, telling me daylight has come.

I follow him, taking in his room's almost Scandinavian, Ikea style, and minimalism. He likes space and neatness, with very few items cluttering it up. Neutral tones, light woods, plants and a lot of floor space, and open calmness. It's clean and airy and almost obsessively organized.

"Carmen just needs to know I brought you in here, and she'll go nuclear. It's best if I appear downstairs with you, where she's contained, because my ears, and my head, can't handle her gifts right now. She still thinks we have a future, and I need to talk to her about that." He carries on focusing on clothes, his tone level, as though he hasn't just caused me pain with careless words.

It quietens me, and that distant heartache and pang of jealousy find its way back home to my stomach. I wondered if our bond had been dented in all this mess and if I was starting to feel differently about him. I guess I'm not that lucky, as my heart still seems very much attached, despite everything. I'm mad at him, disappointed in him, yet I still yearn for and love him. My soul still wants and needs him.

We dress quickly; although his clothes are baggy on me, it's better than showing up in a rag and a smile. Following him close to his heel, we make our way down another two flights of stairs and two other levels before we end up back where I caused such a scene hours ago. That sweeping staircase to the main entrance, which is now immaculately calm.

It's a lot cleaner and tidier now the debris is gone and the front door closed, with the addition of several new heavy-duty locking mechanisms in place. The boarded glass panels are screwed on with braces over them for now, hinting that the threat of another attack is on Juan's mind.

Colton takes my hand in his unexpectedly, sliding strong fingers into mine, and leads the way across the vast marble floor into a small hallway that runs away from the bathroom he put me in earlier. I accept his touch, needing it now I'm on a comedown from what happened upstairs. Once again vulnerable and out of my depth and clinging to him to take charge while in his domain. Drawing from his strength and ability to swagger through the worst kind of chaos.

We walk down the dark, almost claustrophobic space, with voices, noises, lots of movement cascading our way, and follow two Santos we catch up with inside the most crowded room I've ever seen. It's hard to tell how big it would be empty, for it's packed solid with adult Santo wolves, primarily male, from all over, even the ones who don't live in the packhouse. Easily over a hundred or so, and they're all squeezed in, fighting for breathing space as we join right at the back, unseen.

Right down at the front, several elders and the Shaman are standing on a low podium facing back at us all. Men, I have never seen before in my life, standing behind them, and I guess these are the older generation of retired elders, coming out in our time of need. It's mostly men in here, as is the way when dealing with important matters, or femmes who have no children and are better

137

suited to battle, as all of those who are not are home minding their little ones. Juan Santo is right in the center, and he seems to be waiting for everyone to quieten down before he starts. The overwhelming seriousness of this cascades around the room, thickening the atmosphere with tension.

Colton pulls me in front of him, placing me right at his chest, so he's up against my back, lacing his fingers into both of my hands from behind as they hang by my sides in the darkest of our shadows. He rests his chin against the back of my head, bringing his body to fit snugly into mine, so we are wholly joined without it being apparent to those around us. He's a good head taller than me, so it's a natural position, and I glance around to see if anyone is staring, but they're all too focused on their Alpha king. It looks like two people are standing close due to the crushing lack of space as our hands are concealed in darkness.

"Quiet now." A voice from the front row hushes the nervous mumbling and scraping in the room, and everyone stops talking, the atmosphere somehow heavier with the forced hush. Juan steps forward, although I can barely see him over the people in front of me and have to stand on my tiptoes to get a good view between heads. There's a moment of pause as he looks around us all, his eyes catching his son across the crowds, and I can't miss the brief surge of anger as he realizes I'm right in front of him.

I glance away, instantly scalded, landing back down on flat feet, wounded by the penetrating glare, and scan the room instead to see if Carmen is anywhere close by. I can't see her, thankfully, which means she probably can't see us, and I try to sink further better to conceal myself behind the Santo in front of me. Colton squeezes my hands and holds me closer, somehow letting me know I should ignore it.

Be still. You're safe with me.

He comes through gently, caressing my mind with a tender tone, and I exhale dejectedly.

For now, maybe. While they're all distracted with vampire attacks and end of world foreboding, but my gut says it's temporary.

138

I can feel the hatred lingering in the air from Juan's fierce frown, and it unsettles me in every kind of way.

"You all know why we are here," Juan begins. It's the final push needed to bring a total hush to the room as all completely still, not even the shuffle of moving bodies, and fall deathly silent. It tugs my attention back to him, and I peek around the side of the male in front of me to catch sight of him again. "A long-forgotten enemy attacked us, and quite frankly, we didn't see it coming and were not prepared. Despite the rumbling of recent months, we didn't honestly expect them to rise and attack in this way, and we failed our people. We lost fifty-three of our kind, on the dark side of the mountain, tonight. Forty-seven lost in the battle and six bonded who perished when their mate's heart took its last beat."

My heart aches as he says it, visualizing so many of the faces I know went down in that attack. Unlike anyone else in this room, I'm probably the only one who not only knew their names, but what every single one of them looked like, who they were as people, and their ages not only when they died, but when they were first dumped in that hellhole without their loved ones. Memories with all of them, even if they were not close to me. To these wolves, they're just numbers to measure their failures against.

I close my eyes as the tears begin to fall silently down my cheeks, warm unwelcome rivulets of remembrance. I shudder as I push them away, inhaling heavily as my shoulders start to tremble with the effort of not falling apart. The pain is returning once more, and I can't stop myself. My heart fills up and strains to contain it as images I don't want to relive swamp my mind. The horrors of how I last saw them all trying so hard to invade my brain and cut me down all over again.

I nestle back into Colton as his arm comes up around my body and across my neck as he cuddles me. His comfort because he can feel my pain, my body trembling as I cry, squeezing my eyes shut to gain control. His touch is what I need more than anything, and I stay here in the darkness of my own doing, listening and silently weeping while held tight in his comforting embrace.

"We think it was a test, for this device we found in the orphanage," Juan carries on, and my eyes rip open at his words, shoving my despair aside as I squirm, wriggling out of Colton's arms to see what everyone is craning their necks to look at. Catching a gap as the ones in front move sideways to look where I am.

He holds up a small, perfectly square black box that looks harmless, an antenna sticking up at the top, but a lack of buttons or dials of any sort. Small and compact, no more than the size of a tissue box, with another wire sticking out from the rear about a foot long and doesn't seem to attach to anything to power it. It doesn't look real, more like something a child could make with card and glue and some black paint, and I blink at it, stupefied, glaring furiously, and hating that something so insignificant destroyed my life.

"They chose our weakest and our most secluded and walked right in, depositing this in the center of the first-floor kitchen. We think they wanted to test its effectiveness and still have a fighting chance should it fail. It didn't. We've only one survivor left from the home and only because of the fast actions of our pack. We took down many of their kind, but a few escaped and
will report on their success for sure."

There's a murmur and uneasiness as people glance around at one another, questioning, and I catch the whisper of my name on the hushed wave of sound. A mixture of relief that my survival ensured their own Santo Alpha and the bitter ones, calling me a reject and querying how I was the only one who survived.

I catch the low, body vibrating, internal growl from Colton as his protective instinct kicks in at hearing my name, and a couple of nearby Santos glance this way, eyes widening in surprise, and they instantly stare down at their feet, turning meekly submissive in a flash. Faces darkening with fear and shame at being caught by him, of all people. Realizing he's right here, among them, and not down there with his immediate family. I turn away to block them out and stare towards the front instead, mentally blanking them all because this has always been my life, and I'm not bothered by their remarks.

I catch sight of his grandmother in the shadows when they settle down, a woman who barely shows face but is lingering nearby. Unsurprisingly, there's no sign of Luna Santo, Colton's mother. She's been absent from view since the wars, and, rumor has it, she locks herself up in her room on the main floor upstairs and never leaves. No one has seen her in years, and if it weren't for Colton's memories of her in my head, I wouldn't even remember what she looked like.

Meeting one of the few things in the world which can leave unhealable damage on a wolf, and her mental state has crumbled with the trauma. Some say she was scarred horribly by the battles, both mentally and physically, and is too ashamed to come out and face her people. Only I now know from being inside his head there's some truth to the stories, and there's only a vague blurry visual of Colton being told she's cared for, away from the mountain, because the war broke her.

Those around us turn silent as Juan breaks through the thick atmosphere once again, drawing me away from my train of thought and disrupting my searching of the past for answers to her lack of appearance.

"Testing weapons can only mean we're heading for a war with an enemy we thought we long ago defeated. They're working on a strategy, and this is just the beginning. There have been rumors of stories, but nothing concrete for many months, although this is our proof. Civilization as we know it is about to change drastically. We must protect the packs, join with those from other lands, and prepare for what is coming. We *must* unite and finally have one leader to rule. One voice, to work as one, under my guidance as Alpha, if we are to survive a second war like the last."

I shiver as his words hit home, my brain scrambling to fathom something as massive an undertaking as that. We're a dozen packs in one state, but worldwide there are thousands, hundreds of thousands, and most still do not live in peace with the others of their kind. Rivalries exist, and some are still at war, even now with the history of the conflicts behind us. A common enemy may change that, but there's a lot to do before that can happen.

Packs are destined to want to rule over one another, fight for dominance, forge the hierarchy, and our mountain is not typical when it comes to living proximity. It was a necessity as we recovered from the war of before. Our people, shattered by loss, were more pliable in accepting another pack as our leader. Most of our Alphas never returned to dispute the claim to rule us.

Santo's idea that he will become the only leader and unite us all seems ridiculous, given the vast number of us he will need to unite in this world. I'm sure there are other pack leaders out there who believe themselves far superior to him. Other dominants with way more ability and gifts, and it's not in an Alpha's nature to yield without a fight.

I shiver, my body trembling with all that is dawning on me how terrifying our future now looks, and Colton tightens his hold on me, reassuring me as best he can. Trying to keep me calm and be that rock I never knew I needed before finding his touch. I exhale heavily, submerging myself in his body heat, and try to bring myself peace.

"We need to put measures in place to protect our mountain from another attack—effective immediately. Allocations of groups with leaders will be assigned to those who haven't already had so. We are the reigning pack in Radstone, and they'll all be looking to us now to lead and protect them. Training will begin at first light for all old enough to fight, so all of you eat. Sleep. We've already sent small details to walk the perimeters, and each of the villages has been ordered to do the same. We'll have guards outside at every hour, keeping watch, and we'll revise a system to improve on all of this, set up drills on how to react should an alarm be raised. In the next few weeks, we'll be moving all surrounding packs to the mountain's south side, here among our people, for their own safety. We have much to do. There will be upheaval and chaos, but we must keep our heads. This was the first offensive, and we do not know when they intend to return."

The silence becomes unbearable when his last words fall in the air, and the gravity of our situation sits heavy on us all. Some of these men and women are survivors of the first war against the vampires and had already paid their dues, but most of us were just children or young enough to stay behind. We lost so many, and although our numbers have recouped over the years, we're not living in readiness for a fight. We've had relative peace for years, and I have no idea how we're going to get through this.

Bringing us all to one place to live in each other's pockets, here in the Santo land, will be madness. We're spread far around the skirts of the mountains, and our numbers are high. There are not enough homes to accommodate bringing us all together to this one shaded side, under their command and watchful eye. Not to mention the children, their schools, and their animals on the outer farms. This is insanity.

I feel sick to my stomach knowing that everything I knew before, my idea of empty living, was, in fact, the best years of my sad existence. Now we're dawning on a new age, and I wish with all my heart that I could go back to being that unworthy reject, in a house full of unwanted, on the shady side of our peaceful mountain.

If I could go back, I would. I would never complain again and never crave a different life because what is coming couldn't be worse.

CHANGING TIMES

After Juan has finished making his announcement, the Santos file
out of the room slowly, in a wave of murmurs and noises as they
discuss what he said and where we go from here. You can feel the
tension thickening, the uneasiness, and the nervousness, as it sinks
in that this is real and life as we know it is about to change
dramatically. Colton pulls me aside, tucking us out of the way of the
door to let people pass, and grabs a passing male who is very
familiar to me.

"Mateo, take Alora to our room and wait for me there.
Assemble the pack; I want to talk to you all. I won't be long; my
father wants me." He nods out towards the front of the room, where
Juan's still concealed by moving people, and I instantly feel sick
with apprehension.

Being left with someone and separated from Colton reminds
me that for all the things I am mad at him about, I still feel secure
when with him. His strength, quiet confidence, and air of control
are the calm to my nervous floundering, and it only hits home that
I need his presence more than I want to admit. He's my safety net
and the only person in the world who cares about me in any kind
of way.

"Dude, I don't think that's a good idea. Carmen and Alora in
the same room ... she will ...."

"Are you questioning me?" Colton's tone instantly changes, ha
growling snarl in the undertones, irritation fast to show his
displeasure, and that aggressive air kicking in as Mateo looks away

sheepishly. Knowing he overstepped the mark. Questioning of command never goes down well with Alphas of any sort, especially not by one of his sub-pack, and it shows me that Colton is way more patient with me than even his closest.

"No, *mi alfa, me disculpo.*" Mateo responds in fluent Spanish, lowering his head and displaying his regret. He shows the demanded respect, obviously chastised as his leader is Colton, apologizing and addressing him as Alpha.

We have one major rule in our world. Never query your Alpha for any reason, and never disobey. I forgot what that was like when living severed from any natural pack and only following basic rules in the home. Being here reminds me of how it used to be when my family was alive, and we all followed Samuel Whyte before his family was taken down and never returned.

It makes me rethink Colton's refusal to defy his father and leaves me churning it over in my head, a new angle on a frustrating situation. Reality sinking in that just because I lived outside the restraints and rules of our social norm for a decade doesn't mean he has.

Colton and Mateo are a sub pack, a smaller group divided from the main and lorded over by a single dominant—Colton. They're called Beta packs, or subs, and much like the hierarchy of leadership, even the sub packs rank in order of importance and command, like smaller units in an enormous army, with ranking officers and Colton's right up there in the top five. His father's pack of Beta second commanders is number one. This is how large packs like the Santos keep everything running smoothly.

The order depends on skill, experience, and how battle-scarred they are, and Colton's sub pack was of an age to defend us ten years ago. They all tasted real war on our lands. Even so young. It's why they train together every day and are some of our most capable soldiers when needed. I should never forget that even though Colton is not yet the Santo Alpha, he is one in his own right and his own sub pack, and I underestimate the importance of his responsibilities. He isn't just some nineteen-year-old high school jock with his eye on a future crown. He's already a commander, performing his duty and caring for his pack.

"Go with him. He'll keep you safe. He's as close as a brother to me." Colton leans in, pulling me to him so he can murmur, almost nose to nose, that gentler tone waving through me and breaking down my defenses. That sweet look I now know is only reserved for me, and he reluctantly pushes me towards Mateo until a hand lands on my shoulder. It's an unfamiliar touch, and I flinch at the contact but try to hide it.

"The rest of the pack are not going to like this." Mateo points it out, raising a brow at Colton, but gets a blank stare that I can tell was a move from verbal conversation to mind. Whatever Colton says, Mateo looks away again and gently taps me to nod towards the door that people are filing out of. He flushes slightly, his face reddening high on his cheekbones, and I guess he got a quiet dressing down away from listening ears. To save face, Colton didn't do it outright, showing he cares about his friend, even if he was pissed at him for questioning his authority.

I won't be long. Try not to engage with Carmen.

His voice is like a last lingering stroke, giving me tingles as I move to leave him. I nod at him, not anywhere close to feeling as confident as I pretend, before turning on my heel, steeped in nervous energy, and letting Mateo guide me with that single hand on my shoulder.

Colton's memories show me they're best friends, but Mateo is also one of his commanders, and he trusts him completely. Mateo is as familiar a face in my memories as Colton as they were always together, like brothers or inseparable shadows. He's the one who teased him that day in the lake in the memory Colton showed me, and I guess he already knows that a long time ago, Colton knew who I was. That Colton harbored some sort of juvenile feelings. Even as children, the Fates were trying to draw me to him.

I walk with him now, side by side, a male as tall as Colton and as broad. They share similarities, and I wonder if they're maybe cousins or have a close blood tie because they look alike. Same thick straight brows and black hair that's a little ruggedly messy, like

146

they have a natural curl, although Colton's is shorter, so harder to tell. Same darkest brown molten eyes, tanned Latino skin tone, and square jawline, although Mateo is not as cleanshaven or groomed. His hair is not clipped or manicured, and his eyebrows are not as angular and tamed.

Mateo's like the rougher, less kempt version of Colton, who just rolled out of bed and threw on the first clothes to hand. He has a casual quality, is less pulled together, and sharp. Mateo seems less concerned about his worn faded jeans and gray hoodie, which don't look designer.

Colton takes pride in his appearance and clothes, and it's evident to everyone he comes from wealth when you see him on an average day. He just oozes that effortless polish, expensive labels, and self-confidence.

"So, you're Alora ... from the Whyte clan, right?" he nods as we dodge fast-paced walkers, and I'm not oblivious to how many glance my way, with sneers and weird looks, as we pass them going to their rooms, or wherever they have to be. My presence is noted, and the vibes I'm picking up on tell me that people know who I am or know I'm responsible for trashing their packhouse. I ignore it, lower my chin to avoid eye contact, and silently exhale to blow it all away.

Everyone leaving the room at once causes mayhem in this narrow hallway, and I can't tell which way we're even moving as we're crammed among so many. It's like ants evacuating a collapsing den via the only escape route. It's claustrophobic.

"Yeah, I think we used to play in the same places as children," I answer distractedly, avoiding collision with oncoming traffic, trying to be polite. Still, I'm too busy side-stepping large males pushing by and trying not to get trampled underfoot.

"We did. I remember you. You had a brother, Jasper, about my age." Hearing his name coming from someone else's mouth sucker punches me unexpectedly, and I have to bite my lip to stop the sudden inhale from the slice of pain it inflicts. Even after all these years, I've never really fully mourned their loss. I try never to think of them and push them down whenever one surfaces.

147

"I did. He didn't come back from the wars." It's a fast, audibly painful response, my voice wavering, as I shake my head to expel the vision of him, so like my father in looks, and look to the ground instead to watch my steps. The comment about his age means Mateo is older than Colton by at least five years, if not more, so it's weird that Colton is the sub Alpha and not Mateo. It gives me something else to focus on and not the memory of a brother I will never see again.

"I'm sorry. I didn't mean to upset you. I guess time is not a healer like they say." He seems momentarily uneasy, and I smile his way, bringing my eyes back to his with a sympathetic shrug. It never is the right time to have these kinds of awkward conversations.

"I'm not used to hearing anyone say his name. It was forbidden to talk of our loved ones at home because they were seen as shamed. They failed our people by dying." I grind, tightening my limbs as I churn out the words I hear so many times. Mateo frowns, something dark in the depths of his eyes, hinting at a reaction I don't understand, and then it's gone.

"This way." Mateo changes the topic and points to a hallway veering off to the right of where we are, taking us out of the crush of people and into the near silence of an empty passage. He stands for a moment, looking around, and I can tell he's mind linking, probably calling their pack to where we're going. He takes a minute or so, and then he turns his attention back to me. "The rest are on their way, so we may as well show it to you before they get here." He walks down the dark hallway and opens a door at the very end using a keypad. Pushing open a heavy solid cherry wood door reveals an already lit room inside. It has working lights, so I guess they started replacing bulbs down here first, and we walk in, letting the door swing shut behind us.

It's like a large study from an old-world time, with substantial leather armchairs and a massive wall-hugging fireplace off to one side. There's one large walnut desk with a heavy dark green padded chair behind it, facing out into the center. Matching dark green leather couches by two walls, bookcases lining another, and what looks like a minibar in the gap left by the door. There's a thick animal hide rug under our feet. I think it might be a brown bear or some huge rough-haired animal, and absolutely no windows in here at all.

"Every pack has a communal room for hanging out, bonding, and talking shop. Ours is the best because we're lucky enough to have Juan Santo's son as our Alpha. It's a perk as we get favor." I can't tell if he's serious or sarcastic, and I don't pick up on any actual malice in his tone. It's an odd thing to say if he isn't trying to be an ass. He nods me towards a seat as he strolls to the fireplace, presses a button, and it explodes into instant flames. I thought it looked real, but I guess it's gas.

I sit close to it on an armchair, not cold, but watching flames has always brought me a sense of calm and reminded me of another time and place when my mother would brush my hair by ours. A time when I had no cares in the world. A time when I was secure and loved and nestled in the lap of my family. I try not to dwell on it and stare into the depths, emptying my mind.

"Drink?" Mateo pulls my attention to him, now at the dark wood and glass bar, and I shake my head. I'm already nervous about them arriving, and I can't relax, even if he seems more tolerant of me than most of this pack. The last thing I need is to dull my senses and get drunk with a guy or group that I don't know and have every reason to treat me cruelly.

You okay?

Colton comes through loud and clear, checking on me, and for a second, it warms me that he does, that maybe he felt my nervousness. His voice is that sound of home that I never knew I needed, and I find myself exhaling like I've been holding my breath as I lean back into the chair a little more relaxed.

I am just waiting on the others and sitting by the fire.

I reply, setting his mind at ease and hoping I sound as comfortable here as I am pretending to be.

I won't be long. My father kept all the leaders back to talk about plans and schedules. You know what I mean. I'll leave our link

149

open if you need me. Don't let any of them give you any shit, or they'll have to deal with me.

His deep husky voice has me pining for his presence, and I sigh wearily.

Mateo is being a gentleman and taking care of me; I'm sure he'll intervene.

I'm trying to make him relax, but the overwhelming surge I get back from his emotions that he didn't like what I said surprises me. It's a hint of jealousy, and I blink at Mateo as though I'm missing the point. He has his back to me, pouring his drink, and is nowhere near me.

Right. As I said, I won't be long.

His tone is clipped, and he closes the link before I respond, despite saying he wouldn't. He sounded off and moody, and I swear it makes me want to laugh at how ridiculous he's being. He sent me here with Mateo, and now he's what? Jealous because I said he was being nice. I knew males were territorial and possessive by nature, worse when they mate up, but I'm not even his, and he has nothing to worry about. We imprinted, and the Fates made sure I have no desire to look at anyone else, even if he did reject me.

I inhale sharply, shake it off, and go back to staring at the fire, trying not to let him get to me as the door swings open and two boys stomp in, arguing with each other

"You're a liar. I didn't say anything of the sort." The first male snaps, turning and spotting me and instantly frowning like he's just faced a terrible or vile sight. He stops dead as the other collides into the back of him with an exaggerated 'oomph' noise. He's unsurprisingly dark-haired, tanned, and has your typical native Colombian look. All the Santos originated from there before coming here a few generations ago. They usually mate up with others like them, so the bloodline stays purest, and most of the males get sent back in early childhood to spend time in their homelands, so most have mixed accents like Colton does.

"Hey, watch it," the voice snarls and shoves him forward, exposing an identical face and equal build, and I realize these two boys are twins. If memory serves correct, I can pull out of Colton's mind that this is Domi and Remi. They're younger than Colton by a year, making them eighteen, like me. Both lean, tall, athletic boys with light brown hair and soft hazel eyes. More Santos, and I know for sure they're Colton's distant cousins on his mom's side.

"And she is here because ...?" The first one turns to Mateo with a growl and gets a snarl in response. Mateo, seemingly growing an inch taller and faces them down.

"Because Colton said so, and I doubt he wants to hear you were questioning it!" It's not a friendly tone, and it has the desired effect of dampening down the attitude of one twin, at least.

"He's not questioning. He's just a little shocked that our pack room has someone ... not of our pack," the other chirps in, throwing me a devious side-eye, and I fade back into my chair, aware the waves of prickling heat coming my way are hostility, even while he is smiling on like it's not.

"Who's not in our pack?" That female voice I've been dreading comes waving in as she walks in the door. Thick like honey and sultry, preceding her entry. She sashays in like the Queen of the manor and stops dead in her tracks when she spots me. Gray eyes instantly storm over, pouty mouth forming a thin, tight line and porcelain skin paling as rage ignites under the surface. Her eyes glow intense amber as she growls her dislike for me and lowers her chin to move into an attack stance. Wolves are aggressive by nature, and we jump to fight for every little thing. Bite, nip, attack. It's just how we are.

"Why in the fuck has he let her in here?" Carmen loses her cool, steps towards me fast, but Mateo zaps forward, using his hyper-speed, blocking her in a nanosecond, and zips between us. He stands firm, lifts his chin, and makes a good show of exerting his dominance.

"Colton wanted her here and will be along soon, so pipe down, go sit over there and behave!" Mateo has a tone not too dissimilar to Colton's Alpha tone, only less effective, and she draws her eyes from me to him, not as affected as she would have been had their Alpha said it.

"Don't tell me what to do. You're not my Alpha. Hell, you're not even his Beta." The undercurrent of a snarl between them sizzles, and I tense, waiting for it to get crazy in here. I am surprised that Mateo is not his second in command, and I rake my memories to find out who he is. I swear to god it better not be Carmen, or I'm in trouble.

"*Ahora, que tenemos aqui?*" Another female voice floats in, soft, light, and strangely alluring, with a deep raspy undercurrent as three more wolves stroll in unannounced. I recognize her as Meadow, one of the older femmes in her late twenties, mated to Cesar, the one behind her. Her brother is in tow, Jesús, and they stop to gaze over the little scene.

"*Ahora, chicos,* go sit down before I break a claw reminding you who *is* Beta in this room when Colton is not here. Sit!" Her accent is heavy and thick, clear she's an incomer to Radstone, and English is not her first language. Her accent has never faded, though. It's not uncommon for wolves with links elsewhere to bring in a family pack from further away, to live with them or find a mate, and I know Meadow's been with us for a few years, maybe even as far back as the war.

Mateo and Carmen give one last snarl and separate, walking to the couches, chastised and, surprisingly, not defying her. They're followed by the twins, who avert their eyes from their new member and instantly go into sulk mode, slumping together on one sofa and staring at me with lowered eyelids. No hint of warmth, which adds to my growing uneasiness as I sit stiffly where I was. Meadow walks into the room entirely, confidently, eyeing me up, unashamedly, and I feel like I'm being weighed up as prey.

She's a sight to behold, strong, graceful, and sassy at five feet eight. Black hair, the most amazing pale blue eyes under sculpted black brows, and deeply tanned skin. She has full lips, catlike eyes with perfect makeup, and an outfit of clingy denim with a blouse that shows off her ample cleavage.

She's beautiful but has an aura of terrifying. She doesn't stray out of the Santo side of the lands much, but it's evident that Mateo is not Colton's second in command. Meadow is. I wouldn't argue with her, her natural nails are long, sharp, and pointed, with a shellac of blood-red, so I can't imagine what her wolf claws would be like. She puts fear in me with just her presence.

"Hi. I'm Cesar. This is Jesús and the infamous Meadow here." Cesar nods at me, with no hint of either dislike or friendliness in his blank statement. He's another tall, stocky type, and I see a pattern with this pack. Best of the breed and all alarmingly alike, except Carmen, the only blonde among them. They're all big, strong, and have lashings of aggression and attitude, which are common among our strongest. I'm sure as a pack, they have many a battle of wills and lots of spats.

"She knows who we are, don't you, *amiga*? She has Cole's memories, and I'm sure she knows how to access them." Meadow strolls in front of me, heels clicking on the hardwood floor, her eyes wandering over me as she takes me all in without caring how uncomfortable it's making me—devouring my appearance with a critical eye.

"I do," I answer sheepishly, aware another has entered the open door and praying that has to be all of them. I don't even glance their way, as Meadow has a commanding quality that demands you give her our full attention. This is getting crowded, and I feel like I'm raw meat that's being lowered into a hungry lion's den.

"Oh, how did the Fates get this so wrong?" Jesús sneers at me, appearing beside her, not too dissimilar in looks to his sister, only masculine where she is feminine, and instantly shuts up when Meadow throws him a pointed glare with a subtle growl.

"The Fates are never wrong! Don't you know that?" Before taking a calming breath, she snaps, lifting her hands, making motions in the air as though to accompany deep breaths. She smirks when she catches my eye and bends towards me, almost dropping her massive boobs from her low-cut top in my face. "I don't know. I sense something in this one. You think, *Papi*, she has a little summit, summit?"

Cesar doesn't seem impressed or unimpressed - totally blank, and I can only assume he is who she calls *Papi*. I know it's a name for your lover or mate. She reaches out, picking up a strand of my wild, unbrushed hair, and slowly runs her fingers through it, tingling my scalp as it tugs gently. Putting me on edge and making me so uncomfortable, I feel like calling on Colton, but I don't. I expect his pack to be like this at a first meet. I mean, he just threw me in with them amid all that happened today, and they're sizing me up to see how much grit I have. I can't show them weakness, or they'll shred me.

"Is it true she came from the home for the rejects? The ones the vamps all slaughtered." One of the twins can't conceal his disgust, and Carmen sneers, a look of anger crossing her face, and throws him a side-eye glare.

"Yes. And our formidable Alpha lowered his standards and tried to mark this mutt. He needs his head read." Carmen is quick to chirp in with her dislike of me, seething hatred my way. The room feels like it's closing in as anxiety builds and my panic grows, and I wonder how long before I get cornered and chewed on.

"*Oye* ..." It's a sharp sound given out to shut her up, Meadow standing to roll her hair between two fingers and facing them with a look of 'I'm getting so pissed.' "Don't disrespect our Alpha's *compañera*. Don't make me mad, Chica. I won't tolerate it, and neither will he. I don't like when I get angry."

Meadow is the scariest femme I have ever come across, and I don't know why she's unnerving me so much because she seems pretty sane on the surface. It's just she has an aura that screams 'certified psycho,' and every single time she moves, I flinch internally, getting antsier by the second as she stands so close to me.

Carmen recoils, obviously knowing only too well that Meadow doesn't make empty threats, and Mateo clears his throat to distract her. He, too, seems like he knows he should diffuse things, and it only heightens my wariness. Some femmes in our packdom are worse than the mates in terms of volatile aggression and ability to maim, and I think Meadow is one.

"Drinks anyone? While we wait on him." Mateo glances around for takers and gets a couple of quiet nods.

"No, we have *otros planes* for our little *compañera*. She needs a little help over here." Meadow clicks her tongue at me to catch my attention, and when I look up at her, she extends her finger and motions for me to come. It's creepy and yet an order, and without question, I slide up in my chair, heartbeat elevating and wondering what she plans on doing to me.

"You look like a bag lady who dresses out of the trash, *novia*. If that's what Colton has you looking like, you ain't gonna last long here. It's not a good look. Come, we have to fix this before I can sit and look at you for any length of time. You're offending my eyes.... What he do to you? You look like you been working out on our man, huh? Maybe practicing getting marked, huh? Saying goodbye to your poppies and letting his seeds blow up your wind tunnel, eh?" It's a dirty raspy laugh following a dirty remark, and I flush with embarrassment at her brazen statement as I catch her meaning. Knowing I probably look a little chaotic, I can almost taste Carmen's seething rage winding my way.

"No. I haven't let poppy seeds blow or, umm ... err, I ... no." I retort, face flaming, mumbling, babbling, as excruciating shyness almost kills me. Face reddening and unable to look her in the eye. I can feel Carmen's eyes boring down on me, waiting for my answer with vicious suspicion. I can feel her poised body getting ready for my takedown if she thinks Colton has touched me sexually. "We've done nothing ... nothing." How can I tell them I turned, ripped him half to shreds, and then called him weak? I don't think that would go down well with his crew.

"Hmm, disappointing. Well, I can help with that." She gestures again for me to follow and when I hesitate, eyes roaming the enraged Carmen sitting near the doorway, she catches my sleeve and yanks me. Carmen is poised with a reply to what Meadow said, but I can see she's holding it in and simmering, despite the knives she's throwing with her eyes. I'm not sure what the story is between Meadow and Carmen, but I don't get happy, loving pack mate vibes from either of them.

"Colton will be a while, and my room is not far. We look around the same size if you slightly roll up the legs. I'm sure I have something that makes you look less ... *vagabunda*."

"You'll help her with nothing. She's not and will never be his mate. You know who he chose and that he rejected her, so stop playing games, Meadow, and leave her be. The trash look suits her because it's what she is." Carmen couldn't hold it for much longer, and that flash of rage has Meadow spinning her way, almost taking me with her.

"Green is not a good color on you, *puta*! I don't think you are in any position to make demands, considering whose bed I caught you in. You should thank your stars that I've not excised my right to punish such a betraying *putilla* as you. Don't make me reconsider it!"

There's a shocked silence, and Carmen's eyes dart around the rest of them, apparent shame written across her face as all the others avert and avoid her. They all know, of course, they do, and the silent, tense moment tells me they're mad at her for betraying Colton as much as he is. In the eyes of wolf law, she committed a sin that is non-comparable to his.

He was bonded, and he kissed his destined mate. She had sex while promised to another, to wound him. She was linked to Colton, and she punished him by defiling their union after he had already rejected the mate the Fates gave him. It is how this works, and our laws on commitment and betrayal are clear. It doesn't matter how double standard it is.

Packs are weird in they can fight all day long, get aggressive with one another, nip, and tease, but you wind one of them up, they will turn on you even if you're one of their own. They have a special bond with their Alpha, and I can see Carmen is in the doghouse. None of them like her right now.

"You have less than half an hour before Colton most likely shows. You know Juan likes to keep things short." Mateo points out, and Meadow claps her hands happily.

"Plenty of time. Come, we have some girl stuff to do. Carmen isn't welcome. She can sit over there and think about what she's done." Meadow tosses her hair back, that long sleek hair shining as it flies over her shoulder sassily, throwing her a pointed look and leading the way, yanking me with her once more. Cesar and Jesús, still standing in the entranceway, move out of the way, and I catch the slight up and down appraisals as they size me up in passing.

The twins' eyes follow me, and although it's not outright hostility, I can tell none of the males, except for maybe Mateo, are sure they want me here. I'm an outsider to them, an intruder to their pack, and not worthy of being bonded to their Alpha.

As soon as we get to the hallway, Meadow slides her arm in mine and hauls me close, a little aggressively for my liking. Leaning in, so her perfume and natural wolf scent mingle and hit me with a heady concoction.

"I know we're supposed to follow Juan in his hatred of all the orphans he threw behind the mountain, but I lost family in that war, and it could well have been me. Some of us were lucky enough to see some come back. I don't believe that only our strongest bloodlines came home for a second. You can trust me, *amiga*. I'm not like most of the pack. I have a mind of my own." She whispers it in hushed silence and throws me a soft look that, despite feeling her crazy vibes, rings true. She has an underlying kindness, and I can feel it when we're this close. "Colton's a good boy, but he's also Juan's son. He knows his place in the pack, and he knows if he defies his father and breaks that kind of respect for our laws, he'll never have the respect when his time comes to lead. I know what he wants, and I know why he can't have it. But it doesn't mean I don't want to have a little fun and make him suffer." A smile, wink, and almost mischievous laugh, and I frown in confusion. Unsure if I should question her or not. If she is close to Colton, I have no idea what she means about having fun and making him suffer.

She leads the way, pulls me with her up a stair and then down a left hall before we come to a polished wooden door with her name staring back at us from a polished and engraved gold plate. The scent up here is mainly female, and I guess they keep the sexes on different floors, although Cesar's scent lingers around the door, and I guess because they're mated, he gets to stay in here, too. Being mated is marriage, and once you're marked, no one has the authority to stop you from being together in every way, every second of every hour.

"I'm the queen of hair and makeup, and you, *mi amiga*, need a little Santo makeover because, like it or not, you're now our pack and our problem. As long as you live, so does Cole, and it's our job to keep it that way. That means you need to fit in and look the part ... not like this." She gives me an up-down eye flicker of disapproval and an exaggerated expression of 'yuck.' She scans her palm, pushes open the door, and leads the way inside. Flicking on a light switch and grinning when it comes on.

"They finally replaced mine, thankfully. That was some show you put on in the hallway and some mess you made. Impressive! I think you smashed every glass bottle I owned." She wiggles away from me to a dresser and rifles through the contents, throwing me a devilish smile. I relax a little, nerves winding down and anxiety untangling my internal organs, easing into the aura that surrounds her. There's something infectious and alluring that pulls you in and makes you feel like you can open up to her, and I stand awkwardly by the door, watching her.

"I'm sorry. I honestly don't know what happened or how I did it. Colton thinks I ..." I revert into excuses, ingrained from years of being a reject.

"I know what he thinks. Colton tells me everything, and I mean *everything!* I know he thinks you have an absorption gift, and I'm guessing his lack of presence this afternoon was when he came to you to test his theory. How did that go? Or is what I'm looking at the result of getting down and dirty and distracted?" She has the filthiest way of laughing that implies sexual innuendos and the crudest mindset, turning any sentence into a much more loaded one with just a chuckle, and I blush again.

"We haven't had sex. We haven't done anything since the first time he kissed me. He pushed me to turn and figured I can do what he says, effectively." I don't know how much information I should give away, as I don't know her, but I can find nothing in my mind to tell me that Colton doesn't trust her. She's his second in command, and I'm sure that comes with the highest kind of bond.

"No, he won't, not if he ain't gonna mark you. Colton may be many things, but he's very straight in upholding a moral code. He can be spoiled, a little self-absorbed, and the center of his own universe, but he has a code, and he's the kinda guy who would drop everything to have your back if you needed him. He's not like his father, but he cowers a little in his shadow. He's young still. I hope he grows out of it soon. Becomes the man that's hidden inside the boy."

I nod at that because I know it's true, even I can see and admit it, and jump when she spins back at me, holding up seethrough lace scraps. I can't even tell what they are.

"Black or red, *Chica*? A good feeling starts with sexy lingerie, and I've never yet worn either, so you can have one."

My eyes bulge out of my skull a little, and my mouth runs dry.

"Umm." I clear my throat, shifting from one foot to the other, and try to stop gawping at what she's holding. It doesn't look like there's enough of any of what she's holding to cover even a tiny part of me. There is no belief that it's a complete set of lingerie or that she buys the right size to cover her assets.

"Let me guess. You're a tidy-whites and sports bra kinda girl? Do you even own a push-up bra or a thong?" I catch the jest in her tone as she mocks me and rolls her eyes as I shake my head, eyes wide and utterly shell-shocked that we are even discussing my underwear habits. I mean, we only just met, and apart from the fact I thought all Santos hated my kind, here she is trying to gift me her underwear.

"*Ay, Dios mio!*" she mutters to herself, with a hint of disappointment. "Colton seems more like a black lace kind. The boy has hidden kinks for sure. So, we'll go with that. It has a little push to give your sisters some lift." She wiggles her breast with one hand to demonstrate and tosses the black scrap towards the four-poster bed.

"I really don't need ..." I stammer out, embarrassed to the core, but she shushes me mid-refusal of uplifting man traps with a finger jab, and I fall silent, too intimidated to continue arguing.

"Okay ... so now we need something sexy but casual. Not trying too hard, but has to make him think about banging you whenever he sees you." She wanders to a closet and yanks it open. Enjoying this makeover a little too much and getting into it.

"I don't want to make him ... bang me." I point out, unable to believe we're having this conversation, and all I get in reply is a hearty sexy laugh.

"Oh, I know, and knowing him, he won't. Whether you want a man to bang you or not is beside the point, *Chica*. You have sexuality and the goods to make men want you. Work it, play a little. Make Colton regret the day he ever said I don't. I mean, why make it easy on the boy when it's so much more fun to make him squirm." She swings her hips and makes a pelvic thrusting jerk, giggling at her own motion, and goes back to hauling clothes out of the closet and throwing them across to the bed between us. My nerves catapult to the ceiling as I watch an array of small clothing items flying by with low-cut or short-almost-not there-cut.

"I don't want to play games or make this hard for him. He made his choice, and I don't, I mean, I'm not ..." I stammer awkwardly, really overheating with shame at the skimpy choices she's laying out. She shushes me again with a finger on her lips and fixes me with a penetrating look, resting her hand on her hip and leaning into it.

"I get it. A good girl just trying to find her place somewhere she don't wanna be. You're a virgin, and you think all there is, is a marked mate or eternal untouched while you wait to be marked. Why are you pushing yourself into the shadows and becoming invisible? You're a pretty girl. You've more right than Carmen to be in our pack, and trust me, nothing will piss her off more than to see you take your place, making our Alpha more besotted with you than he already is. "

"You don't like her much, do you?" I blanch at her and can't get my head around this. She doesn't seem like she has all that much care in her heart for someone who's run with their sub-pack for two years, since Carmen paired up with Colton.

"She was never my choice. We've never warmed. A stupid girl, far too jealous for her own good, tried to damage my bond with Colton. She made that mistake one too many times, and now, she don't got herself a sister who is sad to see her pushed out. She brings nothing but drama to our unit. She needs to go." Meadow stops throwing items my way and sighs heavily, her eyes darting back at me, and she delivers a soft smile.

"I have an ulterior motive, *Chica*. For this ..." She waves her arms around us at the chaos of clothes and comes back to stand in front of me, reaching out and tugging a strand of my hair through her fingers.

"Which is?" I ask brazenly, feeling somehow deep down that I can trust her. There's something about her that tells me she's not my enemy.

"Juan has given Colton an order. By the next cycle, he has to have marked Carmen and put an end to this. The moon is full in less than two weeks, and he's looking for every reason to delay this and convince his father that he doesn't want that bond. He wants to be with you, and he can't keep denying it. I'm sorry, *Chica*." Meadow seems devastated over her confession, genuine sympathy in that narrowed brow and glistening eyes.

"What?" It overwhelms me, insides churning in that agonizing way I felt when he and I were apart, and silent, painful tears roll slowly down my cheeks. It almost winds me as it falls out of my mouth, her face falling sad as a droplet glistens in her eye more obviously.

"Juan has no right to force that of him, but Colton, he needs a shove. He needs to stop obeying everything he commands and fight for his right to choose his mate. The law is on his side in this. Juan oversteps his boundaries all the time, and Colton is so used to toeing the line and obeying that he doesn't even think he can question it." Her anger simmers below the surface, yet I feel it vibrating from her as it fuels my own.

"Juan is forcing him to mark Carmen before the next full moon, even though they're no longer even dating?" It's almost a sob as pain slices into my throat and threatens to choke me. Legs give out, and I stumble to the bed nearby to slump down heavily, stunned by the reality of this. "He didn't tell me." I heave in some air as the tears wrack my body, and Meadow comes to perch beside me, running her hand down my hair, trying to console me.

"I think Colton is hoping he can convince him of another way before that time comes. That your gift is enough to show him you're special." She soothes quietly.

"Juan will never accept me, even with a special power. Juan hates anything to do with my kind." I don't know where it comes from, but a world of pain floods my heart and twists my insides in such an excruciating way I think my heart stops beating. I can't bear to think about him marking her for all eternity. I don't know what that would do to our bond or how much that would kill me, but suddenly, I see what she hints at.

She thinks dressing up and looking good will turn his head more than it already is. Make him want me more in hopes he will find the will to stand up and claim what is rightfully his. Maybe push his lust buttons enough to force his hand, to mark me in the heat of passion like he almost did that night in the study. When the hormones of imprinting were at their strongest.

Colton isn't like that, though, and I don't think flirting and sashaying around in skimpy clothes will alter his commitment to honor and obedience. Especially not now the insane need and hunger have faded to manageable levels. It only stays that strong in the first days to ensure the mark is made.

That first kiss was hormone-fueled after the imprint was so new. It's calmer now. The feelings settle in, and the raging lust gives way to a deeper connection. That's how it works. It's meant to make you complete the bond with sex and marking because you can't control the need for each other. It then fades to love, respect, and taking care of each other, with a less intense appetite for sex. I can't make him lust crazy like that again and push him to defy his father with some makeup and a pair of booty shorts. He has way more control than most.

"We can't fight this. Colton has to be the one, and he is a little preoccupied with vampire wars and changes to everything now." I point out dejectedly, sighing heavily with my own logic.

"Look, I'm going to level with you. I don't want that skanky *puta* becoming a permanent fixture in my sub pack. I loathe her and have done since Colton brought her in. If sexing you up gets Colton to find his spine and maybe at least delay this somehow, we can find a way to change Juan's mind together. We're his pack. And whether the boys agree with this or not, they got his back and mine. Carmen was never one of us. I saw what you could do in the hallway, and if that was an ounce of untrained, uncontrolled gift, then there's no telling how much power you have inside of you, *Chica*. I know about your eyes, and that has to mean something. There are rumors about wolves from a time gone by with special gifts and blood-filled eyes we cannot ignore."

"I'm not special. I'm scared and out of my depth," I admit honestly, taking comfort from her stroke skimming my hair repetitively. Meadow has a maternal quality, and I think that's the feeling that's pulling me to her. She has the same spirit my mom had, the exact fierce but gentle nature. She takes no crap, and she has an aura that tells you she's loyal to a fault, bold with her opinions, yet a heart that's always at the core of her plans. It's been missing from my life for so long.

Colton may be the boy to follow his father, but I know he's trying to find a way to be with me, even after he rejected me. I have a hold over him that runs deep, that neither can fight. If I gave him more, gave him a reason to throw all in, then maybe he would find it inside of him to defy him and mark a mate on the full moon that isn't Carmen. Until now, I've let him be the one to keep pulling us together. Maybe that's why he's able to resist. Maybe Meadow has a point.

I've been distant, mad at him, and combative. I haven't made any of this easy, and, at times, I've pushed him away. Maybe she's right and not in the dress sexy way, but perhaps I need to strengthen our bond and pull him to me. Apply the affection he shows me and give him a reason to fight for us. Encourage him.

All I have is how he feels about me, and I know that sex with your fated does something more when you finally come together. There's a second level of imprinting when you unify. I should aim for that, seduce him, even if I'm not sure he'll yield, and Meadow isn't sure either.

She doesn't see how hard he tries to keep his hands to himself, and maybe with a push, I can prove us both wrong. Unify my mate, and solidify his mindset into marking me, no matter what Juan says. I belong with him, and my future in this pack, these lands, all rely on getting this out of the way and having him finally unite us.

Juan can go to hell. I need to get Colton to man up. Once that's done, his father can't do a damn thing about it, and it can't be undone without killing us both. His hands will be tied, and then we can focus on the impending war and all that comes with it. This needs to be done.

"Show me how to put these on." I pick up the scraps of lace and wipe my face with the back of my hand, pulling myself together with some kind of plan. Be it a haphazard one. As Meadow said, it's a step to stop hating on him and start encouraging him to find his spine.

Your mate is supposed to help you grow, and until now, he's the only one doing anything like that. It's my turn to help Colton find his strengths.

"Now you're talking. Seduction, *Chica*, is a tried and tested weapon that no man can deny for any length of time when it's from the woman he already loves. Ignore Carmen. Her time has passed, and she broke his trust. She brought shame to our pack when she slept with TJ. Colton can never bond to her."

I inhale sharply, that name registering as I run through my memory bank and stop on a face to go with it. I know who he is, and I can see why Colton's remaining feelings for Carmen died a death. TJ is Colton's first cousin, his direct blood, and was raised as a brother to him. He's Juan's younger brother's son, and at twenty-eight, he's an Alpha to another sub pack. He's always had a subtle sibling rivalry with Colton, and I guess he saw an opportunity for the upper hand. That had to have stung and wounded Colton so profoundly.

I now know why Colton never named and shamed and made their betrayal public. Juan would never allow him to bring a black mark to his bloodline like that, and his insistence to still mark Carmen as Colton's mate is proof, he's trying to act like it didn't happen. He denies our laws to suit his purpose. He would rather see his son bonded to someone who shamed his pack than see him connected to me.

Screw you, Juan.

If learning to seduce Colton puts him in place to defy him, then I'm throwing myself in and not coming back out until it's done. That boy is mine, and I have all kinds of pull to make him beat to the march of my drum, a strong, loud thrum that will drown out Juan's tenfold.

Bring it on, Santo.

A Plan

Meadow whistles at me, almost deafening me with the strength she can emit with just two fingers in
her mouth, and motions with her hand in a circling manner to get me to turn around. She's bossy, but there's something likable about her, and I'm fast warming to her pushy personality.

She's gone to town on me in a short space of time. My hair sleek, combed until it was glossy, and pulled up into a high ponytail that she said made my waves come together to an almost ringlet at the back. She's blushed, pinched, dabbed, painted my face with various products, and squeezed me into clothes she swears are my size, but the restrictions I feel make me doubt it. My bust is surprisingly close in size to what she wears, so no doubt she heavily downsizes for extra 'oomph' in her breast department.

Skintight soft denim jeans, paired with a fitted white tank with a low-cut V. I'm all cleavage I never knew I had, a booty I feel is out on show from sculpted pants, and I'm pulling on the soft mauve velvet hoody she told me to leave open. My feet are in crisp white sneakers because we're going for the 'casual and didn't try too hard' look, and she's thrown some silver hoops in my ears, with a simple dainty necklace holding a tiny green crystal said was the color of my eyes.

Honesty, I spent my life dressing in shapeless or loose clothing to feel comfortable and not to draw attention, and now I feel like I have way too much on show. And a bit too dressed up for a wolf pack meeting in their communal. I know Colton has seen me naked

166

after turning, but this feels more exposed somehow. Maybe because I rarely wear makeup and what's done feels strange on my skin, my lids heavier with the lashings of mascara.

Everything is perked and propped up, held in tight fabrics that enhance my curves, and I wish I could see it for myself to tell how bad or good it is. For all I know, I look like a clown. But no, I only busted every damn mirror in this mansion some hours ago and can only go by Meadows reaction, which seems to be positive.

"I would bang you, *Chica*." She winks, throws me a kiss, and blows it my way dramatically, clicking her fingers and her tongue on the roof of her mouth in unison to make an approval noise.

"Thanks, I guess," I respond with a half-laugh, half nervous cough, not sure if that's the right thing to say, but she laughs airily.

"I like you, girl. You're funny, without trying to be. You're like this little naïve, awkward kid, but with a heart of a vixen, waiting to come into her own. Never change that." She eyes me over once more, nodding to herself with evident pride at what she's created, and it warms me to my stomach. It's weird to have someone genuinely look at me with a hint of pride and acceptance like this. I mean, Colton doesn't count when he did it earlier. He has to feel that way about me as it's ordained by the Fates to be so.

"I'll try not to." I smooth my hands down the soft fabric smothering my legs, and do one last check from my viewpoint.
All I can see is boobs.

"You sure I look okay and not too obvious?" Doubt is already swarming me, denting the bit of confidence she's been building up in the last half hour, and Meadow shakes her head, loosening those beach curls she has going on at the ends as she puts in some oversized gold hoops in her ears.

"Please ... I know what I'm doing, and I ain't no fool when it comes to teasing men. We went for sexy casual, just work it, and trust me on this. One eyeful of that bootylicious and Colton gonna be dry humping your ass into next week like a wolf in heat." She extends a hand, that mischievous glint on those pale blue sultry eyes, straightening her fitted white blouse down over those mega breasts of hers with her free hand, and I hop forward to catch her fingers in mine. Eager to go before I lose all my nerve and wipe this off.

We've only been up here for around twenty-five minutes, maximum, but it feels like hours have passed, and I'm so much more relaxed with her even if I'm not relaxed with how I'm kitted out. I guess having her right in my face with various implements she could have gouged my eyes out with has built trust. I can't explain and can only go by the memory of what being part of a pack was to compare, but this feels like Meadow is bringing me to her as her pack sister, initiating a bond. It makes me choke up a little, suddenly so grateful that she's Colton's second and has her own kind of bond with him, which has pushed her to invest in me. It's nice to have another person who likes me, for whatever reason.

"Let's go find your man and make Carmen's face implode." Meadow sounds like she's a little too invested in doing that, her accent a tad heavier when she's smirking, her lips curling like the cat that got the cream. That smug tone and I can't deny she's lifted my mood entirely in terms of that 'skanky *puta*' which I now know means 'dirty slut'. Eloquent. I guess having someone on your side, who's not ordained by the Fates to be so, makes a difference. It's no longer just Colton and me.

Meadow leads the way, and with a combination of moving fast and giggling at nothing in particular as we play, push, and shove each other around corners and doors, downstairs, back to where we started, we seem to get there in record time. I barely took in my surroundings at all this time. Who knew a Santo Beta wolf could be so fun to hang out with?

The door to the study is shut, but I know before following her in that Colton isn't here yet. I can't feel him anywhere near this room, nor any fresh scent, and swallow down hard as I step in, right behind her, almost hidden in her shadow.

The rest of them are in various states of lounging, uninterested by our return, and did not miss our presence. Someone is playing music in the corner on a cell phone or a small device, I can't see, and it seems they have all had a couple, or a few, drinks in our absence. The smell of alcohol wafting our way and tinting the air with that chemical whiff.

I can't miss Carmen sitting alone at the desk, sulking. She's flicking through a large book, something heavy with aging pages, and glances up hatefully as I make eye contact. She doesn't say anything and goes back to what she's reading and pretending we didn't just walk in.

"I have to admit, she scrubs up well, and I guess I can see why Cole couldn't keep his hands off her ..." One of the twins' remarks as Meadow gets out of my way, exposing me fully to the room. There's a cough as Carmen reminds them of her presence, how much she doesn't like that comment, and Demi shuts up. Romi pushes his brother in the shoulder playfully, shaking his head at him, and eyes me up too. I can tell by the way he flickers over me, nodding with a smile that he agrees.

"Okay, so like this, maybe I can see the potential. I mean, ... Ouch" He makes a motion with his hands as though he touched something hot and then dramatically blows his fingers and makes a sizzling noise with his mouth. Despite the earlier hostility with these two, I smile slightly, giggling involuntarily, screwing up my nose in shyness at being scrutinized as my heats with a blush.

"See, *Chica*, they like. My boys, they know sexy when they see it. I think it's a massive improvement to wearing Cole's castoffs." Meadow walks around me, her final appraisal as though she didn't spend minutes upstairs admiring her handy work, and then sashays away again, grinning. She's congratulating herself on her excellent skills.

"Who likes what?" Colton seems to appear out of thin air while I was too distracted to pick up on him, and I spin in both surprise and instant nervousness, realizing I didn't get any time to prepare myself for him walking in. I'm just standing here halfway into the room like some awkward kid who's been asked to model the ugly jumper her grandmother knitted for Christmas.

Our eyes lock as he hits me with that megawatt cute-boy smile, a hint of dimples, and a reminder of how gorgeous Colton is when he relaxes and lets his charms shine. That's before breaking contact to let his gaze slide down my outfit and back again. I can tell by the raised brow expression he likes what he sees, and that smile turns into a full-on, dimple-enhanced, swoon-worthy sexy smile, with an accompanying twinkle in his eye that melts me to my core. It does weird things to my insides, and my butterflies rise and set my skin alight with a smoldering fire.

Well, I'll be damned. I thought naked was good.

His mental message has me blushing insanely, heat consuming my face, his voice dripping with heightened lust, but it's short-lived when I catch his eyes glancing towards Carmen, and he seems to put his tongue away instantly. Pulling back his reaction and yanks on that serious persona once more. It's like he got scolded, and I wonder if she mind-linked him and gave him what for. In her head, they're still trying to work things out, even if I know otherwise.

"My father gave me a schedule of where all the packs, teams, and such are to report at dawn. We meet in the mess hall at first light. Our subs are convening on the West River, the old basketball court, and we'll be in charge of continuing training with the pack members already learning combat ... and of course, Lorey."

Straight into leader mode, pushing that spark between us aside as responsibility kicks in. I don't know who gasps louder, out of literally everyone in the room. Even I take that last word or two in with a little inhale of 'what?'

"She's training with us? Has she ever done any sort of hand-to-hand or weapons training in her life? We might kill her by mistake!" I never got a good look at the previous silent member, and he steps forward now. Appearing from behind the bar area and I cringe when I catch sight of his face.

He's older than Colton for sure, a little graying of his hair at the temples, and he has one utterly white eyeball that suggests he's partially blind. The other is so dark brown in comparison that you can't help but react when you see it. A raggedy awful-looking scar running from cheek to forehead and passing right through, so deep you can tell he was wounded pretty severely whenever this happened, and it's the first thing you see.

I try not to stare, but it is so scarce to see a wolf with any kind of scars. We selfheal, miraculously, and instantly most of the time, and only one type of wound will ever leave a mark like that on a healthy wolf. Silver dipped in wolfsbane. I heard they used it against our kind in the wars with some success, although it killed most.

If it doesn't kill you, it leaves you forever marked as he is by creating an infection inside you and poisoning the site around it. It eats into your body and flesh and makes you so very sick that healing won't cure the mess. You have to heal like a human. I don't recall ever seeing him, but I guess he wouldn't want to be seen outside much with damage like that.

Wolves have very high egos, and any kind of failure in battle makes them act weird and live in shame. We're all about that. I mean, it's affected my entire existence.

"Where else would she train? She's safer with me, and I'm safer being the one to teach her to fight. This thing is real, and no one has more experience than the combat teams, of which we are one." Colton has an edge to his tone; his gaze flickers my way, and I catch Carmen out of the corner of my eye, throwing him a full-on pathetic and woeful look. Aiming to manipulate him with what I assume used to be a tried and tested method when he was with her. Tears come out to play, and I try to ignore her. Colton's jaw muscle twitches, and he glances away from her, back at his pack, somewhat unimpressed. A frown creases his forehead, and his eyes cloud over a little in glowing amber.

"Radar, I think it's the best plan, and we as a unit can bring her up to speed and teach her how to sync with us, to become one fluid machine with an extra set of teeth. Our pack lost numbers with Karly and Ebony both being with pup and out of action." Meadow throws me an encouraging, warm smile as she backs up Colton's, bringing my attention to the fact there's more to this sub pack usually, bringing femme numbers to match the males. She starts subtly growling at her mate when he opens his mouth to say something, and he shuts it just as quickly.

I blink back at the scarred wolf and click; his name must be Radar. It's weird for a name, but I assume it's a nickname, something to do with whatever gift he has. I know some wolves possess the ability to feel things coming from afar and have insight into certain things in the way a real radar pulse would. I wonder if it's what he can do, although maybe not if the vampire attack was unforeseen.

"And if she's useless and slows us down ... what then?" Carmen butts in nastily, abandoning her pitiful act bitchily because he didn't bite, and instead pushes between us to get in the middle of the conversation. Putting herself between Colton and me and nudges closer to him to mark her territory. Colton steps sideways away from her, turns, walks to the bar, pulls out a bottle of water from a concealed fridge, and takes a slow drink without reacting to her.

"Why would she be? We're good teachers; we've taught many of our kind and started them in their training. Besides, didn't you see the chaos in the house, or were you too busy being blinded by your seething hatred?" Meadow doesn't hold back, her words dripping with venom, coming at her from across the room where she's been standing back to admire her handiwork, and Colton sighs loudly. He turns, perches his butt against the edge of the bar, and it's only now I notice the dark circles under his eyes and the ashen pallor of exhaustion.

"Can you two stop for just an hour? I swear this shit gives me a headache." Lackluster too, and I wonder what exactly went down with his meeting with his father. His usual shine is missing.

"She started it!" Carmen blurts out, like a juvenile, and it makes me frown at her with a subtle shake of my head. Mature she is not. She's following Colton once more across the room as he pushes off and heads for a couch, but he sees her coming and crosses away to perch on the arm of the opposite one, where the twins are sprawled with cans of beer. She looks instantly annoyed at the fact she can't sit anywhere near him, and it irritates me endlessly that she's chasing him around. It's evident to all of us he wants her to leave him alone.

"*She* has a name, and no ... I think your skanky *puta* always starts shit. When are you going to stop trailing his ass and sit down? You're being pathetic." Meadow lets out a frustrated 'arghh' noise under her breath when Carmen doesn't stop edging closer to him. Mirroring my sentiments exactly. She walks over and yanks Carmen by the arm harshly, pushing her into a nearby chair aggressively, so Carmen stumbles backward ungracefully and butt thuds, then she throws a commanding pointer finger in her face. One of her talons millimeters from the end of piercing Carmen's nose.

"Now sit! Like a good little puppy, or I might have to spank you." Meadow is throwing attitude, and with a tone and glare like hers, I wouldn't argue. Carmen's face turns puce with outrage, her eyes darting wildly to Colton to overrule his second in command and chastise her for talking to her that way, manhandling her, but Colton inhales again, sighing heavily, and goes back to his previous position of sipping on his bottle of water. Carmen looks like she may self-implode and make Meadow's and my day, after all.

Meadow slinks over to Cesar on one of the armchairs and crawls onto his lap, curling herself around him and nestling her butt against his crotch. I can't help but watch the way he opens up and accepts her invasion, wrapping her in his arms willingly, and whispers something in her ear before she smiles at him sexily and flutters a kiss on his lips quickly. So fluid, no refusal, and no insecurity in her that he might not want her sat on him.

They're entirely bonded in all ways, and although I haven't seen her mark, I can tell it's done. They have that connection oozing from both of them that says their union is finalized, and they can communicate on a deeper level than what we have so far. A mark can be wherever your mate decides to put it, although most males like to have it on show and put it on a femme's throat, not all do. They're known for territorial possessiveness, so it's more common than not. Cesar is obviously very secure about his fiery hot femme, who can battle off males by herself.

I ache for that, wondering where Colton would choose to place his and have to tear my eyes away from him before Carmen kicks off again. My heart is beating a little too fast, and my soul yearns stronger than before. I miss his touch already.

I realize I've zoned out, blinking back to reality, and they're talking about zones and patrols and something to do with the new containment areas. I try to listen in as Colton explains that they're setting up homes in the valley to accommodate the families from other parts of the mountain tomorrow. That tents and temporary buildings will need to be erected, and they will convert the local bar and school on this side, along with the gym and the community hall. They have caravans and mobile homes coming out of storage for some, but many of the people they want to move closer refuse to leave their homes and unite on this side.

"You can't force people to shift everything and up and leave to move a few miles. I get the why, but these people, they don't want to leave their homes for a tent in the fields, Cole." It's Jesús, and I watch as they all lean forward, seriousness kicking in as they talk this out and freely throw in opinions. Everyone except me, and of course Carmen, who is focused on the conversation at hand and silently listening on the outskirts of the huddle, gazing longingly at Colton.

"We don't know when another attack will come, and it's easier to keep them safe if we have them here." Colton shrugs, repeating what he's been told, but a look flashing across his face tells me he disagrees. I almost will him to stop mimicking his father's words and be honest with what he thinks we should be doing.

"Easier to control, you mean? We all know your father has been angling for supreme reign for years, and this sounds a lot like he's trying to force the packs into one place, so they're easier to police." Mateo verbalizes what I guess I was thinking and feeling, surprising me that I'm not the only one. Colton throws a dangerous look at Mateo, a growl in the undercurrent as he jumps on the defensive over an insult aimed his father's way, but Mateo doesn't back down. "You know it, Cole. You know how he is. Tell me it's better to coral people together when they have a device that can disable us all within one space, and I'll drop it."

Mateo talks sense, and I agree. Bringing the people together means we're a sitting target if they use the same device. At least spread out, we have a chance of escaping the effects and fighting back. They can't attack us all in one go with one of those things, surely.

174

I catch Colton glancing my way, something flickering across his eyes as he thinks, and then he turns back to Mateo. I miss the quick message in his look. Not sure what it meant.

"Okay, maybe. I mean, we always knew he would try to maneuver some sort of union around the mountain. I just didn't think he would physically expect them to move here. The device, we don't know enough to second guess what it would do to us all in the valley. What we brought back has a limited range." Colton is uneasy, and I can tell he doesn't like his pack questioning orders from above. He truly is hooked by the nose when it comes to his father, and I need to figure out how to get in there and remove the darn thing. Maybe I wasn't paired with Colton so he could save me from my life; perhaps I was paired with him so that I could save him from his. The Fates work in mysterious ways, and things aren't always obvious.

"You can't keep tabs and instill fear into people if they're not close enough to feel your wrath." Radar butts in again, and it's easy to see that Radar isn't completely loyal to his Alpha when it comes to Juan Santo. There's a hint of malice in that tone, definite sarcasm in what he said, and I glance to Colton to see if he reacts in any kind of way.

This entire conversation isn't all that friendly where Juan is concerned, and Colton isn't biting back in the way I expect. Outside, if anyone dared to offend his father, he would rip them a new one and leave their remains smeared across the mountain, so I'm a little surprised to find he lets them speak freely. I guess he respects them enough to let them be honest with their opinion, and nothing said is repeated outside of their circle of trust.

I'm envious for a moment, a longing of belonging I used to know well eating at me, and it pushes me to sit in the corner on a stool by the bar. Listening, but not part of this as it's not my place, and they are not my pack. My opinions on this mean nothing.

"Whatever the reason, he wants us out tomorrow afternoon, driving to the other villages and changing minds." Colton gazes at the floor this time. That same twinge of jaw muscle and the color of his eyes glow a little amber for a second. A hint he isn't happy, his emotions in turmoil as I suddenly feel them strongly, and it only takes a second to find out why.

"Is he suggesting we apply force to families and children if they refuse to be re-homed?" It's Cesar who bursts out with it, outrage in his tone, and almost accidentally evicts Meadow from his lap with his aggressive thrust, who looks equally startled, adjusting her position with a frown at him.

Colton remains silent, and the room also falls into silence as they take it in. I can feel and taste the confusion and disgust, but no one wants to be the first to say it. I gawp at him, not sure I heard that right, but looking from ashen face to ashen face of a group of people who all know what he means, I realize that's exactly what Juan wants.

He expects his sub packs to go and forcefully remove people from their homes and into the valley floor on the south side. In the name of protecting them from attacks, the motive is bringing them in and taking control. He will not tolerate refusal, and I wonder what kind of punishment he plans to exact. Juan is a cold bastard of a man, and this isn't even as low as I expect he'll go. Juan always intended to push his agenda, and now he's using the attack as his excuse. He hungers for power and reign across the packs and has been biding his time for so long.

They won't be any safer camping in the valley than they will in their villages under the guard of patrols and watchers. Setting up alarm systems and training all who can fight how is a better use of their time. They can all work together to safeguard and improve security from their own homes. How will they care for and cater to the hundreds who live around the mountain skirt if they dump them all in the center of the valley on this side?

There are enough Santos to spread out successfully and patrol the mountain every night after dark; the only time vampires can come out. They can rest during the day. Raising the alarm is enough to get them there fast. The orphanage is proof that they can span miles in half the time of a human in a car, and if they had a warning, they would move to get there in time. With patrols already out there, the people would have way more expectations of getting through it. It makes no sense to bring them here. Mateo is right; this is about control.

"What good is gathering us all in one place. As Mateo said, they set off that machine, and every one of us, corralled in the valley, will be rendered useless. No one will be able to turn or fight back. It's easier to massacre a race when we're all laid out like fish in a bowl, and no one will be free of its effects if the only area we patrol is the valley. I'm sure they can make bigger, or use multiple, to hit us all at once." Jesús is now on his feet, pacing, agitated, and getting worked up by the second. I'm feeling the restless unease spreading through them all like a virus as they mumble their agreement, and I keep looking to Colton to say something.

"This is pointless. Do you think I don't think the same and that I didn't try to reason with him? Nothing I said made a difference. It never does." Colton stands up, losing his temper, agitated too, and utterly drained. I can feel it coming off him intensely, and his eyes lock on mine again as he catches me across the room, ignoring Carmen throwing hers his way.

"Come on, Lorey. I need to show you your new room. I'm too tired for this, and we all need to meet down at the mess hall for dawn. Go to bed, you reprobates. Stop arguing with me because it's futile, and it's not my place to make you obey him. We need sleep."

I don't need to be asked twice. I jump up, suddenly a little too excited at being alone with him again, and know it's because I've mentally taken another path and have a plan in place. One that hopefully involves those beefy arms around me and the sexy mouth on mine once again. I go to follow him as soon as he makes a move towards the door, and I almost gloat at the way Carmen's face crumbles.

"One of us could show her." She snaps bitterly, and he spins his head back, stares down at her with a blank expression, and doesn't move a step further.

"Yeah, you could, but that's not what's happening. *I'm* doing it." He shrugs with one shoulder, his tone icy cold, and it seems to shut her up. Recoiling back as though she's been burned, and I can tell he's in no mood for more defiance or squabbling. Her eyes mist over with what I expect are fake tears, maybe not this time, and I try hard to figure out what it is he ever saw in her. Carmen's a horrible person with a selfish, spoiled attitude, and I don't like her.

At least I now know why he's this way with her. The indifferent behavior and biting tone. Colton's ego's wounded, his pride dented, and as much as I don't want to believe he had any feelings for her after we imprinted, I can feel the hurt in him radiating outwards. He maybe doesn't love her anymore in the way he used to, but he cared enough that he thought he could salvage their pairing until she hurt him. Her betrayal in that way cut him deep, and he's lost all respect and trust for her, which doesn't bode well in a sub pack.

Colton walks past me on the way to the door, catching my hand in his as he does so, making me jump as I was too busy looking at her, and leads me out amid the happy, joyous coo of Meadow

"Don't stay up too late ... go to bed. Hers or yours, either is optional and fine by me, *Chicas*." She laughs in that raunchy cheeky way she has when she's being brazenly sexual, echoing behind us as we leave the room, and I blush crazily, trying not to look his way as I catch his eyes flick to me. Nervousness envelopes me once again, and instantly I'm back to being awkward and shy.

Soon as we hit the hallway, he shuts the door and gives me a proper smile, swinging my hand in his like we're children, and tugs me closer, so we rub arms as we walk. Working our way out before hitting the central passage.

The closer I am to him, the more aware of how truly drained he is. It's seeping from every pore, and despite the smile and the playful behavior, I can feel his stress levels are elevated crazily, and his body is emitting a low depressive mood.

"You look really good." He says it with a half-smile, one dimple on show and I shrug childishly, still not 'owning it' as Meadow would say.

"I'm not sure about the look. It feels kind of weird to be wearing such tight clothes." I squirm as I try to pull the jeans from my butt gracefully, and he throws me a cheeky look as he watches me attempt it.

178

"Want some help?" it's a grin, a smooth move kind of flippant comment made by the males who walk around like cockerels in a henhouse, and not an actual serious question. It's obvious he expects my usual rebuff, but instead, I throw a smile back his way, swallow down the nerves and butterflies he's hitting me with, and nod in the way Meadow showed me. She gave me a crash course in simple flirting while doing my hair earlier, and I throw on the sexy smile and flutter my lashes, butting in against him coyly.

"If you like." I bite on my lower lip, not sure if I'm doing it right, but his reaction, I guess, says I am.

Colton trips over an imaginary piece of carpet and coughs to cover his clumsy response, immediately less confident, perplexed, and failing at Mr. Smooth, all in one fell swoop. Cocky but not willing to follow through.

"Not the response I was expecting." He frowns, swallows a little audibly, and fixes his eyes ahead of us while he regains his previous composure.

It's not like I couldn't tell, and I throw a one-shouldered coquettish shrug, absolutely dying inside with how weird and fake this feels. I've never flirted or played games with boys. I had no interest in doing it before Colton.

Colton turns away, putting a little distance between us and the opposite of what I was going for, as he points us up a flight of stairs.

"This way, try to memorize the route so you can find it again." His tone is distant, his mood not exactly what I expected, and I sigh at the deflated mood that hits me heavily.

We're away from the main hall, the grand sweeping staircase, and some back hallway with narrow steps to the next floor. Every wall painted beige, dark wood floors, and potted plants dotted around prettily. They have even started replacing windows up here, and one newly glazed one is letting light shine through. Colton leads the way, his hand no longer in mine as he slides in front of me to climb the stairs, and I suddenly feel awkward and shy that my attempt at flirting poorly backfired.

I don't get it. He should be completely hot for me, yet at my first attempt at encouragement, he acts like a coy virgin who doesn't do well with girls. I know for a fact he's not a virgin and not inexperienced with girls.

I have *all* his memories.

He seems all too focused on where we're going and no longer on me. His mood is still weird, and now he's making me feel the same way. Sort of sad, depressed, and a bit testy and unsociable.

"Here, this door on the right. This used to be Taryn's room, but she mated up and now lives with Franko, her mate, on the third floor. The room's all yours." Colton steps in front of a large dark wood door tucked into a tiny alcove in an airy part of the hall that widens out. He motions for my hand when he slides it into the machine using a keycard.

"Hand here, and it'll save your print for future use. No card or key necessary." He throws me a warm quick-lipped smile, takes my wrist, lifts my hand, and holds it on the smooth black panel, pressing in digits, and then yanks the card out before it flashes red and beeps. He lets my hand go quickly, as though he doesn't want to be here holding it anymore, and I can sense his urgency in wanting to leave. It brings me down with a thud and an excruciating ache in the chest.

"Not hidden away in the west wing anymore?" I ask quietly, sounding as melancholy as his mood, looking for something to engage him in conversation with because I feel his intention to sneak away and leave me in my new room, and it sucks. He's disconnecting from me, shutting me out, and it's shredding my soul to pieces as it becomes clear that's what he's doing.

"He wasn't happy that I decided you should be among the rest of us and part of this pack, seeing as he's trying to unite the mountain. Convinced him your showdown was under better control and wouldn't happen again." Colton avoids my eye, obviously not telling me everything that was said.

"And he gave in, just like that?" I hate that I can sense he's being evasive and keeping things from me.

"Not exactly. Sometimes I'm good at arguing my corner. Sometimes ..." Colton looks away, defeated, as though tonight has taken a toll on him. Whatever was said to his father, I can sense his strained emotion and weary mood coming at me like a fog the longer we stand here.

"Just tell me. I'm a big girl, and I can take it." I sigh, desperate with a raw, pleading tone, letting my frustration out, and I catch the flicker of hesitation before he sighs.

"He doesn't care that you have a special gift. He wouldn't entertain the topic. Shut me down and bombarded me with his disappointment in my lack of putting my pack, and my responsibility, first." His crestfallen face and the surge of pain that hits me in the chest tell me his father's words wounded him. It serves to remind me, though, that this is not all about him doing the right thing. It's also about pleasing someone he looks up to and loves and has always obeyed as he's meant to.

He swings the door open and steps aside, making it clear he's depositing me like a gentleman and nothing else. He's done talking about this, and he won't argue about it either. No usual Colton touchy-feely, no intimacy, or any kind of anything. He just steps back and holds it wide as the lights flicker on automatically. Putting space between us and fixing a look on me that screams more of a commander than a boy who loves me. He's closing off, shutting me out, and my heart starts to bleed.

"If you need anything, then mind-link me. There's food in your room. I had it put here before I came to the communal. Enjoy your dinner and get some rest. I'll come for you at dawn." It's empty and devoid of emotion. He moves to leave as I step inside, but panic grips a sudden response out of me. That churning nausea that he's being like this, slicing at my guts and ripping my soul in two.

"Colton ... what did I do?" I blurt it out like a needy, sad Carmen type, and he stops mid-step, frowns, and turns back to me with a very noticeable wince of pain flashing across his face. It kills some of the rigid stance, and he seems to sag a little.

"You didn't do anything. It's me. My father wants me to stand up and take my place. He wants me to mark Carmen at the next moon and resolve what he calls our little issue. Nothing I say makes a difference, he won't bend, so maybe we should keep our distance and hope that something changes or that marking her kills our

181

bond." He's deflated, as broken as he's making me, looking so much younger and vulnerable than his years at this moment and giving up so easily. My instinct is to get mad and yell at him like I've done so many times already in our short acquaintance, but my plan of earlier pushes through, reminding me he's lost and set afloat right now. He's in pain, too, and struggling to navigate it as much as I am. So much weighing on his shoulders that I don't understand and can't see.

I need to bring him in and secure him to my harbor. Stop letting him pull all the ropes alone, stop expecting him to sail against the storm without direction, making all the moves. Don't push, even if my instinct is to feel disappointed in him and seethe with anger. I need to stop, breathe, and look at him another way as someone who needs gentle coaxing and nurturing. He's stubborn, he's bound by duty, but I have his heart, all of it, and I need to help that power grow from inside out.

I lower my tone, gently whispering as I cross towards him, fighting my nerves and inexperience and putting faith in the fact I know he loves me. Taking my cue from Meadow.

I step across the gap and raise myself on tiptoes to reach him, laying one hand flat on his muscular chest and gently lifting the other to his jaw. Eyes resting on his, locking onto him in the way that always makes me feel safe. My heart swelled, and my body tingling with the nearness of him.

"Don't give up on us." I breathe it out, almost against his lips. I get so close. Insides somersaulting with the need to kiss him. I run my fingers up his cheek and cup his face, pulling him close so softly my mouth grazes his lips, and I feel him physically sag into my touch. Melting against my briefest connection, his pupils dilating as I bring his forehead to mine. No matter what he says or how he acts, his truth is always in our touch, and he cannot deny its effect on both of us. That need to pour into each other and inability to fight when we touch.

"I'm not worthy of you. Today showed me that." It's husky, strained, and low. It's self-pity and exhaustion. Defeat because his father knocked him down again and left him reeling from cruel words. I refuse to accept what he's saying is true to what he's feeling, and instead of anger, I lean up and press my lips gently to his. Startling him with the sudden contact and refusing to back down.

It takes a second of pause, his body going rigid before he relaxes, pushes his face forward to kiss me, and his hand comes to slide around the back of my neck as he takes over. It doesn't take much to ignite a fire in him, and I groan as he gives me what I'm yearning for.

Kissing him is so familiar, and as I open my mouth to let things progress quickly, all those feelings and crazy urges rush back like a massive tidal wave hitting the shore. My lips part wider to give him access as his tongue slides against mine, and he kisses me with passion and expertise that makes my toes curl and my stomach tingle. So easy to become consumed and intoxicated with need when we're touching this way.

Colton stirs against me, his body easing against mine, relaxing into the hold we have on each other and meeting my groan with his own murmured growl of enjoyment. Neither can deny our bond when we kiss. It's potent and all-consuming. We're made for kissing, and I can't imagine anyone ever tasting this good or making me feel this complete.

Just as his hands slide down my back and over my ass, bringing my pelvis to his, hinting at his sexual excitement, he stops abruptly. Catching himself, he pulls away fast, so suddenly he rips us apart. I'm stunned by the sudden release; my eyes flicker open, and I totter on unsteady legs. He steps back, fully releasing me, almost letting me topple with the sudden loss of support, but I catch myself on the nearby door frame, breathless and panting with how hot that make-out session was, and glance up at his shell-shocked expression.

"We shouldn't ... it's only going to make this harder." He closes right back down inside his head. That softness of his expression, the dilated pupils and stirring body. It all reels back at speed as he regains perfect control. I, however, am fired up and burning with crazy heat, which triggers severe frustration at the sudden halt.

"I disagree. I think we should take what time we have and have no regrets about it. My body yearns for you, and I could feel it was mutual. We're doing nothing wrong in the eyes of the Fates. This is what they wanted for us. Stay with me tonight, share my bed, give us something more than this." It's brazen for me, and I swear I hear Meadow's voice in my head, egging me on as the words tumble out. Confidence growing that I never knew I could possess, and a shameless need to see this through. I'm all in and willing to lose my virginity tonight. I want it badly.

I don't care if I'm not marked; I'll let him in my bed and make him bond to me in other ways if it makes him fight for his right. Sex will bind us, and I'm willing to use any tool to get my mate's head out of his ass.

"I can't. I'm sorry." Colton can't look me in the eye, and I can feel the agony waving his way from me. The turmoil, the regret, the confusion as he fights his willpower. My boy's screwed up in the head and fighting with his own emotions and morals. I realize this will be tougher than I thought, and it's not just Juan's command. Colton's fighting with his inner voice about what's right and what he should do. I can taste the indecision, as it's thick enough around me to color the air.

He steps forward, eyes still downcast, and surprises me with a quick yet soft, fleeting kiss on the forehead that renders me mute. A moment of his gentle, affectionate side to let me know he cares, even if his refusal makes it seem otherwise.

"It's not that I don't want you ... just, please don't hate me." He doesn't wait for an answer, turns on his heel rapidly, and heads back the way we came, at speed, not looking back, wounding me with how much he's fighting this. My heart thuds through my chest, stomach in knots as I watch him go, but I remind myself that I'm not a girl who falls at the first hurdle, and I won't give up.

If you change your mind, my door will always be open for you. I'm not giving up on us.

My mind-link follows him out of sight, my heart aching harder the further he gets away, and I'm close to tears but bite them back.

Refusing to break down and be weak over this. Colton needs strength, and I'm going to prove I have a lot of it.

I survived my family's death and my makeshift packs. I'm tougher than I ever gave myself credit for, and it's time I owned that.

I wait for what seems like an eternity of agonizing silence in the air until he's far out of reach emotionally, and the sounds of his footsteps on wood have drifted hopelessly away. I almost break down and cry when no response comes at all, desolate and alone when he delivers that one little ray of hope.

I love you, Lorey. I won't give up on us either.

THE AGONY

I bend double, stomach twisting itself inside out, and dry wretch as my body tries to vomit out the contents of my early breakfast. A washing machine motion makes me spasm as I gag once or twice. Sweating profusely, limbs shaking with exertion, and heart working so hard, I think I'm having a heart attack, and it's about to explode through my chest. I can feel my pulse inside my ears and in my throat while I use my hands on my knees to brace my body and gasp for breath to fill my laboring lungs. I feel like I'm on the verge of dying.

"Here, drink some water, and it'll pass. Take a breather." Colton holds out a cold bottle towards me, foggy with condensation and straight from the ice bucket, at eye level, and I can't even muster up the ability to reach out and take it. I cough up phlegm, my throat burning painfully, and exhale wheezily in some sort of response. I can't believe how unfit I am.

"It'll get easier; you're just at the start of building stamina." He carries on, placing the bottle on the grass below me near my feet within my eye line, and sinks onto his haunches to gaze up at me, tilting his face and smiling handsomely. A bead of sweat runs from my messy ponytail down past my ear and somehow travels across my cheek to drip off the tip of my nose. I can feel more running down the center of my spine, between my shoulder blades, and I shudder.

"If I ... make it ... that ... far." It's an effort and a half to get the words out, and he grins at me, amused by my uselessness. We've been out here for hours. Stretching, running, exercising, jumping boards, climbing obstacles. I never knew physical training could inflict so much agony.

"You're doing fine. The first time my father put me through this, I blacked out and woke up at his feet, covered in my vomit." He shrugs with that cute-boy smirk as though it's some sort of proud memory, and I squint at him. Not sure why that's a helpful or encouraging thing to say, and he chuckles, that sexy half-smile of his bringing out his dimples and pats me on the back firmly. I feel like he's being more condescending than sympathetic and inhaling with effort, sure my lungs might no longer be working to total capacity, and then blow out a long hot exhale. Trying to recover enough to take the damn drink I sorely need.

The noise of a field full of people of various ages, all in different stages of training, is all around us, voices echoing among the rumble of vehicles and building work in the further distance. It feels like a school sports day, with more shouting and yelling and older people. Also, a lot fitter because I don't remember my class ever taking on a course like this and doing it without dying.

The entire valley is in movement, orders being carried out, and there's been an ongoing stream of trucks all day so far. Bringing supplies, materials, and wolves from further down the valley outskirts of its furthest point. They started construction further down, and there's been rumbling and thudding noises coming from that direction on the wind. They were quick to assemble and put things in motion at the crack of dawn, and it's humbling to see the force that is Santo in the flesh.

The worst of the internal burn inside me calms down with the non-movement of my limbs and the three minutes of rest. I grab at the bottle and manage to straighten up, if somewhat painfully. My body trembling and my legs weak, I can't take it anymore, slumping down on my butt ungracefully and accepting fate. I'm done. It doesn't help that we're moving from spring to summer, and the sun is hitting its highest point of the day and slowly roasting us all to a

187

crisp. Not the best time to take your unfit self and put it through military-style athletics.

Colton looks up and towards a podium where senior wolves stand, issuing orders at the masses, and nods silently. I guess someone is talking to him, and he flashes me back a sympathetic smile.

"You'll be pleased to know you have a two-hour rest and refresh session to go easy and lie face down on your bed." He extends a hand to me, straightening up to stand up himself, and I bat it away with another frown.

"I'm going to lie right here, thank you very much, and hope to god I wake up, and this was all a bad dream." It's a better attempt at verbal conversation, but I still sound like an asthmatic dying pig. If only that were a strong possibility.

I let myself slump back into the short prickly terrain cushioning my ungraceful fall and stare up at the cloudless blue sky, so utterly relieved to let my body finally stop. It would be a beautiful day if I could appreciate it.

The fatigue washes over me and highlights how done my limbs are and how unlikely they're going to cooperate or recover anytime soon. I can't take any more even if I wanted to, and hours of physical exertion have highlighted how unfit I am, while Colton barely broke a sweat.

"Do you need me to go get a wheelchair or give you a piggyback?" He's mocking me now, his tone light, that air of cheeky, and I can tell his dimples will be on show. I shove at his foot weakly as he gets up, comes close, and toe digs me softly. Trying to push me into action. He towers over me, offering a little shade from the direct sunlight, and I take a second to admire the formidable build of my Adonis. He's in a gray tracksuit that molds to his perfect muscular body, and, even in this heat, he has it zipped up to the top of the stand-up collar. There is no hint of being overheated, sweaty, or even reddening, and I wonder what's up with that.

"Nope. Go away and leave me here to become one with the daisies. I've decided this isn't the life for me." It's humor on my part. The atmosphere between us today is a lot less strained than last night. He seems brighter, more like his usual self today, working and training in the sub pack. I can tell he is back in standard form. Carmen even managed to irritate him less, as we were all so focused on what we had to do.

This morning, at dawn, I started with a twenty-minute yoga-type bunch of stretches, a warmup, followed by a two-mile run that was a major shock to my system. I've now added sadist to his list of less desirable traits because he's a bossy asshole who kept running behind me and pushing me along by my butt when I lagged, refusing to let me stop no matter how much I begged him. Or maybe it was just an excuse to put his hands on my ass. Either way, I didn't appreciate it while panting like an old person trying to climb a stair.

"Can't. The grass cutters come out at noon, and I don't think you would look good shredded and decorating the field. Come on, lazy. We need to shower, eat, and head out this afternoon. We have things to do."

That brings me back to reality and hits me with a note of seriousness. I know what we have to do, and whether I want to or not, I'm being dragged along. Luckily, his father hasn't been around today to see me among his best because I know he will not like this slow integration Colton has me doing. He believes that, from yesterday, I became part of his sub pack.

The plan this afternoon is to split into trucks to start visiting the villages around the mountain. Juan wants us to issue notices and has given orders to 'deal' with those who disobey. Colton convinced him that force wasn't necessary or advisable in the end. I guess Juan slept on it, and this morning, he issued new orders among the pack leaders. We've to deliver face-to-face written notice that might give them time to come around to having them up and move the few miles to the Santo domain. I know it's because of Colton standing up to him.

Colton has a good heart, and despite years of thinking him arrogant and careless of people below him, looking back, I realize he just stuck to his kind; in his old mindset, the packs were rivals.

189

He had his close-knit circle, and he didn't like entertaining anyone new. As everyone else did, he saw me as one of the cast asides, and he did not attempt to interact with me. His defense of the people around the mountain tells me I had him all wrong.

I reluctantly roll over onto my belly and lay my cheek on the grass, enjoying the cool feeling on my previously overly warm skin. It's a little prickly but a welcome relief to climbing nets, sprinting, and jumping hurdles again. The rest of the pack is still off in the distance, carrying on, and I keep hearing Meadow issuing commanding directions to them as they tackle a colossal wall they're climbing. As wolves, it would be easy, but today's training was human only. Stamina building, apparently.

"Just five more minutes." I moan softly, genuinely giving up on any form of movement as my body shuts down completely, deflating with a heavy, dramatic sigh. I yelp when his firm hands slide under me at speed, around the waist, him jumping over me and planting a foot on either side of my hips as he lifts me in one short sharp maneuver.

My arms flail, my legs curl and swing under him before he pulls me wholly with him and drops me on my own feet. Clinging to his upper arms, making all sorts of desperate sounds, and end up with the back of my head in the crook of his neck, my butt embedded in his groin intimately. He doesn't let me go straight away, just pulls me in tight with a sneaky hug and lowers his face, so his mouth comes level with my ear. As always, my body reacts even when I don't want it to, and I goosebumps all over, internal explosions and tingles going off inside my stomach so easily.

"You should never turn your back on your mate. Gives him all sorts of dirty ideas." That husky tone ignites hot and fiery feelings in the depths of my pelvis, and it magically revives me.

"Mate, huh? I thought you dumped my ass and were sulking over the fact we would never be." I point out a little sassily, his arms sliding up around my ribs as he hugs me in against him fully. Taking advantage of the moment and initiating a different kind of contact.

"It's such a nice ass that I realized my mistake and am groveling at your ... rear." He chuckles in my ear, that telltale cheeky sound, and I know he's only playing, but it strikes a chord in me that dampens the sexy mood, killing it dead. For a moment, that bitter pang of annoyance hits me in the stomach hard, and I push away from him hastily, freeing his hold on me and stepping out of his embrace, elbowing him in the abs as I get away.

"Don't." It's a moody bite to my tone, death of playful, as now stiff, and prickly, heart pained while he's making light of this. I catch him out of the corner of my eye, sighing too, his whole fun demeanor changing as swiftly as mine.

"Hey. Don't be like that." He reaches for me, but I step away again, picking up the discarded water bottle, and turn on my heel to march to the main house. He said shower and food, and I think we need some breathing space. Maybe I'm being too sensitive, but I can't help the overwhelming urge to punch him in the throat while sobbing my eyes out.

"Lorey, baby?" He follows me, obviously getting the waves of wounded mood and sulkiness coming his way. I know I chastised myself last night to be more patient and reel him in, but I'm so sick of this hot and cold thing he has going on. It's up and down, touch, don't touch. Mate, not mate, and it's messing with my head. No wonder I'm having a hard time even sticking to my own plan.

I ignore him completely, annoyed at myself for once again turning hostile when he was genuinely fooling around, but the fact I know we have two weeks before he marks that bitch has me feeling all kinds of foul things. It doesn't help that she spent the last few hours watching me, laughing at my attempts to keep up, and cartwheeling around me like some sort of gold medal gymnast, showing off, showing me how much better she is. She tried to make me look inadequate and kept interfering whenever he got too close in showing me what to do.

Hey, I didn't mean to upset you. Talk to me.

His voice invades my mind as I try to put distance between us, but it just irritates me all the more.

Just make up your mind, okay. Stop messing with my head and giving me mixed signals. It's not fair.

191

The pain in my tone is obvious, and I flinch as he speeds up and catches me from behind, yanking me back by the upper arm and spinning me to him a tad aggressively. His little muscle in his jaw that twitches sometimes is working overtime, and I stare blankly at his chest to avoid eye contact.

"You told me we should take the time we have and do what the Fates wanted us to do," he frowns at me, defensively, pulling me back a second time when I try to back off and gain distance, his voice edged with the same low irritation as mine. He has no right to be touchy in this, and it's not the way to handle my change of attitude.

"Yeah, right before you stopped kissing me and walked away ... again; you're blowing hot and cold!" I point out, frustrated beyond belief, and stupefied, he doesn't see how he's being.

"I'm not being hot and cold. I told you I love you and want to be with you! It's just the shit keeping us apart that's getting to me. I don't want this to be harder, but at the same time, I can't not be with you. I'm drawn to touch you, be with you, constantly. That's not mixed signaling." He doesn't see it the way I do, and I almost yell it in his face as the good old inner temper explodes at him.

"YES, it fucking IS!!" I shove him away hard, aware some around us have stopped to look up, engrossed in the hint of drama going on over here, but I pull my head up and glare at any I catch with eyes this way. Downright combative, and not like me at all. Surprisingly, any I challenge looks away fast, and Colton hauls me back for a third time, oblivious to his wrongdoing and feeding on my spreading anger.

"Look ... I'm sorry." It's delivered through semi-gritted teeth, and I know it's probably more from the fact I'm drawing unwanted attention and publicly challenging his authority than being pissed at me. Still, it's not the right way to handle me when I'm already overly tired from hours of physical torture and sensitive because I love him, and this whole thing is shitty as hell.

"Aren't you always?" I raise a brow, sarcasm oozing like molten lava from my lips. I slap his hand off my arm, not caring if it stung, and make a fast dash to put distance between us before he reaches out again.

Leave me alone!

I shout it at him mentally and don't let up, taking a sprint for the door and dashing forward as soon as it comes into view. At least super speed has its advantages sometimes, and I almost collide with a group of young teens coming out the main door and have to skid to a halt. Someone large and familiar, crashing into the back of me with equal speed and emergency braking in such a way it almost sends me flying. Colton catches me around the waist as I topple headfirst from the impact and rights me just as fast, pulling me up, so we weirdly end up back in the position that started this whole bickering argument. Me in his arms, as he's wrapped around me from behind and his mouth at my ear. Only this time, it doesn't ignite a desire to snuggle in. Fuming and ready to claw his eyes out, I turn in his arms to face him down.

"You want me to ignore all this and just go with my heart? You want me to share your bed every night, act like everything is rosy and perfect, and my father won't do everything in his power to end this if I try to defy him? You don't know what he's capable of, Lorey. You don't know the lengths he will go to stop someone he loves from doing something he deems wrong for our pack. I may be his son, but that means nothing." His biting tone and flash of fierce in that usually relaxed expression snap me to attention at the strained way the words rush out. His eyes, softening from almost angry amber to that dark brown under lowered brows, knock a little wind out of my sails.

"Like what?" Tears bite in sheer agitation, my emotions getting the better of me that here we are, arguing over this again, caught suddenly with the pain in his eyes, and he lowers his voice.

"You never stop to wonder where my mother is? Our Luna, who should be here for her people, being the heart and glue that tends to our vulnerable, in all these years?" That low, raw question that brings amber to his eyes winds me with the unexpectedness of it, and I try to claw at the memory banks for an answer. Remembering my suspicions from before.

Sometimes accessing his memories is not that easy. There are so many, jumbled together, out of sequence, so sometimes it's better to know what or who you're looking for if trying to find an answer. There are snippets of confusion and nothing concrete that I can pull out in a second, except she was unwell.

"Well, where is she?" My fury dies a little, curiosity shining through and toning down this row. I can't sustain that kind of mad when my lame heart gets upset over him. Colton is a weakness, and he seems to know how to disarm my fury and cut right to the bone without trying. People seem bored we've stopped yelling and go about their day, bypassing us once more as he lets go of me and takes my hand instead. Tangling fingers intimately, his warm, strong, and solid in my smaller, softer, and looser one.

"Maybe we need to talk somewhere private. I thought you would have seen all this in your head, but maybe not. I guess because I have so few memories of her to share. Come on."

That quietens me into submission, and I don't fight him. Colton leads the way, grasping my hand, and tugs me with him through the hall. It's busy, filled with Santos coming and going from the mess hall, in all states of sports attire as training started today, and everyone seems to be rushing about or completely immobile in groups, chatting. There's a sense of confusion with some, an urgency with others, and a holiday vibe with more. I guess some don't realize the seriousness of why everything has changed, and some are overwhelmed with anxiety and rushing around doing whatever they're told with prompt action. It's chaotic and overwhelming, and I close down and allow him to lead me through.

Colton takes me away from the swarm of moving groups and heads towards the hallway to the communal room on this floor. He walks fast, and I fall in step obediently. It only takes a silent minute to turn into the passage and head down towards the room, where everything seems strangely hushed.

As soon as he hits the digits on the keypad, the door clicks open, and the lights flicker on. I blink at the change from dull to bright and follow him inside quietly, waiting for him to move me in and shut the door. He locks it behind us, and it only adds to the tension rising inside me that he doesn't want anyone else to eavesdrop.

He motions for me to sit, his manner different, Mr. Serious on show in the form of the commander that came here last night, and heads to the bar. He pulls it open and grabs two sodas for us before coming back and choosing to sit on the floor in front of my armchair. He hands me a can once he opens it for me and opens his own, taking a long drink before saying anything. I can tell he's delaying this, regaining composure, or turning something over in his mind, and I wait patiently. Perched in the seat a little stiffer than I should be, cradling my drink between my hands.

It's something he thinks I should know, so I won't rush him. Trying to scan my memories in the long pause between us, but it's such a jumble when it comes to his mother, of snippets and bits of conversations, so I don't get a clear understanding of where she is. It's something I noticed, but I assumed it held no fundamental importance in the grand scheme of things.

"She's not here." He points out blankly as though reading my thoughts after a moment of staring at his can. I don't recognize his raw, raspy voice and the strangled way the words come out, telling me this is more painful than he can bear. "I haven't seen her for nine years."

It's not the answer I expected, and I gawp, heart skipping a beat, my eyes widening with surprise, and I have no words at all. Head trying to pull that together and wondering if I missed some sort of public announcement that the Santo Luna had left the mountain that long ago. I mean, I was still a kid. This was something the people had a right to know. I just didn't realize it had been that long, almost a decade, without our Luna.

"She's in a ... place, sort of ... care home, I guess. A medical facility. Has been since a few weeks after they came home from the war." He leans forward, so his gaze is more heavily focused on the floor, yet I catch the glow of amber before he tilts away, enough that I can only see the top of his head. His emotions spiral out and consume me as I feed on his despair. My stomach clenches with it.

"Why?" I can sense he's distancing emotionally to stop me from feeling his pain, cutting off to save me, and I can tell it's because this causes him a mass amount of it. He isn't pushing me away because he's ashamed. This is something that rips him up inside, and he's aware he can't control the intensity. I still get a massive wave of grief, regardless, not too dissimilar to how I felt when my parents never returned.

"Her mind's broken. My mom never came home as the person she left. She isn't who she was, and my father said it's because she wasn't strong enough to endure the horrors of the war. That it was too much, and she faded away. She doesn't talk, move, or do anything anymore. He said she stares into nothingness, and it's like her body lives on, but her soul's gone." He chokes on the words, his eyes glazing over, and it slices my stomach in response.

It winds me, my insides clenching up with the gravity of what he said, and I stay sat in mute silence staring at him, trying to get my head around that. Figuring out what I should say to that. Mental illness in wolves is rare, considering we can magically heal everything inside of us when we turn, even our brains.

"He sent her away ... my mom, his mate. Cast her aside because her condition could hurt the pack. Show how weak she was and unworthy as a Luna, and cause them to doubt his command. He won't tell me where she is because he knows I would go to her, and he doesn't want me to. He says it would scare me. That it would crush me." Colton stares at the can in his hand, exhaling heavily as he deflates and seems so lost and young right now. A little boy pining for the mother he can never see.

It's clicking into place, even if Colton doesn't see it himself. He doesn't realize the link between him rejecting me for not being what the pack needs and the fact his mom fell at the same hurdle. Maybe in his head, it's messy and all jumbled up, and he doesn't see it, but I do. It's not just his father's command holding him back. It's a deep-rooted fear that maybe I wouldn't be able to handle things either. I've never heard of wolves breaking down this way, and I can't even imagine what she must have seen to end up a shell of a person who abandoned all she loved. Locked in her mind, silently and eternally adrift.

The Luna is meant to be the gentle touch of her people. Her focus is on the young and vulnerable, while her Alpha mate is the strength and protection of the many. Our Luna is not here, and for ten years, her weakest has suffered under his command. Her absence is the sole reason my kind were pushed aside and forgotten. She would never have allowed the orphans to be cast out; it's the job of a Luna to protect the young, the innocent, the unloved, maternally. It all makes so much more sense now.

Juan focuses on keeping the pack powerful and promoting unity among the strongest. He wasn't interested in the weak and condemned them to the dark side, so he didn't have to take on his mate's role and care for them. He even sent his own away because she failed to fit his expectation. That's how power-hungry he is.

No wonder Juan has become so much colder and crueler. His softer voice of reason, who could sway with her bond to him, has been gone for years and offers no conflict to the decisions he makes. Only a mate can honestly argue, sway, dispute openly, or try to reason with an Alpha without real backlash or punishment. He rules with aggression now and logic and has no tender care for anyone who isn't worthy. Her warm eye on her people is missing, and her heart in their wellbeing. It's why they pushed so many of us out.

"He didn't even let me say goodbye. He said it was for the best. Just had her moved and didn't tell me until she was gone. I feel like he's ashamed of her for being weak." Colton's voice croaks a little, his emotions pushing through despite trying to shield them, and it pains me to feel that kind of broken anguish. He was her only child, and from what I can feel, they loved each other deeply, as a mother and son should. It's an almost unbearable pain as it swarms me, but I can relate. I knew this pain and have grieved with the same intensity. It's the mourning of a parent's death, even if he hasn't lost her to the underworld.

"And that's why he hates me because he thinks I'm the same." I point out, watching for the reaction on his face, his eyes still glowing amber as he stares at the floor over his crossed legs, unable to look me in the eye when caught in despair. I think Colton is ashamed of being so broken by this, another pointer of Juan's parenting skill. Colton has been lacking a mother's touch for half his life. The most critical years while he was forming. The one who should've nurtured and softened him after being forced into battles as a child, to teach him not to follow his father blindly, the way he does, and instill the strength to be his Alpha. That was Luna's job as his mother. He's been at his father's mercy for years, bearing down on him and conditioning his outlook without restraint. It's any wonder Colton's as caring as he is and not more like Juan. Teaching him the cruelest of lessons about loyalty and compassion to your mate and the unimportance of love.

He discarded her as weak and put her somewhere to rot because her inability to handle what they threw at her shamed him. He chose the good of the pack over the mate he was destined to care for. No wonder Colton is screwed up. His role model and moral guide taught him that love is secondary to duty, and his heart has no value in what his decisions should be. It taught him that to love is not enough, imprinting is not an excuse, and the pack must always be the priority even if it goes against his own needs.

"He just wants to protect me from the heartache he's endured. A mate in bond who still plagues his mind, but it's like she's dead. I don't think he goes to wherever she is anymore as he hasn't left this place in over five years." He shrugs with one shoulder, glancing to the side of us as a tear rolls down his cheek, and I can tell he feels awkward at showing that kind of softness, probably hearing his father in his head, sneering and scolding him for it. Wolves are macho, and, as men, they try not to cry much. Juan probably chastises him for any kind of compassion, empathy, or show of care in this way.

Impulsively I slide from my chair and mirror his pose on the floor in front of him, so our knees touch, and we sit face to face. My hand slides to cover his thigh, and I lean in, my heart exploding with the need to console him. My mind is racing with many thoughts and reasons and explanations and seeing not a strong dominant Alpha before me, but a scared young boy who wants to let go of the choices that are too hard for him to make on his own. In so many ways, he's still that eight-year-old kid who went from joyous ceremonial turning to a battle-scarred warrior in the space of a year.

"I'm not her. This isn't about us." I point out, knowing that he has those doubts somewhere deep inside. He saw my gifts coming through. He's starting to know me, and I hope he can see that, as vulnerable as I may appear, there's strength in me. The vampire attack hurt me, left my heart weeping for those I've lost, left me with horrible dreams and a fear of the dark shadows, but it didn't crush me. Neither did the loss of all I held dear when I was only eight years old.

He needs to know that this situation might have a completely different outcome from his mom's. What happened to her is so rare I never knew it could before he told me.

"It doesn't matter what I think. If I believe you're stronger than her or not. He thinks the bond blinds me, and he doesn't trust my judgment. How can I know if he's right or wrong when I'm so inanely in need of you, it pushes logic out no matter how I reason? He's right in that our people need a future leader with a strong Luna by his side, but he can't accept that you're her. And I don't think my head's clear enough to know without my heart always changing it."

I get the full whack of his confusion and despair as he lets go of the floodgates he's been holding back, and I'm swamped instantly with the chaos that's been living inside of him since that night. It's overwhelming, and I am drowned with the urge to sob, tear my heart out, wail, kick someone and scream all at the same time. I have to cling on like I'm on a rickety raft on a turbulent sea as his emotions devour me and almost snap me mentally with the force of such chaos. I breathe through the surge until it settles inside me and calms enough to reel my thoughts into calmer waves. Rationale pulling my brain to him.

"Tell me honestly. Deep down in your gut, your instincts, without questioning it, just answer impulsively; do you think I'm capable of being that Luna?"

I need to know his true feelings without his foggy mess coloring them. Need to understand what our future holds. If he believes, deep in his heart, that I'll be wrong for his people, I know no amount of time together, kissing, or even sex will sway him from doing what's right. His father's voice is in his head, and his mom is a shining example of the result if he chooses wrongly. His people matter more than I ever gave him credit for, and his head is full of the vampire wars that will start all over again. If he believes in us, I can't let him stray down this path without fighting.

He's afraid of having me, only to lose me to a broken mind when our worlds turned upside down or maybe even death, which ends us both. His father's filling his head with all of this doubt, and it's all so apparent now why he's struggling with what he should do.

There's a part of him who's strong enough to defy his father if he chooses to. I was wrong about that. I see that now. He swayed him over the villagers and them coming here under force.

It's Colton's insecurity over whether he can put his feelings aside and make the right choice, not just for his people but for us, that's screwing him up. He's terrified of what might happen to me if he puts me in a place that his mom was, carrying the burden of many, riding into battle ahead of the hordes, and expecting me to hold myself and them together, as a Luna should. He's overthinking all the possibilities, with many others whispering in his ear. The men who are wiser, older, influential in our midst. This is way more complex, and it all feels so hopeless. It's not just about a wolf deciding on a mate ... it's so much more hanging in the balance. He's our future, where all eyes look to lead us when Juan no longer does.

"I'm not going to lie ... I don't know." He flinches as the words spill out, screwing up his face and hunching down in disappointment at his inability even to answer that without confusion.

I can't even be mad at that because I've no idea what's coming with this war or what his mom went through ten years ago, but he does. He fought on our lands as a warrior, defended us from smaller invasions, as an adult should, even though he was only a child. He's seen the reality of what's coming and still bears the scars.

I think I have the strength and courage to deal with it, but maybe I'm just a child with a stubborn head and a foolish heart who thinks the Fates would never steer her wrong. Perhaps I'm the delusional one, grasping at hopes and being ridiculous. I have no words, and my hand slides back into my lap with the weight of realization punching me in the gut. Screwing me up emotionally, mentally, and physically.

"Now, do you understand? Love, it's not the issue. I'm yours, heart and soul, every beat just for you." Colton reaches for my hand, enveloping mine in his but failing to warm the icy cold seeping through me with his touch. Sad desperation in the air as I nod hopelessly, accepting the absolute truth as it stretches endlessly between us, like a gulf we can never cross. Head filled with so much, and yet my heart is empty, desolate, as numbness overtakes me to save me from the pain it can't deal with.

There isn't an answer to this, a way out, a ray of hope in the darkness. The Fates should never have let any of this happen to either of us. I love him, but I'm not enough.

TIME

It's been a few days since Colton told me about his mom, and I swear she keeps plaguing my thoughts. It's
like a tiny itch in my brain I can't shake, and I keep coming back to it repeatedly for no apparent reason. I even dreamed of her last night, and it was the weirdest, most confusing thing ever. It came after I finally located a memory of her in this shared library of thoughts and couldn't shake her soft face from my visuals. I must have tried too hard and implanted her in my brain to mess with me. It's the only explanation.

I vaguely remember her without Colton's influence, only in my memories, she's faceless because I couldn't remember her all that well, so it's nice to apply features to her. She has Colton's flawless beauty, his black hair, darkest chocolate eyes, and sallow skin, with a soft ambiance that's less masculine than his.

She used to come to the library near our farm every weekend to read books to the children. I remember her being a caring, quiet lady, well-spoken, well dressed, and she had no prejudices against wolves from rival packs. The children were all one to her. She always wanted to see us live in peace and harmony, and she had this warm pull that I see in Colton sometimes when he isn't closing up on me and freezing me out.

The dream lingers in my mind, despite being up for hours, and now, I'm sitting on the grass taking a break from training and can still feel her voice filtering through from the recess of my mind. Fatigue letting it slip back in as I cool down and catch my breath, and her haunting melodic tone, filled with pleading, rings through again, the words which woke me this morning.

"Save us."

It's all that comes through, and it gives me the same shivers it did when I dreamed it. She walked up to me, in a bright white, sterile, wall-less space, with no one else around me but blurred nothingness of light and stale air. Standing in the middle of what felt like a hospital, I don't know, unsure where I was meant to go or how I even got there. Confused.

She appeared in the distance at first, catching my eye, almost hazy and surrounded by a fog that cleared as she came closer. Dressed in a light shapeless gown, almost like a medical covering, except it was pure snow white, not blue or patterned. Her hair was loose, free, and hung longer than I can recall from my memory bank, almost touching her waist, whereas she always kept it jaw length in even Colton's memories.

When she came into focus at first, I could see her cheeks were wet with tears, eyes bloodshot, her skin streaked where they had fallen repeatedly, and her smock was soaked through, as though they'd been absorbing thousands of them, for an eternity. Her desperate sadness consumed and overwhelmed me, and I was rooted to the spot, unable to breathe with the heaviness of her pain.

She was eerily pale, beautiful still, but only the shadow of the woman from Colton's memories, thin and worn down, as though her life were being sucked away. She touched my face softly, startling me with the sheer heat she exuded, leaned in so close that she almost kissed me, her warmth invading the coolness of my air, and whispered it right into my face, startling me to wake in the dull stillness of my room.

Those two damned words.

Shuddering again, aware the memory of her touch on my skin has pushed a physical sensation on my cheek, and I touch it to remove the feel of it. The dream felt real, and I hate that it won't leave me alone in waking hours, replaying on a loop and deeply affecting me. The total opposite to Colton, though, as he's been practically absent, physically and mentally.

203

Something he's been doing for an infuriating number of days. It's like opening up about her reminded him of all the reasons he chose to reject me, and he backtracked at a hundred miles an hour and ultimately pulled away. He's been on active avoidance ever since, and it's both broken me and pissed me off beyond the limits of my boundary.

He comes to training, barks orders at me from a safe distance, and has permanently closed the door to our mind-link. It's making me madder than hell, infuriating that he has done another U-turn once again, but whenever I try to talk to him, he walks off and blanks me. A big fat 'stay away' from me aura, all around that dense head of his, and he won't even look me in the eye. He makes sure I can't get close, I can't touch him, and he either sticks with the sub pack so I can't get him alone or leaves before anyone else does, so I can't follow.

I know what he's doing, and as much as I want to punch him in his genitals for it, I understand, but it's just so frustrating. What makes it worse is Carmen has caught onto the strained atmosphere and is laying on the oozing flirt mode with all her might, driving even the males of the pack to eye-roll every time she baby talks him. I think she sees it as hope or an opening that she's on the path to getting him back, and it's making me sick to watch her smugly move in on him at every opportunity she gets.

Colton still isn't tolerating her, but it doesn't mean I'm not having visions of turning and ripping her throat out multiple times a day. Killing a fellow wolf from your pack is a mortal sin, no matter the excuse, but I would happily pay the time for that crime.

Meadow is the only thing keeping me sane, and last night she camped out in my room to cheer me up and distract me, watching movies and having girl time to throw off all the stresses of everything going on around us. She brought me clothes and makeup, not that I need them now my belongings were left at my door when I came back from training a couple of days ago. I suspect Colton went and packed up everything with my scent on in the orphanage, but I can't be sure, and he won't stick around to let me ask him at all. It adds to my fury because it shows he still cares, he still thinks about my needs, but he won't face me at all. His mind is set, and I know what this means for us, he's already chosen his course of action, and he's biding his time until it's done.

He doesn't come to mess hall to eat either, just shows up at the park to train and leaves as soon as we're done for the day. He spends the rest of his time with Juan, patrolling the lay of the land and overseeing the training camp and the new buildings. I've seen them walking together many times, and I almost couldn't control my loathing growls or the hatred I have for that man.

The pack is getting uneasy, and Meadow mentioned he hadn't called any kind of communal since, as though he's avoiding any real dialogue with any of us. He knows the pack will have questions about this. He brought me to them, made it seem like I might have a chance, and then snubbed me as they were beginning to accept my presence.

He's caught inside his head as he tries to work things out, but we're losing time. Ticking away slowly as the full moon approaches in its cycle, I don't think I can take much more. Logic is telling me to give up on him, but I don't want to accept it. That he's done and given up on us after what he said to me, my heart doesn't want to believe he could be this way.

I've been lost in my thoughts, anxious, obsessing, crying, and worrying myself sick with the chaos of this lack of closure. I'm not being a cold idiot, cutting him off, or avoiding him like he is with me. I would talk to him in a heartbeat if he let me. It's like he just abandoned me after dumping me in his sub pack, with no idea what I'm supposed to be now, how to feel, and what I'm meant to do after the full moon.

If he marks her, where do I go? What do I do? I'm only here because of my link to him. I'm not a Santo, I don't belong here, and although the sub pack seems to be warming to me, I'm not bonded to them. I'm not one of them, and Carmen will kick my ass to the curb the second he marks her.

She'll be his Beta until she takes her place as Luna, pushing Meadow down the ranks, from merely becoming his mate. She'll have more say than any of them, and I can see Colton allowing her to move me out for the sake of their pairing. She hates me passionately and spends all her time either drooling after him or throwing me shade. It's just a waiting game until she finally has that power to eject me. That's how it works.

I exhale heavily and pull myself up off the grass where I've been sitting cross-legged for the past ten minutes, ripping at strands absentmindedly, letting my mind run riot, as Meadow strolls on up beside me and slumps down, too. She's barely flushed, no evidence of panting after scaling thirty-foot tree climbs, and almost no sweat has formed on any part of her at all. And she's unaffected. I'm over here looking like I rolled in a puddle, red-faced, and having a cardiac arrest some twenty minutes after I did it.

I have to admit, though, that my stamina is improving in only a few short days, and I no longer hit the shakes and near vomit like the first time we did this. I'm getting stronger.

"What is it when men today? I swear, I must be getting my cycle because I want to stab idiots in the head. It's like the haze is coming in and making them all stupid, or *loco*." Meadow falls back on the grass, looking very athletic in pink leggings and a matching sports bra that enhances her natural assets. Cesar has been driving her mad the past few days, with his overprotective side kicking in as Juan upped the training schedule and started pushing his agenda a little harder. He's been all over her, shadowing her through the course, stopping her before any he thinks might be dangerous, and meeting her fury at mollycoddling her. Males can't help it. Even if their femmes are capable, they need to shelter their mate.

The haze is mating season, and yes, it's fast approaching and can make the males a little crazy possessive, over-sensitive, and willing to wrap their mates in wadding. It's an inevitable part of our year, which thankfully is short-lived, but sees every male and femme who've turned go into horny overdrive. Most mated couples don't leave the bedrooms for days on end. The unmated are fair game and result in rushed unions after it's over. Many markings, out of unwanted pupping, have been made in the past. It's craziness. I'm not looking forward to it coming at all, seeing as this will be my first year on this side of the fence, and I have no idea how it's going to feel, especially with a head and heart invested in a guy who intends to mark another.

Meanwhile, the villagers around the mountain refuse to budge, with only a few moving to the makeshift accommodation Juan has been building. I know this is angering him, and it's denting his ego that these people don't see him as the authority he thought they did. After all these years of swanning around thinking his transition to 'ruler' was set in stone, and no one would dispute it.

His anger is apparent and the show of force yesterday as trucks came in, depositing screaming women and children in the camp, hinted that he's snapped and took them against their will. It's horrendous, and I watched in horror as women with bound wrists, roped so they couldn't fight were hauled out and unclamped to be reunited with hysterical children from another truck. He separated them. Took babies from mothers to keep them compliant. Their mates followed soon after, giving up the fight and coming to submissive control to be with their families. Who does that?

It left a mixed feeling among the Santos, and everyone has been on edge, nipping at one another, having to police the new additions in case they try to return home. You can feel the utter disgust in the air around us. No one is questioning their Alpha, but no one agrees with this. The Santos aren't as bad as I used to think they all were, and it's evident that many are not like Juan at all.

Colton was beside him on the podium when the first trucks came in, and he couldn't stomach it for more than seconds. Saying something to his father, I could see his aggression mounting, his expression thunderous, his eyes glowing even from this distance, and his actions animated as though showing his disapproval angrily. They argued, and Colton stormed off and stayed out of sight for the rest of the deposit. The elders all looked on in silent agreement with Juan, showing exactly who was the empty-hearted and power-hungry with all the control in this hierarchy. Traitors to their kind.

It feels like this place is turning into a prison, much like the home was, with wardens, and it's quickly collapsing around Juan's ears as wolves begin to question this in the corners and hallways. You hear the whispers, but they soon fall silent for fear it'll get back to him. Everyone knows he's ruthless and will punish any of them, blood or not. He has his lethal pack of war-bitten psychotic wolves that do his bidding. His elders, his brother, and his Beta. Four deathly loyal sub packs at his beck and call if you dismiss Colton's. A mini army, strong enough to get wolves to fear them. Juan's untouchable and has the force to back up his claim to being the uniting Alpha. He rules with fear, not respect. There's no care in his heart.

There's been no word of any vampire attacks beyond ours since the orphanage, or at least none that Juan has let anyone know about, and there have been no new hits or hints of a threat. Apart from my new living situation, it's like it never happened, and no one mentions the lives we lost that day. I didn't even get to bury them or pay my last respects. The cleanup crew moved in, and their bodies were burned outside the city limits, with no one being told until after it was done like worthless trash that needed to be disposed of. A black mark Juan wanted to wipe clean and push out of sight because *he* can never be seen to be failing at anything.

Juan hides more shame, the same way he hides his failure mate, Luna Sierra Santo. It seems he likes to keep secrets and pretend history is not what it is. I wonder how many of the stories of our war victories have been exaggerated and twisted. No one talks of the fallen or the battles they lost. They only teach us about the heroic wins and the wolves that came back.

"Tell me about it. Colton is high on my hit list today, not that I'll get close enough to do anything about it." I sulk into my lap, answering Meadow, depressed and exhausted with this situation, and Meadow leans up on her elbows to look at me.

"He won't even talk to me about it, *Chica*. God knows I've tried, but he's inside his head. He does this sometimes, although not for so long. Goes into lockdown and pushes everyone to arm's length until he figures it out on his own. Been this way since the wars made him grow up way too fast. I think the impending full moon is only making him worse as the clock ticks down, and his father is still messing with his head. I swear, if Juan left him alone for just a week, maybe even a couple of days, that boy would soon

208

see right and do what his heart is telling him." Meadow spreads star-shaped across the grass and blows out a massive lungful of air as though to expel her frustration, staring at the sky.

"Has his father said anything more about Carmen?" I ask outright, afraid to have these conversations with her as they always leave me feeling worse, but she's the only person I have had to talk to, and I know she's on my side in this.

"Only that Colton needs to think of the future of his people. Honestly, I don't even know why Juan is rooting for Carmen. A month ago, she wasn't good enough when he constantly told him he needed to get serious and find a better mate. I don't get it." Meadow shrugs, rolling on her side to perch herself up on one elbow, picking out some daisies, and twirls them between those talons she calls nails.

"Wait, what? I thought Juan was invested in her as the best femme for Luna? He's sure as hell fighting her corner hard enough!" I blanch, my head spinning to her entirely as rage ignites inside me, pushing self-pity down.

"Nah, you got that all wrong. Juan has never warmed to her. He only seemed to take any kind of interest in their relationship the second the Fates brought you to Cole as his *compañera*. Until then, he was one reason Cole hadn't yet settled and marked her. Always whispering in his ear that he wasn't ready, that he's too young and had time, that he should sew some wild oats and live a little. He only started with this marking shit when he knew Cole had his sights set on you."

"So, his dislike of me contradicts even that. Screwing with Colton's choice even before me. I swear, I wish I knew why he was so against me. It can't just be because of the home and losing my family." I exhale, grabbing at the grass in exasperation and yanking out some more stems before watching them blow from through my fingers on the wind. Set free, roots severed, to find their own path, wherever the wind blew them, and it stirs something in my head.

"The man is all about honor and power; it's totally about you being one of the unwanted. It's like a black mark on his bloodline to accept the Fates bonded one so unworthy of his only son. He's obsessed. I don't think he's all there, you know, since the wars, a little *loco* if you ask me." She points at her temple and rotates in a circle, leaning up further to gaze at me with crossed eyes, jesting that he's crazy, but it doesn't bring any lightness to the conversation.

"I hate him. Even if he *is* mentally unwell, he's the reason nothing in my life has been good for a long time. He's the one who called the packs to unite and go to war. He's the reason my mother left me to follow his call when they asked for warriors to protect our lands, even though he wasn't our Alpha. My father tried to stop her ... he knew they had little chance of returning. He wasn't a warrior; none of my people were. They should have stayed behind and protected the ones here, not left it to the children like Colton to take on a man's job." There's no point in dragging over the failings of the past, but I can't help it. The wars were a shambles for our people, even if we did end up coming out on top. The packs had no tactics or pulling together until it was almost too late. So many who should never have left our weakest vulnerable to be watched over by young wolves or newly turned. We were lucky to survive attacks on our homelands at all.

"Juan isn't the man he used to be. Cole didn't just lose his *mamá* in those wars; his father came back a changed man. The battles, they got inside his head. He wasn't exactly soft before, but he only got worse. I think it's why Colton clings on so hard, trying to win his approval, clawing to stay connected to the only parent he has left. His father single-handedly raised him and molded him into a man these past ten years. Cole's loyal to a fault; he may seem tough sometimes, but he has his *mamá's* warm heart and inability to see the worst in people. It's his biggest strength, and yet, his worst flaw." Meadow and I stare intensely at each other, sad moods reflected before I break contact and gaze off into the clouds to try to find some peace. My head's a mess with all of this, my heart aching badly, as it has done for days now.

"Do you think Juan turned this way because of the Luna too?" I desperately want to understand why someone who was once held high and respected among his pack is now feared and questioned. Why his own hide in corners to disapprove of his tactics, where the 'loyals' would never challenge, that's not the sign of a healthy, united pack. That's the sign of a failing Alpha clinging to his power. It is a sinking ship, and it doesn't bode well for what Colton will inherit.

"I don't know. All I know is, he's not the uncle I knew as a girl, and I don't recognize him anymore. Cole tries to pretend he's still in there. Maybe he sees it and looks for the best in him. I think he fears being cast away like his *mamá* was and forgotten by all who love him if he pushes it. His father likes to throw it out there that Colton has her weak genes, and it's probably why he tries so hard to do what Juan wants of him, to prove him wrong."

"Colton isn't weak ... he's confused. Even I can see that. What do you think Juan would do if he defied him and marked me on the full moon? Do you think Juan would send him away, send us away?" I have to know if there's any hope of changing his mind, that maybe Colton will still come through for me. Even if his behavior tells me that he's already pushed all indecision aside and chosen a path to take. I need to cling onto a tiny little ray that there's still time to sway him.

"I didn't until Cole told me he believes his father would find a way to take you from him if he defied his decision. Juan hasn't said it outright, but he's implied it. Cole worries that they'll take you in the night the way his *mamá* was and kept from him, with no way of finding you again. God knows he hasn't stopped trying to find her, but there's no trace, and those who know, don't speak about it. He's no idea which of the elders helped. The Shaman had no part in it. He's also baffled as to where she is and has been helping to trace her."

I always wondered about the Shaman. Colton seems to trust him, and he doesn't seem to spend his days by Juan's side, as the elders do. The Shaman hides away until the turning ceremony each month and rarely comes out.

"How can he still blindly love a man who can do that to him? She was his mother." I despair at the thought, sinking into my crossed legs and perching my elbows on my knees so I can lean my chin into my palms. Propping myself up while my body sags in deflation.

"Love, *Chica*, it does *loco* things to rational people, and no matter how cold Juan is, Cole still loves him as a son should. He's all he has in terms of a real family. His grandmother has a weird aversion to her grandson and barely looks at him. She's Juan's mother, and since birth, she never bonded to Cole. It's bizarre." Meadows sighs heavily, too, and I can taste her hopelessness in the air seeping into me. She frowns down at the grass and goes back to picking daisies, throwing them over her shoulder listlessly in distraction.

"There isn't any hope for us, is there? Colton cutting me off ... all of this ... it's to protect me. He's going to mark Carmen, and that will be the end of it. I can feel it in my bones. Whether he loves me or not, his duty, reason, and stubborn nature, all point at doing what's expected because he thinks it will be a resolution that secures the pack's future. And he cares about that more than about us." As much as I go around in circles in my head, I can't see any other outcome.

As much as I want him to be strong for me, it's not really about that. He is strong; he just cares too much about the people he's *meant* to care about. Alpha's in his blood, and putting the people first is part of that leading nature of his type. As much as his gifts, personality, looks, and DNA, he's programmed with this preset need to be bound to his duty for them.

He faces all these paths and possibilities and, even if he chooses me over all of them, he fears his father will either take me from him, and I don't doubt he would, or that I'll be so damaged by life as his Luna, that he'll scar my mind in the process and lose me in other ways.

I need to face facts. Seeing how Juan's been treating his kind these past days has sickened me to my stomach, and I need to start putting myself first. Colton won't endanger me with the possibility his father will snatch me from him. I think he has more faith in my ability to be mentally strong, though, although it's not that clear cut in his head, and I don't doubt he isn't aware of it.

Colton is fated to lead his people. He's known it since birth. He'll do what his father wants because his hands are tied. He can't run from that, and his father holds all the ropes where he's concerned. He's bound, unable to free himself no matter what way he turns, and his future has never been his to command.

Colton is going to betray the bond out of love for me. As crazy as that sounds, it's evident in his behavior and the way he's again shut me off. He's trying to make it easier because he knows what he must do. He knows that if we continued to stay close, he would keep fighting for us and not fully submit to what his father wants.

I can't keep being mad that our bond should be stronger because I know this isn't about that. The bond is strong. It's solid in a way; it's what keeps pulling him to me, fighting his willpower, and messing with his head repeatedly. It's what'll push him to mark her, hoping to break me free and keep me safe from harm. His need to protect me.

The only problem is that I shouldn't be here once he marks her. I may still have a link that endangers his life, but without his heart and eye on me the way it is now, Juan might make a move and take me away, anyway. I bet Colton hasn't even factored that in because he doesn't want to see his father as that wolf. Juan may still make me disappear and go wherever Colton's mother is to ensure his son doesn't get tempted. I'm the enemy in Juan's eyes. Nothing changes that, not even his marking.

I just wish I knew why he hated my kind with this force of passion. We were all the same once upon a time. It's not my fault my family died. It's his.

"I wish I could argue, but the last few days, Cole being like this, I don't think there is. I know him, *Chica*. His mind is set. He thinks he's protecting you." Meadow sits up entirely, hugging her legs as tears mist her eyes, and she reaches out and strokes my hair. Her desperation rises as she too accepts that this is how it is. Neither of us has wanted to say it in the last few days, but the tides are changing; we can feel it in the air. Our people are perched on a cliff, and change is coming, whether we want it or not. The threat thickens the atmosphere, and we both know this is futile.

"I need to accept it before then. Just not let Colton factor into my plans and focus on doing what's right for me." My voice is strong, my words direct, but my heart wavers in blinding agony. A burning pain spreads through every vein because I know what I must do.

Meadow begins to cry softly, pretty droplets rolling down her flawless skin, and I can tell she knows where this is heading. Her silence is her agreement. Her sorrow is her blessing.

"You'll always be my pack. No matter where you are. I love you like blood. You were meant to find me, *mi hermana*, and I'll never stop caring about you." Her statement tells me she knows and will not argue about it. She's a realist, and she knows my life won't improve when Colton marks Carmen. I'll be this problematic issue stuck in the way of Carmen's 'happy ever after,' and we both know she's too spiteful to let that fly.

"I know what I have to do to ensure my safety and my future. I love you too, Meds. I'm sorry." I guess deep down, I've been churning this over for days, knowing it's where I was heading, but I didn't want to face it or say the words until now. I've pulled my head apart and churned my mind in circles over this, and it all kept coming to the same blank spot I didn't want to fill in. You have to cut the roots to let the grass fly free and find its place to seed and grow.

Meadow's soft tears turn to fat, shuddering ones, and she scrunches her body into a ball, cuddling herself tighter to console, so we won't draw the attention of the sub pack who are racing around the run track nearby, chasing one another in high spirits for once.

"I wish there was another way, but I know what you're saying is true. You were never welcomed, and there's a chance the marking will completely sever your bond and leave you as Juan's prey. He won't leave loose ends to come back and mess with what he wants."

If Colton marking Carmen does sever my tie to him, Juan will kill me and burn my body with the rest of my rejects. That's how little I mean to him. It's all the confirmation I need as a plan clicks into place, and she verbalizes the fear that's been gnawing at me.

"No one will notice if I go, and Colton, maybe in a few days, might question it, but the full moon will swoop in, and he'll do what he has to." His avoidance has meant he hasn't linked in any way, doesn't come by my room, and avoids any interaction. Besides Meadow, he's the only one who would care if I didn't show up for training.

"Don't make me say goodbye, don't tell me when. I don't think I can handle knowing I would stop you. I don't want to keep that kind of secret from Cesar. He would know. I can't lie to him." Meadow sniffs from within her body cocoon, desperation all around her as her heart bleeds. I understand, and I reach out and touch her gently on her knee, my own eyes misting over, the pain just as bad, but I hold myself together. Apprehension circling in my gut, but my focus is clear, and I've made up my mind.

"Sisters, don't say goodbye. They say laters, *Chica*. I have things to figure out and plan, so I'm going upstairs." I use Meadow's pet name. Our eyes meet as we smile damp, emotional smiles, and in that instance, I know a love that I've needed for the past eight years, a true friend, and it kills me that I've found it only to leave it behind. I'm going to miss those blue eyes and that sassy spunk of my beautiful wild femme sister.

I pull myself to my feet, head determined and surprisingly free of tears, despite her breaking her heart and crying floods as she watches me move. She stays immobile like she's stuck on the grass, unable to do anything else for now.

It hurts more than anything in the world, not too dissimilar a pain to having Colton reject me, but there's something inside me pushing on and keeping me calm. I can't sit here and wait for the inevitable and then cry when it all goes how I expect it to. I need to take control of my own life and do what I always intended. I had a plan! A chosen path before I imprinted.

To leave Radstone and the Santos behind and make it on my own. If the Fates wanted me to be mated and stay, they wouldn't have made me his. They knew this would happen; they know everything, and yet they threw dynamite in the fishpond and sat back as chaos ensued.

"Tell him I don't want to see him for a few days if he asks that I need headspace. That I don't want to train. I'll leave sometime within that, so you don't know. Give me a couple of days after I don't show for meals in the mess hall before you tell him I'm gone. My scent has to have faded before he finds out."

I don't want anyone tracking me, especially not him, and as our scent fades fast, I need at least twenty-four hours to get far away from here before he finds out I'm gone.

Of course, I'm terrified. I mean, over the last days, I've become marginally better at turning at will, my fitness improving, but I haven't perfected anything, haven't gotten to grips with my gifts or how to use them. I'm going out there with no experience or skills to keep me safe, but I have to. It's safer than what I can feel is coming.

I grew up taking care of myself and knowing the basics to get by. My father taught me to camp, to hunt in human form, and cook; even if I was a little kid, I still remember. He taught me how to make fires and fish ... it was his favorite pastime. Going rural as a human and living off the land was something he liked to do with Jasper and me, daddy time with his children. I can't have forgotten *all* of that.

Now I have the bonus of being able to turn. I can hunt for food that way, eat like a wolf, nourish my body with things a human couldn't digest, like raw meat. I can sleep anywhere I find shelter because we don't feel the cold, get sick from the elements, or die of exposure. I can keep moving until I find somewhere to stop. I don't mind being alone. I'm not afraid to be isolated from others and do it myself. I've felt that way for ten years—until Colton.

If I have to venture into the human world to get a job or somewhere to settle, then I'm sure it can't be that hard. I'm hardly a vulnerable, weak girl with no way to take care of herself. I have my senses, strength, speed, and inner wolf to protect me even in human form. I can heal when I get sick or injured. I just need to find my courage and go.

Time will do nothing in this situation anymore, and as much as leaving him will kill me, it will also set me free. It will set us both so.

216

Him to focus on his responsibility and lead his people, and me, to hope that our bond will fade or die in time, that I may never forget him, but that I may learn how to live without him.

Despite what I said to Meadow about needing a couple of days, I don't. I've already decided to leave at dusk; I just couldn't tell her that. I need to move before dark, as no one wants to be out there while our enemy can move around. I have time to run far and find shelter before the sun fully sets, and I'm done wasting time with this.

RUNNING

I pick at my tray of food in the mess hall, pushing my salad around, completely distracted. Counting down
the minutes before I can head upstairs, already on edge, unable to think about anything else despite telling myself I'm only making it worse. My nerves are already shot.

Meadow keeps her distance and sits down at the far end of the long table because she knows she won't hold it in if we sit close. She isn't doing a great job of acting naturally either, and I can almost taste her tension waving this way. I catch her eyes on me a couple of times, but she looks away quickly, as though we've had some sort of lover's tiff, and I wish she would stop before someone picks up on it. I think she's why I'm on such high alert because she's adding to my stress levels.

The rest of the sub pack is dotted around me, although still grouped in an obvious unit. I'm stuck between the twins, who decided they were flanking me in here today, and they are arguing about who got more coleslaw with their baked potatoes while reaching over me trying to steal each other's food. Radar watching them silently across the table, like an amused parent who is not inclined to intervene until I can't take it anymore.

"Here. Just take mine, okay. I'm not hungry, and you're making me crazy." It's a despairing snap as I push my tray at Remi on my left and skid my chair back to escape this nonsense. Not caring if all eyes turn to quiet little me in surprise; they're behaving like a couple of toddlers.

218

They behave like this at every mealtime, but I'm on edge and tetchy, and my nerves are pulled taut with the knowledge I have to get going soon if I'm going to be ready by dusk. I have so much going on in my head, my heart is in eternal conflict, and I just need some timeout.

Everyone has been feeling the strain of late. With more trucks arriving this afternoon, more prisoners carried in from around the mountain so that they can forgive me for the random outburst at the two most irritating of this sub pack. They may be older than me physically, but it's obvious the twins are the two most juvenile among us. I stand up, ignoring the inquiring glances, but no one questions, probably guessing I finally got as fed up with them bickering as everyone else, as they do it almost daily.

The mess hall is full of Santos chowing down at this hour before they get called out to assemble for evening chores and duties. Patrols get pulled out onto the main field an hour before dusk, giving me a window of opportunity. Pack, get out and move before the first patrol walks the perimeter. We have a rest and refresh hour in our rooms after meals, and, for me, that signals the last time I carry out the routine I've fallen into the past few days. That's my chance.

I'm supposed to help with the cleaning crews every day after our evening meal, and tonight I'm in the laundry room for the first time, as they like to rotate duties. It says so on the checklist I got given a few days back, but as I've never been in there before, I doubt I'll be missed.

"I'm going to get changed and freshen up before chores begin," I say to no one in particular, trying to act natural and weirdly, Jesús is the one to reply. Eyeing me up in that odd paternal way he has become accustomed to doing lately.

"You should eat. Keep your strength up. You've been looking pale these past few days." It's more of a stern command than a suggestion. Blinking at him, unsure if I heard him right, I throw a subtle smile his way. Confused but appreciative of the unexpected care. He sounds like a dad or a big brother. Something I'm not used to.

"He's right. You look tired, and eating well is part of fixing that. Here, sit. We'll behave." It's Remi this time, pushing my plate back at me, and as I glance from him to Domi, who is nodding in agreement, both equally apologetic guilty, and it hits me so hard it makes me choke up. I catch nods around the table as all eyes fall on me, the subtle expressions of agreement that they've noticed I've not been myself these past days and telling me they care enough to point it out. There's no malice or deviousness in their expressions. They genuinely are trying to advise me for my own good.

They've accepted me as part of the sub pack, while I wasn't even paying attention. This is pack care; this is how it's meant to be. Watching out for one another and guiding one of your pack when needed. Being a family.

I almost break, tears hitting the back of my eyes, and I have to try so hard to push them away and stay visually unaffected. To not crumble and show them it's gotten to me because, for them, it's natural behavior, and they don't know how overwhelming it is or how absent from my life it's been. No one cared if I skipped meals in the home. If I looked pale, tired, or even just plain sad. No one mentioned it; no one pushed me to take care of myself. So invisible for so long, and now I feel like these people see me, really see me.

"I'm okay, and you're right ... I'll eat later. I just need some quiet time to think." I play it off coolly, but inside, so many warring emotions are kicking me in the ass, ripping my heart to shreds at the realization I have a chance of a real pack family with these people, and I'm leaving them behind. It's hard to swallow, words sticking like glue in my throat, and my face aches with the effort of keeping my expression neutral.

"Are you coming to the com room after chores?" Cesar startles me with this one, and I blink at him, completely non-plussed. Panic setting in that we might have some sort of meeting I have to show up for, or Colton will suspect.

"Yeah, we decided we needed some pack hanging time, a few beers, movie ... all chilling together." Radar finishes it for him, all eyes on me, standing awkwardly, poised, and I hesitate. Struggling to think up an instant refusal, while dying inside, I'm being asked to initiate, bond, and I can't. If ever there was a moment I wanted to kick the Fates in the ass, it's now.

"You know the whole Carmen ... Colton thing. I don't think ..." I stutter my feeble excuse, hoping they take pity on that messy triangle of heartache and release me from the invitation.

"He won't be there; he's avoiding all of us, so screw him. And 'Car-moan-all-day' is following his ass around like she's in the haze already. She won't be there if he isn't," Remi said, adding more weight to my already trodden down soul, which is about to snap under all this pressure. I can't formulate a reply. Sweat beading at the back of my neck when Meadow swoops in and saves my ass. Her eyes darting to me, concern etched on her brow.

"Give her some breathing space, guys. Girl's had a tough week, and she's tired. Let her see how she feels after her first time down in laundry. We all know how tough that shift is, stuck down in the sweat room." She throws me a supportive half-smile that doesn't reach her eyes, and I could practically kiss her. My foggy mind grasping onto that little reason to bail without actually rejecting the invitation.

"Yeah, I'll see how I feel after that. I hear it's pretty exhausting, and I might be wiped out after. Don't want to ruin your viewing with my snores." I make light of it, exhaling softly with relief that she gave me an angle, and the urge to kiss her all over again calms me down.

"Well, you know where it is. We'll be there after nine." Now Domi, and I honestly feel like this is some sort of sign, but I have to ignore it. I have to stay steadfast with the plan.

"Sure, I'll catch you guys later. I better go." It's a fast exit, saying it as I make a turn and head away, so I don't get sidetracked with any more conversation or unexpected invitations. Hoping not to get caught in another offer I can hardly refuse, and I'm so busy looking back, smiling at them guiltily, that I don't look where I'm going. I crash into someone's chest, 'oofing' with the sudden contact, and wind myself lightly, bouncing, almost sending myself and them flying with the force of the collision.

221

"Ouch!" I yelp out in response, winded momentarily, and inhale sharply, catching my breath in my throat when I realize who was standing a foot back from me now and looking equally surprised. That swoon-worthy cute-boy face, dark, sultry eyes under a furrowed brow, and I want to melt into a hole in the floor and disappear. It could only be me and today that this happens.

"Hey. Sorry." Colton tries to avoid looking right at me, the awkward tension deafening, and for a moment, I feel like looking up at the sky and screaming, WHY??? Heartbeat a hundred times faster, palms clammy, and legs weak, as I get hit with the usual Colton effects. Someone up there is testing me now I know what I'm doing, and I can't deal with this on top of everything else.

"Hey, and bye." I throw the words in a hurried, almost sassy breath, duck around him fast, avoiding looking at him any more than I need to, and head on my way at speed, not wanting to get into this with him. He affects me in all forms, and I can't stay firm with him in my head. It's already too raw, and I don't want to lose my courage. I don't look back, almost fall over Carmen, running along behind him, ignoring her completely, and shut off my hearing when his voice echoes after me.

"I guess ... bye." He sounds wounded but screw him. He's no right to be hurt at my rebuff because he's ignored me for days. He's the reason I'm running. I try not to let myself react, just tuck my head down against my chest and keep going, pushing it all away.

I stop thinking about him. Will my brain to focus on the steps I'm taking and hyper-speed up the stairs as soon as I get out of sight. I need to file everything into one little box in my head and focus on doing, not feeling. My emotions are not helping. I have to take from logic to deal with this. I can fall apart later when I'm out of here and miles away. I can break like a dam if that's what I need to do, wail to my heart's content, but just not right now. I have to be strong to see this through.

Despite telling myself that, it doesn't stop a tiny, slight murmur of insane jealousy in the corner of my brain, shouting questions at me anyway. Why was he heading in there now, after days of not? He doesn't eat with us anymore for some unknown reason, and where was he with her? They didn't look like they just bumped into each other. She was following him into the mess hall, although, to be fair, she's been following him for days, anyway.

I push the green mist aside, chastising myself for it, and get my ass up the stairs, along the hall, and down to the end where my room is. Wasting no time getting inside and breathe a sigh of relief when I lock it shut from the inside and sag back for a moment to pull my wits together. I turn to walk to my bed and unexpectedly kick something light across the floor, looking down as it skids to the center of my rug and stops. I scoop down to pick it up.

It's an envelope, and I recognize Meadow's gentle curving cursive on the front. I turn it over hastily, inhaling her heady scent and perfume as I pull it open and gawp at the stash of cash inside. There's a note tucked in behind the money, and I pull it out to read it, hands shaking at my discovery, once again overwhelmed.

Hey, Chica
This isn't much, but you need it more than I do.
My number is on the back of this. Keep it. You know where we are if you need us.
We are your pack.
I'll miss you.
XXX

The tears mist my eyes, my throat swelling so I almost can't breathe as ache hits me low in the gut and threatens to make me crumble. I push the note back inside quickly, trying to combat it and flick through the cash, mentally counting almost two hundred dollars, and it breaks the wall holding in tears. I slump down onto the floor like a disheveled sack and cry, holding it close to my chest and breaking down. It's not just for this. It's for everything.

Why did I find my pack now, at a time when I thought I had no other option? Why would the Fates give me something closer to a real home, only to make it unreachable by the tiniest stretch?

I have to pull myself together and stop being weak. None of it matters, and it doesn't change things. I have to get my crap together and stick to what I decided. I have to stay strong and determined. I can't break because I won't be able to put myself back together if I do.

I pull myself to get up and walk to the closet, despite heaving with wracking breaths sniffing as I try to stop the tears. I have to find a bag to pack my shit up and focus on doing, not feeling. Luckily, whoever brought my things from the orphanage packed some of them in a large backpack that had been Vanka's. I drag it out of the bottom corner, holding it for a second, a fresh wave of pain twisting my insides as I stroke across the corner where she wrote her name in a black marker pen. Bold, jaggy letters that somehow represent who she was in life. I numb it out, swallow it down, haul out essentials, and stuff them inside.

I need basics, like a couple of changes of clothes, toiletries, the money, the snacks I have in my room. I need something to sleep with, too, like a blanket to lay on the ground, and something to carry water in, just in case I can't find a stream or river in hours. I don't know what else to pack, and I end up shoving things haphazardly. A book I never got round to reading, the iPod that was among my belongings, and then I realize I probably won't be able to charge it if I stay in the wilderness and put it back on the shelf. I find a lighter, the Swiss Army knife that I kept among my treasured items from my father's possessions. Some old camping matches and his flint stick for making fires should I run out of matches.

I push through my stuff and come to Colton's gray T-shirt, pausing painfully, recognizing it as the one he gave me to wear when I shredded my clothes. I thought I'd given everything of his back to Meadow for him, but this remains like a scar on my heart. His human smell still lingers in the fabric, despite it being washed, or maybe I'm just conjuring it up for myself, his scent so ingrained in my head that I will it to come back at me. I impulsively push it in the bag, stroking it for a second too long, and zip everything up inside. I shouldn't take a part of him with me for my sanity, but I can't bear to take it back out.

I keep checking my watch, even though I know I have another 3 hours before they assemble for dusk patrol. I have to kill time without going back downstairs and acting weird. I need to occupy myself without obsessing and driving myself crazy until it's time to go.

The thought hits me. A shower!! That's an idea. And a nap if I can force it. Refresh myself change into more suitable clothes than this sports pants and T-shirt duo I have sweated all over. Tasks will pass the time and keep my brain centered.

I pull my clothes off without hesitation, throw them in my wash basket, and quickly head to the bathroom. Yanking my hair down from my ponytail and turning on the shower, testing it before I go to step in.

Lorey? You there?

Colton's voice hits me in the center of my forehead, the last thing I was expecting, and I almost slide with surprise as I lay my foot on the wet shower floor, grabbing onto the door to stop myself falling, like a newborn fawn on unsure legs, almost crashing into mayhem.

For the love of all that is holy, why are the Fates screwing with me today?

Yes, what do you want?

I snap, a little harshly, instantly remorseful at my knee-jerk reaction to him, then not, when anger kicks me in the butt and reminds me what an ignorant asshat he is. That he's all good to reach out now, after an unexpected brush with me downstairs, pushed his 'need to contact me' button a lot harder. I rub my bruised shin, which bashes the shower screen, and jump in under the hot water instead of standing like an idiot.

After seeing you downstairs... I just wanted to make sure you're doing okay.

I can pick up on the hesitation, the agony in his tone, and I sigh heavily. Madness wavering because I'm a fool when it comes to him sounding like this, this boy, and against all my better judgments, I soften my tone when I should cut him off instead.

Why are you reaching out? We both know what you're going to do. Can we just not do this?

He's killing me, making all those emotions spiral up and mess with me all over again, and I need to be stronger than this. I need to bring back the bite to my voice, the steel to my resolve, and end this before making myself even more confused.

I can't seem to stop myself. I can only go so long, and the need to see you or hear you gets too much. I have no willpower when it comes to you.

Back to his hot-cold bullshit, and I know if I let myself get drawn in again, it will only go like every other time. After a couple of days of pulling close and then, he backs off and leaves me feeling desolate again. I get it. I do because the need for him is always stronger when we have some contact, but I'm not playing anymore. It's not helping either of us, and, as much as I love him, I have to do this.

I have a solution ... every time you feel you have to talk to me ...

go talk to Carmen. I'm sure she'll love that.

I focus on something to be pissed about, and it does the trick. Moody, bitchy tone setting in. I can always count on my brokenhearted jealousy to find the fire in my soul. I sound as bitter as he makes me feel, and I'm glad the water is pouring over my face and camouflaging the tears falling of their own accord. I have zero control of that right now, and glad he can neither see nor hear them.

I deserve that. I don't know what to say to you. I've been a coward for days because I can't face you. I don't know how to say the words to you or how to say sorry for what I'm going to do. I guess we both know what's going to happen next week.

He confirms my worst fears and solidifies my decision in that one brief statement. Ripping what's left of my shredded, mutilated heart out and stomping it all over the floor until there's nothing left but a mess. He's chosen to go through with marking her, and this is his goodbye. His confirmation.

Then don't. I need to go. I have to do chores. Maybe just leave me alone until it's done, and then we'll see what happens from there.

I lie, trying to sound tough. Mentally scathing in tone, even if my body is shaking with the buildup of the sobbing that's coming. Trembling as I try to hold it in, breathing fast and shallow. Throwing cold and snappy in there while my limbs are quaking with the effort, but I can't let him know what it is I am planning on doing. He would stop me, even with his mind made up. His need to protect me would overrule everything else.

Right ... chores ... of course. I have to go assemble for patrol in a couple of hours too. Enjoy your chores. I guess I'll see you around.

He lingers, saying it slowly, as though looking for a reason to stay.

Yeah, you too. Now I gotta go. Bye.

I don't give him a chance to linger more or reply, sensing his hesitation, so I take control. I'm the one to close the door on our connection and shut it down dead as I do. Doing something I haven't ever done to him, he always did it to me, metaphorically shutting it, bolting it tight, and pushing the soundproofing button on our link so he can't come back anymore. I don't want him getting through. I mentally lock it and toss the key aside. I'm not going to lie, it feels like I just stabbed myself in the chest with a dull object, and I gasp sob when the dead silent noise consumes that part of my mind. It's horrendous to know I'm the one to cut him off, but I have to do this. I can't have him popping into my brain anymore. Never again.

I stop for a moment to process the conversation, and despite trying so hard to be strong, I end up sitting on the floor under the full force of my shower head and sobbing my heart out until I can't breathe with the effort. The doubts slide in, and I have to chastise myself for being so stupid.

This is why he's stayed away. It makes both of us weak and clouds our judgment. I should have known seeing him would push him to contact me. It's harder when we do, especially touching, and we did when we collided. I probably played on his mind after I left because of that simple moment, and I'm just as pathetic, sitting here crying over him. I shouldn't have responded to him at all; he shouldn't have reached out. It's just proof that our bond is powerful, no matter what we try to do, and neither can control the way it keeps bringing us back together.

I hate the Fates and this infernal bond. It's messing up everything, and I've no longer any control over my feelings. I thought I was strong, but I'm an idiot regarding him. I'm a fool for him in every way, and I can't even stay mad or hateful, no matter what he does, because the second I get a chance at connecting, I let him. I shouldn't have left the link open all week; I should not have allowed myself to get taken in for even a second. It should have been done the second I decided I was leaving and not given him a window of opportunity. I won't make that mistake again, for sure.

I yank myself up, pull my head out of my ass and aggressively wash down while refusing to break down anymore. It's the past. It's not where I need to be, mentally.

I wash my face until it feels raw, wiping away tears I don't want to cry anymore, and shampoo my hair with vigor, as though cleansing my head of thoughts and feelings. I finish up fast, pull a towel on when I step out, and focus all my efforts on drying quickly, rubbing my hair as dry as I can get it, before combining it into a sleek ponytail and pulling on fresh underwear and clothes. I slide on jeans, a tank, and a sweater, pull on some socks and sneakers. I look around the room for anything I want to add to my backpack.

I tidy my room, make the bed, and lie down on top of it to force myself to take a nap to kill some time, staring blankly at the ceiling and refusing to let my mind wander back to him, us, or this crappy situation.

There's a noise outside my door that makes me flinch, and I pause and stare at it, praying to God he hasn't decided to come here and start this shit all over again. It's what he does. I hold my breath and listen, my own heart beating loudly in my ears as panic sets in.

I can't see him. I can't let him sway me, touch me, or get close. My heart will betray me if I do.

It's followed by the squeak of one of the cleaning carts, and I exhale when it rolls right past my room and fades into the distance. My body weak with relief, and I sprawl out star-shaped on my bed, exhaling so heavily I let out a whooshing noise and then moan at my stupid despair.

Stop freaking out, Alora. You're going to get yourself in such a mess and not be able to follow through. Relax, breathe, count.

I put everything into doing just that, remember the techniques I used when I stayed in the home and couldn't relax or sleep on nights when everything got to me too much. I picture a meadow, a sweet-scented field full of pretty flowers, and one by one, as I walk through them, I count the heads, picking them out, touching them as I go. I visualize the colors, the feel of their soft, silky petals on my fingers, and how the subtle scent blows around on the breeze. They all dance and sway in ripples, coming to me in mixed smells. It helps me drift into a calmer state of mind. The noise of nature drowning out everything else in my mind's eye. If I can just focus my energy for a little while, I can get through this. Once I'm out of here, and on my way, it'll be easier.

It seems to work. I drift into a semi hazy state of rest, and before I know it, an hour or more has passed, and it's getting dull outside.

I come to, aware I've lost time and must have slept, blinking at the sudden light change of the space around me and checking the clock on my wall. I'm shocked that it's been more than a couple of hours since I came up here already. I guess I spent a long time in the shower, and I hop up woozily, pacing to bring the nerves firing up and awakening my senses back in line.

It's early yet, but I don't think I have it in me to wait any longer. I stalk to the window to look out over the back of the packhouse. It's deserted back here, still too light for the guards to take up position, and maybe it's a sign I shouldn't wait until dusk. Perhaps too many will be out there, and I might not be able to make up excuses if I get stopped trying to make my way out. Everyone should be running around, doing chores right now, so I might have a better chance if I do it now.

229

A quick plan comes to mind, and I turn, picking up my damp towels from the laundry and wrapping them haphazardly around my backpack, adding my sweats, so they look like a bundle of dirty clothes. I had intended scaling down my window later if I could, but this way, I can walk through the house as though I'm late for laundry duty. If anyone sees me, I'm just collecting clothes, and I can use the exit in the hall before the laundry room to access the rear of the house. It's a solid plan, and I don't waste time pulling myself together.

I bundle my faux pile up in my arms, checking in the new mirror hung in here the other day to see if my backpack is on show. Satisfied it isn't, I head to the door, take one last look around my room, and take a deep, steadying breath.

It's time to do this.

I use one hand to haul it open, slide-out, and turn left towards the back stairs down to the first floor. The one closest to my door and brings me out is the same narrow hallway leading to the back exit and the laundry door. It's perfect. I don't know why I didn't click on this before, and maybe this is the Fates trying to make up for messing with me.

I pass a few people lugging carts and vacuums from room to room and keep my head down, not really noticed by them, wishing I'd worn a hoody so I could pull it up, but it's too late now. I stick on my route, turn into the stair, scale it in seconds in hyper-speed and then head along the final hallway to freedom.

Soon as I get near the door, I look around, see no one is out here despite the hustle and bustle and steam coming from the nearby closed door to laundry, and head out the back door instead. No one is back here either, oddly. It's either good fortune or someone up there giving me a break. I'm aware many windows look this way, though, and I'm still not free and clear.

I unwrap my bag, pull it onto my back, and shove my dirty clothes and towels in a nearby bush. Look around before sticking up against the house, my back sliding along the rough brickwork, eyes darting all around me to check no one is around. I almost crawl under the window to the room I should be in right now, holding my breath every inch of the way. My heartbeat's crazy fast and racing, my breaths shallow and hurried. My face is sweaty because I'm scared to hell of being caught and marched to Juan Santo.

I stick to the flower beds, stepping over them so I don't trip, stay tight against the walls, and duck under every window I get to. I take it slow, try to remain silent as I do, and battle my own shaking limbs. I'm heading for the tree line, which runs along one side of the manor, and once I get in there, I can run as fast as my body allows me relatively unseen in its dense woods. It extends for a couple of miles right out of the valley and into the farmlands beyond. I can't turn, as I don't want to ruin my clothes now. I only have two complete outfits, but I should be able to speed out without doing it.

I hold my breath when a door swings open behind me, freezing in place, half crouched, and eyes widening in horror. I glance back, seeing it swing out into view, and my heart skips a beat, sweat rolling down my forehead from my hairline. No one comes out, though a voice waves my way closer than I expected.

"Yeah, leave it open. It's like a goddamn sauna in here. It's inhumane making us work in this shit for hours on end." I don't recognize the female voice, and whoever opened the door mumbles in response, retreating inside and fading in volume level.

I exhale, relaxing heavily, thinking my legs might give out with that little shock, move my ass back into gear, and run crawl the rest of the way, feeling lightheaded.

As soon as I hit the tree line, I pull myself behind the biggest trunk I can find and use it as a viewpoint to check if anyone saw me come over here. I take a minute to pull myself together, breathe properly, and lean against the rough bark until I regain my strength and the wobbliness in my legs fade. I check my surroundings, surprised that there is no one out here. But as Juan has made it clear for days, the vampires can't be out in daylight. I guess that's why. Everyone is busy doing what they're doing, and I can hear voices on the wind from the front of the manor, hinting that many of those with no chores are assembled in the front field. I won't get another chance like this.

I put my head down, turn in the direction I want to go, and set my legs in motion with no intention of slowing down, stopping, or looking back until there are at least five miles between Radstone and me. I may have a heart attack as soon as I set out, but I keep one strong thought at the center of my mind –

I'm finally free!

.... And I don't let up until I'm sure of it.

Survival

It's been around eleven days since I left the valley, and I can honestly say it's finally getting easier in some ways,
but not all. I was a fool to believe it wouldn't be hard on so many levels, and I still can't get my head around my naïvety. Knowing then what I do now, I don't think I would have left at all.

It's not just the survival factor that gets to you; it's the isolation, the loneliness, the living on constant high alert as you have to be aware of all that is around you, and the gnawing fear that sits in your gut hour after hour. I'm on edge, hyper-aware at all times, and mentally exhausted with it. I cannot stop watching my back and surroundings, always listening to make sure I'm safe and afraid of even the tiniest noises or movements near me. There are so many enemies in nature that I was oblivious to when living in the mountain bubble.

I rarely sleep, so tuned into the noises of the forests, the gullies, and caverns I have walked through in recent days. Always listening for something to come out of the shadows at me and have endless dreams when I do of vampires and monsters pulling me from my tiny crawl spaces before devouring my helpless body. Every time I'm paralyzed with the same useless inadequacy as that day in the orphanage and completely unable to defend myself. I see Sierra often in my dreams too, my infrequent naps, and that repetitive sentence she utters on her breath, which always wakes me with a start. Always the same damn thing.

"Save us."

I don't understand why she haunts me still and can only imagine it has to do with my broken heart and the dregs of Colton in my memory banks that get through the steel door I'm trying to force them behind. She was one of our last conversations, and maybe that's why she plays so heavily on my mind.

The first few days were the worst and thankfully behind me now, and I think it's finally sunk in what I'm actually doing. The first night, looking for shelter, eating Doritos I had hastily packed in my backpack for supper, and trying to find a comfy way to lie in a shallow, hard-floored dugout on a hillside that barely concealed me. It was a shock to my system, having come from a lifetime of shelter and home-cooked meals I took for granted. Even being myself all those years, I was never alone or without food and a roof over my head, whereas now here I am, indeed in solitude.

I didn't sleep at all at first. Everything was swirling in my head, and the cravings for not just Colton but Meadow, the sub pack, my room in the packhouse, and the safety of the valley. It was all crying out to me, reminding me I'm barely grown and only newly turned and still so vulnerable in so many ways. I sobbed so much in the first few days; I thought it would break me and send me running back with my tail between my legs, but it didn't.

I weathered the storm, wandering south aimlessly with no plan, and after getting the first few miles clear of the Santo lands, I didn't see the need to run anymore. There's enough distance between us and no signs they'd picked up my scent to track me because, quite frankly, they would have caught up with me already if anyone had been looking. I stuck to rural areas, stayed away from roads, and moved through forests and woods, farmlands, and rougher areas to avoid humans.

I can still see the mountain in the far distance as it gets further away with every day I trek, but I'm probably not as far as I think. It seems so much further because I took so long to get here. I'm afraid to turn in daylight if I'm seen, afraid to travel at night in case I run across vampires. I have to use human legs and human speed, and without your heart and soul pushing you on, progress is slow.

Day four was the worst day of my life, and it alone was almost what ended this adventure of mine. Just when I didn't think it could get any harder mentally, my heart already breaking with the need to see another person or hear another voice, a pain that came out of nowhere, sideswiped me.

I thought I was dying. It was like someone reached into my chest cavity, grabbed my heart in the middle of my soul, twisted it around sharply, and yanked it out, breaking every bone. I crumbled to the ground, gasping for breath, every part of my rib cage, lungs, and core slicing in agony, unable to catch air within me. Clawing at the ground as the pain shot through every limb and nerve ending.

I rolled around in the mud, clutching my chest and wailing like a wounded animal, as tears flooded my vision and my brain nearly shattered. It was the single most terrifying moment I experienced, apart from the night the vampires attacked, and I was wholly helpless again.

It felt like the ultimate betrayal, the severing of my soul, and the only thing I could connect it to Colton. It is the only logical answer to something so all-consuming, yet for no apparent reason to its sudden happening. He must have done something strong enough to our bond to inflict this kind of hell, as was sure as hell was not his death, as I'm still breathing.

Only two things could hurt your imprinted like that, especially from so many miles apart. Severing the bond, which he couldn't have because I would be dead, or betraying the bond with an unforgivable act.

Sleeping with Carmen and marking her.

It has to be that. Nothing else can compare to this agony! The thing they taught us about in school, about carrying that heartache when your fated mate destroys the bond. It all makes sense, and, for days after, fighting the fatigue and desperation it still makes me feel, I barely covered more than a couple of miles in total, before breaking down into a crumbling mess and sobbing again. It felt like he had taken a knife himself, cut me open, and ripped everything out before setting it alight. The emotional devastation was as bad as finding out my entire family had gone when I was just eight years old, and it still lingers like a shadow, weighing heavily, keeping me in the dark, even now. It broke me in so many ways.

Mentally, as I wore on over the following days, I became numb, and my will to run far from the mountain died a death. I was going primarily to outrun him and what he had to do. To try not to let it get to me, to distance myself from the pain and leave him to walk his path without me. And yet the Fates delivered a blow that almost stopped me in my tracks completely, killing my will to find my future at all. They left me with the heavy sadness that consumes everything and won't lift. There's nothing to run from anymore. It's done. He did it.

I'm just going through the motions now, without really engaging any kind of effort under this black cloud, my new constant companion. I walk, find something to hunt and eat; I wash in rivers; I find shelter, and sporadically sleep through the dark.

The noises, the movement of nature, should bring me peace as a natural wolf, but it serves to remind me how very alone I am and that wolves are pack animals. We don't thrive alone, and it's wearing me down slowly. I can't seem to ever really get any clear sign of where I belong in life or what I'm supposed to do. Just that discarded, worthless kid who wasn't good enough to be mated, even when the Fates imprinted me on someone. What hope is there for me?

I don't have a reason to go back anymore, anyway. Not even for the sub pack, who never really belonged to me. I need to push on and find somewhere to settle, accept it, man up, and stop crying like a stupid child, but nowhere ever feels right. Colton made his choice; I can feel it, and we're done.

On day eight, I stumbled into an unknown dense dark forest at the base of a smaller mountain that was relatively secluded, finally finding somewhere that seemed easy to defend, was pretty, and had a good cave for a possible long-term dwelling. Dense enough to feel safe and a nearby water source. Sheltered and a good supply of wildlife for hunting. No humans around for miles, and no signs that any had been there in forever.

It didn't take long to be chased out by feral wolves who caught my scent in their territory, though. Natural wolves, not my kind, though, because my kind would probably have strung me up and gutted me for straying there. Outside of Radstone, the packs still have deep ingrained rivalry and feuds.

They chased me all the way to a cliff edge before I had to jump into the river below to escape unscathed. I don't think I could have fought off more than a dozen rabid wolves on my own, and I don't have the energy to turn and heal myself right now. I'm spent. I guess I'm not eating enough, not resting enough, and all I do is travel from dawn to dusk half-heartedly and flop down again. Maybe it's not energy but a lack of willpower when I'm stuck in this mindset of hopelessness.

I had to find a quick place to build a fire, dry everything I owned that day, and throw away the leftover snacks I opened as they were soggy and inedible. The money Meadow gave me had to be laid out in the sun, and her note was ruined entirely, which meant losing her number on the back because the ink bled out and disappeared.

Eating raw meat isn't sitting well with my human form either, which came as a shock, as I expected it to be a natural transition, but I don't feel great most of the time. My wolf side isn't all that in touch with my body, and maybe it will take time to adjust, like building stamina and developing my gift.

Just more failure, and I feel it's all getting to me. The dark, empty loneliness in my head, telling me I'm not good enough and never will be. I don't feel like being a wolf comes naturally, and somehow being in human form is easier, which is probably normal, considering we spend the first part of our life that way. I thought it would be a fluid transition, with few bumps, like learning to float by jumping in the deep end.

Sunny today, with no breeze, and the atmosphere has an almost serene calm to it. I sit staring at the little fire I pulled together in the basin of the clearing I found. My ass on a fallen rotten tree, feet at either side of my rock, circled mini campfire. Somewhere caught in the unremarkable depths of another dense dark wood, in the middle of nowhere, is not as far from the mountain as I would like it to be.

I'm far enough that fires no longer make me nervous, even when sat in an open clearing like this, as I doubt anyone would see the smoke now. I have no idea where I am anymore; I only know how to go back to where I came from.

That's the thing about us ... we can always find our way back to places we've been or left, but without a map, I don't know how far I am from where I started, or where I am if someone asked me. It all started to look the same to me after only two days, and finding landmarks in almost identical forests is not that easy. I have to keep climbing trees to check where the mountain is on the horizon, so I stay heading south of it.

Lord knows I would probably accidentally do a Uturn and head back if I didn't. I don't seem to have a sense of direction that I'm sure most wolves should. I just have this constant pull to go home, and I'm not convinced it's entirely because of homesickness.

Sierra's dream keeps haunting me, even in daylight now, and, for some reason, keeps replaying whenever I have to choose a direction, swaying in the canopy and gazing at the miles stretched out around me. More than once, I've noticed that when I come to a crossroads in my path choosing, she becomes prominent in my mind, and my gut tries to pull me east. Not even back to her son, but off to the left, into the unknown. I'm not sure it's related or why my mind keeps wandering that way.

I've wondered what would happen if I said screw it and just went that way more than once, but I know it's probably nothing more than my being dumb and imagining it. I'm lost emotionally and physically, so it's no wonder my mind is trying to give me some sort of guidance, or fake purpose, to get me out of this funk.

My plan was always south, my instincts keep on trying to sway me away from the south, and I shouldn't ignore my gut, but if my instincts are as faulty as the Fates, I'm better off ignoring them completely. Look how wrong they were about Colton. He did it ... ignored them despite our bond. He marked a mate and forgot about me. I guess it wasn't as hard as he thought it would be in the end. He just needed me to get out of his way.

South is where my mother said her family came from, not that I know much about them, as she never really spoke of her roots the way my father did. My mother was not a Radstone wolf, nor a Whyte pack. She came from somewhere else, shrouded in mystery, and always said meeting my father was fated and magical but never really told us the details or expanded on it.

I was not overly invested in love stories as a small child, so I never pushed. Father would shrug and tell us that their story was much like any other and brush it away, evasive, but then he wasn't the gushy romantic type. I know that she said she came from a place where the weather was warmer, land flatter, and her pack never kept in touch or reached out in all the years we lived on the mountain skirt.

My grandparents were my father's family, and my mother never brought hers up. We didn't talk about it. My family was small because my father was an only child, born late in my grandparents' mating life, and older generations had passed away in my early life before I knew them. Like vampires, wolves live longer than humans, but not for hundreds of years.

It never used to make me think or dwell, but now that I have red eyes and a strangely rare gift, I wonder what I knew about my mother. Memories are mostly her in human form, and on the few occasions I glimpsed her as a wolf, I don't recall ever seeing her eyes. There isn't much need for a pup to see their parents in wolf form when you live on a peaceful, settled farm, growing vegetables and raising cattle. Turning used to be a personal thing when there was no need. Like recreational time for yourself, activity among the peaceful dwellers who didn't have to fight, defend, or lord over anyone. The Whyte pack leader was equally stable and calm, and I never saw him turn at all when I knew him.

My father never mentioned it; no one did, so I doubt they were red. I mean, she was a snow-white wolf, which was mentioned enough over the years as though it was a bad thing. I knew it meant she was different. I'm sure her eyes would have been a talking point too, if they had been like mine.

They said her fur was white because she lacked a pigment, like a flaw in her genetic makeup, and I wonder if it's why my eyes are red ... like a person with albinism. Although my wolf is half gray, I'm sure people with albinism have pink eyes, not blood red. It's all so confusing, and I wish Meadow had told me more about the legends or that the Shaman had taken time to talk to me. It feels like they should have some relevance or that my gift should. Maybe all it means is what Juan said is true. I'm a diluted, impure bloodline and ultimately flawed.

It's afternoon, the sun's still high, but it's doing very little to warm me through and lighten my dull mood, not that I care. We have a gift in that we're not affected by the cold the way humans are, and we don't need the same temperatures to survive. We can feel it, we can enjoy being warm and cozy, but we can sleep in freezing surroundings and not get sick. And if we do, we turn and, voila, healed. I'm not worried about getting ill or injured out here as long as I can muster enough energy to turn for a few seconds, but my mental state worries me.

I keep thinking about Luna Sierra and her broken mind, and I would be lying if I didn't have a deep-rooted fear that I may not be strong enough to endure an oncoming war. It's always there in the background of my mind. I can hide and avoid it as much as I want, but one day, I'll find myself in the midst, and I won't be able to escape it.

There's a crack in the undergrowth behind me, and I spin around to focus my eyes on the dark, shadowy depths of the trees in the direction it came impulsively. Breath pausing, heart rate increasing, as my adrenaline instantly spikes and I train everything on that one spot, poised like I'm ready to bolt, and my butt hovers over the log I was previously perched on. I catch sight of a small deer running through, parallel to me, as it makes a skipping path to find its little herd and relax again, exhaling heavily with relief and sitting back down. I don't think the jumpiness will ever subside, and I need to learn to calm down a little when it's bright daylight.

The forest is never silent, and it's something I need to get used to. It's noisy as hell, and when darkness moves in, it turns spooky and thick with atmosphere and feels like a million eyes come alive. There's always some animal running around, some tree creaking, the babbling of water, or the rustling of the wind. None of those is anything to worry about, but try telling my hyper-senses and scared stupid, young girl's mind. However, I should give myself a break and lighten up a little. I mean, it's been eighteen years of being a shadow in a pack who maybe didn't want us, but they met our needs and kept us relatively safe. Well, minus that one night. Now I'm on my own and responsible for my safety; it's okay to be on edge. I guess it's a good thing to be aware of.

I found a cave here for tonight that seems secure enough, with no rear entry, and even though I should still be walking, something in me said it's time to stop for a while and just ponder stuff for a day or two. I'm shielded here, and there's a water source a few feet away, in a little tumbling brook that heads out to a more significant river further down the way. I feel like I earned it, and after patrolling this area earlier, I don't think I'm encroaching on any pack territories.

I choose a spot near my makeshift bedroom for the night, haul out some of the rabbit I caught during my last turn and didn't feel like eating, out of my backpack. I start a fire to make a proper meal of sorts because I need something warm and decent to give me a sense of comfort, in that I'm winning this and not just scraping by.

Cooking the meat that I wrapped up in leaves to carry with me, instead of eating it raw, will trick my brain into a sense of achievement and less desperation. I foraged for some berries and mushrooms when I found this spot, and I have everything sitting on the flat stone I picked up nearby and stuck in the hottest part of the ash. If I can pretend I'm doing well, able to eat well, with some relaxing cookout time, maybe I might sleep well later when the sun goes down, and maybe my dreams will give me just one night of respite. At the same time, I try not to ponder on this unearthly belly ache of longing.

I miss proper food. Cooked dinners, hot drinks, snacks. I miss milky cocoa, walking around barefoot on the carpet, and having a light switch to illuminate the shadowy corners. I miss having a soft bed and a safe room to close off at night and not worrying about always having one eye open. I miss the noise of the others in other rooms and down hallways. I miss Meadow and the sub pack, and I dare I say it ... I miss him too.

If I'm honest, I miss him more than everything else combined, and then some. Even if I hate him for all of this and will never forgive him for marking Carmen, I can still admit my need hasn't wavered. I can't even think about it without bringing back the agony which shadows my every move and pushing it back down in the depths to shut it off.

I watch the fat seep out of the meat as the stone heats up and it sizzles, giving off an aroma that reminds me of the mess hall. Not that rabbit was a typical smell, and I have to swallow back that instant choking regret I get often. I've identified it as homesickness, even if the packhouse was never really that for me. I guess it's just a general longing for the mountain and the ties to my long-forgotten family. The farm still sits empty. Although I always knew it was there, waiting, I never dared to go and see it. I've never been good at facing my pain, walking away. Closing it off always served a better purpose. Jasper used to tell me you had to face your problems head-on to be free of them, but then, he never lived to prove that was true.

I miss my brother most of all, even more than my mom at times, even if he used to tease me, call me names, and pull my braids. He was a few years older than me and never let me forget it. My first real male protector in life never let me down - until he left me.

I wrap my arms around my legs and lean forward, self-comforting, trying to enjoy the heat of the flames warming my face to shut off my mind and its straying, unwanted thoughts. Another loud crack in the shadows behind me has me bolt upright, and I spin around to see where it's coming from. My eyes narrow and wolf vision successfully flicks to adjust and surprises me with the clarity of seeing in the dark. I wonder if the deer is coming back again and peering into the depths, hoping to see it happily trotting back out.

I gasp as a thundering, giant, black bear comes crashing through the nearby tree line suddenly, entirely unexpectedly, downwind from me, so no scent warning, almost soundlessly until that last moment. "Shit!"

It must smell me or what I'm cooking and probably followed either scent to investigate. It doesn't look inquisitive; it seems mad as hell, with raging eyes and bared teeth, and I can tell how it rears on its back legs and wails at me that it's probably my scent ticking it off and not here to say hello.

Bears don't like my kind; it's a well-known and documented fact. They deem us a threat, and we never wander into bear territory alone. Those monsters are strong, relentless, huge, and weirdly capable of taking one of us on as long as it's a more petite femme like me, with little to no combat skills.

I get up and start backing away fast, knowing that this is some nasty shit to be in right now, eyes darting around for a weapon, or escape route, as it wades towards me through the underbrush, kicking rocks aside with its massive clumpy paws. I swallow hard, pull my wits about me, and start pulling off my clothes slowly, keeping my eyes trained because I don't want to lose the very few items I have to wear. I only have two outfits, and they are already worn and ragged from constant use, so I can't afford to lose a single item by shredding it to scraps by turning when dressed.

I know I can outrun this demon with its head on killing, but I can't grab all my stuff and food and run if I do. I have no time, and it's nearer to my possessions than me. I can't leave it all behind me as this asshole will chew it all to shit. It's mine, and I need what little belongings I have. It's all I have, and as it tramples over my backpack, a little gray of Colton's T-shirt peeking out, something inside me refuses to take this crap from some overgrown, mangy, flea-bitten teddy. It's all I have left of *him*, and I'll be damned if I'm leaving it behind.

It comes crashing at me, pulling my full attention back to its enormous face, eyes raging, yellow teeth, baring in all their massive, pointy, terrifying glory, and I know there's no way out of this. It's four times the size of me, effortlessly, three times as wide, as black as the sky on a moonless night, and completely deranged. I yank the pant legs off, discarding them with my other off-casts, leaving me in my underwear as I run out of time. It lurches at me, and I instinctively turn to counteract the attack, shredding the only good lingerie I ever owned in my life. Black lace Meadow gave me, and it pisses me off on another level.

It happens so fast, like something inside me snaps and takes over, and I move in a flash, somehow ending up wrapped around the upper front of that smelly, panting beast, rolling across the basin floor and crashing into fallen logs and rocks. Its claws and paws bashing down on me, except it doesn't feel of anything much because of my surge of adrenaline, and I latch onto its neck with my teeth, biting hard until I taste salty, metallic blood running into the back of my throat. Digging my claws in where I can get them. My mind is on one thing only: to maim and hold my own until I come out on the other side of this, no matter how long it takes. Strangely focused, entirely in control, and yet fighting back with a fierce I never knew I had in me.

It hollers dislodges me with a well-placed swipe across my head and side with its massive paw, claws digging into my skin and ripping as blood sprays across the landscape, sending me rolling across the debris. The pain is like a distant dream and heals almost instantly, soothing into nothing, like a mild, far away throbbing while blood rushes through my head and my pulse bashes inside my thundering thoughts, pushing me on. I'm quick to my feet, finding energy I've lacked for eleven days, running straight back at it, and flying hard into its mid-section, with front paws and claws extended fully, ready to start ripping, almost psychotically, as I collide. Determined to leave my mark on it more permanently than the way it just did to me.

There's an inner fire in me that knows no bounds, as fear dries up and fades away and this need to fight for my own things, my safety, becomes all-consuming. Nothing else passes through my train of thought, and all I can smell and taste is this sudden need for blood. Like a hunger coming from deep within that tells me I won't relent until I take it down. It fills me with a complete disregard for anything else. I feel it surge through me like a force I can't explain. A shot from an energy drink or being zapped with a power outlet that springs you across a room.

The bear counteracts my aggressive maneuver, and even though I gash its front ruthlessly with one paw, ripping flesh once more and almost blinding myself with a face full of splatter, it body slams me with the other, crunching my internal bones, and sends me flying through the air like a limp rag. That winds me and renders me temporarily dazed.

I'm still not anywhere near its size, which is its biggest advantage in this, but I won't let it beat me. I have speed, strength, and the ability to heal, as long as it doesn't kill me with an instant puncture to my heart or brain or rip my goddamn head off. As long as I have a few seconds of not imminent death, my body will bounce back quickly. Although each time is throbbing more than the last, I guess my initial adrenaline surge is waning as bones readjust and crackle under my skin to be reformed. It hurts like a bitch, and this time I elicit a howl and yelp as it does so.

My anger grows with this fresh pain, disabled only momentarily as I scramble to right myself, finding my balance and quick reflexes. An inner rage builds up so intensely that I can taste it, becoming almost like a solid mass that I can feel and touch around me.

The bear lunges at me again, and this time I'm swift, see it coming and sidestep, jump out of reach, and pounce from ground to an overhanging rock that levers me up enough to take a jump right onto the bear's head and side. I jump high and get it at an angle, right at the side of its face, clinging on devilishly by puncturing its shoulder and neck with gripping talons, and sink my teeth into the top of its skull, trying to crush it with sheer willpower. I realize too late my jaw can't stretch that far, and without a good amount in my teeth, I just rip off a clump of the scalp and dirty, foul-tasting fur, which makes me gag.

The bear, as furious as I am and yowling in agony at removing a sizable chunk of its skin, reaches up, catching my hind leg with its claws digging in brutally, and throws me clean across the forest floor. My body hits a fallen log side-on with the force and velocity of a cannonball. Ribs are cracking under the assault of collision, spiking, stabbing into my lung, crushing, crunching, and holy hell balls. I gasp out with a moment of agony that renders me unable to make an actual sound. Air leaking out and failing me because it hurt worse than turning for the first time, stunned with the brutality, and I'm going to rip that motherfucker's goddamn throat out.

Somehow, I manage to inhale a breath, so my lungs inflate and push my shattered fractured bones back together enough to heal again, but that internal energy I could feel building suddenly encases me fully with every step it takes towards me. My anger knows no bounds anymore, and I focus on a rage comparable to the fiery depths of hell right at that monstrous asshat. It's around me, shrouding me, like a veil I can almost see, translucent, yet it's tingling my skin, urging me to wrap it up and pull it in. Feed on it and use it. I can't explain it, but it's like the air becomes a thin fabric of something tangible and touchable, something I want to grab and take in my hands.

The bear moves in at me, growling and wailing high into the sky with a wave of blood-curdling anger that probably translates to 'die bitch', and I struggle to get up, still recovering, still dazed, with this milky, not entirely clear, air invading my space. Without understanding the why, not questioning where the idea comes from, but having a second of panic action as he makes a final death lunge at me, I grab it from midair, surprised to get a physical handful, like a hot, hard bowling ball in my palm, and throw it at the bear impulsively.

I don't know what I thought I would achieve, and honestly, I didn't have time to ponder either the science or the stupidity, but I throw air at a bear to save my hide. Then groan as logic slaps me in the head for being an idiot.

Like something out of a Hollywood movie, I watch in wide-eyed disbelief as an almost invisible force hits the bear and ripples the air around it, sending the milky veil into a shimmering, flowing movement, like mesmerizing water after a rock is thrown in. It makes its body indent crazily like I just rammed it with a truck at speed, and for a millisecond, time slows down as I take this all in. It's thrown back over three times in the distance it threw me, flying high in an arc through the clearing, and lands spectacularly with a shuddering thud on the floor below the tree line. I swear the ground quakes with force and reverberates through my healing body, bringing a calm to the forest that was not there before. Complete silence as everything stops, and all of nature pauses to say, 'What in the hell was that?'.

The air pulsates around it silently, the veil moving over and away like I blew a candle, and the smoke disperses in the waves of breath into nothingness. With an erratic heartbeat, panting, hunched up in my poised pose but dumbstruck and blinking at it. Disappearing like it never was, and I'm as shocked as the damn bear at what I just did, sitting stupefied, watching in complete disbelief.

It seems stunned, rolls, crawls to its trembling legs, blinking my way, and then turns and takes off at a prolonged speed, no longer willing to combat whatever I just did. It's not recovered, though; it's clumsy, swaying, and crashing into the undergrowth.

As I watch from my perched semi kneeling position, it doesn't get very far. It staggers sideways, then slows to a bumbling uncoordinated mess of a stop, falls over its own feet, and slumps face down on the ground. It's like it is drunk, and as it lets out a long noisy, groaning exhale. I pull myself to my feet and watch as it falls completely silent.

I can hear a heartbeat in the air, so suddenly it makes me jump; slow, labored - one ... two ... three ... and stop. I'm shocked that it was so clear while so far away. It couldn't have been its heartbeat, surely? It had to be mine, but I can't hear it anymore, and I check my pulse to be sure I'm not dead and already crossed over to the other side. Nope, still beating as I press my clawed paw to my breast and snort out a thankful half growl.

I blow out a lungful of air and give myself a few seconds to fully heal every single tiny injury it inflicted, stretching out my ribs to be sure. I stay in wolf form and slowly edge forward to see if it's still alive, trying to recover my wits and focus for a second attack. Surprised to see my fire and food were free from our thrashing around and still smoking away gently, untouched. It smells pretty good too, and my mouth waters with how hungry this has suddenly made me. Weird.

My bag is kicked to one side, but nothing looks ripped, and I catch sight of the T-shirt still sticking out, bringing a sense of calm to my internal rage, which had still been simmering away all on its own. I pass it and come up at the bear from the side, veering left cautiously and keeping my distance in case this is a ploy to get me close.

The bear has its eyes wide open, glassy, tongue hanging from an open mouth, framed with teeth, eliciting no breath, and blood streams from both nostrils. It's vacant, staring at nothing, and I realize whatever I did, it messed the bear up inside, and it's dead. I can tell without touching it that its life force and aura are entirely gone. My senses are tuning in and finding nothing.

I did that. I killed the bear with whatever I threw that I couldn't see.

I don't know whether to feel relieved, proud or devastated because I did that alone. That I pulled some weird power out of my gut and took down a bear with nothing more than air. My heart constricts, my gut twists, and I suddenly have the overwhelming urge to throw up as human emotions kick in and slight shock takes over. I begin to tremble, heart pounding against my chest wall, mind racing over the fact I just had my second ever, real full-on battle with something capable of killing me, and this time, I didn't almost die at his hands – um, paws. I didn't need Colton to save me, either. He'd be proud, not that it matters or that I care about what he thinks.

I push my paws out in front of me, moving to stand on my hind legs and stare at them, unsure how to feel about it. Just gawping at these strange clawed, fur-covered, rather blood-soaked weapons of destruction I never knew I possessed. Of course, I knew I had paws, but these did something weirdly special that I can't explain. They also look ... whiter?!?! Under the mess, and grime, and red stains, but maybe I never really paid attention to how pale they were before. I was sure they were grayer when I first turned.

I try to muster that sensation again, that physical veil thing that I could touch, and hold, and see, but nothing happens, no matter how many weird grunts and noises and odd faces I pull, and I shake my hands away, feeling stupid for not knowing how to control something I can do. My legs shake, and I can already feel my energy waning and signaling I'll return to human form soon if I don't hurry. I don't know if I could do this as a person, and I'm not ready to forget it.

I forget the bear, forget the battle, the shock, the pride, and walk back to the clearing, extending my hands and trying to grasp at the air again, to no avail. So focused on this that nothing else registers in my brain about what just went down.

Whatever that was, I have to figure out how to do it at will. I have to understand how to conjure it and make it appear like that, so I know how to use it again or perfect it. Like the day I shattered everything in the house. It happened when I got mad and ... I got mad!

The thought hits me like a slap as my brain clicks into place, and I recall how crazy angry with Colton I was right before I did that. Just like I was a mass of seething fire, sweat, and despise, with this idiot grizzly. That has to be the key to what I did at the house, and now this.

I don't think it was the same as this, though. He proved it was an absorption gift, mainly when he tested himself against it. I definitely did not have Colton's strength, speed, and power this time, or the bear would have been toast in seconds. I saw what he did to the vampire that night. So I did absorb and deflect his gifts. This isn't something else unless that bear had weird powers and was some sort of shapeshifter and not a regular black bear at all.

I glance back at its lifeless form, a hint of apprehension and circling questions, and shake my head, removing that doubt completely. Shifters would revert to a person after death, and it's still a pretty sizeable black fur rug over there. Creating a dark mass against the trees.

I felt anger and rage, and instead of fear, I wanted to exert my dominance. I instinctively protected myself with something I conjured up, and I haven't come in contact with anything like this that I can ever recall. Not recent enough to absorb anyway, and I know it wouldn't have stayed with me. Absorption doesn't last like it hasn't with Colton's gifts.

I look down at my hands once more, weighing it up in my mind, and realize that it's exactly how I did it. Raging with Colton, like I was with the bear, must be the source of harnessing it. I need to learn to use my rage to control my gift. Not that it will be hard to find a reason to be mad, I just need to remember the pain of four days after leaving, and bingo, I could fuel rage for eternity while cursing his 'skanky, *puta* ass' name.

If I leave the self-pity aside and remind myself that on the full moon a few days after that, I felt no new agony ... so no new betrayal, then I know the answer. He must have marked her before the turning ceremony once he was sure I was long gone. Out of sight, out of mind. He didn't even wait.

I sat up that whole night waiting and watching the moon and felt nothing. Slimy dog.

It ignites rage, but I don't know what to do with it. I stare at my limp hands, slowly turning back to human, failing to conjure the milky mist and give up. I guess without something to direct the rage or have something threatening me somehow, I have no idea how to conjure it up properly. Maybe if Colton was standing in front of me ...

My head falls back as I sigh up at the sky and exhale heavily. Standing in the wood naked, and brain jumps back to reality. I have an opportunity here if I put gifts and rage aside. I just killed a bear, a big one, and his fur shouldn't go to waste when I'm trying to make rural survival more bearable. I was aching for some home comforts and a soft bed. That fat, chunky ass has a perfectly thick piece of warmth going to waste now. I need to remember what my father told me about off-grid survival that it's essential to utilize everything you can at any given opportunity.

I turn my attention back to the beast, a sliver of guilt finally cutting into my heart a tad painfully, reminding me I am, in fact, human, as I watch its still, pathetic, pose and try not to fall back into a weak girl with too much empathy. I've had to do this a lot these past days when hunting for food, and I need to accept that life can be cruel, and in nature, it's eat or be eaten. I ignore the growing knot in my heart and chest, push away the thoughts, and find inner grit.

I pull out my pocketknife from my backpack and flip out the knife section, gleaming in the sun, hitting the clearing and shining back at me. I've been using this to skin rabbits and such for days, but it's small and not the sharpest, even though I have tried to use flint rocks to keep it so. It will take a month to skin that damn bear.

I extend my hand, stretch it out, and turn it to my wolf paw. Lycanthrope can use their paws like hands or feet, and I extend my claws fully, measuring up mentally the size and sharpness, knowing I have the only tools I need right here. I don't bother dressing, as I'm filthy after that little battle and about to be more so. Dried blood from my now healed body and the bear's wounds covers my skin in disgusting patterns and smear marks. I probably look as feral as this makes me feel. I'll need to bathe before dressing, and this is going to get messy.

I cover the ground between us and close the gap with the bear, extending my claws fully, with my mind set on a stomach-churning task. I'm leaning in to salvage what fur I can and maybe a trophy claw as a reminder that I just earned my first warrior stripe. I push down the urge to vomit, suck up the sudden surge of emotion that makes me feel slightly vulnerable, as I stand over my kill and survey what I'm about to do. I don't even know if bear meat tastes good; it might when cooked, and I guess I'm about to find out.

It's the first day in the last eleven that the sadness and hopelessness abate, and I feel like I might just learn how to get through this in one piece with a little more resolve than the last two weeks. I might learn how to grow and be strong if I give myself more time and some faith. If I can take on a bear, maybe I can take on something paler, faster, deadlier, with bloodlust, should I happen upon one.

I need to figure out how to unleash my potential, and for the first time, I wonder if Colton saw it before I did. That he could see through what everyone else did and caught a hint of a spark when he got closer to me. Maybe I am special.

Wolves can't throw air.

CHANGE OF DIRECTION

I lie on the makeshift fur bed I made last night, resting on my stomach lazily with a good size of the pelt over the top of me, hands crossed under my chin as I watch the early morning birds peck at the scraps I left on my cooking stone. Dancing around and merrily, eating what little I left behind. The fire has long smoldered out, and everything around me is dewy with early morning moisture. Everything still and peaceful, in the morning glow of a newly rising sun, and oddly still. I made it through another night, and I'm still here, waking in a better mood with every day that pans out.

I didn't find a cave or shelter last night, so I curled up in the bear pelt, which took me a full four days to scrape and clean and dry out in the sun on the hottest rocks I could find. I'm no expert in tanning or preserving pelts, but it works enough, even if it is stiff and smelly, and it's worth lugging with me every day, despite the added bulk and weight. I sliced it into four manageable sizes for rolling and binding on my back, two for under me at night, spread out like a thin mattress with some comfort, one rolls up as a makeshift pillow, be it a stiff one is currently off to one side. The largest piece I flip fur down and lay over me as a weatherproof blanket, covering on top of the single blanket I carry with me. It keeps me dry anyway because I don't need the warmth, but I do like its coziness, even in caves.

It gives me a sense of security and not feeling as exposed when caught in a black surround made of slightly rough fur.

I've been sleeping a little better since that battle. I don't know if it's because I learned something about my strength, and it boosted my confidence, or if it was just having some small comfort to use as bedding, and the knowledge I did this all by myself that helps me sleep a little easier. My senses are not as unstable and panic-wired lately, and I feel less on edge.

I mean, I still keep one eye open at all times and stay alert, but I'm not as nervy as I was, and I don't feel quite so barren in terms of low mood. I feel capable, as though I've gotten through the worst, and I know I can do this. Newfound self-respect in my capabilities that are changing my whole outlook. Maybe skinning a bear and dealing with that disgustingness showed me I have way more stomach than I thought I did.

I'm learning to turn at will, too, improving that ability, and I can almost turn in my sleep without a second thought. The more I do it, the easier it gets, and I can sustain it for longer as my stamina builds. I can even turn singular parts, like my hand, without a complete body turn, which means I'm gaining the control I need. Like Colton, who uses his eyes to warn when he doesn't want to use his Alpha gift or turn entirely, I'm learning how to do it. I can physically feel when I make my eyes change now.

The weird thing, though, is my paws and stomach seem to be whiter than I remember. With each turn and without a mirror to thoroughly inspect myself, I can't tell if I am losing the gray. It sounds stupid, but I think my gray fur is falling out or getting lighter, and I don't know why. My legs, I'm sure, were entirely gray, but now my feet are white too, and I don't know if maybe I just remember them dirty, or it was dark the first time I turned, but they're snow-white now.

I yawn and stretch out lazily, rolling over under my makeshift cocoon, the rough fur grazing my naked skin, which is oddly comforting, and turn to gaze up at the clear sky this morning. Almost tropical blue and cloudless, with no hints of bad weather or rain like a few days back. An excellent day for an early start, and as I've come up against some uphill terrain in a pretty thick part of the forest, I should savor some of this before I hit the shadows of the canopy. It's dusky and gloomy in the dense parts, and I like to find clearings to settle at night to wake with the light.

I made a direction change after I set off from my bear battlefield. Maybe it was the newfound self-confidence in my abilities or the adrenaline clouding my brain, but I embraced my instinct and headed east, just like my gut kept telling me to do. It's not like I have anyone dictating otherwise or any destination I aim for.

It paid off, and after I did a spot check tree climb to see which direction the mountain lay, I surveyed the land and noted that south was taking me towards the clear landscape, fields, and open grounds with the hints of a town or city ahead. East was taking me into the mountains, with dense woods, lower hills, cliffs scattered in continuous canopy cover, and many forests to get lost in. I don't want to be among people if I can help it, so I decided. East it was, and since then, I've felt strangely peaceful.

It's like the stirring aching feelings were not *all* about Colton, home, and being alone. As soon as I hit my new direction, something inside me stopped praying on my thoughts, constantly filling me with a sense of wrong and despair. It's almost like I answered something that had been bugging me, and maybe I should just embrace the fact my instincts were telling me east made more sense. Which it does, even if I'm no longer heading away from the mountain, but sort of parallel to it now. I feel like I'm far enough that I will never accidentally stray into the path of a Santo, even if they come miles for whatever reason. It's a big world, and a chance encounter would be unlikely.

There's no wind today, and I have enough scraps from a deer I felled last night for breakfast. I smoked a lot of it in a makeshift canopy I stuck over the fire through the night and let some dry out in the sun before it went down, so I don't need to stop for food today at all. I can eat the semi-cured or dried meats and push on. I also packed enough raw in my backpack for later. Now I have a goal in mind and a new plan, I'm raring to go. The sense of feeling lost is momentarily quiet, and it's a good feeling to have some respite in a small way.

The last tree I climbed, I caught onto a sizeable distant mountain, not too dissimilar to ours, with a base dipped in the luscious green of the forest kissing its feet. I want to get there. The trek looks a couple of days, and in the woods as dense as this, I can hyper-speed with no fear of being seen. There are no people, but the trees are so closely grown that I may have to take detours into clearings to push through some of them. It's proper wildland, not artificial and spaced out, and barely grazed by human intervention. Perfect for a lone wolf who wants to disappear into oblivion, never to be found again.

The mountain is the goal, and I hope that I can find a more permanent dwelling so I can start improving my home comforts when I get there. I can be crafty with my hands, and if I find a cave big enough, I might be able to fashion some necessary things, like clay pots, maybe a chair from woven branches. The more I can make my final landing spot seem half-civilized, perhaps the more certain of my future I will be. Eventually, the homesickness will stop, and maybe one day, thinking about *him* will go away too. I can't deny I've still cried in low points and woken with him in my dreams, his touch on my skin, his lips on mine, his voice bringing me home.

Those have been the most challenging points, where I woke with longing to find he wasn't here, and reality slapped me in the face, the sound of him still lingering in my mind and weakening me to want me to reach out and link him. Just to hear that sultry, husky, reassuring tone for real. It would break me for a moment.

I'd cry it out and then feel numb for a while until the sun came up and reminded me why I should only hate him and never give him more than my anger.

I need to stay strong for myself. So far, I've kept the strength to not open the link and just touch him, even for a tiny fraction of a second. I don't want to feel him in my head because if I do, my strength will evaporate, and I might give up entirely at a time I'm just starting to come into my own.

I won't lie and say I don't miss a real home, beds, carpets, and all the luxuries of the valley, but I'm free. I can go where I want, answer to no one, and it's not like I have any desire to find a mate now, so there's no point in being around wolves. My heart will always belong to him, even if he's denied it and moved on. I would rather be alone than lie about my love for someone new, just to have company. Resigned to the fact, I'll love him until I pass, no matter how many years that takes.

I quickly get up and pull my now dry clothes off the rocks. I washed everything yesterday and slept naked in my fur bed, hoping to feel less grubby today, less scraping by, and more pulled together. Washed myself head to foot with the last of my soap braided my hair into two plaits hanging down each side of my head to let it dry. I felt neglected and feral lately and needed to remind myself that I'm still part human, and the little things, like grooming, can make a world of difference. I feel somehow determined and cleaner like I have an actual purpose.

I pack my things, roll up my furs, and eat some of my dried meats as I encase them in large leaves to get ready to go. Binding and tying everything in and to the backpack with vines I corded yesterday, dragging it all on my back, bouncing the weight up to adjust the straps, and re-acclimatizing the weight.

My sneakers are getting scuffed and worn, and soon I might have to find tree sap and make minor repairs to make them last, or venture towards the human spots in time, to use what money I have for something longer lasting. I didn't expect them to give out quite so soon, and in hindsight, I should have brought boots and not these when going off-grid. That's the only downside to all this. The human part has specific requirements that nature won't provide unless I get creative. Shoes are not in my skill set, and I'm not sure my human feet could handle the forest floor debris without them. I would have to turn to go any distance and probably pull a thousand pieces of grit and broken wood out of my feet every night.

I fill my belly with meat and water and head off, leaving no trace behind me after scattering the remnants of my fire and burying the ash. It's something my father always ingrained into me, that when you leave a camp, it should bear no evidence you were ever there. We should respect nature and leave it as untouched as we found it.

I'm always careful to bury or burn the carcasses of my kills, clean the blood from where I skin them or eat them and keep everything neat and clean. It's served me well so far.

Mentally, I feel lighter, not that I've forgotten any of my previous wants and desires or heartbreak, but I'm getting better at handling it. My dreams vary but always around the same things, and I still dream of Sierra most nights.

I thought it would have faded into something new by now, but she's persistent, and since I started turning east, it's almost like the dream becomes more prominent, the vision stronger. Last night, I swore I could smell a scent in the white space around me, smell her, and it had a familiarity I couldn't quite put my finger on. It was like a long-lost distant memory, always out of reach, and it gave me a headache trying to claw for it when I woke up in the night at the utterance of her same old two-word command. If I didn't know better, I would think I know how she smells, but maybe it's from distant memory when she used to read at the library when I was tiny, and I somehow retained it. And her voice, like Colton's yet not, lingers hauntingly, so equally known to me.

"Save us." It's only ever that, nothing else.

The weirdest thing I've noticed about the dream is that I'm not as I am now in it. I've seen my own hands while in the white room when she clasps them in hers. My hands are that of a child, small, delicate, dwarfed in hers, which makes even less sense to me. I guess, though, just like the almost forgotten sense of familiar smell and sound, maybe the dream is also a nod that this all comes at me from way back when I was a child, and I've forgotten. Confused into a senseless moment, reminding me I did once upon a time know who she was. I have given up trying to dissect the meaning, though, as there doesn't seem to be one.

I come to a relative clearing in the wood, hot and achy from covering miles of ground at a fast pace, and stop to catch my breath. I drop my bags by sliding them from tired shoulders with a heavy thud and stretch my body out with a fantastic amount of crunching and cracking in the depths of my skin and bones. It feels good, despite the worrying noises. Extending my arms fully and stretching out, extending fingers and limbs to full capacity, making an 'arghh' sound as I do so, relieved to lose that weight and straighten up without it. I curve my spin and bend my neck from side to side, cracking it satisfyingly.

I roll my shoulders and pace around the clearing to ensure it's a safe spot to stop, eyes darting, ears honed in. I can hear water nearby and walk into the tree line by a few feet until I find a tiny shallow bubbling brook heading downhill. I take my fill quickly, still cursing that I broke my water bottle a week back and have no way to carry any and head back to my bags, pulling out my smoked meat and slump on the floor while chewing on it to take in my surroundings.

The sun is high, so it must be around noon now, the day's heat at its strongest. Rustling wind, so gentle it's barely there, as it sends the leaves swaying on the branches around and above me. Birds are circling in the sky above, adding a pleasant, peaceful calm to the not-so-quiet of the day. Small forest animals chatter busily, sing and chirp in the distance, while the nearest remain silent as they watch me and try to second guess if I'm a threat. I can almost hear and feel the wildlife paused in their tracks, eyeing me up, little hearts beating fast to see who this stranger is among them.

That's the one good thing to come from all of this. My senses, instincts, and wolf side are growing and developing fast, and I couldn't ever have come this far naturally if I was still back in the Santo packhouse. I know I'm changing, becoming independent, so sure of myself as the days roll by. Less convinced I'm a failure and afraid of my own shadow now. I feel like this experience is doing something for me that no time in the valley could have. It's taking my wolf and bonding us as one instead of just being another part of me that occasionally shows up. I guess I'm finally seeing and feeling what Colton mastered in his abilities and embracing my other side. No longer two halves battling for one space but instead merging to flow fluidly from one to the other.

Maybe I had to lose Colton to find myself. To learn what I was capable of and harnessing it alone. Perhaps that was always the Fates plan. Teaching me a lesson and setting me on a path. Maybe, right now, he has his new direction, his new strengths that came from our brief crossing of paths. Perhaps he was always meant to lose me to find himself, too. Like somehow, this is some minor detail in a bigger plan, and our hearts may have been broken, but in the grand scheme of things, it was necessary for something else. Maybe Carmen was always his destiny, and they gave him the strength to betray our bond for that reason.

Who knows? I don't think I ever will. I don't think I will ever find the ability to forgive him for it either, even if it was all in the Fates' crazy masterplan.

Maybe I'm trying to find a reason to justify all of this because I was always taught that the Fates are never wrong. They always have a purpose for everything they do, even if we can't see it. Even leaving lonely little girls as unseen shadows in homes for unwanted, and then showing her a light of hope before crushing it in her face and throwing it far away.

I don't dwell for long. If I do, the bitterness, sadness, and anger will consume me and destroy my mood. Before the dark moves in, I have to move and find somewhere to settle tonight. I want daylight hours to set up my bed properly find leaves and dry grass to pad it first. It's become a ritual daily to help keep me sane. One thing I'm finding is instrumental to my mental wellbeing is taking the time to make my camp comfortable and a little homely and have some downtime before dusk. I sleep better, which helps my overall emotional state.

I get up and gaze around, slightly disorientated from walking in circles and going off to find water, and decide to check my directional progress before I keep moving. I've covered some distance and want to keep that vast dark mountain in the far distance as my central point to aim for. If I have a plan that I don't sway from, it helps me stay focused.

I look up at the trees, walking clockwise in my clearing to find the tallest and thickest of them to climb. It's better to have one with a substantial trunk right up to the top so I can get above the canopy and peruse my land. It's easy to climb when you have claws and super strength to aid you and a complete lack of aversion to heights that I didn't know I possessed.

I pick one and waste no time kicking off my shoes to turn hands and feet into sharp climbing accessories and scale to the top in the blink of an eye. Lycanthropes have many skills that natural wolves don't, and this is one of them.

I push my head up through the leaves, breaking through quickly, and even with this beast swaying as I scale to its terrifying height, I cling on and look out over what I can now see. The trees up here form an almost solid carpet surface that looks like you should be able to step out and walk across. All are swaying in waves and dips on the wind, like a green mass moving on the water's surface, but with more texture.

It's not as gentle when you're this high, and it's almost mesmerizing to watch. The lay of many shades of greens, moving to browns, some yellows, the peaks of the odd rock formation or small hill, and the sporadic clearing. It's a sight that's not comparable to anything else, and I revel in its beauty for a moment, the sun thoroughly warming my head and face.

The mountains in the distance are so faint they almost look light gray and, as I turn to see where I came from, it's weird to note my mountain is now also of a similar color and distance away, but also surrounded by a fog that makes it almost invisible across the large expanse. I get that same aching quench of gut twist when I look at it and shake my head, bringing my focus back to my new destination to combat those feelings. There is no time to dwell on where I've been when I should only focus on where I'm going. Gazing back at my new mountain thoughtfully, something catches the corner of my eye and makes me turn instinctively.

The sun dazzles a little speck, a tiny flicker of white spark which seems to bounce at me across to the right, but when I turn to look properly, I can't see where it came from. The trees sway, covering any chance of seeing it at first. I wait for them to swing back again, wondering if I imagined it, but there it is, a tiny flicker of reaction in a pop of clearing, almost like a light shining Morse code sparkles at me, and then it's gone as the trees sway back again. Their movement's organic flow closes and opens the gap where it peeks out.

Holding myself as steady as I can on my moving perch. I focus on it, waiting for the movement of the wind to show it to me again, and this time, I hone my eyesight on what it might be. I catch the tip of what looks like some sort of pole or mast, and when the wind kicks a bit harder, the leaves part wider for a second, and I catch the top of something flat and dark gray, just below whatever is catching the light, and then it's covered again. No matter how long I perch here watching, it's the most I can see, and I wonder what it is.

It's manmade for sure, but I don't know if it's a mast, a building, or some sort of rural construction used by power companies, or maybe something else. It's piqued my curiosity, as it's not far from the path I plan on taking, and now I want to know if I'm straying into human territory in a place that seemed idyllic and people free.

I sigh in exasperation, looking towards the mountain, then back to my little flashing light, head forming so many questions and doubts, and try to see something I just can't. It might be a supply post, seeing as we are well off the beaten track and people do that. I've heard of it, seen it on T.V, and saw them in the books in the school library. Rural buildings sat alone and open, filled with survival kits for lost hikers and injured campers, especially in winter. This place is nestled in a dense part of the forest, absolutely miles into the center of a massive overgrown part of the area. It could be a supply hut, with dried foods, supplies, maybe even shoes and water bottles.

I look down at the ground far below me as though thinking about the possibility of what I might salvage there, something in my gut urging me to investigate. It wouldn't be a bad thing to pick up items I could use if that is what it is. I can't imagine it would be anything other than a hut or a mast.

It couldn't hurt. I mean, I'm not exactly on a schedule, and if I get close and it's not occupied, or not a supply hut, and just a mast or something pointless, it'll remove any suspicion of people running into me. It might be nothing more than an unmanned power plant

262

building, and I might gain nothing more than a few hours wasted on a detour. If it's staffed, I get the hell away from it, change path and head for the mountain faster, and hope they never venture the way I'm going. It might still be a source to swipe some essentials, though.

My gut says go, and without stopping to debate it any longer, something inside me egging me on, I slide down the tree to recover my things and see what is out there in my new discovery.

THE BUILDING

I sit watching, from my safe distant and secluded viewing spot, the large singular building nestled in an
unnatural clearing, surrounded by ten feet of barbed wire fencing that stretches all the way around, save for a set of enormous gates at the far side. All closed and locked tight and looking deserted. There are dirt tracks showing signs of infrequent visits from offroad vehicles leading up to it, coming from the south, and I'm perched here for watching for signs of life for an hour now, as I try to figure out if it's safe to get closer.

It took the rest of the day to get here, following an imaginary line from my last camp spot, in the general direction and sticking to hyper-speed for most. I'm tired, my back agony from keeping on trekking at an hour I've grown accustomed to being the settling down and making camp stage. Sweating, breathless, hot, and sticky, and currently sat on my backpack as I try to figure out how stupid I would be if I went and further investigated.

There's no sign of life, no new tracks, or lingering scents of anyone being around the perimeter from this distance. It seems silent, but then it's a large white windowless building with a rough cast of fine white stone and looks exceptionally clean for being out here in the middle of no-man's-land. It has an aura of mystery, and my gut tells me to be wary, even if it urges me to investigate.

The mast on top is a substantial metallic construction, like the Eiffel tower almost, and sits on the roof of its custom platform, stretching some thirty feet upwards. I thought at first it was a telecom mast, or maybe power, but nothing connects to what looks like a radio antenna coming from the top of it. There's a steel box generator, almost half the size of the building, within the compound, yet sat apart from it; it is low humming within its encasement, suggesting this building has constant power.

There's something off, even if on the surface it looks how I imagine an unmanned power plant substation would look, and despite that, my weird inner voice that kept pushing me east it's telling me to get closer. My mind and instincts are battling with what to do, and it's why I've sat here staring at it for so long. The sensible part is screaming danger. The less logical me is telling me how harmless this looks and that there are no life signs. The weak part is aching for connection to civilization and a longing to touch something tangible and manufactured after so many weeks alone. It reminds me that I've still been crushingly lonely despite doing better. I'm a pack animal, which goes against my nature to be solo.

I can't see any way in from this angle, so the door must face those giant gates, which means it only has one entrance and nothing else. Not exactly a layout for any kind of worrying military base. I mean, it's not even that big. It's not big enough to be anything much else. At most, you could park two of the Santo trucks inside, so I doubt it homes any more than some power grid equipment for maybe some of the further rural homes. Perhaps it's a radio station with sporadic visits or something. I don't have a clue, as it's hardly my area of expertise.

After an hour sitting here, I have gotten no signs of life or any reason not to have a closer look, and the only thing stopping me is my terrifying level of suspicion. It seems wholly deserted. I'm being overly cautious, my feeble side wading in, and even with the wind blowing this way, I'm not picking up any human scent.

I can see cameras at the corners on this side of the building, and they probably have them at the front too, but they are all pointing down at the ground within the fences, so I can at least get that close without being caught on them. I guess they're to pick up on wildlife getting in. I might see more if I go around the other side and figure out what it is. It might have signs or hazard warnings if it is just a power plant. If I know for sure, I can stop tiptoeing around and relax.

I exhale heavily, wiping the rolling beads of moisture from my brow, and look up at the fading light in the graying sky. I should find a place to make camp and stop wasting what daylight I have left. Come back in the morning, but that means trekking further, as this is the first clearing I've come across in hours. Nothing nearby looks like a good place to set up, so maybe I might have to sacrifice a restful night and roll up in the bear's fur right here. I can't think of anything else to do.

It's either go check this out and walk on when I know what it is and if I can salvage anything or camp and look at it on the new day. I'm exhausted, need to eat, and don't have the energy to do much of anything.

I get up, mind in two halves, and pull my backpack up, lugging its heavyweight as I try to decide. I would prefer to stick to my usual plan of picking a site and staying there until dawn. I don't want to be out in the open when darkness falls, as despite not picking up on any creatures of the night, I can't be sure there aren't any lurking in caves or underground tunnels, many of which I have come across these past days. I remember the stories of the vampires coming out of the ground during the war.

I don't wander far, realizing it's wall-to-wall, closely-knit trees in all directions but one, moving towards the building. It is the only part here that has space to lie down, and I'm not about to sleep in the clearing near it.

I doubt any passing big cat, bear, or such, walking its perimeter will bypass a sleeping me without fuss, so I decide to pick a tree with excellent leaf cover and climb one. It's better than being a sitting duck on the forest floor, and I doubt I'll get any proper sleep when I haven't found a good place to hide. Up a tree, I can tie myself to the trunk and at least dose off and on through the night and wait to investigate this in the morning. It'll give me a little security, and at least up high; I can defend myself if need be.

I end up walking a full circle and finding the right kind of trees nearer the main gates of the building. One's with broad bases, multiple branches from mid-way up, with extra amounts of foliage and twisting crisscrossing boughs for platforms. I squeeze between two that are close together. About twenty feet up, their branches merge and curl to make a wide landing place, and I have to haul myself up with my backpack on, finding it a little more labor-intensive than usual.

When I get up there, I find a flat enough spot and roll out one of my pelts. I snuggle into a dip between two parallel boughs and can properly lie down without anchoring myself to anything. I hang my backpack on a broken stump on the trunk and lie out on top of my makeshift bed, stretching and wriggling to see how comfy I can get, satisfied that this isn't too bad as long as it doesn't get windy or rain tonight. I don't want to unroll pelts that could slide off if I roll in my sleep and draw attention to lurking wildlife. I won't have a fire to keep some natural creatures at bay up here, so I have to make do with cold meat, a bumpy bed, and the rustling and swaying of the trees to lull me into slumber. Not that I think it'll be an issue as, now I'm up here, my eyes are heavy and my brain cloudy with fatigue. It's been a long day.

I sit and watch the building through the foliage for a while, sitting at my safe distance, watching as the shadows lengthen and become part of the dark surroundings as the light fades fast. I'm already exhausted from my extended trekking, so settling down and drifting off is more manageable than usual. Not the usual spew of weighty things on my mind to keep me awake, and it feels like only seconds of blinking and drowsiness before I zone out.

I wake with a start, jumping slightly and sitting up fast, banging my head on rough wood and silently yelping as I properly come to. I must have drifted into a deeper sleep quickly because it seemed only a second ago I could still see my hand in front of me, and now I'm in the pitch dark and can't even make out what I'm sitting on. Disorientated at first until I remember where I was and how I got here, and my belly rumbles because I didn't eat. I woke with fright for sure, and my heart is thundering through my chest as my nocturnal eyesight kicks in, frantically bringing the surrounding area into focus.

I'm not sure exactly what woke me yet, and I slowly sit up, sliding my legs up, my knees touching my chest as I rub my now bruised, lumpy forehead while scanning my surroundings for a cause. Taking deep breaths to calm down and center myself, letting my senses take over, rather than my scared brain.

It doesn't take me long to see what brought me around once I settle down and look. There's a shiny black truck parked in the undergrowth beside the fence, nearer the back of the building where I first stood. It's about ten feet further down the makeshift road. They must have just pulled up. Maybe the noise and headlights are what roused me, and I watch with bated breath as someone slides out and makes their way around the fence to find the entrance. An eerie, solitary figure shrouded in darkness. It's both a joy to see another person and a massive alarming worry that I'm seeing another person.

They, much like the truck, are all in black, wearing a hood pulled over their head, so I can't see their face at all, but I can tell he's male. Tall and stocky, he moves around the gate, focusing on his task and eerily quiet on his feet. The wind picks up gently and blows this way, guiding his scent towards me, and I recoil in complete shock like someone tasered my ass.

He's a wolf ... like me. There's no denying that particular scent we all carry, and it red alerts me and wakes up my brain immediately.

I have no idea why the hell a Lycanthrope would operate a power plant in the middle of the forest. I mean, maybe it's not that big a deal. Some packs live and work in the human world and have regular jobs as they try to pass off as one of them. This could be a guy who works for the power company and, for some reason, likes to frequent his unmanned building in the middle of the night. I'm sure that's probably a regular thing, for unconventional hours, or maybe if he has a special task at this time of night.

Probably not likely, and it's too weird that all the way out here, alone for weeks on end, the first person I come in contact with is one of my kind. It's a little too coincidental, especially as I came here after following some deep gut feeling and stupid dreams of Sierra Santo.

I watch, squinting through the foliage as I try to see his progress and get a better look, but the gates are obscured from my angle, and he disappears behind trees that sit between us and out of sight. I don't want to lose track of him in case he somehow heads in here without me seeing and shows up at the foot of my tree. I doubt I would be a welcome discovery.

I don't hesitate. I slide off my perch, silently climb down the tree, and crawl closer until I see him again from another angle, ducking down behind a rock and keeping low. I'm relatively safe from this distance if he doesn't see me moving around. My senses are on major high alert, and I'm taking comfort in the fact the wind is blowing this way, so he won't smell me the way I did him.

I have to creep on all fours, keeping still and wedging behind a fallen log to get a better look as I track him. By the time I figure out where he is, eyes scanning the fence and truck, he's already inside the compound and up against the door. He moves fast, and it confirms that he's one of my kind.

I hear a beep, a click like he opened something or had some sort of key, and the door slides to the side in front of him. It doesn't open out as I would expect, but more like that of an elevator door that slides out of sight, back on itself, which is weird for a low-tech building.

I can see inside from here, though, and there doesn't seem to be anything in the doorway, making it all even weirder. It looks like an empty concrete box, with no big inside room, control panels, or anything from what I can peer into. That just makes the sliding door stranger if it's concealing nothing. I move a little closer still, not convinced I'm getting a complete picture, hitting the last line of trees before the clearing, and stand tall to side-slide behind one and peek around. I know getting this near to him is stupid, but I can't see, and this place has me so confused about its purpose or importance to my instincts.

He walks inside, turns, and faces something to the left, just behind where the door is. He leans in, ducking slightly, so his face comes level with an out of sight panel.

"It's me. I'm back. Bring me down." A low growl to his masculine tone, most definitely a wolf. I can just tell.

He stands tall and turns to face the open front door. There's a crunching noise, the humming of the generator revs up in ferocity, and the entire building emits a long grunting moan. My heart rate escalating as nerves consume me and my body trembles. I swear, for a second, I think he looks right at me and I dive back, flattening my back to the bark and close my eyes, as though somehow that'll make me invisible. I'm not sure though, as he didn't seem to react at all, and I'm probably being paranoid because I'm scared.

I look back, holding my breath to steady my shaking self, quick enough to see the door sliding shut as he slowly lowers below the level he's standing on. It clicks instantly that the floor is moving, and he's going down. Like some sort of elevator for sure, and it explains why, on the surface, there's no sign of life, and the building is small. It's deceptive, and the sliding door conceals a car-sized platform to a lower level. That means whatever is down there is big enough to accommodate vehicles should they need to be taken down, making my blood run cold.

I don't think it's any kind of power plant, and I shouldn't be here at all. It has more going on below, and now I know a wolf is crewing this station. I have absolutely no chance of finding anything worth stealing and getting away without a trace. Not that I want to anymore. Everything inside me tells me this is a bad idea, and I need to get far away from this place as soon as possible.

When the door fully closes, I walk out in front of the tree where I've been hiding and peer over to where he left his truck, wondering if he may have left anything of value. If I'm cutting my losses and running, he might have something. Maybe a medipack, food, clothes, or something I can use. He didn't lock it, and he was alone.

He probably isn't coming out right away, and I should make the most of his absence before returning. He might not stay, and judging by the fact he abandoned his truck and never brought it into the compound; I don't think he is. I have to be quick and go.

I run along the tree line, keeping to the inner side and within its shadow, and dash his truck, using hyper-speed to get to it fast and look inside when I slide up against the door furthest from the building. It's an off-road four-by-four covered in mud and debris and the perfect vehicle for moving around this terrain. I can tell right away there's nothing in it. Nothing in view that I would want, not even general trash. It's clean and free of anything worthwhile. It is not what I would expect for a truck used frequently, so it makes this even weirder. He obviously doesn't use it very much to come and go. One last fleeting run-over with my eyes convinces me he has nothing of worth.

I dash back to the closest border of brush and start making my way back to my temporary camp without looking back, keeping behind the trees by two rows. With the heaviness of mounting panic growing inside me like a warning signal, my breathing is labored. Heartbeat pounding in my ears as it batters my rib cage and adds to my terror. I don't feel safe being this close anymore, and I should never have ventured to find this building. I don't know what I was thinking, and the last thing I need is complications from wolves and James Bond type buildings in the middle of forests. This has a spy movie written all over it, and I'm in no mood to be dangled headfirst over a vat of sharks for information I don't have.

When the noise of the building cranks up again, I don't know if it's the floor moving up again to reset or if he's coming back. It stops me in my tracks, and I instinctively drop to the dirt and turn around. I crouch where I am, watch and wait, peering through the trunks and bushes to see the door, until the moaning cranking noise of heavy innards moving comes to a halt. Yet the door doesn't open. Nothing happens at all, except the return to a previous hum. I don't think it was him; I think maybe the floor comes up again when they reach a destination, and I relax a little, blowing out my breath with relief, moving again from this tree to the next to make my way back to my perch.

I almost make it all the way in when another loud thumping noise stops me in my tracks and makes me look back nervously, so jumpy and on edge, with all my senses heightened for more efficiency. This time the noises are less intense, less mechanical, and more like regular people noises.

The building appears to be coming to life as it increases. The doors make a swishing noise, but nothing seems to open. There's a bang, sliding of bolts; I can't tell. A beep, a whoosh, like a piston's noise, and then I can make out the swing of a heavy metal door and gravel rolling and slides from it.

Suddenly, lights flick on all around me from concealed posts further out in the trees and make me jump. My heart skips a beat, and ice flairs in my veins; I find myself illuminated in the previously dark space. Blinded by the sudden solar strength, a burning pain hits me in the eyeballs. I blink, shielding my eyes as my night vision craps out and gives me an instant headache, like a rabbit caught in the headlights.

I wasn't expecting this entire area to illuminate, like standing under a sunlamp and pulling my wits around me; I dart as fast as possible to the nearest spot of darkness and hope they didn't see me. The lights must be extended above the canopy on masts further out that I didn't see, as everything around me is brighter than daylight, and I have no one direction to go to that will get me out of it faster. The entire space is bright as hell. I run, heading towards my mountain in the far distance, concentrating on nothing else except escape. Screw my backpack and furs; I don't need them right now.

I sprint, dodge, jump, clearing fallen logs as twigs and leaves scratch my face and hands and rip at my skin in passing. Breathing labored and loud as I pant. I aim for the shadows without looking back in case this is because of me, that maybe he did see me out there and, whatever this place is, no one should know about it. I put my head down and hyper-speed to the best of my ability, only making it to a skidding halt into darker bushes when a scary, piercing noise fills the air. It has a horrible effect on my body and senses, rattling my brain inside my skull as my physical self crunches up, instantly immobile, and I grab my ears.

It's a siren, honking hard and loud, in a pitch that causes me physical pain with its sheer volume, echoing in the air and making the surroundings shudder in trembling response. My heartbeat elevates until I think my chest will explode, my body straining to turn to a wolf to get away faster, but I don't let it. I need to keep these clothes more than ever now, and I need to get back to my tree to grab my stuff.

My gut tells me to abandon it all, forget about the clothes issue for now, and just run, but my logic is telling me to calm down, stop reacting, and be rational about this. As the cameras pointed down, they couldn't have seen me, and I didn't venture near the fences. Maybe he just looked my way, but I saw no sign of a reaction or recognition that he knew someone was out there.

This could just be a coincidence and something they do, even without someone like me lurking nearby. They couldn't know I was there—if there is a 'they'—and why would they react like this? What could they possibly be hiding that a young girl like me posed a threat to?

That wolf might have been solitary, although he talked to someone on whatever that intercom was, so maybe there are only two of them, and this is a power plant. I know a lot of that contradicts what the other parts of my brain are telling me, but self-preservation has a funny way of shaking you into being less manic. Lying to myself can help lessen the fear and get me moving instead of freaking out.

I try to take some calming breaths as it all filters through my head, and I keep telling myself I'm overreacting. This is just a drill, or a thing, or expected. I'm fine. I'm sure I am.

A whizzing whistle of air that skids past my left ear and inflicts a searing pain with the high-pitched velocity it passes me with makes me jump sideways and crash into bushes as I run at speed. I almost swallow my tongue; my stomach lurches and jumps out of my body with the scare. It gives me a near heart attack, and I scramble in stinging, scratching bushes to fight my way out. I get caught up in heavy thorn vines and trip over my unsteady legs.

The fall makes me tumble and roll, knocking my shoulder on rocks, and stops my scrambling for a second. I take a moment to look back at the surging, bright sunlit area I left behind, gasping as I see the outpouring of men dressed in black coming from a concealed ground-level hatch near the main door. Four, maybe five, bodies appear on the ground above. There are already two outside the gates, and both are facing this way, looking intensely into the trees where I ran and pointing big ass guns with their sights trained in here.

I don't know what flew past me—I don't think I want to know—and the doubt that I was in any kind of danger dies an instant death. The blood drains from my body, so I turn cold and statue-like as it sinks in: they are looking for me. I don't stop to wait for even a blink longer, terror once again ripping through me at speed and activating my 'run like shit' button. They all face this way and come thundering after me as soon as they see the rustle of the bushes I dart from.

Gifts that are remarkable or not, I can smell them from here, wolves, and they are all armed. A little patrol of male wolves in black uniforms, and they're coming at me. I don't care who you are, what story you're in, that never bodes well in any situation, and I don't think they're trying to invite me in for coffee and cake. I've stumbled across something I shouldn't have.

Pure instinct takes over, and the urge to turn is almost killing me with the rate my human body is pounding itself to shreds with sheer adrenaline. I run, I trip, I fall, and I know that human form is only slowing me down and making it more likely they catch up with me. I know only too well that wolves will not be kind and show me mercy at being caught in their lands. I have one set of clothes ... and that's it.

I need to think about survival now, even if that means ending up naked and backpack less, miles further into the undergrowth. I just need to find another way to gather the things I need later and curse myself stupid for venturing this way, near this damned building. It's not an inconspicuous power station. Those men were guards, and whatever they were guarding was important enough to carry weapons and stay in the multiples.

I'm so goddamn stupid. Fuck you, Sierra, and your damn dreams and pushing me east. Fuck the Fates. Fuck Colton for making me leave the mountain, and fuck Juan for being the root of all my woes and how shitty my life has been for a decade. This is *all* his fault!

I turn. My inner wolf almost howling with an intense release, glad to be free, finally. Head down, clothes shredding pitifully as I leave the last of my worldly possessions in the dirt and run like the wind. I can do nothing else about it now, and they are in fast pursuit.

I fall, wedging between trees too close to get through and break free noisily with sheer strength and willpower. Wood splintering, branches crackling, but being silent is no longer my concern as the noise of their pursuit out sounds mine. I can feel them coming, hear them, smell them. I can even feel their heartbeats synching with mine as scent follows me close on my heels.

Panic spreads through my veins, and I hope that the angry numbness I gained with the bear kicks in soon, or I'm screwed. I can't even stop and try to use any gift right now, especially when I don't even know how. The last few days of trying to conjure it up proved futile. I'm scared now, not angry, and I have no hope of conjuring any other feeling.

Something else whizzes over my head, like a small shooting tunnel of air that makes my hair tingle and pulls as it passes. It shoots directly into the tree several feet in front of me and stabs viciously into the trunk, standing proud and straight as it comes to an instant halt. I only catch sight of it for a split second, a transparent tube filled with watery liquid, a red feather tail, embedded deeply in the rough wooden skin of the poor tree. It catches my eye and draws my attention, and before I can run past it while still trying to figure out what it is, something stabs into my spine, right between my shoulder blades, with a stinging pain so intense that it makes me howl involuntarily. A loud wailing noise that hurts my ears.

The impact is hard, the pain is unexpected, and the combination makes me trip and crash face-first into the branches and rocks on the ground I'm crossing. I roll, hitting the rough floor of the forest like a dead weight, and skid ungracefully, pulling debris and dried leaves with me, kicking up a cloud of dust and choking on it, across a tiny clearing knocking off whatever was sticking in my back as I do. I feel it being yanked out with a stomach-churning tug.

I land on my face, legs sprawled as my body betrays me and turns back into human form without my say-so, and my eyes focus on the tiny thing a few feet in front of me. Dazed, I try to catch my breath as this unearthly warm and strange sensation pours through me from the spot in the center of my back.

It's the same as what hit the tree. A clear tube, only empty this time, with a red brushtail. Only now can I see its long, silver, and highly pointy tip. It looks a lot like a dart for taking down large animals. I've seen them on African game reserve documentaries. The needle is thick and massive, so no wonder it feels like something stabbed me with a big pointy object at bullet speed—it did. I let out a groan and try to roll and move, aware that an empty tube suggests the contents are inside me.

I attempt to get up, but my limbs give out like useless heavy weights of flesh with no control, and my vision spins. My head turns woozy as everything around me sways crazily like I just got on the deck of a boat amid a rolling storm.

I don't like this, and I can feel the thundering of feet fast approaching me as wolves' growls turn to human voices. I can make them out ever so slightly, coming at me on the gentle breeze of the rustling trees as silence takes over. My hearing and head faded out despite trying to fight it.

"I hit her ... she's to the left. Split up and spread out in case we need to double dose her."

I can't grasp anything as my hands claw at the dirty muck strewn ground below me, desperate to keep trying to run. As futile as I know it is, something in me is refusing to give up the fight and urging me to get to my feet. Like a tiny warm voice in my mind, softly calling out to me.

I swear, I hear Sierra drifting my way in the wind as she reminds me of the same thing she has been saying all along, yet it somehow means something else in my drugged state.

"Save us."

In my oncoming delirium with weak grasping fingers, sure I see her face in the canopy above as my eyesight obscures.

"I can't. I'm not strong enough." It's a pathetic whisper at no one as my eyes blur with tears at my failure, and my heart aches that, somehow, I let her down, even if it makes no sense. Maybe it's a pain of failing myself. Weeks of running and hiding, and I can't do anything about what I've gotten myself into. I was stupid to think I was special.

I can feel them close now, and as I try to lift my head and shoulders from the soggy earth in one last-ditch attempt to save myself, my vision blanks out entirely, and I lose consciousness.

WHERE AM I?

My head aches with the weight of that damn bear sitting on my skull. My mouth feels weird and furry, like I just ate my socks, and I blink at the bright white piercing light as I slowly try to open my eyes. Flinching at the assault and screwing my face up in reaction. My body is heavy and disconnected as I try to come to and figure out where I am and what happened to me. I feel like I just survived a train wreck, and I'm not entirely sure I'm not dead and in the afterlife waiting room. I'm altogether disoriented, everything spinning, and I can barely move my body as though I've somehow I feel vacuum pressed to the surface I'm flat out on, and it's the most surreal sensation to wake up to. It takes a minute for my eyes to grow accustomed to the brightness of my surroundings, and, much like having a torch shone in your face, it's painful at first until it levels out and an actual ceiling comes into focus. Watery eyes blur to clarity and blink repetitively to figure out what I was staring at.

White square tiles and a gray, wooden ceiling fan that's on slow and hitting me with a gentle breeze. The tiles are large and grubby and pull my focus enough to let me grasp the reality of my situation: I'm inside a building and no longer on the forest floor.

My gut twists, and my insides sink as that filters through. It all comes slowly back, the memory of eating dirt and passing out, and I try to sit hurriedly as panic comes kicking back into play. Straining with all I have in me as mild panic sets in.

I can't move, a tightness across my chest, arms, and legs, yanking me down painfully, and when I attempt a second time, trying to figure out what's wrong with my body, I realize it's not me ... I'm restrained. It's not some weird malfunction of my body after being tranquilized.

I manage to tilt my chin, still dizzy but able to drag the exaggerated weight of my skull up enough to look down my body and exhale at the sight I see. Laid out flat on a hospital bed, dressed in a light medical gown. There are leather straps across me at several points of my torso and legs, keeping me down, and both my ankles and wrists are shackled in wide black fabric to the sidebars of the bed. The guards are up, holding me in place, and try as I can to wriggle, I can barely move an inch. They're tight, thick, and impenetrable while I'm in human form.

I turn my head to the side, dizziness making everything sway, getting a blank white painted brick wall and turn the other way, opening up my view into a small medical room. Brick all around, no windows, and one white door closed shut with nothing but a high square glass panel in the upper half. There are cupboards, trolleys, and worktops in here, with all manners of medical kits and supplies, some posters on the walls that remind me of the doctor's surgery in Radstone, and an array of panels up near the door that look pretty high tech. The floor is tiled in a weird blue-gray vinyl and, apart from the information posters on dressing wounds, the predominant color here is white. It's stark, stinks of disinfectant, and has the usual low hum of electrical outlets and the whirring fan over my head.

It's almost eerily silent and deserted, but I know that's far from reality. There is nothing overly out of place for a sick room that causes me any extra alarm. I mean, it's not like I'm waking up mid-body slicing in an alien abduction story.

I feel nauseous, my heart pounding through my ears already, even without the added anxiety of waking up and finding myself captive in a strange place. I'm obviously inside the building now, somewhere below ground, and I have no chance of getting off this bed. I can't get up, probably not even without the straps, while I haven't come all the way out of my drugged stupor. My energy levels are low as hell.

My first attempt at turning is entirely futile, but I try, hoping to wipe the residual drug out of my system with sheer willpower. It's like I have zero ability, and even breaking my promise never to link Colton again, I try, desperate for some kind of help. Just his reassuring voice, always knowing what to do, his words to calm me. I get a black wall of nothing, meaning something is blocking all of my gifts and abilities, and I'm no better off than a mortal with no gifts.

I wonder what the hell they've done to me to subdue all that is supernatural, and I don't have time to ponder it when a tiny buzzing sound draws my attention above my head, behind my line of sight. Wriggling around until I can tilt my head back far enough, arching the very slight amount I can, to see a camera repositioning in the top corner over my head and focusing its attention on me. I guess my movements alerted someone that I'm now awake, and I glare at it hatefully, visually doing what my body can't and rebelling in some small way. I try harder than ever to get out of these straps and give up as a wave of fatigue washes over me and leaves me breathless.

It's futile. I have no strength, still groggy enough that my little energy wanes fast, and I jump internally when the door across the room beeps loudly, reverberating through my ears and clicks to signal someone coming in.

"I see you're awake, dear girl. I've been waiting impatiently and ready to come to introduce myself to such a marvel as you." The heavy accent is foreign, almost like the Queen of England that I've heard on television in the orphanage, and I screw my face up at the man who strolls in towards me, smiles weirdly as though eyeing up a special gift someone has left for him by surprise. I'm momentarily taken aback by the almost caricature way he has of talking.

He's in his older years with graying fluffy hair, glasses, and a balding head. His midriff is round and portly, making his white lab coat look restrictive and emphasizing that he's wider in size than in height. The second he walks in, I can tell that he's not a wolf; you would never see a wolf in a bad physical shape, and we definitely do not go bald. Gray over time, but none of the human aging flaws like developing weight or saggy bits. Definitely no hair loss. Wolves stay in their prime until they crash out past the hundred and so years we live for, and this guy looks like he's maybe hitting human sixty at a push. He has a striped baby blue shirt on, a peek of green braces, but a dark red polka-dot bow tie that just adds to his peculiarity.

I stare at him pointedly, eyes steeped in mistrust, and give him no response.

"Quite." He says absurdly for no apparent reason as his eyes travel up and down me in the most disturbing way. I'm being sized up for some sort of alien autopsy. Either that or he's lost in his head and marveling at some wonder that has him smiling like a weirdo.

"Where am I?" I blurt out boldly, not caring about being polite and friendly given my current predicament and the fact this asshole has me lassoed to a bed while bobbing nearby Willy Wonka style. My spine is agony at the point of that damn dart, and it feels like I'm black and blue all over. Only just beginning to feel my fingers and toes, and despite regaining some alertness, I feel like I'm not quite here fully yet, and this still has an aura of dreamlike to it.

"Oh, of course ... silly me. How rude and utterly awful. Let me introduce myself first. I'm Doctor George, William Robert Adams. I'm the resident chief scientific officer at this facility, and you, my dear, are our guest. Sadly, we've had to take certain measures for both your safety and ours, seeing as, like my acquaintances, you seem to possess a certain wonderful gift. But it's a temporary arrangement until we become better acquainted. I hope you won't hold it against us that we acted hastily in a preventive manner without knowing your character or purpose for trespassing on our doorstep. And your name is?" It's a whoosh of ridiculously precise, queen's English in an exaggerated and somewhat foolish sense. I'm at a loss. I didn't think people actually talked or behaved like this, let alone ones who survived living among the aggressive, low patient, temper driven, wolf kind, like me. He's a little absurd.

I blink at him, stupefied at that whole upper crust, marble-mouthed mass of weirdness that came out of him. He seems like some eccentric Mary Poppins type character, and I'm sure I might still be high from whatever they darted me with. I stare blankly at him, dropping my head back on the pillow, and don't say a word.

"I know. I know, you must be thinking the absolute worst after Mr. Deacon took you down with an elephant dart, and they carted you in here and trussed you up like a Sunday roast on an oven sheet. Truly, we don't mean any harm. We would just like to ascertain who you are, where you came from, and exactly what you were doing snooping around this rather top secret and out-of-bounds facility. A boring informality before we can be more hospitable. Please don't hold it against me." He raises his brow at me, still smiling like a demented person, and removes his glasses to clean them on his coat, only breaking eye contact for a moment before returning them to his face and renewing that creep smile. I'm starting to wonder if this one is a sandwich short of a picnic, and maybe this is what happens when you live in a box underground and don't see the sun for prolonged periods.

"Passing through. I don't know what this place is and have no interest in it." I point out blankly, not willing to elaborate, but only get a strange 'hmm' noise in return as he nods at me.

"I see. The minor issue with that is that you were very clearly caught snooping around on our surveillance and checking Tyron's truck out before high-tailing it into the forest—*oops*. I believe you, but they don't, which is rather disastrous. May I add, though ... wow, just wow, I've never seen, literally ever, in flesh and bone myself, an actual full and pure white-furred wolf. It truly was a remarkable sight, not to side-track the main point and negate the seriousness of your current position, but I just had to put that out there." He raises his palms in a quirky little jazz hand movement that perfectly matches the happy, wide-eyed, lifted brow thing he does. The dude is strange.

Who the hell is this guy, and did he swallow a thesaurus in his formative years? He sure takes the long way to say anything, and it throws you off. I honestly can't tell if this is a tactic to disarm you and pull information or if he really is a conversation starved oddball and tends to offload. Maybe he's just weird. He has the whole odd outfit thing down to a T for being a weird one.

282

I'm also shocked to be told my fur is now entirely white. Although I've had hints and suspicion it was turning that way; he just solidified the fact for me. It's not like I've had a mirror or an ability to take my head off and use it to look at my whole body when turned. I have no idea why my turning white is happening, and I wonder if my mother experienced the same thing. A flaw, just like everyone said it was, maybe some kind of disease that spreads.

"I thought he might have food," I add, eyes darting around the room past him as I continue to come back to the land of reality and start looking for something useful to help me get out of these straps. Trying to muster up the willpower to turn again, but nothing happens. Something is seriously screwing with my abilities, and this individual doesn't seem like an imminent threat. Unless talking you to death is possible. My nerves quickly dissipate in his presence.

"Oh, so you're hungry. How thoughtless of us. Well, we can do something about that, can't we? No need for us to be rude and unfriendly. It makes perfect sense that you would be drawn to a concrete building searching for supplies in the center of this green utopia if you were out here lost. I just would like to know your name for a start, and possibly where you originated from, and maybe, if you have any more friends lurking out there. A pack, a mate. Someone who might not be very discreet about the whereabouts of our sensitive location. I know it's a bothersome formality, but they won't let me feed or untie you without it."

I ignore him completely, too occupied with the why of the fact I can't seem to muster any kind of ability. Even my strength is only that of a regular human. It's frustrating me, as I can now move my toes and feet and rotate and wriggle them to test the strength of the straps. The power and speed I have, even in human form, are absent.

"What have you done to me? Why can't I turn?" I snap it at him aggressively, temper rising as it sinks in, but it isn't helpful in terms of ability. I hit him with a pointed look under lowered brows, and his happy little face drops to an almost impressed 'ooh' look.

"Ah, well caught. You're an observant one, aren't you? This facility is a life-sized isolation tank, so your kind can't use any unwanted force or abilities on my staff when we require your presence or when we have guests such as yourself. It's remarkable that they can make a building completely capable of dissolving any supernatural ability, isn't it? I don't have the engineering science, but I can assure you it is quite ingenious." He talks way too much. He also gets way too excited over the most minor things, and I eye-roll and shake my head at him, trying to draw him back to the Intel that I need.

"Once again ... Where am I?" I'm losing my cool quickly, annoyed at being held down, and I wriggle manically to attempt to escape this crazy one, not giving a crap he's standing right there. The noise of the door beeping and clicking behind him snaps my attention back to it and the dark uniformed figure that comes stalking in as he pushes a trolley with what seems to be a food tray to one side.

"Pipe down, Princess. You know where you are because you hauled ass up to our door and tried to take a look. The question he asked ... Are there more of you out there?" It's a commanding deep, almost growl-like tone from a serious-looking man with a foreboding glare. That feeling of intimidation returns as he makes my braveness pipe down, and I return to still and calm mannered and stare directly at him.

He's a scary one and most definitely a wolf. Not that my sense of smell is working either. Tall, broad, physically hunky, and good looking in that bland, typical, dominant wolf way, and unnervingly very Santo. This in itself is weird.

He's Latino in accent, dark, tanned, handsome, and I swear he almost has Colton's dark chocolate eyes, although his have hints of green that lighten them overall, and it somehow kills the whole smoldering look. He has an arrogant look and a slight downturn to his mouth— whereas Colton's turns up—which gives him an air of aggressive superiority. Even when being a pompous ass, Colton always has a smiley quality to his face. Pretty boy ... cute ... dimples ... God, I miss him.

"Guess you'll find out soon enough," I remark bitchily, not willing to give them any information until I know what will happen

284

to me. So far, it seems that tests, experiments, and pulling my insides out are unlikely. I'm probably more in danger of ben 'fan girled' by the dude in the white coat who has a severe leg hump for my whiteness.

If they know I'm alone and have no one tracking me, they might think nothing of disposing of me. He said this was a top-secret facility, and I'm guessing making promises not to tell doesn't hold a lot of weight with these types. I shouldn't tell them anything and pray they believe I'm a no one and let me go on my merry way.

"Not the sensible response, sweetheart. Name ... Pack name. Don't get smart. The quicker we know who you are, the faster you *might* get out of here." He eyes me viciously, not friendly at all. I snort at that, half laughing sardonically, and roll my eyes, noting how much emphasis he put on the word might.

"Sure, I will. I mean, it's totally normal to be an asshole, drug people, and tie them up, right?"

Now is probably not a good time to realize I developed a bad attitude and sass while living in the wilderness, but something about him riles me up. I'm guessing the Santo look and that hint of an accent reminds me of so many smug dickheads I grew up around, and his tone is getting on my last nerve. Sick of being pushed around by these Alpha-type wolves and their damn superiority complexes.

"Deacon, here, is our head of security, and you must excuse his abrupt manner. He's just very concerned that the delicate nature of our work might be compromised if some random yet very pretty rebel wolves should happen to disrupt our facility. We have sensitive materials that require the utmost protection. I beg you to understand our predicament and disregard my friend's hostility in such an unfortunate matter." He's flapping, looking flustered and trying to give an air of friendly.

"Doc ... too much Intel for a bratty girl who's giving nothing in return. How about you go polish a stethoscope over in the corner and leave this to me." He snaps, and the poor little doctor reddens in the cheeks at the verbal telling off. His eyes drop to the floor in submission, and it's no surprise to see which one rules this roost.

Deacon is not that much older than me physically, yet he acts like he could totally be one of Juan's arrogant, nasty bloodline, with a massive chip on his shoulder. He looks like the type to love pistol-whipping people and probably gets off on the power trip. He probably got stationed here against his own will and takes it out on everyone around him.

"Maybe, if I weren't chained to a bed, I would be more inclined to talk." I point out sarcastically, raising one brow to drive the point home and showing none of the fear that's still simmering in my belly. I guess being out there alone for weeks on end gave me a sense of fierce and confidence I never knew I could ever get back, and this time it's Deacon who eye-rolls.

"She has a point. It's not very polite of us, especially when she cannot do any physical damage within these walls." The doctor seems to be a soft touch, and the dark glare Deacon spins and throws at him makes him pipe down immediately. He almost turns crimson from the neck up and shuffles back, slightly away from the big brute at his side.

"She gets loose when we get some answers!" He digs his heels in, turning back to me with an unamused frown that signals he's exerting his dominance, and I sigh heavily, knowing I've no choice but to give them something if I want the use of my limbs at least. It's not great being interrogated by two men standing over me while I'm set out like a sacrifice to the gods. Mentally, it makes me feel at a considerable disadvantage, and being free would make this less intimidating.

"Fine!! Carmen!! My pack comes from the east, and I'm taking a little trekking holiday from them after a fight with my mom and stupidly stumbled across your little building. I was curious, that's all." I lie convincingly and stare straight at Mr. Security, long and hard to drive the point home. My stomach is trembling, my nerves getting the better of me, and I can't tell if the waves of cold are the aftereffects of the drug or my anxiety piquing. I've no idea why I chose her name. I mean, I do blame her for a huge portion of how I got here. I guess on some level, if I get free, then I want her name to be the one they put on the 'shoot on sight if seen' list.

"Carmen? Hmm ... Nope." He replies and crosses his arms across a muscular chest, trying to appear in the know, but it only serves to irritate me further.

"Umm, why nope? Carmen is my goddamn name. I'm sorry it doesn't meet your expectations. Freak." I huff, wriggle aggressively, and exhale heavily when I make no headway in loosening anything.

"You're not a very good liar. You have about fifty tells, and the only part of that which was true was that you stumbled across us. The rest was bullshit. Look, we just need to know who else is with you and who you linked and told about this place before we took you down."

"What does it matter, for fuck's sake? No one, okay. I'm alone, and this bullshit is getting old. Untie me if you're all so fucking nice and friendly, as it might make a goddamn difference to this conversation! If you want me to talk, get me off this goddamn, uncomfortable, infernal fucking bed you have me strung out on like I'm awaiting dissection!" I lose my cool. My temper snaps with sheer frustration at him, riled in a way only Colton could ever make me. I blame the fact that he somewhat resembles him and has that same pig-headed, stubborn ass manner that made me crazily hate the Santos. That know-it-all, bullshit mind game, and ordering me around.

"How alone?" He completely ignores my femme tantrum. Deacon steps closer, pressing his hands to either side of my head on the bed, and it dips as he leans into me, bringing his face close enough he locks on me, eye to eye, and blocks out most of the light over my head, casting his face in shadow. It has the effect I guess he was going for, in that I lose all fight, recoiling back inside myself, wholly affected, and a little fearful, and lift my chin not to show it. Backing down subtly, but not without a bit of fight.

"Like all the way alone. My pack isn't with me, but I can't be sure they aren't far behind." It's not really a lie, as I don't know if any of my pack has ever caught any kind of trail and followed me. I doubt it, as they would have caught up by now, but I'm not going to say I know for sure they haven't. I just don't know, and it seems to be a believable statement as he leans up and pushes himself away from me after a minor scrutinizing of my face at close quarters.

"No one with you? No mind-linking?" He repeats sternly, and I shake my head as stupid as I am for admitting it. Deacon seems satisfied I'm not lying and turns back to his submissive oddball.

"You can untie her, Doc. She can eat, but she stays confined here until we decide what we should do with her. I still want a name and pack. I need to know what kind of threat she, or they, pose. I'll be back soon. I need to contact Alpha Santo and get directions concerning our intruder. He'll want to be informed."

My heart stops beating in my chest, and I have to stop myself from gasping out loud at the words that come out of his mouth. My insides self-combust and the blood freezes in my veins as my mind comes to a complete standstill on those two little terrifying words.

Alpha Santo! Juan? There is no other Santo pack in these parts, and his resemblance isn't coincidental. Why Colton kept coming to mind is now glaringly obvious. This is Juan's facility, which can only mean one thing. Deacon is a Santo; it explains the asshole's lousy attitude and shitty behavior. And possibly, Sierra is not an invading dream because of Colton telling me about her before I left him. She's been calling me somehow, from these four walls, and led me right to her. There's no other explanation for how this all ties up like this. The Fates wouldn't just let this casually happen.

I don't understand why or even how she managed to do it from inside an isolation tank, but there's no other logic for this kind of crazy coincidence. This is a Santo building, a facility, so many miles and days away from the mountain, but close enough for Juan to have his reach. Doubt he has many facilities in our lands, and I didn't just come upon this by chance. I wonder how much of this the Fates orchestrated, and I don't mean from the second I turned East. I mean, all of it, and how I was led here from the day of my turning.

I'm so screwed, though. Once Juan knows I'm here, it will be game over. He might actually send me to the same fate as Sierra, wherever she is, and leave me to rot in here along with her for the next ten years. It'll be the answer to the dilemma of my pairing with his son. Keep me locked up, and keep Colton safe. It's not like anyone will miss me if I disappear for a decade.

The doctor moves over me as soon as Deacon leaves us alone, his face apologetic, with a softness to his gray eyes that I overlooked before. He has kindness in the wrinkles and lines around his eyes and mouth, which suggest he genuinely smiles a lot in his life. With a worried glance at my face and a smile that doesn't quite reach his eyes, he whispers in a shaky voice, revealing his fears.

"Please, don't react when I remove these. I don't want to sedate you again, and I don't know if I've got the strength to match you, even in human form. I swear, I mean, you no harm. Let's keep this civil. You play nice. We play nice. It doesn't have to be hostile." He doesn't trust me, and even though I have no gifts here, he's wary of me. He's human for sure, and he knows what we are capable of, which means he's probably witnessed it to be this kind of afraid. I find it weird they even have a mortal here, but I guess the wolf world has a shortage of crazy doctors to keep Juan's mate hidden with. Packs are family, and it's rare to find sub packs that keep secrets from the rest, especially among one as big as the Santos. I guess humans are easier to keep quiet.

I nod and relax my body, showing him I'll behave, and he seems to pick up on it, his smile strengthening, and his face softens. I can almost taste the tension seeping out as he leans in to undo the first buckle.

He makes fast and light work of releasing me from the bed and jumps back cautiously when he unties the last ankle strap, eyeing me from a distance as I slowly sit up and regain my bearings. It takes a minute, and my head swims as I level up, aware I have only this gown on to cover my modesty, and it falls forward off my shoulders as I move, telling me it's not even tied at the back. They must have thrown it on before restraining me, and I reach back to pull it together again.

"Just let me go. I'm not interested in this place or your work. I have plans of my own and a route. I'll happily get back to that." I point out, trying to sound sincere, but the older man's eyes narrow, and he frowns at me, shaking his head apologetically.

"Oh, my dear, I'm afraid I'm not the one who makes those kinds of decisions, or I would show to the door with a wave and a sandwich. The problem is, we can't let you go without being sure all of that is true. No one's come up here in ten years without invitation, yet you are not just a regular silly trekker or lost hiker—but a wolf. A solitary femme, which is quite unusual in itself, given pack hierarchy and the female role in your world, but a rare white form, at that. Remarkable. I'm afraid it's all a little too suspicious given the circumstances." His voice is hushed, as I guess he doesn't want Deacon or whoever watches the camera to hear, and the genuine serious concern etched in his eyes shines out. He has a trusting quality about him that's tingling my sixth sense and telling me he's not one of the bad guys.

"What circumstances would that be?" I match his expression, a little churning of suspicion of my own as I take in his manner and how he seems to deflate a little, his posture sagging as he turns towards the wall. He stops at the food trolley and pushes it towards me with a fake smile.

"We've been testing such unusual DNA for years, and a rare specimen falls right in my lap. It's almost like the Fates ordained it, or maybe a little spy came to gather Intel for a rival pack? My work until now has been a secret and protected, but you found us. An elusive, rare white." He raises his brows suspiciously, and I fiercely glare at him as his tiny accusation filters through and offends me on a deep level.

"I'm no spy, and I have no idea what you're talking about. I'm white because, much like my mother, I lack pigment. It's not rare because it's special. It's a flaw! Diluted bloodline, or some nonsense, and not desirable at all." My inferiority issues piquing and taking the form of rage. It's an angry outburst with a basis in old wounds and heartache and I croak with a raw, harsh tone in my voice, biting back a surprising tear as it comes out. "In my world, I'm an outcast because I'm inferior, so screw your theory. No one cares about that kind of intel, least of all me."

Like I said something ridiculous, he laughs, his wide eyes startled; his expression completely unnerves me and throws me off.

"A flaw? By whose standard, dear child? Hybrid blood is spectacular and a masterpiece of engineering science, my dear. I don't know who's kept you in the dark all these years with such nonsense, but being white is not a flaw. In a breed where you own physical perfection and can self-heal the worst of wounds and illnesses. Do you think your DNA would allow such atrocity by defect? No, of course, it wouldn't, it couldn't. Your gifts work out the kinks in your makeup from the second you're born. It's the bonding perfection between two species and happens only when the biochemistry of a particular set of genes lines up magically. Two species, two blood types, merging beautifully in one captivating dance that produces a new third, equally magnificent species. You, my dear, are what I have been dying to test for the last decade! It's a near-impossible combination to make work without awful deformities or even loss, and your kind is few and far between. Whoever first engineered your astounding DNA must have been incredibly talented. Tell me, are you a first-generation, or are you a natural-born?" That grand speech, and whooshing of excitable words, floors me. I try to absorb half of what that word junkie threw at me, and I'm still sitting blinking at him as my brain catches up the translation from freak talk to plain English.

"You're lying. I don't know what you're talking about or half of what you said, but I know hybrids aren't a thing." Terror overtakes me as his words filter in, and my mind refuses to digest what he's saying because it's simply wrong. The wolves pride their bloodlines and purity; it's a massive part of our being and hierarchy.

Mixed breeds don't exist because, if they did, the purebloods would destroy them. They don't want dilution and mongrels among our blood. They're bad enough when weak DNA, like my family's, infects a pack, and those people become calm land workers with no urge to fight and dominate. It's why the Whyte pack never had any kind of claim to the mountain as a ruling pack, and the Santos own it. Our kind thrives on dominance. We need alphas and purity to survive.

The doctor clutches a flat hand to his chest, aghast. Eyes wide, an expression that translates offense.

"Lying? I never lie when it comes to science, my dear. I'm a biochemist of the highest order with a special interest in your kind. I've dedicated my life to it, and it's all I research. Hybrids are my specialty! I would so love to get your samples under my microscope and see if the stories are true, and show you for yourself the absolute wonder of your genetics. Warring species in one body, yet they seem to have completely bloomed! I mean, look at you ... utter perfection."

My blood runs cold, my eyes raking him and trying to understand what he's saying, so many questions forming and gathering on my tongue. My head is scrambling with the uncertainty that he might be telling the truth. But that would make my mother ... I can't.

Deacon reappears unexpectedly, interrupting with the beep of the door before he enters, and throws us both a strange look that suggests he doesn't like whatever feeling we just gave him. The atmosphere is tense, and the doctor seems to lose his enthusiastic energy and slinks back out of the way, probably afraid to admit he told me way too much. Despite co-habiting in this place, I can tell that there's no genuine bond between them, and he is as wary of my prison guard as I am.

"Alpha Juan will be here in two days. This one ... her name is Alora and, interestingly, from our own mountain, so take from that what you will. She isn't going anywhere." Deacon turns to me, a look of disgust rippling across his face as he scowls at me, and everything inside me seems to disperse in a wave of numbness. The fear claws through me that Juan knew precisely who I was with just one call and is coming here personally to decide my fate. That's not a good sign.

"The mountain ..." The doctor whispers it so lightly under his breath I doubt Deacon hears him, but I do and catch the slight hint of recognition flitter across his brow before he pushes it away, replacing it with a blank expression.

Damn me for being a white wolf! That had to be the defining detail that gave it away. Maybe also the fact he knows I'm missing

292

now, and one lone femme, this close to home, was probably a no-brainer.

I raise my brows at Deacon with false bravado, saying, 'so what?' His eyes narrow at mine, and the scowl gets more prominent.

"So ... You're a runaway from our pack? Juan said he's been looking for you, traitor. How coincidental you end up here. Clearly looking for something you shouldn't be! You're going down to isolation until he gets here, and then you can be someone else's problem. Hopefully his, and I'm sure he'll find the perfect punishment for a flawed failure who betrayed her kind." I don't doubt Juan has conducted a whole new story about why I'm public enemy number one and arguing it will be futile. Deacon is a believer, loyal to Juan's sub pack, and it's boringly obvious. He was put here, probably because he is one of the brainwashed who does exactly as they are told and questions nothing.

Deacon grabs me by the upper arm ruthlessly and hauls me off the bed forcefully. My body is still dead weight, and I almost fall on the floor with the sudden demand to use my limbs. Grabbing out to catch myself and instantly overwhelmed with dizziness at being bolted upright.

"Careful, careful. She's an exceptional specimen and still a young lady. Kindness does not cost extra, Mr. Deacon. Compassion. A little human dignity. If we have her for two days yet, then I need to harvest samples for my studies and could use the time to learn more about her very unique blood. I can't let this opportunity go to waste, and I certainly can't stand and watch you damage her." The doctor is torn between genuine human concern for a person and that of a scientist with his eye on a prize lab rat. I can't even be mad about it, as it opens a window of opportunity.

"Doc, she's our prisoner, not a study volunteer. She's a betrayer of my blood, and I'll handle her as such. The only place this chick is going is down beside that mindless corpse they keep in bay two and out of bounds for you and your quack colleagues in the lab. If we're lucky, she'll stay as quiet as her new roommate and gone before she messes up any more of my week." Deacon is an asshole, for sure. He pulls me with him, not waiting for my legs to catch up, and, despite my inner desire to not touch this idiot, I have to grab onto him or be dragged along behind him.

"Sierra is not mindless. She's sedated and detained by you thugs and your lack of vision. She's a work of art, a person with feelings and thoughts, and if Juan would only allow me to awaken her and ...."

"Enough!! Shut your mouth!! That's a dead name. Just like you will be if you talk about her again." Deacon barks at him hatefully with a harsh tone and pins him with a fierce glare.

The doctor recoils, scolded, and red-faced, but I can feel his simmering anger at the mention of Sierra. The spark of absolute rage in him before he was shut down and paces off to bubble under the surface, grabbing a nearby rag and twisting it between his hands as we pass him. I can tell he's trying so hard to hold his tongue.

I'm speechless, though, my mind racing at the confirmation she's here, and my mouth runs dry. I don't fight Deacon as he bodily hauls me out the door at speed. No consideration that his grip is leaving marks on my skin or that I'm tripping over every step as I try to regain control of my legs. His fingers bite into my arm as my legs, like jelly under me, try to keep up with his long, fast stride. I end up clinging to his side like a needy child, aware my gown is sliding off, and I catch sight of the doctor one last time as he follows us out into the hallway, and I strain back to see.

He looks sad, defeated, and as he watches me get dragged away, I lock my eyes on him one last time as I piece together a plan of sorts in my head that might give me a tiny hope of getting out of this. I throw him a desperate backward glance in an attempt to communicate.

"I volunteer. Take your tests. I want to know why I'm white, and I'm not going to be doing anything else for two days." I lie impulsively, loud enough for my voice to echo this hall. The doctor is a soft touch and knows something about Sierra. Maybe I can convince him to let me go or see her and determine why she brought me here. It's clutching at straws, and my brain is trying to figure how this will help, but it's all I have now. Deacon falters, stopping us with an exaggerated exhale of annoyance. He turns us back around.

The doctor's face lights up with a glow that tells me he might be my key to getting out of here before Juan shows up in two days, or at the least, he may be a valuable ally if I can keep him latched onto my unique so-called 'hybrid blood.' Might be able to manipulate him into revealing more or getting lax with keeping me locked up. Deacon, I can tell, is a lost cause, but the doc might just be the weak link.

I don't believe anything he said about being a hybrid, though. I think he's a crackpot scientist who has sampled too many of his test tubes from being in underground isolation, but if it gets me an angle to lever a possible way out, then I'm going to play on it. I'll play along, nod my head, and let him stick me with as many needles and swabs as it takes to win him around.

"See, see, she has no objections, and it's only some blood and smears and such. I will barely touch her, and it won't interfere with her time here. Juan will never know." His enthusiasm and surge of newfound joy are energizing and solidifying my plan. Deacon scowls at him for the longest, tensest moment as I hold my breath and pray.

"She stays in bay one. You don't take her anywhere else, and you are to be done before Juan gets anywhere near here. Not a word to him about it, at all!" Deacon lays down the law, relenting, probably for a quiet life, and it's not like he'll have to do anything.

The doc nods enthusiastically, like an excitable puppy, and I remain calm and neutral, shielding the sea of nerves rippling up inside me. My heart is pounding, my insides trembling, but I'm cool and calm on the outside. I have a chance of breaking out, and it's keeping my wits about me.

I allow Deacon to turn me manually and haul me off through the door ahead of us to a second hallway, pushing through the swing door with haste. I blink at the drastic change to lighting, opening my eyes onto a white sterile passageway with glossy surfaces that shine bright, blinding with the force of the daylight LED lights. It creates an optical illusion of a vast white wall-less space that blinds your corneas half to death with the intensity of the snow-white environment.

It's like being in my dream, creepily so. The one in which I saw Sierra, and I'm dazed a little by its surrealness. My heart rate escalates, my eyes raking around us as it pieces together and brings back memories and details of that light space where I met her. Being pulled along mindlessly as my thoughts repeatedly drift to her standing ahead of me, with no real sense of boundaries around us. It's too striking a resemblance to ignore.

The Fates brought me here for a reason; they pushed me to run from Colton and hauled me east, so I can't ignore it. Meadow always said the Fates were never wrong, and all of this is way too coincidental to be an accident or to keep me as a nonbeliever. I'm here for a reason, and the dreams I've been having about her suddenly make so much sense.

Save us.

She meant it ... she meant us ... her and me. And Colton. He's wavering without his mom.

We're both here, and I seem to be the only one that can do anything about getting us out.

SIERRA

Deacon is a brute of the highest order who probably got his training in Juan's school of charm for asshats. He

half drags me and half lets me walk on my own feeble legs down the hallway to an elevator. Only stopping to bark orders at another guard sat at a desk nearby before shoving me inside and taking me down to a level with an aircraft hangar air. The doors slide open to reveal an ample, empty space in semi-darkness, with concrete floors and strip lighting on the ceiling, which stands a good twenty feet above us. The area is vast, and there are three trucks parked at the far end on what looks like a platform, which I'm assuming raises up. It's dull, definitely many degrees colder, and seems like a part no one frequents all too often.

As we walk, the lights flick on automatically over our heads, and I note in the middle of the wall on the left, a low glow is already illuminating from what seems to be an open alcove. From this angle, I don't see what it is until we walk level with it and turn right, my head snapping to turn back, even while being dragged away from it, so we head in its exact opposite direction, where I catch a glimpse of what it is.

A room behind an entire glass wall stretching its width for ample viewing that looks like, at one point, was a sectioned area for parking and has been repurposed. Tire grids are running up to the window, but the inside room has smooth concrete floors as though they have been resurfaced. It houses a bed in the center, surrounded by machines, carts, and equipment, all making flashes, low beeps, and hums, keeping the solitary figure within the bed silent.

A motionless brunette woman, hard from this angle to tell if it's Sierra, lies out like sleeping beauty, amid wires and tubes, under a single dull spotlight hanging directly over the bed. She's so still, pale, and lifeless, tightening my stomach in knots, choking me with emotion. It's almost like an art piece of a priceless mummy in a museum.

She's in full view of this entire area in her glass box, yet completely unmanned and with no caregiver monitoring her, which speaks volumes. I guess all the monitors and machines are doing the job of people, and it breaks my heart to see her so alone, even if she isn't aware of it. Colton would die if he saw how she's being kept, with no human contact, no care or interaction ... just machines and isolation, in a goddamn basement. My heart aches for her, for him, and I'm glad he doesn't know this is what Juan has done to his mom.

Deacon gets annoyed with my straining backward to stare and jerks my arm cruelly, snapping my face back around, and I give him a hateful scowl, scared of him less and less the more I'm in his company. He's a typical Santo bully and not unlike a lot of the pack was my whole life. Pushing people like me around to exert his dominance in the hierarchy. He's a dumb jock type with a bad attitude and the need for a dart gun to take down a running femme. He would last ten seconds out there if he made me mad enough to throw air at him, as stupid as that may sound. Loser.

I focus back on where we are heading, and I can see my room mirrors hers, and I'm about to join the glass casket crew. I'm guessing it's the backup room should they need to move her to do whatever, or maybe in case something happens in there and she needs moving over here. God knows, but it's almost identical, and I wonder if there was ever a second person like Sierra here. Or maybe Juan has plans to add one—me.

Mine is not full of tubes and machines, but it houses a single hospital bed in the center, which appears to be bolted down, and a wall of units and cupboards behind it. One corner holds a very public portable toilet that the other room lacks, and I don't struggle when Mr. Security pulls me level with the transparent wall. There's no privacy or places to hide with its matching glass barrier, and as we stand here, I see the almost invisible outline of a singular door within its vast transparency.

"Is this so you can watch all day and night without opening the door? Getting your freak on and watching defenseless women!" I snark at Deacon, who has avoided saying anything more to me since we left the doc in our wake. The only words he uttered were at the guard outside the door when he informed him my three meals a day were to be added to the rota and reported to the cook until further notice. Another Santo-looking douchebag upstairs who glared at me like I was something disgusting he found stuck to his shoe.

He glares at me with that sardonic asshole expression, scans a swipe card against a panel on the wall to our right, and pushes me inside aggressively when the door slides open. It's a bit sci-fi tech, and I refuse to react in any other way than hostile bitch. I almost trip over my own feet and slap my hand on the wall to steady myself before turning my head with a half turn to snarl at him, wishing I could turn because that boy's throat would be in need of repair given half a chance.

I have so much aggression inside me that I can't contain the sudden hatred for him. I can almost taste his blood and feel his pulse beating out of his jugular as I focus on what I could do, given half the chance. I spin back to him, my robe flapping around, so he probably gets an eyeful of naked ass as I do and throw the angriest, most vicious sneer I can muster right at his smug face.

"I'm so glad I got to shoot you at least once. God, it made me hard to see you go down like a sack of shit." He smirks as the door slides shut, and the urge to punch him in the throat overwhelms me to the point I jump angrily at the door as it slides between us. I end up palm-slapping it level with his face, panting heavily as fire consumes me.

"You were clearly too slow to catch me then if you needed a gun, you moron. Probably the only time you've ever been tougher than a girl or got a hard-on over one!" I stick my middle finger up at him and return the smirk he's dishing me as he turns on his heel to go, face grim with a darkening mood. I can tell I pissed him off on every level, but he's trying to act like I didn't.

"Enjoy your cell ... Carmen!" He snorts, using the name I gave him, and I throw sass right back.

"You know, you should remember that name. A mountain wolf with no standards and loose panties ... right up your street. You and she would be perfect for each other if you were ever allowed to leave. You might get laid for the first time in your life. She's a prize bitch which matches your prize assholeness!!" I yell it after him. Temper unleashed a little and furious for the sake of being furious. Annoyed to find myself banged up in this hellhole and under the care of a sanctimonious Santo like him.

Colton would rip his head off if he were here. God, if I could link him right now, I so would. Just to see him roll on up and tear Deacon a new one. He would beat seven shades of shit out of him without even needing to turn wolf. That's the difference between an asshole looking to be Alpha and one who is naturally born that way. Colton never needed to push me around to exert his dominance; you could feel it whenever you were around him. He was gentler than most wolves once you got close to him, but you knew he could turn savage and destroy anything in his wake if he needed to, like vampires in a courtyard.

Deacon blanks me completely, waves a dismissive hand at me like he has the last word, and leaves. Stalking back the way we came, like an arrogant shithead who needs to go choke.

I honestly cannot stand that guy, and if I could turn, God, he would be first on my hit list to air punch across the room. I have enough rage bubbling through my veins to ignite it, but unfortunately, no actual ability in this weird futuristic building. All I need is a tiny bit to link Colton, tell him where his mom is, and bust everyone's ass in here. I have enough rage that I think I could, maybe. I wish I'd been bright enough to find and use that gift when they chased me through the damn forest. I only have myself to blame for not being able to harness my given talent.

As soon as I watch him storm off into the elevator and completely disappear, I turn my attention back to the room across the floor from me and focus on that lifeless, sleeping body. She's twenty feet away at the least, maybe more, but these glass walls, although thick, don't keep the sound out. The low beep, beep, and swish of her life support machine are humming and repeating subtly in the air now that the asshole has gone, and the place is almost silent once more. I lean forward until my palms touch the glass, only this time softly, and press my forehead to it so I can steady my still, pretty weak self and stare at the side profile of the figure laid out over there. Instantly enveloped in a feeling of hopelessness as I watch her lifeless form.

She's been down here like this for God knows how many years. I can't believe Juan would do this to his mate. It's like he just put her aside and forgot about her, and the only reason she's still alive is that their link would kill him if he let her die. So, this is what he does—breaking the bond and rules of being mated. He's not protecting her or caring for her in sickness and health. He isn't allowing the pack to nurture their Luna the way they're supposed to. He's ashamed and hiding her in a place no one knows about. There's no dignity in what they've done to her, and the doc slipped up and made it clear there's nothing wrong with her mind. Juan obviously has other reasons for keeping her down here if madness is not it, and I will her to give me some sign that she knows I'm here.

"Hey! Luna Sierra, can you hear me?" I yell as loud as I can, hurting my throat in the process with scratchy rawness. It doesn't elicit any response, not even a change in heart rate on one of her many machines. I observe, listen to the sounds, but there's nothing. "Can you hear me?" I try again, not as loud, but my throat aches with the effort, and I cough dryly, quickly giving up on that method.

I sigh, sliding down the glass and watching her desperately, trying to figure out how someone in a building that blocks gifts, in an induced coma, could somehow reach out to me and guide me to her with the weird dreams and urges to come east. It doesn't make sense now that I see her and know she can't call to me. She

301

doesn't seem like she can do much of anything except breathing independently as she doesn't have a ventilator. She didn't urge me here. There's simply no way in hell it could have been her. She's all but a vegetable down here.

The only answer I can think of is maybe the Fates did this instead, and it wasn't her at all, but I guess I'm not about to find out. If I thought she had answers, it's pretty clear she won't be giving me them, and this is a dead end. The Fates delivered me back to Juan for absolutely nothing. And when he gets here, knowing I found this place and saw her like this, he isn't going to let me get anywhere near Colton ever again.

Everything in here is bolted down, probably because they don't want prisoners throwing things at the window, and I am not about to kill myself by hurtling my body through it to see if it breaks. I hate being stuck in human form and completely powerless to even get out of this dumb glass. Without being able to turn, I would probably bleed to death. Be that unlucky girl who brought down a shard over my neck or something and still be stuck here. A shriveled, empty corpse to stink the place up.

That jerk didn't even let me eat, as he said, and my stomach growls at the lack of having food since God knows when. I don't even know what time it is, morning or night, or how long I was sedated in that room, considering there are no windows underground. I last ate the day before sleeping in that damn tree, where all my possessions are, and I'm starving. It's no wonder I feel weak and shaky. I'm running on empty.

It's weird, but maybe it's my years of being bossed around, held captive in a less than caring home, and treated like a reject at the hands of my so-called pack, but I'm not even afraid anymore. Being here held captive, I know that the worst will come with Juan, but even then, what's he going to do to me? He can't kill me or inflict too much pain because his son will bear the brunt, and lord knows his legacy is always at the center of everything. I guess he could do what he's done to Sierra, but it's not like she seems aware of anything, and maybe that wouldn't be a bad thing—no longer tied to Colton, carrying this burden of heartache while he lives his life with

302

that 'skanky *puta.*' Maybe a long sleep would be better than being stuck in a glass box for a lifetime.

I abandon the glass and walk across the cold concrete floor on shaking legs. I need to lie down and finally get rid of the rest of this drug in my blood, so I can at least walk around normally and not feel like I'm on newborn legs. Maybe I'll feel better if I take some time to let it work out and sleep off the rest of it. My body is shaking internally, and I keep having minor bouts of dizziness that remind me I'm in no state to take on the likes of Deacon if I ever get a chance. Before I leave this place, my first goal is to knee him in the balls for shooting me in the back like a coward.

I don't get to the bed before the noise of the elevator whooshing open sways this way, and I stiffen instantly, expecting Deacon to come back and grace me with his toxic personality. I mentally try to figure out the likelihood of being able to kick him between the legs for the sake of it. I climb on the bed, turn around and sit with my legs dangling off the edge in readiness to give him more attitude and lure him inside to my perfect level of height. I hear footsteps and the squeaking of wheels rolling across the hard floor, coming my way.

It's not Deacon. It's the doc and a female in a white lab coat. I frown as he appears in front of the glass door, pulling the food cart and carrying a bag in his other hand, while she pushes another behind him. He waves at me before accessing the door and slides it open with a smile.

"My dear, we never fed you, and I couldn't let you go hungry down here in this bleak nightmare of a place. I brought you some clothes. They're nothing fancy, just the smallest size from the supply closet that I could find and a fetching shade of military gray." He pushes the trolley inside, the sudden smell of food filling the air, and my mouth waters with the reminder I'm near famished. He drops the bag just inside the door but hesitates about coming in, and I sit here waiting patiently. His female companion stays back, arranging some medical implements on a tray on top of her trolley, and avoids looking my way completely. She's young, maybe early twenties, and seems a very small-town white girl, medical student, and human. Blonde and blue-eyed, so definitely not a Santo.

"Thank you." It's a genuine response because this gown is not exactly great at hiding things or offering comfort, and maybe eating will help straighten me out a little. In human form, I'm suffering from the effects of not eating and probably have low blood sugar to boot. The female seems interested in me but keeps her distance, and it's easy to tell that my kind makes her nervous. She pushes the trolley near to him, then turns and walks away without a word.

"It's nothing too adventurous, just a chicken salad and bread. The cook is normally quite wonderful with our hot food, but you were an in-between-meals visitor. It won't be long before lunch is served, and it'll be something hot as always. I believe today is carrot and coriander soup, followed by delightful steak tartare. A fabulous, talented chef, and we are most grateful to have one here." Despite his overly friendly chatter and enthusiasm over food, he seems awkward now that we are down here, and I catch him glancing over his shoulder at our sleeping beauty, watching our departed medical student walk into her room and check on the equipment and levels. The door closes behind her quickly and dampens the noise back to a low hum that intensified when she opened it. I catch the doc pause for a second longer before a slight sag gives away a little tell.

"You knew her?" I ask brazenly, seeing a sadness as he turns back to me and a fake smile pops up to hide his obvious reaction. His expression clouding over a little, and despite my senses not being on form, I can almost taste the change in his mood. He looks at me oddly, eyes narrowing, and it's as though he goes to say something, then stops and falters, his mouth opening with no sound before he draws back, looks around once more, and leans in a little, lowering his tone. Only too aware of the female across the way.

"She was my friend. This was her project long before the war—the hybrid research. The learning about the rare wolves no one talks about. I never imagined she would end up being one of its inhabitants." His face reddens, and he shakes his head as though he can't quite believe he told me this. Mentally shaking himself, but

I won't let an opportunity pass me by, and I have to show he can trust me.

"He just left her here to rot. Juan, I mean, ... because she got sick?" I ask innocently, fully aware that upstairs he said there was nothing wrong with her mind, but I need to draw him into this gently. I need to win him over slowly.

"Sick? Hah! If that is the sickness to which you refer. Her mate has no interest in my research, but we serve a purpose that he needs to fulfill—keeping her alive and quiet. So, he pays the facility's bills, funds my grants, and leaves us to do whatever we want as long as she exists here, and we don't ask questions." His low, hushed voice signals that maybe he doesn't entirely trust either the female across the way or there are cameras down here. I sit up a little, pushing my hands under the edges of my legs, and change tactics. A common ground to show him I'm not about to run to Juan.

"I knew her too ... and her son ... I know him. Colton." I don't know why I hesitate to call him my destined mate, but the sharp, piercing stab to my heart before the word comes out stops me. Maybe because all I can think of when he comes to the forefront is that he has betrayed me and marked that bitch and is now her mate. I can't bear to say the word out loud. I swallow it down, the bitter taste almost making me gag.

"Ahh, yes, little Colton. Such a blessed boy. So many years since I laid eyes on that beautiful child. She was so very proud to bear a son, you know. She always wanted a child of her own, and the Fates blessed her, finally, with that little bundle of cheekiness while providing Juan the heir he was pressing for. His future legacy. He was such a little rebel as a pup, always climbing and running around when I visited the manor. I can't imagine what her being taken did to him. He loved her so very much." The faraway look, the distance as he locks onto a memory, and I slide down from the bed, motioning to the food tray so as not to make him think I'm coming at him, but I want to be closer, so he feels more able to talk freely in a hushed tone. I want to lull him into a sense of security and kill him with kindness.

"She struggled to conceive him?" I ask innocently, trying to direct the conversation and keep him engaged in what he assumes is a neutral topic. Get him talking. If I'm going to win him over to my side, I have to make him feel he can talk to me and not like I'm prying too much for answers to Sierra's current predicament. ' *You move around the prey to suss out the best angles and lull it into calmness before you pounce on it*' is something my grandfather always used to say. I'm curious, though, why a wolf would have issues with fertility, as it's not something we suffer with. We're physically perfect. Fertility is a given when the Fates decide it's your time to pup.

"Curse of some hybrids, I'm afraid. It's that when they mate with a pureblood, sometimes the pure genetics destroys the hybrid cells, and the child becomes non-viable. In vitro cell death. It's been so hard to reproduce with your kind because, as I said, your DNA destroys imperfections. An invasion of another species in the makeup is exactly like a virus in your body. It has a little war of its own and diminishes the fertile egg. Fascinating, yet heart-breaking, especially for her. Colton was her seventh, and I think it would have finally broken her had he died. Such a special boy." Not where Juan is concerned, he's not. That's a whole other thing.

I know he's said it twice now, but he can't be right about the hybrid thing. I mean, my mother had two planned pups, and she never mentioned issues in pregnancy or carrying us, so neither of my parents could have been hybrids, which means I'm not. And then there's the matter of Sierra ... she is a wolf.

"She can't be a hybrid. That makes no sense at all. Juan Santo is a pureblood who wouldn't tolerate that kind of union. His son's a pureblood; it's all he ever goes on about." Rolling my eyes without meaning to, a little anger spiking through as memory replays the whole superior, lording over the mountain bullshit. Juan's constant lord and king kick and preaching to the packs for decades about his family's traced pure line of genetics. The Santos pride themselves on being from the strongest lineage of wolves. He would never willingly take a mate who was anything less. I mean, look at his reaction to me and Colton's imprinting. That says it all!

The doc looks behind him, checking his assistant is engrossed in dealing with the machines before stepping inside my room, so the door slides shut behind him, lowering his tone.

"My dear, I fear I have said too much and inadvertently made your hope of release a less plausible outcome. You must forget what I said, especially about Luna Santo. It's in your best interest that we never had this conversation, and you do not repeat to anyone that we did." There's serious concern etched into his face that deepens the lines around his eyes, and he locks a direct gaze right on my eyes, a hint of warning in his tone. He's closing down our line of communication because he thinks what he's telling me puts me in danger. An indication that I was right about his character and him being the weak link in this facility. He's a decent man who cares, and I need to show him I'm already screwed so he doesn't lock me out.

"I imprinted on Colton, and Juan forbade it. We're fated, but he forced him to mark another for the pack's sake. I'm not getting set free. I'm probably going to end up like her, or worse. I'm a reject of the pack, a diluted bloodline that brings shame to his people, and the only reason he's coming here is to be done with me once and for all. Nothing you say makes a difference to what he's going to do to me. I'm not getting out." It's a harsh, hurried whisper, and I fall silent as I catch a glimpse over his shoulder of his assistant coming out of Sierra's room. Nodding her way to alert him, he seems completely dazed. Stiff and still and staring at me intensely.

"I'm done. I'll go up to the lab and run the new bloods they sent us from the south, Doctor." She calls to him from the hallway across the bay, and without looking back at her, he waves a hand dismissively, eyes locked on me most alarmingly. She takes that as an answer, nods, and walks off towards the elevator briskly to head back upstairs. The air in this room is suddenly heavy with tension.

"Imprinted? By the Fates? As in that rare form of bonding two souls, so they become insanely lust and love-driven to be forever together? I didn't think any Alpha had the authority to undermine that. It means you're linked to ... Sierra's bloodline?" His skin tone seems to pale noticeably, and his eyes darken weirdly. His mind is

307

racing over a million thoughts, and his forehead wrinkles deepen as his frown does—an air of mild nervousness kicking up around him.

"Yeah, well, Juan doesn't give a rat's ass about anything except his own authority, and Colton, he's so stuck in his shadow that he chose to let me go instead of honoring the bond. So I left, didn't look back and something brought me here instead. This wasn't a chance find ... this facility. I dreamed of her almost every night, and something pulled me here. I'd headed south, but something made me change and come east from my path. Sierra's voice calling or some stupid memory of a dream that wouldn't leave me alone." I offload on him now that his companion is in the elevator, and it feels good to say it to someone rather than be caught up in my own head—a gush of chatter that I've been turning over for days.

"Stop. Don't." The doc waves his hand at me, snapping me back to attention, and a wild-eyed, terrified look on his face as though I just told him I have a bomb under my ass. He turns abruptly, panicked, and slams the card against the wall panel to slide open the door, lacking graceful coordination. He steps out of the doorway, shaking his head and hands, and I follow, unsure why he's recoiling. His whole body is trembling as he emits a crazy amount of fear. I can taste it.

"What? Why? Do you think I'm lying?" The sudden rise of emotion in him has me on edge, too, and I panic that I'm scaring away my only ray of hope of escaping. He appears to be running away, but as he turns to close the door, the tear I catch in his eye silences me, and he pauses, taking a deep breath and lowering his hands. The open door between us keeping us a couple of feet apart, but his sadness overwhelms me.

"Eight years of silence. Eight years watching her sleep, eight years hoping that one day the things she said ... I'd accepted that my friend had lost her mind completely. Eight years ... and I convinced myself that her visions and stories were that of a madwoman, broken by a battle that convinced her that her mate was an evil player in some bigger plan, and her confinement here was a betrayal to silence her. Eight years justifying that she was better off asleep than to be tortured by an illness of the mind." I don't know if he's saying this to himself or me. His eyes are not on me, just glazed and distant as a single tear rolls down his cheek, and I'm so very confused.

"I don't understand. Upstairs, you said she was fine. She's been here longer than eight years. Colton said nine." Or was that including the war when he didn't see her in that timeframe because he never saw her when she came home? I don't know. Oh, God, please don't tell me she truly is broken, and this is all for nothing.

The thought crosses my mind. Things not adding up to what he said, and going around in circles, unable to piece it together logically. Maybe Sierra was sick, but then what the hell is he saying? He smiles sadly, his pale gray eyes finally landing on mine, and gives me a watery half-smile.

"If she was crazy, how could she tell me that one day a solitary she-wolf from the west would come to save us all from something coming? A future leader of her people, joined to her blood by the Fates. Maybe it's a coincidence, and maybe it's not. Maybe it's wishful thinking and guilt because I've let her lie there for eight long years. Don't you see?" He's babbling, but I pick out the points I think he's trying to connect.

"I came east from where I was, and I'm linked to her son," I repeat robotically, still looking at him with a quizzical expression and trying to figure out what his vague statements mean. He's lost in his head.

"Tell me. What does the name Marina mean to you?" He narrows his eyes on me, leaning in as though telling me a secret of the utmost importance, and her name falls off his tongue like a lead rod that stabs me in the heart.

I gasp at its utterance on this man's lips, my blood running cold as he says it, and I openly stifle a sob at the unexpected pain of hearing it. It was a name that died when she did, and no one has uttered it in a decade.

"She was ... my mother ..." I whisper painfully, that same rise of heartache anytime I think of her and have to stop my tears from breaking free.

He clasps a hand to his mouth as though I've uttered something sinful. His eyes widen in alarm, and he begins to breathe heavily. Backing away from me as something seems to click into place.

"I can't hear this because if this is what she said ... I've let my friend suffer in sleep all these years, alone; I failed her. I let him convince me she was mad, don't you see? I broke my oath. I broke my promise as her friend, and I'm a terrible person. I need to go. I don't want to know about any of this!" He pulls away, shaking visibly, crumbling, and avoids looking at me as panic grips him mercilessly. He's visibly distressed. His words falter as he babbles them out and he's once again running from me mentally.

"Wait ... don't go ... what about my mother? What do you know? How do you know her name? What did she say about her?!" I'm yelling after him, grasping for something I don't even know I'm chasing, as panic rises with being left with nothing but her name. My door slides quickly shut as he departs and traps me inside this chamber because I was too slow to lurch forward. He isn't looking back but fleeing across the concrete floor until he gets mid-way between mine and hers on the way to the elevator.

"I'm sorry. I truly am." He cries it at me as I slam my hands on the glass, trying to get the door to open, pressing hard against it so I can see him as he runs off to my left.

"I need to know what she said about my mother!!" I scream it like a wild banshee, my emotions overwhelming me as so many racing thoughts rush through my head, and I'm consumed with suspicion, pain, and heartbreak, all weighing down like a house falling on top of me. My breathing is erratic, and I pound the glass aggressively in sheer need to follow him. It shudders and quakes but doesn't budge an inch.

I can't calm down. The craziness of that interaction has me all wired and panting as emotion wracks me, and my thoughts spiral crazily with so many possibilities for such little information. The mention of my mother, his reaction made me react in ways I never have before. I start pacing, pulling at my hair as I try to self-calm and focus.

I upset him, so he ran off, but maybe he'll come back; perhaps he needs time to process and calm as I do. Maybe it was a shock that something she told him now appears to be coming true. He said visions, but wolves, they don't have those, and maybe that's what triggered him. A fear that she could, and did, and now I'm here, and I came east, and I'm linked.

Oh, God, it's all so messy in my head, so I can't even imagine what's going on in his if this is something she told him over eight years ago. I mean, to us, the Fates and coincidence are common, and we trust in the paths they lay for us with so little questioning of it, but humans have a more challenging time accepting or believing. So many nowadays don't even believe in God, let alone some supernatural higher power that always has a plan. He'll calm down, rationalize, and come back to explain why he knew my mother's name. I mean, that's what he'll do, right? That's what I'm praying for, anyway.

Something strikes a chord in everything I said, and now I need to know more. I have to learn more. I need to find out what Sierra told him all those years ago that got her sent here and pushed into a coma. Juan keeps her quiet by convincing people she's crazy, so I want to know what that is. Especially if my mother's name is in there somewhere, and she knew I would come, be linked to her son. How could she know that? Wolves can't see the future. Only witches and seers and ... Oh, God!

This hybrid crap and Colton being a long-awaited child. None of that could be true because Juan would never value a mixed breed child the way he does his son. Especially not a witch. They are the sorcerers and demons of the supernatural world with a kind of voodoo you don't fuck with. Unless he doesn't know. But that can't be if he knew about this place and the research and left her here. She wanted to know how she could be both witch and wolf and find others like her for whatever reason. Maybe she wanted to know how to conceive a child without it dying. Juan had to have known she wasn't pure, which made even less sense given how he acted.

Witches and seers are more like humans but with insanely powerful gifts. Sierra surely couldn't be a half-witch. That's crazy.

She couldn't hide something like that from the pack all those years, and why doesn't Colton have any of those gifts? You would know if he could conjure magic and catch visions. But then she's here. A witch has power, so why didn't she save herself?

Maybe he didn't know when he mated to her, and perhaps when he found out, that's why he banished her here, so the pack would never know and revolt against an Alpha mated to an impure. I've never heard of anything like this, and it explains his obsession with making sure Colton has the right Luna. Maybe he's afraid Colton isn't pure enough, and it will show in his offspring if he mates badly. Colton can't have any knowledge of it; I would have seen it in our joined memories.

None of this makes sense. Luna Sierra was in the pack for decades before she had Colton, so surely that can't be the reason Juan brought her here. He would have known. You can't hide anything from your mate. Her memories in transference when he marked her would have made sure he knew. Which means *he* hid what she was. But after decades of living that lie, why would he then suddenly banish her to the back of beyond. And what the hell has my mother got to do with any of this?

My head spins with all of this, a pulse hitting my brain's center with overload and aching so badly I feel like my skull might explode. I end up pacing back to the bed and falling face down on top of it with an 'arghh' noise that reverberates through my entire body it's so loud. All the doc has done is give me more questions than answers, and I roll on my side to see her across the gap. The lights have shut down out there, so she's illuminated in the light from her cell.

"What are you not telling me, Sierra? Why am I here? What are you, and what the hell am I?" I call to her as though somehow it will give me an answer, but she remains still and silent in her cocooned state, and I exhale heavily. My body is trembling with adrenaline as I begin to calm down, but tears fill my eyes. It's not sadness, really, but confusion, frustration, and a gnawing pit of unease that there are things I know nothing of, which have everything to do with why I was guided here in the first place.

I've lost my appetite, no longer interested in the food he left while my head is going crazy with all of this, and I know one thing for sure—I just lost my ally. I chased him away, and I only have two days before Juan shows up to deal with me.

I have zero chance of romancing Deacon in that time, even if I wanted to try. Not that I could. He physically makes my skin crawl, and I don't think I have it in me to be nice to the asshole that darted me in the back like a white liver-bellied coward.

I cross my arms over my head and face to smother out the light and noise and sigh at the situation I find myself in. Willing my brain to stop spinning around, turning inside out, and to give me a few seconds of peace to get my bearings. For the love of the Fates!! It feels like it's been the longest day in history, and, according to the doc, it's not even lunchtime yet.

What I wouldn't give to be anywhere but here right now. Maybe reverse the clock, go back to my Awakening ceremony, and run before I turn to save myself from all the bullshit that has happened since. It was the worst turning point of my life, and I can blame all of it on the bloodline of Santo. I curse that name forevermore. I should have left a long time ago and never waited to turn.

No Colton, no imprinting, no running to the mountains, and no attacks by vampires playing on my mind. Just sheer ignorance of a girl running free and turning alone, knowing none of these people or caring. I should have found the courage to go long before I did and saved myself the heartache.

"Alora?"

I nearly jump out of my skin at the sudden closeness of the doc's voice and almost topple entirely off the bed as I realize he's right beside me. My lack of wolf sense let him creep right up to me with zero warning. My heart misses a beat and almost kills me in the process.

"You scared the shit out of me!" I snap impulsively, taking in the bloodshot eyes, the pale pallor, and the strong hint of alcohol on his breath that I'm sure he knocked back hastily to level himself out. He looks a little chaotic and shell-shocked, to say the least, and there's no sign of his female companion.

"Quite." He replies tartly, and I can tell by his manner that he isn't okay. Or it's his weird British response to what I shouted at him.

I pull myself up to sit and eye him warily as he stands stock still in the center of my room, staring at me as though I have two heads. He twists his hands together, wringing his fingers, and I give him a moment to pull himself together.

"There are no cameras down here. They like to pretend she isn't here, you see ... the wolves, upstairs. They don't venture down very often, so they don't have to acknowledge their shameless purpose of guarding this place. Lord knows we didn't need chaperones when Luna Sierra was in charge. Just me and my staff to take care of her, mostly from upstairs. They weren't here before she was put to sleep, so they think she's in a coma and life support of her own accord, and her rich husband benefactor is paying to keep her comfortable." He walks around in a circle, and I watch him quietly, feeling the anxious waves and deep emotions coming from him intensely. I'm wary about sending him running once more, but he came back, and I have one question I need him to answer before we go any further.

"Why did you ask me about my mother ... Marina?" I say it solemnly, heart hitching at the use of her name, breathing in slowly and deeply to stop the spiraling emotions that run through me, and I note that my hands are trembling. I'm nervous, reacting in a subtle wave of anxious anticipation like I'm perched on the edge of a cliff, and one tiny breeze will knock me off and change everything I have ever known about my life. I don't know why, but I can feel it weighing down on this moment like I should stop, turn, and run far away.

He stops his frantic pacing and turns to me completely. Eyes wide, face serious, and he implores me with a widespread of palms as though apologizing as the words come out clearly.

"She's the reason Sierra is here. Juan executed every one of your bloodlines so they would never return to your mountain, and she tried to stop him."

THE PAST

"What?" it's like every cell in my body stops as a deathly silence fills the air, shock stilling my thoughts, my lungs ceasing to move, and you can hear a pin drop as his words sink in slowly—so fucking slow.

Juan executed my family. They didn't die in battle.

That's a lie. It can't be true because they weren't the only pack never to return. The entire Whyte line, among others, all died protecting our kind. For God's sake, it was a war, and we had many casualties. Did Juan kill them all, too?

The doc has to be playing me, lying to mess with my head for some kind of ulterior motive, and I'm falling for it. Perhaps I was wrong to trust him, and this is all a ploy to break me down and get intel he thinks I may have ... but how would he know her name? Maybe it's a test to see if I'm strong enough to turn, despite being in this isolation tank.

I take a much-needed breath as I begin to suffocate under the pressure of my mounting emotions, realizing I wasn't inhaling or letting it go. I take a moment to let it sink in, my head spinning as my brain tries to dissect and make sense of each word and how it comes together with what he just said. I don't know how to react; cry, rage, scream, laugh? I sit here like a numb deadweight staring at him as though he just told me the world is ending and we're to wait here to die. Momentarily devoid of feeling as shock fills the void.

316

It has a different effect on my body, though, and I think I might throw up for a second. I wretch, my body lurching, and as it all spins out of control, I have to lift my heels to the edge of the bed so I can prop my head between my knees to ground myself. Swallowing down the rush of salvia that clogs my throat and breathing through the waves of nausea.

"I'm sorry ... my memory is not what it was, but the gist is that Juan was eliminating the possibility of a prophecy coming to fruition ... a white wolf Queen, rising from the shadows to reign the people in a victorious and united future. Juan believed your mother would dethrone him after she proved herself a worthy warrior on the battlefield and led many a victorious attack on your enemy by uniting the packs. Your kind was losing the war, and she turned it around ... your mother. She was gifted, special, and more powerful than he could ever dream of being. The kind of specimen I could only dream of being able to study." He sounds concerned, regretful, apologetic, all at once, but it's all meaningless noise, and I just keep coming back to it, over and over.

Juan ... he killed them all. My whole family. All those that mattered to me. My past ten years have been a lie, and I suffered, not because they failed, but because he took them from me. This can't be true, especially not if she was so powerful.

"Then how did he ... if she was ...." The words die on my tongue, hastily uttered in a breath as my brain tries to rationalize the details, as warm salty tears roll down my cheeks, and I sit absorbing a history I never knew as the pieces are laid out before me. I am confused by the conflicting statement of what I've always been told, and a fire of rage is building inside me slowly to overcome the icy cold that has spread through my nerve endings. It's like a drip, drip, as it's fed and allowed to grow slowly. It warms my belly and spreads across my pelvis and down my limbs, something growing inside me so all-consuming that I almost welcome its warm, fluid expansion to my cold, empty soul. My brain just cannot seem to filter and arrange it to make sense.

"Your father was her weak point. Just a peaceful land-dwelling wolf he murdered to get to her. Your kind's devastating ability to

317

kill both mates with one blow, and sadly an uneven pairing as that was her only downfall. It's a rather sad travesty that even your strongest is only as strong as the mate bonded to them in the end and highlights the importance of why they shun the impure. He then ordered his sub-pack to hunt down and kill everyone from the pack she was residing with in case they linked in the last moments and knew of his treason. He had to tidy up loose ends, you see. He had to cover his tracks, and only his 'loyal' knew what he'd done and aided him."

I inhale sharply, my heart constricting as tears bite my eyes and the words wound my soul. Sliced open and ravaged with a more devastating truth than the one I lived for ten years.

None of the Whyte pack returned from war, as they were apparently cursed as warriors and fell at the first battle. They are not strong enough, fast enough, and unable to hold their own because they are weak land workers and not warriors at all.

All lies.

All slaughtered by Juan and his trusted sub-pack, his elders, his closest. Those he now wears like a shroud to lead from behind on the mountain. Which meant Sierra saw it all too, as his Luna; she was by his side at all times and followed him into battle. None of them jumped to defend her because they were just as guilty as her mate.

My mother, father, brother, and grandparents are all gone at Juan's hand, and I cannot contain the fury growing within me as my mind puts the pieces together, and it all adds up. The return of the wolves saw everything change, and they ripped children like me away from guardian families who had vowed to care for us and pushed us into that home, except for me. Vampires slaughtered my guardians, the last of the Whytes, in the middle of the night. I now wonder if that was a lie, too.

We went from being cared for, cherished by wolves who opened their homes to us, all while our families fought, to being almost outlawed in a way. By Santo wolves who spread the word that the war was nearly lost because of our bloodlines. They told them not to respect us as the remaining legacy of fallen heroes but to leave us to fade out and kill an impure invasion on future generations. They started the second they returned, pushing all of us into that dark side of the mountain and maintaining we were cursed.

Why didn't he just kill me, too?

Words fail me, and I stare at the doc as I lift my head, catching the wariness in his eye as he sees my expression and hesitates about moving away a little.

My heart is pounding, my breathing shallow, and a twisting knife of pain devours me as it sinks in and courses through every cell of my body that Juan did the most unthinkable thing of all: broke our laws and killed his own. Killed mine and my own! For what fucking reason!!

A prophecy about a rising wolf? A story? A fable that hadn't even come to fruition. He thought *he* could overpower the Fates, take what he wanted, and push things in his way?

It's almost as if the doc can feel my questioning, or maybe it's my silent, deathly manner as I sit up stock straight and lower my chin to glare hatefully across his shoulder at the Luna beyond. It's not a look at her; it's at everything I'm now finding out and can't control. He betrayed her, just as he betrayed his entire people. My family. He betrayed his own son.

"Sierra was meant to be his answer—a hybrid witch and wolf. He thought that searching out this white queen and mating her would assure him the power he longs for. Sierra is a black wolf, though, something he overlooked as a minor detail, and when their tale did not push them into the path of the story he thought was rightfully his, he took matters into his own hands.

The rising of your mother made him insane. Upon returning from the wars, they wiped the books free of any hint of a prophecy, forbidding the Shamans from teaching it to the young. He rewrote history to hide it. He pushed all traces of what he did into a coma to silence her for her treason." His voice is tight, tension hitching, and I can taste his nervousness as he backs away, shuffling out of my way to give me a clear view of the lifeless soul I'm fixated on.

My whole being poised like I'm on the verge of lashing out and ripping this room to shreds, such is the crazy hate and anger coursing through me, and I clutch the bed viciously to hold myself in check. I am torn between mounting fury and heartbreaking, crippling devastation. If I could turn, I would already be ripping this facility apart with the intensity of everything I feel inside me. A storm raging to be set free, yet my heart aches to the point I think it may stop beating under the force of pressure. An agony incomparable to anything, and my entire truth crumbles like ash around the ruins of my fire.

"He knew Sierra was a mixed breed. He knows he destroyed something decided by the Fates. Does he think he has that power? That worth?" I snarl; my voice is unrecognizable as this feeds my desire to combust in a tornado of destruction. I never knew I could harbor so much longing to find one man, hunt him down, and enjoy ripping him limb from limb. Slowly and painfully.

I can almost taste it, that want to have it. The bloodlust is coursing through me in hot waves as I visualize that narcissistic asshole and what I'm going to do to him when he gets within an inch of me. Body bristling and goose bumping, my heart rate rising, and my lungs quickening to accommodate my rapid breathing.

"Yes. It was by design that he sought her out and traveled far to find her. Sweeping her off her feet and mating to her so he could possess her for eternity. He thought he could fulfill and control the prophecy and further his desire to rule. She was a relatively isolated wolf, naïve, unloved, her pack rejecting her because of her roots, and she fell straight into the arms of the first genuine love shown to her. She was known as a witch, and you know they're as much a wolf's enemy as the vampires, which made her a cursed and fearful species. She told me she fell madly in love and didn't find out about his ulterior motive until she had been his for many months and already bound by the mate bond." He looks towards her, a sad, distant glaze to his glassy eyes as he remembers their conversations and the regret of not believing her when he should have.

"So, how did she end up here? If she had powers ... witches are strong. You said she tried to stop him, so why couldn't she?" I'm

320

devilishly low-toned, controlled, the growl coming through in my voice, leaning to anger to avoid the pain inside me, and I can feel my inner wolf tossing and turning with the frustrating need to be set free. It's sharpening its claws and begging to be uncaged.

"She betrayed him by sacrificing her own life to protect a child who can regain the balance of things. Sierra is a seer and a witch. Yes, she has powers unlike any wolf, but they are not strong like a warrior. They are useful for protection on a small scale, and she has abilities to control certain aspects of others. She's a healer, not a fighter, and she did what she thought could make a difference."

"Meaning?" I turn to him fully and lock onto him, seeing him swallow hard. His mistrust of my current behavior is written all over him. At this moment, he's afraid of me, and he's nervously spewing words to try to diffuse it or to keep me focused on anything other than turning on him. Even without my wolf sense, I can smell the terror coming in waves from him. It's not intentional, but these feelings are bigger than me, and I have no will to reel them in right now. It is fractured and seeping, and I don't know how to stop it from pouring out and pooling around me like a dense smog.

"She got to you before Juan did. Ran and left the pack on their return to your lands. She bound her blood to you, so you became linked to her and completely protected from being slain, too, thus meaning he could never kill you. And if he tried to isolate and imprison you, his pack would have asked why. What did a child do? All these years, this story haunted me as nothing more than the imagining of a fractured mind, torn by the horror and atrocities she witnessed, and yet here you stand—the child of Marina. Just like she said you would. Alora, I am so sorry. Please, you must understand that had I known there was any truth in it, I would never ... " His absolute honest despair comes through in torn rawness, but it's not my concern right now. I can't feel anything for his sorrow or his heartache, while there's only chaos and a need to avenge them all.

"Why can't I remember that? If she bound to me, then why don't I see her in my memory?" I snap, interrupting his apologies, too caught up in my pain and misery and needing to hurt something, to care about him and his regrets. It doesn't change the now or how I got here.

"She bound your memory, your gifts, and that of her son to protect you all, for she feared Juan would even see challenge to his position in his child, should he have inherited her gifts too. As I said, she has certain abilities. She said the time would come when she would give back to you that which she took. I assume she means those. Not just yours, but Colton's too." He falters, his voice trembling, wringing his hands in nervousness, and I jump up and stalk past him to push my hands against the glass. My head is torn with the addition of even more to this story.

Colton has other gifts too? Bound? And me ... is she the reason I can't seem to grasp my skills and gain any control because I'm always fighting some kind of spell that keeps them dormant?

How is that helpful? Especially now, when she's like a corpse, sleeping through the years and can't do anything to help physically.

My body is aching to turn and trying to revert to wolf, but this damn building is strong and keeping it in check, no matter how hard it wails and howls within me. I bang the glass, the torture of it getting too much, and watch the shudder traveling from my palm and spreading out the whole expanse of the invisible wall. It does nothing to ease the inner war.

"Bound my gifts? My memories? How could she ... that's impossible. I have gifts. I'm still learning, but they're not tied down completely. Colton has his gifts too, and he's more than capable of using them. His Alpha strength, his speed, his dominance. He can command with a tone. It can't be true. No one has ever documented a witch binding a wolf's natural gifts." It's a rebuff of what he's saying as I mentally try to dismiss them as lies, focused entirely on her and willing her to get up and tell me this herself— lying there like a weak, powerless fool who let her mate destroy everything in our lives.

Get up, Sierra! Get the fuck up!! You owe me this truth yourself, from your own mouth!!!

It's anger at her, but it's born out of fear, churning up to douse the inferno of molten rage. That all of this is too much and bigger

322

than me. I don't want this burden of weight or this story to be mine. I want to go back to the mountain, to the home, to disappear into the shadows and be a girl no one noticed again. I was safe and ignorant, and it didn't hurt like this. It wasn't some precipice of danger and had me teetering on the edge and looking down into the abyss, knowing I'm never going to be safe or okay ever again. It's all too much, and I'm only a child. Eighteen, barely grown. I don't want this!

"No, my dear. Colton will also carry the gifts of his mother. Our research has repeatedly proven that hybrids have a mixture, every time—just like you. His non-wolf side is in there but bound up tight. And you, you cannot harness your full potential if she has bound you. The gifts are maybe strong enough to show at times, but she was a capable witch. I don't doubt her spells serve the purpose she intended. Her spells brought her a child when her body failed to carry Juan's seed. If she can overcome that, she can bind a child in protection until she's ready to release you." He whispers it, such is his fear of me, of being heard telling me, of these people, of Juan, and I glance his way to find him almost pressed into the corner and watching me in wide-eyed apprehension. He, too, knows that there is no coming back from this now that he's opened Pandora's box.

"Then how do I get her to do that if she's over there sleeping her life away?" I fix him with a stare, sniffing back watery tears I hadn't noticed were pouring down my cheeks, my heart numbing out and my mind moving into a state of shock. Calming me but making that sense of hopelessness grow.

"I don't know. This facility has a guard count of nineteen. Even though none of you can use your gifts within, I'm sure you will be no match to nineteen strong men—armed ones—even if you are somewhat terrifying when mad." It's a nervous half-laugh as he tries to lighten the tension. It dies on his lips as I continue to stare at him and lower my hands from the glass as I try to steady my breathing, so it's less erratic and self-soothe, wiping my face with the back of my hands to pull myself together.

"You need to let me out. I need to find that son of a bitch and show him what my mother failed to do. You don't mess with my family! I can't stay here. I can't be here when he comes now." I snarl again, a spike of anger returning, knowing my emotions cloud my judgment and are all over the place, but I don't care. I was just told that everything they led me to believe my entire childhood was a lie, and my bloodline wasn't diluted and weak. My mother was a prophesied warrior destined to lead her people.

And Juan murdered her.

He killed all of them. Every single person I loved, cared for, and knew as my pack. A clan of Whyte wolves. To silence us.

That sniveling, slimy, power-mad freak slew them all. He's going to rue the day he chose to leave me alive. Now it all makes sense; why they threw me with the other orphans and shunned us as a whole. That was our punishment for him being unable to get at me the way he wanted. That was how he figured he could keep me down and separate from the people, so I would have no chance of rising and leading them against him. And if I did, he could put it down to me being hateful and holding a grudge for ten years as an outcast and nothing more than an impure taste for revenge at her failings. So clever.

He made sure I was alone and didn't care if he smeared many innocents in the process. None of the rejects deserved to be thrown out there with me. They were just a cover to enhance and strengthen his lies. He convinced the packs that our fallen heroes were cursed blood to conceal his actions against my people further. No one would ask questions or defend us if their Alpha was telling them we were the failed diluted lineage of weak wolves. He's deluded, cruel, and so consumed with his own need to rule that we were all pawns and had no real value. He's no Alpha. He doesn't care about the people, and he never did. He just wants to rule them in whatever way he can.

It must have wholly enraged him to near madness when the Fates imprinted me on his son, despite his multi-level plan's measures and precautions, and it's all falling into place. He knew they didn't saddle Colton with a useless Luna. He was afraid that in a position of being absorbed into the pack, and as future Luna to my Alpha mate, I would still find a way to rise and dethrone everything he's worked for. Juan was afraid that I would outshine him and tear his power from under his feet with very little effort at all, much like my mother.

Colton was my way in, and he does what he does to that boy to stop him from ever finding his strength. He manipulated him emotionally; he used Colton's devotion, loyalty to his father, and compassion and love for his people's needs to get in his head. The fact that he tore his mother away has always kept him to heel and lingers in the back of Colton's mind. He was afraid I would leave our people alone like she did, leave him when he still needed me. He was scared I wouldn't be strong enough, that he wouldn't be able to keep me safe like he couldn't keep his mom safe, and he couldn't accept the Fates' decision.

Colton was protecting me, believing the lies and the manipulation same as everyone else and seeing no other way. He's young, unsure about his worth and power, and he listened to someone meant to guide him for the best. His faith in his father's intentions is not a flaw, just naïvety that comes from a good soul. His father has been playing him since the day he was born, and his mother had to conceal who he really is for fear his natural gifts would make him the target of his father's hunger for power.

My heart breaks at how angry I've been at him when seeing it from this angle makes so much sense. Colton is nothing like his father, and he doesn't know that his father has no intention of ever relinquishing his position to his son until death takes him.

I'm going to be the last thing Juan sees, no matter what it does to me in the process. I'll get out of here, and *I will* level the balance. I'll kill that son of a bitch. Even if Colton tries to stop me because his own heart won't be able to let someone destroy his father, no matter what he did. I'm going to rip that mountain apart and shred every single wolf who knew or had a part in the demise of my bloodline. Even if Colton never forgives me.

"Dear girl, calm down and be smart about this. Your Fates wouldn't have brought you here just to leave again and start a one-woman war. You came for Sierra ...." The doc's words die on his lips as the beep of the elevator interrupts, and he flashes a look that way, panic overtaking his expression as he jumps up and shoos me away from the glass at a pretty impressive speed for a human. It's so rapid he makes me jump back from the wall in reaction.

"Get on the bed and lie down. NOW!" He snaps it at me, losing that feeble, weak cower he had going on, and I listen, despite my turbulent mood. His haste and urgency moving me.

I turn, take a few steps, and jump on the bed as the doors make that whooshing opening noise of the elevator and approaching footsteps. He comes to me quickly, yanking up my arm as I lay down and pushing the stethoscope from his neck under the edge of my medical gown neckline.

"Heart's racing, my dear; you should practice counting to ten and take deep, relaxing breaths. That kind of anxiety is not good for the heart. You're in a safe place, have no fears." He's facing me, his voice joyfully fake, but his eyes dart to the side as someone approaches the glass, and I try to focus all my attention on acting normal.

"I've been looking for you. You're needed upstairs right now. Leave this mutt alone; you have an actual job to do. Some of your fresh samples have been delivered in iceboxes. I'm sure you don't want to leave them to go bad." It's Deacon, my most favorite person in the whole wide world, and with the pulsing rage I have going on, I tense and try to sit up, instincts taking over and ready to take him on more than ever. The doc slams his hand on my chest and aggressively flattens me down.

"Just a moment!" He grits it through his teeth, eyeballing me wildly and mouthing the word NO. That scowling frown of a paternal telling off, and he keeps me under control. He gets a narrow-eyed snarl in response, but I obey and lie back down. I watch as he moves out of my line of sight and exposes Deacon on the outside of the glass.

"Now! We haven't got all day!" Deacon snaps at him, obviously not happy when the doc questions his authority. I glare directly at the jerk, catching his eye and making a point of staring right through him. He takes it with no expression and stares right back at me, not breaking contact.

"Of course. Miss Alora, please eat and dress as it will make you far more comfortable and ready for my return to continue our tests. We have so much still left to do." He throws me an odd look, and I glance his way for a second, impulsively nodding before he turns and heads out, leaving me with a strong sense that was a hint.

I watch him walk out, and as he gets to the door, he turns and nods at the trolley and the bag as though reconfirming it, and I frown, unsure what he intends to do, but obedience seems like a good idea.

GET UP

It feels like it's been hours since the doc left, and I did exactly as I was told. I ate the food, dressed in the grey sweatpants and sweater, and put on the socks and oversized boots, which baffled me entirely as to why I needed them and all the undergarments in the bag. I'm now pacing my cell, wondering if I imagined they had any importance. Maybe he was just being thoughtful and giving me items to aid comfort, and I was looking for something that was not there because I was so desperate for an out. I rummaged in the bag and food, wondering if maybe he left something for me, like a key card, and came up with nothing except confusion, convincing myself I imagined it completely.

I can't stay here like this, watching her sleep the day away, and if all he is going to do is take tests and fill me in with stories that screw up my head, then this is hopeless. I'm trying to process all of it, and I can't swallow it right now, so I do what I do best and push it to one section of my brain for a later date when I can handle how awful it makes me feel. Right now, I need to stay focused and find a way out of here on my own.

When Juan gets here, I'm useless against him and his men and can't do crap about anything, especially not him, as long as this damn building holds my ability to turn captive. And Sierra over there 'hey, thanks for rendering my gifts useless at a time in my life that I could actually really be using them, and then getting yourself knocked out so I can't access them. Stellar planning!'

328

What kind of seer is that? A seer who doesn't predict the possibility of not being able to give a girl back what's hers if your beloved mate comatose you! And what kind of witch binds her child and leaves them motherless for ten years if she saw it all coming? If Colton could see things and not be bound, maybe he could have found her a long time ago and avoided all of this. None of this was smart planning on her part. It's seriously messed up.

I try to stop my erratic mind brewing, only to watch that same female come and tend to Sierra's machines, stopping my manic foot-stomping around my small space. She disappears just as quickly, without looking my way. I can sense her apprehension the whole time she's in there. Keeping her eyes averted, obviously uncomfortable they have a prisoner down here, and I watch closely what she does before scampering off, acting like I wasn't over here staring. Not that she did much to watch. Pressed some buttons, checked some fluids, moved Sierra's bed up and down, and rearranged her position to avoid sores. Prop her pillows, turn her on her side before pressing more buttons, change her bedsheet, and leave her alone again—basic care and nothing too exciting. I guess I'm thankful they do at least show her some compassion and tend to her frequently, turning her and such.

No matter how much I stand and glare at Sierra, like some kind of creepy psychopath, nothing is waking that woman up, let alone willpower. I can't imagine what eight years in an induced coma has done to her, to be honest. What state her mind and body would be if we woke her up and now? I doubt if that is plausible at all. For all I know, the drugs over the years have wasted her mind to mush, anyway. Her body has been inactive for so long that I'm assuming instant recovery is not going to happen, or if it's even possible to wake her after so long. In a building where her powers are bound, she's basically mortal and susceptible to all the damage and harm an induced coma could do to a human in eight years.

Not to mention the fact she's lost almost a decade of her life; what would be the consequences of waking her now? The last time she saw Colton, he was a nine-year-old boy, and now he's a stocky, arrogantly handsome man ... or has the makings of one, at least.

That's bound to confuse her and disorientate her if she wakes up, and ten years ago was just yesterday in her mental timeframe. The world has changed so much, and her mate has brought our mountain to ruin during that time: class and worth divide our people, and the Santos rule with fear.

Maybe I'm not supposed to wake her up. Perhaps she left another way to get back my gifts, and I just had to find her?

My train of thought is interrupted as a lunch trolley is pushed down from the elevator and left outside my door shortly after the woman exits, but the guard, another Santo looking asshole, shrugs at me with a distasteful smug expression, butts up against the glass with his shoulder and lets his eyes walk over me lazily. Pure creep oozing from every pore. It's the idiot who was sitting at the desk upstairs when Deacon informed him I was to be fed the same mealtimes as the rest of the facility.

"I was told to give you lunch, but Doc stopped me and said you can't eat anything until he's taken some sample, so ... I guess I leave it here and it gets cold—enjoy. Not that I would advise eating it later." He smirks, clearly happy with his sad position of power. He is a total omega wolf, low pecking order, and looking for any kind of upper hand to scrape him from the bottom.

I scowl at him, the smell of steak and soup wafting through the glass, and even though he thinks he's getting some sort of power kick by leaving it out of reach, I don't even want it. I ate the food earlier, and it confuses me that the doc would insist I ate that and not this. It's not been long enough to feel hungry yet. I don't get the sudden urge to tell me *not* to eat now.

I guess Deacon has briefed his sub-pack on who and what Juan says I am, and they are all part of the Alora fan club right now, given the way this asshole is acting. I can almost taste his dislike and the creepy way he's eyeing me up like the main course on his dinner menu, giving me bad vibes. He reminds me of that jerk Damon who used to watch me all through school and tried to get at me in the hallway for a grope and forced kiss. He was a perverted creep who liked control over girls, much like this idiot.

"Why don't you have it? You could use some extra energy boosts. I mean, if the chase in the forest was anything to go by." I give him the same friendly passive-aggressive attitude that I give Deacon, and he grins, ear to ear, as though he's too stupid to realize it was a dig. Annoyingly smug, and if he weren't such a jerk, he would be kind of cute, in the whole Colton way.

Damn, I need to stop doing that. Comparing every hot dark-skinned Latino to him then finding fault because it's not him. I get it. I still give a rat's ass, and I still miss him constantly, and every dark-haired, dimple-cheeked, and dreamy-eyed, hot Colombian, brings him back to the forefront; but God—timing. If he were Colton, he would let me out in a heartbeat, and he would never throw such a smug look at me for something so absurd. If Colton were here, he would know what to do about this whole mess. He always seems wiser, like he has all the answers, and would probably be handing this idiot his genitals back about now.

I can't fault that part of Colton, even when he was a jerk in our youth. Apart from that one time when he shoved me out of his way for epically tripping in front of him and his entire rabid crew, he was never an ass to people for no reason. He was always so effortlessly superior and seemed aloof and quiet like he was better than us. It was all in the looks he gave rather than the verbal content, but I guess he has an intimidating way about him, even when he doesn't mean it.

He was a proper bro type who hung with his pack, played sports, and walked around like Danny from the movie Greece. Everyone looked up to him and kissed his ass when he waltzed by. I guess maybe he was not very sociable with those outside of his sub pack because that's not who I know now, and his memories don't show an asshole like that either. Colton doesn't like to get close to people outside his circle. I guess it's because he lost so many in the war and his mother.

He has a wall up and keeps everyone outside his pack on the other side of it. I think it's why he tries so hard to make his father proud; he loves him, even if he's not worthy of being loved, and that's not Colton's fault. That's Juan's. Colton's flaw is trying to be

331

this perfect Santo wolf, with a weight of responsibility on his shoulders that one day he will lead. He follows the rules, the laws, and the Alpha's word without conflict, as he's meant to, and even puts all of that over his own desires. I guess a leader has to be that way, innate greatness, where his heart can't always lead, and it only further cements the fact that he'll be the best for his people one day, but for us, not so much.

I get back to my previous activity when smiley, smug guard walks off, getting bored with my disinterest in him, and I go back to pacing the room and looking for any kind of tool, or valuable item, to get out. It didn't last long and enforced that he's an omega and low on the scale of things. Used to being ignored and dismissed, he quietly slinks off. Thankfully, as I have no mind space for asshats. I'm uptight, worn thin, and agitated about my current predicament, with so many warring emotions coming at me from my mind.

The cupboards are full of medical crap, bandages, and nothing even sharp or useful. It's practically an empty room, and anything with real weight is bolted down into concrete floors with steel pins. There's nothing that could be of any real use, let alone as a weapon of sorts, and I end up throwing my cushions against the glass in frustration when my anger bubbles up and I can't contain it anymore.

I have so many swirling emotions I don't know what to do with. Vibrating energy pulsing through my core, and I'm mentally up and down and all over the place. One second, I want to cry, lie down and sob, and then the next, I'm angry, furious, boiling over, and want to slash Juan into a thousand tiny, bloody pieces for everything that brought me here and my entire life since they went to war. Just when it feels like it reaches overwhelming levels and I can't breathe for the suffocating need to expel this hatred physically, in the next breath, I'm calm and logical and trying to plan a way out. I can't keep up, and it's exhausting.

Time alone to think and let it sink in has done nothing except get me riled and upset, and yes, I've cried buckets. I sat in a huddle in the corner for a good twenty minutes and sobbed my heart out while it felt like it was breaking again, much like when I left Colton

332

and found myself alone without him and had no choice but to keep going. Soon as the doc left, it was all I could do—for me, my mother, brother, and father, family, and pack. For the mate I can never have.

I cried until my nose ran, and I couldn't breathe, and I drenched the upper part of my gown because I was still wearing it at that point, and the cold wet spreading across my chest on thin fabric was strangely comforting. Mirroring how my soul felt and how it was seeping into every pore. I felt hopeless, weak, and broken, and I have no idea how to get past that.

It was for Colton and Sierra, too, for their pain, loss, and this whole goddamn mess. For the life I should have had, the family I should have still been with, and the mate I would have imprinted on and been allowed to be with. It would have still been Colton. That's what the Fates decided a long time ago, but I would never have had to leave him, and I would be with him now, safe in his arms and calmed by his touch. Guided by that wise part of him that always seems to know what's going on. Only it failed him when he needed that gift the most.

I miss him so much it kills me, even if I can't get past what he's done to our bond, and he still breaks me. It adds to my urgency in looking around for some kind of pointer on what to do. I shake myself and remind myself that the girl I was she's dead. Little Alora of the Whyte pack at Elren farm, peacefully living a carefree life. The war saw her parents' unplanned departure, and Juan saw they never returned. She died a long time ago when her life was turned upside down, altering everything she knew. Her path disintegrated, and all those dreams and hopes fluttered away in the breeze.

That unwanted, rejected, and feeble little no one who imprinted on a boy ten years later, who stood in her place—also dead! She couldn't be allowed to love her fated mate because of what she was. She never really existed anyway. She was a lie that was fed to me and made me live under a mask of my own making because I never knew the truth, and this girl, this one right here, she's the Alora who's been holding her breath and waiting for me to find her.

She's the daughter of a warrior. The daughter of a prophetic Queen who was slain for her power. She's the heroine of a prophecy, and she's a goddamn white wolf with red eyes, which makes her some kind of hybrid with gifts. Gifts that a witch thought so powerful, she bound them until a time came when she needed to get them back. A witch who sacrificed her life and her son's sanity to protect her. She's someone to be reckoned with; she needs to find a way to bloom.

That doesn't sound like any kind of weak no one to me, not a reject, or unworthy of an Alpha mate, and I need to own that shit. A black cloud of shame and failure has overshadowed everything I've done in my life for the past ten years, and believe I was never good enough because they told me so—but now it's gone. Almost like someone lifted that lid and finally uncaged my soul. There's nothing over my head weighing me down now, and that little voice that second-guessed it all—it's dead, too. That was never my voice; it was theirs in the world around the mountain. I am deaf to their sounds now.

This girl has a right to stand up and be counted as someone worthy, and the Fates, for whatever reason, led me here, and I need to see it through. They knew me before I existed, and I was part of the plan. They know what I'm capable of, and they set me on my way to ensure I showed everyone else. If they got me this far, they might have a plan, and I should stop fighting and listen. Close my eyes and let the Fates send me some message through the cosmos and the air because this is *not* how it ends.

The noise of the elevator interrupts my train of thought, a noise so perfectly on cue. I blink and open my eyes, and my head spins towards the source. Half expecting Deacon to stroll in and make my day worse, if that's even possible; it's the doc, and he's pushing a cabinet on wheels with all manner of things sliding off the top as he dashes to Sierra's room. I'm drawn to the wall to watch him, suspicious of his behavior, and forgetting my pep talk and internal boosting of confidence.

He seems different somehow. Wired maybe, a little erratic, his walking around and hurried movements abrupt. He drops a scattering of implements on the floor, the noise of cascading metal and hard objects clattering and echoing in this large space as he abandons the cart outside Sierra's door and swipes the panel to open it. He stops before entering, picks them up, and throws them back on top. Scooping any more he disturbs with his ungraceful and somewhat rushed movements and then runs into her room and starts frantically pressing buttons on machines by her head.

I can't do much else but watch, and as he picks up small mobile devices and sits them on her bed, his face severe and ashen and entirely focused on what he is doing, I realize he's not just checking on her. Something's up. His expression says it all; there's no hint of the gentle, pleasant, eccentric doctor at this moment. He looks frayed and afraid.

Even from here, I can see he's sweating, his forehead blushed and shiny, and his white jacket's underarms are darkening with excessive body heat. He's in a state of panic, and I look around, expecting his staff or the guards to come flooding down, suddenly worried about why. My nerves hitch as my stomach ties itself in knots, and I end up flat to the window, palms pressed by the sides against the glass, breathing heavily as I watch, anchored to my spot.

Maybe Sierra is crashing. Maybe all I was to do was witness her die. God no, please, Colton needs to see her one last time. She can't die; he needs her! I can't stand the thought of him losing her without saying goodbye. I need to know what I'm supposed to do now.

The doc unhooks her from the machine, keeping her heartbeat monitored loudly, and I hold my breath, inhaling sharply as the beep, beep stops so suddenly the air becomes unbearably silent. I don't get why he would take that off, but when he yanks another box from under the bed and plugs her into that instead, I exhale, slightly confused. That familiar beep, beep, starts up again in a subtler tone from a different machine, and he moves to the next and the next, replacing everything he can with smaller mobile devices as my brain pulls together amid my frantic fear and gives me a shake.

He's not trying to save her or take her off the machines; he's making her mobile so he can move her.

He stops, rushes off out of sight as he heads into the elevator once more, abandoning everything he's left in chaos. A moment later, he comes crashing back ungracefully, pushing another bed. This time it's on wheels, back to her room. I press my cheek to the cool, smooth wall in front of me, eyes locked on and heart rate hitching as it filters through. He catches me watching him, notices me with a second snap of his head as though he didn't see me the first time, and makes a weird waving gesture with his hands that translates to nothing. I don't understand.

"What?" I yell back, unsure what he's doing, and he does it again, waving two fingers in the air, which I can only assume means two minutes. I move back, confusion taking over, but intrigue is the dominant feeling. A thousand questions about why he's moving her replaces everything else that had been coursing through me. I watch as I've nothing else to do, and over here, it's all I am capable of anyway, as he struggles to get her from one bed to the other and shakes his head in defeat, face getting redder and sweatier as he does. He pulls out a handkerchief from his top pocket, pats his face, and puts it back while he seems to take a moment to size up his plan. He clicks his fingers in mid-air like he just had a 'Eureka' moment and then abandons her, turning and heading towards me at speed. A complete look of determination on that furrowed brow, an overly serious expression, as he dashes at me.

He crosses the bay so quickly and without hesitation, opens my door, and gestures with flicking hands for me to come with him. His face is almost beetroot and soaked with sweat. He looks like he's just run a marathon.

"What's going on?" I eye him warily, unsure how to feel about his current behavior, and try to figure out if he's drunk. He's breathless as hell and can barely talk.

After blowing out an incoherent sound that I assume was words, he gestures again for me to follow. I shrug and do it. I don't see any reason not to, he's proven himself to be a half-decent human who isn't out to hurt me, and a voice at the back of my mind is telling me this is how I get close to her. As soon as he knows I'm with him, he turns on his heel, and we head back to Sierra.

"Help me ... here to here," he motions wheezily when we get in her room, from her bed to the new one he wheeled over. His voice is low and labored, and he's struggling to get sound out. He's definitely been running about like a maniac before coming down here, and I can feel his heart rate pulsing rapidly in the air. He's composing himself as he works, but it's obvious he's not in the best physical shape.

I look at our sleeping beauty, surprised by how unwell she looks and a lot less ethereal. Sierra, up close, looks like a porcelain doll, so silently still and unresponsive, with flushed, rosy cheeks on a milky whiteness. Dark lashes fan her face under smooth dark brows, and I can immediately see Colton in her features. I don't argue but take her upper arms under her armpits as firmly as possible without hurting her and lift her over while he gets her legs.

She's light, surprisingly so, nothing to her, and painfully thin as the blankets pull away, and I see her body under her flimsy medical gown. Her skin is almost translucent from lack of sunlight, yet she seems so very warm and alive, and I'm convinced she will open her eyes at any moment. It's unnerving, and I can't stop staring at her face as we place her on the new bed, brushing her dark hair from her face as he tends to her limbs and tubes and settles her neatly.

"What are we doing?" I whisper it back, keeping my voice hushed as it's pretty apparent with the lack of helpers he's not meant to be doing this. As soon as he fully arranges her on the gurney, he takes a moment to inhale, calm his breathing by pressing a hand to his chest, and points at the door.

"We're taking her and leaving. I drugged ... fixed ... phew ..." He struggles, wiping his brow with the back of his hand and takes another exaggerated breath; annoying me to the point of getting frustrated with his lack of vocabulary, and he tries again. I raise my brows at him and throw a 'and?' look his way. "I drugged dinner. We don't have much time. A few hours at the most." He wheezes and goes back to picking up tubes and arranging them around her hurriedly.

"You did what?" I gawp at him, this unassuming feeble little doctor who wouldn't stand up to Deacon earlier, and now it registers how quiet this place is when he's making so much noise with carts and beds and no one's appeared. My face pales as my blood drains away, and my brain catches up with exactly what's happening.

He nods at the bay outside her room and motions to start pulling her bed. I'm not dreaming, and we are, in fact, staging a bust out and a heist, in that Sierra is the gold, and we're taking it. I swallow hard, pull myself together, and throw a glance up at the roof and a silent 'Thank you.' to the Fates. They answered my prayers.

I do as he motions, tugging backward out the door with all my might to get it rolling as he throws machines and such almost on top of her as we move. He picks up and dumps more items on the bed as we pass a couple of free-standing trolleys, pulling the saline drip and the bag feeding her fluids with him and its trolley at the end while stretching all her tubes almost taut.

"I drugged the soup and pretended to eat in the canteen to watch that they did; we always eat together. I had to wait for them all to pass out. To the truck over there." He nods towards the truck, and I pull the bed and aim for it, gaining speed as we go. He grabs the medical trolley in passing to tug behind him, making it awkward for him to keep hold of the bed, and I end up pulling it alone as he deals with that and the other wheeled necessities he's hauling, dropping things as he does so.

If this is an escape, it's a haphazard one, and he's the worst kind of saving hero ever. He's making enough noise to wake the dead, and I'm not convinced he won't keel over and have a heart attack with how unfit he is. He's puffing and heaving and losing more than half his body weight in sweat; I think he might need to lie down. Humans really are a weak race.

"How are we meant to get out of here? We're on the lowest floor, and the elevator is that way?" I nod with my head in the direction we came from, a growing tight knot of anxiety that maybe his plan is not the best. He waves at the trucks again, reminding me of their presence, but I'm not sure how they will help down here.

"The one on the end is a medical truck, and that platform lifts to the ground above. It's how we store them and transport things in and out."

As soon as he says it, I spin my head, eyeing the last green military truck that looks like its half-brother was a tank, and see the gears of the platform on the space behind it. The poles and hydraulics lining the steel wall in shadow and look up into a cavernous space that opens over your head when you get up close to them. I couldn't see it from my room, but this space goes up some hundred or more feet to a set of closed metal doors on the top ceiling.

"And then what? We drive around until she wakes up?" I gasp, bumping the bed onto the platform's edge, still helping while dissecting this absurdity, and he shoves it fully. We come side by side with the truck we are aiming for, and he motions for me to keep it going to the rear. I eye him warily, real tension ripping through me as panic rears its ugly head at his lack of a proper plan.

"Yes, sounds right. She's been in a coma for eight years—we need time. I need to wake her slowly, and even then, I don't know what state she will be in, physically or mentally. All I know is we can't stay here and do that without getting caught, and I owe her. I won't fail my friend again!" He has regained some of his equilibrium and leaves the bed with me to run to a metal cabinet on the wall that houses keys and scoops up a set, coming back to open the truck and motioning to bring the bed around.

"So, what you're saying is, there's no plan beyond getting out?" It's a dry, unamused response, and I stare at him as everything inside me grips tight. I have to swallow the rising panic, and he half-heartedly shrugs at me.

"I'm a doctor, not a masked villain who kidnaps people for a living. I figured your Fates would somehow ... I don't know ... help! I mean, you came and ... you're here!"

"Oh, my God!" It's the only response I have, as words fail me. I bite down on my lower lip and try to focus everything on helping him and not on the fact that I have no goddamn idea what we're meant to do after we get out. The guards won't sleep forever, and they *will* come after us. At speed, with guns, and lots of them. And inform Juan.

We get to work using the ramps inside the truck to get the bed and trolley in, and he braces them in place with special metal clamps, hanging her saline bag on a hook coming from the interior wall and pushing the mobile one into a corner and ties it down. He pushes the devices into clamps, clips them along the wall parallel to her bed, and settles everything free-standing into holders or ties them in place expertly. Making light work of it, as I can only stand and frantically race a million ideas through my head about what we're going to do.

"I have a cabin, my home when I'm not here. We should go there and try to wake her. They'll track us, but we have a good head start, and I don't know if we can lose them. No one knows about my cabin." It's a weird look, a half 'happy he came up with a plan' mixed with a heavy dose of 'please tell me that's a smart idea' look. I can only shake my head and stare.

He's not thinking this through or envisioning how well a wolf can track or how much faster they can be on foot when needed. They won't just dawdle when they find us gone, they will come tearing after us like demons on the warpath, and Juan will, too, with his four crazy, loyal sub packs, who annihilated my entire bloodline and got away with it. has no idea what I'm talking about..

"That won't work. You have no idea how well they can hunt us. And as for Sierra, if Juan killed people to keep his dirty secrets silent, he's going to send a tsunami after her to make sure we don't wake her up." I point out, tucking Sierra's blankets tight to hold her neatly while he applies straps over her body to keep her in place. All I can do is keep helping, even if nausea almost strangles me with so many possibilities and ways to die at Juan's hands.

"Well, do you have a better idea? We need to protect her until she wakes; we need to find a place we can fortify. I don't know people outside of these walls. I can't fight or shoot an army of wolves."

No place can be fortified against a pack of angry Lycans. Especially not when all you have is a bound wolf who can't use her gifts unless against a serious threat, an aging, unfit human doctor, and a sleeping witch. We are so screwed.

I wrack my brains trying to think of a million places I passed these past weeks alone and how none of them would be any good to hide in. Besides, no amount of hiding will stop them from tracking us. It was different when I ran. I was solitary, and only Colton had reason to follow. I also had a couple of days' head start to let my scent fade to nothing.

Colton! Of course!!

I can't believe how stupid I am not to see the most obvious answer to this question. Of course, the Fates would bring me full circle and back to him. They've never stopped tormenting me mentally when it comes to that boy, making sure I couldn't forget him even if I wanted to. This is why—this moment of need.

Colton's mom. Colton has an undying love for her and a need to find her. He also has a sub pack and some fierce ass wolves who would do anything for him—one of the most aggressive in the valley. Colton is our protection, and I just need to get outside to link him so he knows I need him. We need him.

"Yes, I do. I have her son and his pack, and I know he won't leave me to fight this alone if I tell him I have his mom." He won't fail her; he's been looking for her. I know his heart, and it's not like Juan's.

"You can trust him? Even after ten years with his father?" He flashes me a wary look, and I nod with no hint of hesitation. I know why he would query it, assuming under his father's guidance that he might have twisted his son into a mini clone all these years, but Colton is far stronger than I ever gave him credit for. He is his own mind, and he disagrees with how Juan hurts his people.

"Colton won't let me down. If he knows I need him, that she needs him, he'll come. I do not doubt this. We're linked; it's not hard to find him." Unless the Fates took that from me when he marked Carmen, I guess I will find that out. I don't think they would be so cruel in taking away something like that when I need to use it to get Sierra out of this place in one piece. In all of this, the Fates

341

have been trying to address the balance and bring us back to what Juan destroyed.

"Okay, once we get free of the building, you should be able to use your gifts. So, I tell you where we are and where we are going, and he can help. Plan? Yes, I think so. I don't fancy dying tonight, so we better make it snappy." He's losing his adrenaline rush, his panic panting, and instead seems in the 'regret and what have I done, but to hell with it' mode.

He ushers me to the front of the truck, pulling the doors shut behind us, and locks them in place from the inside. Without crouching, I can walk straight through the dark confines of the small space to the front seats and sit down on the passenger side with a quizzical look aimed right at him as he gets settled in the driver's seat.

"How do we go up, if we're in here?" I point out, assuming he forgot the minor detail we're underground, but he picks up a very heavy-duty looking radio device from the dash and waves it at me.

"This is a very high-tech and expensive facility. They like remotes. Boy toys." He presses a button in the center of the military green controller, and I almost have a heart attack when the entire platform shunts into motion, jerking us harshly, and lifts. We slowly start to raise and leave the bay level behind, not just this truck, but with all three on the whole floor.

This is when my panic sets in, and nerves get the better of me as I realize our escape will probably go down in history as the worst attempt ever.

It's louder than hell. Crunching, groaning, and echoing around us like crazy, probably scaring off all the wildlife above ground in a three-mile radius. I cover my ears, cringing, and recoiling into my seat, and have to resist the urge to shut my eyes in the hope this is a bad dream. I hope to God he was right about knocking those guards out; otherwise, they will know we are running away.

"Once we get up there and out into the open, the building no longer has any bind over you. The walls work on some sort of inbuilt frequency that's impossible for us to hear, but it doesn't work out there. It has to surround you, you see." He yells over the noise, telling me facts about something I currently couldn't care less about, but it hits a nerve, and I sit up, blinking as my attention piques.

"A frequency?" I turn to him, startled. A memory from before tingles in my brain, and I don't know why that's important, but I feel it should be. My moment of fear dissipates when suspicion starts hiking up inside me.

"Yes, years of research have shown that certain frequencies alone are some of the biggest weapons against your kind's gifts. Truly fascinating. We stumbled upon it when looking at the the ability of some to emit ultrasonic sounds as a weapon."

That's it—the weapon. The one the vampires used to attack the home was frequency-based, too. I blink at him, not sure if I am piecing it together right or if I'm way off. The doc is off on a nervous tangent, babbling away like a runaway cart as a reaction to stress, I guess, and I have to butt in on the meticulous details of frequency being used to detain and disable my species.

"Did Juan ever use this facility to make any sort of small portable isolation tank that throws out the frequency instead of putting it in the walls?" I don't know how that would work, seeing as they almost killed me too and in turn, would have killed Colton, but it seems a little too coincidental that this is how an isolation tank is made. Clutching at straws as I try to fit the puzzle pieces that I'm sure belong together.

"No, my dear. However, he sold the research a few years ago, claiming it was a profitable but harmless discovery." He casts me a confused look, and I can tell he has no idea what I'm talking about.

"Harmless? The vampires attacked our mountain using a frequency to disable us all from turning. I almost died because of that stupid black box, and if Colton hadn't ..." I shudder at the memories, warmed slightly by the notion that Colton is where I'm heading once more, and even though it's stupid and I should hate him, there's a tiny ray of hope inside me, an aching to go back to him. My foolish weakness is kicking in, and finally, after weeks of being heavy and hurt, it's raising a tiny little beam of sunshine in my dark days.

"It was turned into a weapon ... by vampires? I thought their kind were driven underground long ago and no longer a threat. Forgive me, my dear; we don't get any kind of news here." He seems clueless, and the shock evident on his face, eyes wide, mouth gaping slightly as he takes that in and looks out of the window in front of us as he wraps his head around it, resting his hands on the wheel of the truck and shaking his head so very slightly.

"A month back, give or take, maybe longer now. I don't know. I lost track. They attacked out of the blue and sent the mountain into chaos. A war is coming, and the wolves are all being dragged back to the mountain for Juan to control." I sink back in my seat and watch as we climb the last few feet. Climbing the darkness while surrounded by eerie tones of groaning and grinding, I try not to overthink how high we are on this rickety-sounding platform. The roof begins to open, and the dull gray of an ending day shows through the cracks and makes me aware I'm about to taste fresh air once more. The urge to leap out and feel it on my skin distracts me, and I turn to face the now silent doctor instead.

"Using a device not too dissimilar to what we created? And they attacked Juan's mountain and *his* people." He mumbles more to himself than me, and it seems he did not know. I can almost taste the suspicion in his tone as he, too, concludes as I did but realize it's stupid, and I'm letting paranoia and hate cloud my judgment.

"Yeah, but if you think Juan had something to do with it, then, one, we hate vampires, so no. It's unlikely he would coerce with them, and two, Colton saved me when I was almost toast. If I died, then Juan would have lost his son and heir, and no, that's just no. I don't care what kind of monster he is; he puts Colton on a pedestal and always talks about his ruling one day. He wouldn't let his son die. No matter what. I believe his legacy is the most important thing next to being king of all he sees. He only has one son."

"But hear me out. If Colton died, then Juan would have had reason to tie up the people in his control and use the attack to rally the wolves to unite as a pack. If he fabricated a war or even gave them the means to start one, it all plays into what he wants to be— the prophecy. Uniting the packs against war and thus forcing his position to fulfill what the prophecy wanted. A wolf to reign over the people. He's still so obsessed that it should be him!"

My blood runs cold, and, as crazy as it sounds, it starts to fall into place. He has a point, and yes, Colton dying would push those loyal to Colton to rally with Juan in avenging his death. A common enemy is a great way to instill fear and make the people look to a leader to save them. Something doesn't sit right with it, though, and I'm trying to decipher it.

"You think he enabled the vampires and prompted them to hit the orphanage hoping Colton would die when I did? As a catalyst to get the people under control and mount an arsenal."

I'm instantly nauseous, my skin prickling with goosebumps, and my breathing shallow as I try to swallow all this down. Even for Juan, it seems insane, but then he culled an entire bloodline for his chance at taking a crown. The doc nods his head, looking up as our freedom comes into view with an increase in grinding and crunching in the mechanics, and he starts the engine with the turn of a key. The truck roars into life and vibrates through the seat under me as I reach around and pull on my seat belt. So eager to get out of here, I'm almost bouncing in my chair with nerves.

"He sedated his mate and left her to rot. You tell me if killing his son to manipulate an outcome is something he would do?"

"He went to war against them and lost so many of his people. He hates the vampires with a passion." It makes no sense. He wouldn't willingly negotiate with them, but it does make sense that he didn't care who he sold the research to, and maybe it came their way via another avenue. Perhaps the vampires took it or bought it from whomever Juan sold it to. There's something just not there that I feel I should see, and it's leaving a hole big enough to cast serious doubt, as much as I want to tar him with that brush.

"A war against people that should never have happened. Lycans and vampires used to dwell in peace not so long ago." He confuses me with a ludicrous statement, and I frown his way, half snorting at his gross misinformation.

"No, they didn't. I don't know who told you that story, but I can assure you, we've been mortal enemies since the dawn of creation. We were never peaceful allies." They taught us that in school and in my life, I have never heard any other version. It's ludicrous to imagine our two species living on the same lands and not tearing their throats out.

"No, my dear, that's not true. Sierra was very good at her history and very vivid in her telling. Her people, the witches as her mother was, predate the first of your kind. They tell the stories amongst their own." He lifts his brows in a paternal manner, nodding towards me as though he is one hundred percent certain in this, and I can't grasp it. It's all they ever taught us; vampires are the enemy and always have been.

"So, what are you telling me? We used to be friends? Had morning coffee and bake sales together?" I almost laugh at that, sarcasm kicking in, and as we finally hit the upper ground, he throws the truck in gear and reverses at speed right off the platform and then backs us into a clearing in the middle of the dusky forest we find ourselves back in. We're already outside the compound, further than the dirt road that came up to the fence, and I realize we are a fair bit from that completely. Underground must spread wider than I figured it did, and he hits the makeshift road and puts his foot to the gas, heading out and switching on headlights to illuminate where we're going. The sun has not yet set, but the forest is gray and shadowy, and I have to cling onto my seat as I bounce around on the rough terrain, trees hitting the windshield and roof as we skim under low branches.

I cast a glance behind us to check on Sierra, and although the insides of the truck are rocking and bouncing around like mad, she is secured, and her machines are still beeping away, all the tubes swinging wildly. She seems okay.

"The Lycans were the daylight guardians of the vampires and, in turn, the vampires protected wolf lairs in the darkest hours. They were created to complement and protect each other, not war and fighting. It's why you're almost matched in power and gift. Each with a special, unique gift, of course, but neither meant to be used against one another. A peaceable arrangement born at conception, between light walkers and dark, both with different needs and not even a shared food source, so there is no reason to feud. Your kinds were from the same lands, and some even procreated. A bite from either side can kill the other, so it's not exactly smart to rage fights with an enemy who only hints at your demise every time."

I return to facing his side profile as he watches the road closely and maneuvers around fallen logs and debris, focusing all my disbelief on the side of his head.

"Procreated? Now I know you're insane, and you need to up your meds, Doc. A vampire and a wolf ... had babies? Nah, now I know you're high. That's not a thing; there is no such thing. We're enemies and always have been." It's a half-laugh, shaking my head in humor and disbelief as I turn in my seat to face the fast flyby of the forest, entirely convinced he has a screw loose somewhere.

He throws me an alarmed look that I catch from the corner of my eye, frowning and screwing up his face like I'm the crazy one, and almost swerves us into a tree before looking back and saving us the near-death impact. That makes me jump, and I snap my eyes at him fiercely as if to say 'watch where you're driving' while gasping and panting for breath after that near miss. My stomach is now lodged in my throat, and I brace my legs against the dash and push myself back in the seat, trying to calm down. My wolf hasn't yet figured out she can come out to play now we are free of the facility, but another fright like that, and she won't hesitate. So tired of shredding and losing clothes, and it would be awkward sitting naked with this man.

"Yes, Alora. It's hard to digest, and as I pointed out in Colton's case, crossbreeding is not always successful given your masterful DNA and its ability to heal, much like the vampires can, but how can you disbelieve when you are sitting here, the very proof of that union? Your own genetics are waving their hands at you and saying, 'Here I am.'" He looks at me as though I'm being completely preposterous, and his words are like a punch in the gut. Spinning me to him, eyes gawping wide at what he said.

"What?!?!" that's not the response I expected from him, and I blink at him, my mouth open, and I frown intensely. "I thought you said I was witch and wolf." I let it out slowly, precisely, as I remind him of how ridiculous what he's saying is.

"No, my dear, I said you were a hybrid. Assuming your mother was a perfect half and half without knowing her history, of course, but it was very clear from your turning what you are. You're white. I guess that witches generally make black wolves, like a kind of racial thing. You know, like humans - where a dark-skinned Latino and white makes mixed race, and then a white and white human makes white ... add in a splash of color, and their baby's shades are wonderfully diverse. Vampires, however, lack of sun and being the undead, fascinating in biology by the way, they make white. Interestingly, though, it's always the prominent characteristic in all hybrids where wolf DNA is present. Amazing, strong genetics the wolves have. And in some rare instances, where the vampire gene is equally strong but still of no match to that powerful beast, the babies are lucky enough, gifted enough, down the generational tree, to have red eyes. Remarkable." He's way too pleased with his storytelling, and the utter joy on his face only heightens my horror.

I don't know if my mind leaves my body completely or if shock and numbness knock me for six, but I swear, I have an out-of-body experience and get so close to passing out as I just stare at him, blankly, deadpan, not even remotely able to react to that little tidbit of information, that I say nothing at all.

I'm a vampire hybrid. No! Just NO!!

COLTON

"Are you okay, my dear?" Doc's voice waves at me from what seems like a long distance away, and I realize how, in my head, I've drifted into a state of numbness. We're still rumbling along this dark makeshift path carved through the dense forest, and I was so zoned out in my mind I completely faded to dark. My cheeks are damp with the tears that sprung out of me, and I'm staring blankly ahead, in a state of disconnect, like everyone I know suddenly died a horrible death, again, and I had to watch.

"I can't be one of those ... those ... creatures. They killed everyone in the orphanage." It's a soft, pitiful whispering tone, and I can't bring myself to look at him. My head is full of confusion, pain, and questions, and I keep picturing Colton's face, his dimpled smile, those deep, dark, sexy eyes, and what he will think when he finds out ... Meadow, the sub pack. How will they look at me now?

I'm the enemy, and I've been among them this whole time.

"Alora. Those beings were not always the blood-thirsty wolf murderers you view them as now. Vampires serve a purpose in the grand scheme of things, and their kind has as much validity as the wolves. There are those among them, much like your kind, who are peaceful and land-loving as some wolves are. They don't even hunt humans and never wanted the battles and wars to happen. A feud so ridiculous that history books fail to record it correctly, and no one really knows why the species raged a war against one another in the first place. It's a forgotten cause. You are not a creature, and this does not change who you are inside.

You are the same fearless girl sat before me you were ten minutes ago."

I break down and sob, falling forward to cradle my face in my palms and try so desperately to catch my breath, to calm the storm of feelings hitting me hard and twisting me up inside. It isn't fair, and why do I get to be lumbered with every kind of bullshit the Fates can throw at me. What did I do to deserve any of this?

"They won't see it that way. Don't you understand?" I sit up, snapping to face him with fresh tears rolling down my face, dripping from my chin as my heart breaks again. Soul ripped wide open. "The pack can't ever accept me if they know, and Colton ... He'll be disgusted with what I am. He fought them; he killed them and survived that war, too. He hates them with an unmatched passion." That much was apparent when he ripped the head off the one who had me in its clutches and threw it high over the orphanage wall. I feel nauseous even trying to conjure up how he's going to react or even how he's going to look at me. I can't bear to pull him into my head and see his face change from that cute-boy, cheeky happy, into something hateful and Deaconlike. Seeing me as some crude mash-up of vile parts. Disgusted by my existence.

"Dear girl, you said the boy imprinted on you. That means you share the purest kind of love there is, so special, and I'm sure that means he'll accept it as part of who you are, especially if he takes after Sierra. It doesn't define you; you are that same girl. Besides, he has to figure out he's half-witch, and I know from wolf lore that's just as bad. He might have to get over that with a little more effort than your news." He shrugs at that as if to point out Colton will probably have more significant issues, and I shake my head at him.

"Why me?" It's not a question, more of verbal despair, and I sink back against my seat, lifting my head to stare at the ceiling above us and trying so hard to pull myself together. Sniffing back the emotional breakdown to stop crying like a vulnerable idiot. None of this will help our current situation, and as much as I want to scream and rip that part out of me, I need to put it aside and focus on the now and our bigger issue.

We need protection, and I need to link Colton to get it. Scared about how that's going to go, and I don't even know if the link will work. Or that he hasn't blocked me on his end, too. I don't even know what to say to him, especially now with this in the forefront of my mind.

"Maybe because you're important and being part vampire gives you something that adds to the prophecy. Your Fates always have a reason, isn't that what your kind says? Maybe there's a reason, and Colton is half-witch. Imagine the tribrids to come from your union. Your children will be three strong species combined; if your body allows them to come to fruition. That's simply mind-blowing. I don't think there's ever been such a breed." The tinge of excitement in his voice inevitably pushes that knife he's stabbing me in the heart with a whole lot deeper.

"There's going to be no children and no goddamn union! Colton marked another, so that part is over!" I snap it, alarmingly hostile, sitting up poker straight to glare at him as that extra searing pain rips through my chest at a speed of knots. Reminding me of all the reasons I was mad at that asshole in the first place and why I haven't reached out to him since I left.

Screw you, Colton. You weak-ass daddy's boy who should have just manned the fuck up and realized this was bigger than us! I was the one, not her. How could you?

I don't mean it, well, almost not fully, but I'm still devastated that he betrayed our bond. No matter the reason. Even if it was justified in the grand scheme of things, I don't think I can ever forgive him for wounding me this way and destroying what should have been a perfect union.

"Oh, dear. Are you quite sure he ma ...?"

"Yes, quite sure!" I snap, mimicking his English accent haughtily and cutting him off. He's riling a very tender and open wound, and it's doing nothing for my mood. Like I wouldn't know that pain hitting me in the chest and almost killing me that day and what it was. Have still not recovered fully and carry that weight

351

constantly like a heavy shroud to remind me I'll love someone I can never have for eternity.

"I see. So, if he has another, how do you know you can ...?" he gestures at his temple, locking eyes on mine, making circular motions and implying a mind-link. I roll my eyes. I am exhaling to curb this sudden need to punch things and getting rattier by the second, tension rising, making me stiff and uptight.

"I don't; I have to hope," I reply, gritting my teeth, my mood getting sensitive with the current topic of conversation. I know it's a genuine concern, given that Colton is the key to us getting out of this and surviving. I'm just scared to try now while everything is so new and raw. I'm out here, and all of this has smacked me in the face at once. Add that to the gaping gash of heartbreak he rubbed salt into, and you have one utterly irate girl who isn't pulling herself together as quickly as her life is unraveling.

"Then maybe you should, you know ..." Again, with the rotating finger at his temple, I huff loudly in exasperation, willing him to stop pushing and give me some ever-loving, goddamn breathing space for a minute. This is hard for me. I erupt, breaking under pressure—spectacularly.

"YES! I KNOW!! I'm going to do it. Excuse me for having a mental breakdown with everything I've learned in the last six hours and a reminder that my destined mate is a cheating asshole. It's a lot ... A LOT! I'm an eighteen-year-old girl who hasn't linked her cheating, asshole ex-so-called-mate in weeks, not since I ran from him. Give me a fucking break already." I push my fingers and nails through my scalp, pushing my wild hair off my face and gripping it with force at my temples, trying hard not to self-combust under the extra weight of everything hitting me at once.

"I do say." Doc raises his brows at me in a completely ridiculous British way and then softens his expression and holds out his handkerchief to me in a white flag apology as more tears roll down my cheeks against my will. I hate that I'm so hopelessly connected to him, that this rules everything I think or feel. Colton always ruins me.

"I'm sorry. I need to breathe for a few minutes. Colton is ... it's tough. He hurt me. This, all of this, just hurts."

Colton is the one thing in my life that has the power over everything else to screw me up with minimal effort. Even finding out I'm some sort of half creature, my first thought was, 'how will he look at me?' He's right in there, deep inside me, and he can make everything feel so good, or everything worse than bad, that I can barely breathe. Without him, I survive, but I wouldn't exactly call it successful. There's a need that never leaves me, a longing that never stops calling to him. I miss him, of course, I do, and I dream about him. I see or hear him at stupid points of my day, even when it's not related. Reaching out and physically connecting is a whole other kind of torture, especially knowing he's not mine and never will be now. It was easier to have no contact at all.

I never knew you could both love a person beyond a shadow of a doubt and crave them constantly while at the same time hating the ground he walks on and wishing I never had to see him again. Such is my dilemma.

I need him, yet I don't want to, but right now, I physically *need* him to come and save our asses from this situation. Doc was right. I can't take on a pack of Santo wolves, especially ones who don't play fair and use dart guns to subdue my kind. My gifts are worth shit without having complete control of them. Colton needs to be in this, no matter how I feel, as Sierra is *his* mother, and I owe him to give her back to him, where she belongs. He can protect her in ways her own pack failed. Her son will never let her down in that way.

"You can have some time; this road is a good long drive to get out of the undergrowth, and by my calculations, we have three hours minimum, depending on the metabolism of the wolves before they start to come round. I'm hoping for six, which is probably a human response to the drug, but your kind is always a little more geared to outdoing us, even in an isolation tank. You can take a little headspace before you contact him. Just, you know, not too long, as we don't want to be driving in the wrong direction or anything."

He isn't helping, and I turn and stare out the window, watching the trees flash by in the hopes it will numb my brain out with mindless mesmerizing images flashing by, the light fading with every minute we drive, and Sierra is still as immobile and silent as she was.

I need to swallow this, bite the bullet and do it like ripping off a Band-Aid and not sitting pondering and building the moment into something worse. He's out there, doing god knows what, and the sooner I link him, or even see if I can, the sooner we can figure this out and head for a safe place, and all of this no longer rests on my shoulders alone. Some control of this situation, someone else to make the decisions, and I hope to God I'm not being a fool and putting my faith in Colton, only to have him deliver us back into Juan's hands. I truly believe in my heart, despite everything that's happened between us, Colton will come through for me—for us.

This isn't about marking or obeying the Alpha and respecting the laws. This is about his mom and intervening in something more significant than the rules of the packs. This is about betrayal and what his father has done, and I have no idea how I'm going to tell him. It's not the kind of thing you can just rock up in his head and say, 'Hey, I have your mom here, and your dad killed everyone I love; do you want to hang out?' Once he knows, it'll hurt him the way it hurt me, irreversibly, and I don't know how he will react.

How do I tell him about the bigger picture, my family, the prophecy, and how Sierra was kept and has nothing mentally wrong with her? How do I fit all that in without having some mental freak out while in a head link with a guy you have been so afraid of linking because of the unbearable pain he can inflict on you? I didn't only blank him out because I left, and we were done. I closed the door because I couldn't handle ever being able to link with him again and hearing that familiar voice inside me. That soothing, husky melody can find its way deep down into the most intimate parts of me and warm me from within in the most basic way. No one will ever be able to make me feel things the way he does, and he has so much power over me, even with his words, at any distance.

Stop, Alora. This is bigger than a broken heart. Colton will help, and you're just stalling.

I catch Doc looking at me, eyes glancing from the dark, rough road to me, bouncing along this track and back again, but he says nothing. I think he's checking on my mental and emotional state, and I need to get this over and done with. Stop being a wuss and getting overdramatic with a female tear fest, and man up.

I inhale, sit up as though that makes any difference, and push my forehead against the glass of my side window. Fixing my eyes on nothing and drumming up the courage I so badly need. My insides immediately start tying themselves in knots, my stomach cramping with the tension, and I swallow apprehensive nausea as best I can. I let my breath out slowly, misting the window with the heat and condensation of the cold dark glass, and draw a heart absentmindedly in the steamy patch before rubbing it out and frowning at my stupid reflection. Now or never! Rip it off, bite the bullet. Be strong.

I know if I stall, I might lose my nerve completely. I screw my eyes tight shut, conjure up some darkness to clear my brain, and mentally slide open that heavy locked door I put between us many weeks ago. Afraid of the sudden precipice I need to step off, I throw it out there, hoping he's listening.

Colton? Are you there? I need your help.

Please be there. God, I sound so pathetic and weak. I don't get time to regret the break of silence or feel anything about doing it. A paused breath and then ...

Lorey? Is that really you? Baby ... oh shit, baby, God. I can't believe it's you. It's really you ... you're really ... shit.

There's a second of pause, but before I can respond, he's off again, quietening me with his torrent of verbal diarrhea.

Where are you? You have no idea how hard I've been trying to link you for weeks and couldn't get through. Not that I blame you, and I know I hurt you, and you're mad. I'm angry too ... at me, not you. I'm not in any way mad at you for leaving, so don't think I am because I'm not... Please, tell me where you are.... I'm an asshole; I know this. Are you okay? Are you hurt? Are you coming back? ...

Please say that's a yes, and that I didn't completely screw all this up. And, umm, yes, I'm here, almost crashing my truck, but here. I was always here, waiting, hoping, and you know I'll always help you. That shouldn't even be a request when it's a given. God, I miss you. Tell me what you need. Tell me what to do. Say something.

The whoosh of babbling completely catches me off guard, and the tone, changing from relief to disbelief to relief again, and the sheer emotion almost cripples me. He can't hide any of it from his voice, and the surge of intense feeling that comes with it tells me our link still exists, and I pick up on his even through this form of communication. It chokes me up, the obviousness that he's missed me and is as broken about my contact as I am. There's no anger; just complete overwhelm that he can finally hear me in his head.

My initial response is to tear up, my throat closes tightly as if it's going to choke me, and butterflies escape within my stomach and go bashing around my insides, hitting every orifice and organ they can fly at. I'm feeling the same as him, aching with the sudden waterfall of feelings I've been trying to fight for weeks.

Colton, listen. I don't want to do this over the link, but there's a lot, and, for right now, we need somewhere to go, and you need to be there. Somewhere safe because we're going to have a pack on our ass soon, and I can't fight them alone. There are too many. For now, I need you to tell me where to go so we can meet and for you to show up with enough of you to hold off some crazy, mad wolves.

My hands shake with the ferocity of overwhelming pain I'm experiencing at being in his head and having him in mine. It's like the weeks apart drop away instantly, and it reminds me of everything I miss the most about him. The intimacy of it. His voice, overprotective need to take care of me, and his presence, even in my head alone, makes me feel suddenly safer, cherished, and he's only making it worse by saying everything I've wanted to hear. Why did he have to be stupid and mark that bitch?

We? As in ... you're with someone else?

The crumbling of his tone and the hint of hurt that seeps through shakes me out of my rose-tinted stupor, and I realize he thinks I might have found someone, as in a mate. I don't get why he would jump to *that* conclusion unless it's guilt because he knows what he's done to us, and I'm well within my rights to find a mate and say screw him. It's unimportant, and it irks me slightly that he would home in on that little word as though more important than the rest.

Yes, WE. Look, he's helping me; he's a friend, and we need to go somewhere safe.

It seems to completely sober Colton up, and I almost feel him draw back a little, the link falling silent for a moment as he seems to disconnect and then comes back an agonizing long-ass minute later. I guess it's a moment to pull his head together as jealousy eats him, but good, maybe it's karma, and he can feel an ounce of what I've been going through all this time. Let him hurt and think there's someone else. He deserves some pain. If he jumps to stupid conclusions on limited information, then he can suffer.

Right. Where are you? I need to know so I can find you or guide you.

It's that business tone of an Alpha moving in as logic prevails, and he sobers up with that whip in the face. The babbling, happy to hear from me dropping off to wounded male who's trying not to sulk. I know it hurt him, I can feel it radiating through, and as much as it pains me, I'm not going to correct him and tell him the 'we' is a human in his sixties and his mom.

I turn to Doc with a severe expression, my head getting back to business and ignoring that my legs have turned to Jell-O.

"I need a location so Colton can help us." I sound odd, strained, and my voice is husky and hoarse, hinting at tears I'm refusing to shed. I can't deny this is awful, but we need his help.

"Oh, goodness, that was quick, and it worked. Clever girl. Yes, location, of course, we're fifteen miles or so from the Hackuuh mountain base, north of Rennington. We head south for a good forty miles from here, and we meet Route 10 to Normansville. Is that accurate enough?" He scratches his head and goes back to grabbing the steering wheel with both hands before peering back out into the darkness, illuminated only by our headlights. I shrug at him and turn away to focus on the link.

357

Colton, we're fifteen miles or so from the Hackuuh mountain base, north of Rennington. He has us heading south; he says we're forty miles from getting to Route 10 to Normansville. Does that help?

The directions mean nothing to me as someone who never ventured out of the valley until recently. I try to focus on details and not the overwhelming emotions he's passing this way or the way my heart rate is pounding sky high, and my legs are trembling at being connected to him. It's a bittersweet agony, and I'm totally helpless to defend myself from it.

The Hackuuh? You're not that far, goddamn it, Lorey. You're the feeling that I should go south-east? And yet, I still didn't find you! Tell him to stick to that route. We can meet you as soon as you hit Route 10 and escort you to where we've been staying. It's not very far. If we get there first, we'll head towards you and, hopefully, meet sooner.

I knew Colton would push everything he was feeling aside and pull through. It's what he does and why he'll make a formidable leader one day. His heart was always secondary to what he feels is responsibility and what he must do. The curse that made him choose her over me. Despite everything, even thinking I've someone to replace him, he's still helping—no hint of malice or telling me to go away. I feel guilty about letting that deception stay between us, but I can't quite bring myself to put him right, and I sure as hell can't tell him over a link that his mother is with us. I don't have the words. He's going to find out soon enough as it is.

"Stay on track to Route 10, and they'll meet us, show us where to go. We're going to be okay." I pat his arm, seeing the sag of relief as my words filter in, and he nods, exhaling the breath he's probably been holding all this time. I guess I do, too, because we can't outrun the facility pack, but they won't have a chance of getting at Sierra with Colton and the subs. It is safety and success with minimal effort. We need to get to them and let Colton take over.

It feels weird to know he kept looking, though, and admitting something was pulling him to where I was. That's odd. Maybe it was his mother finally calling to him too, and nothing to do with me, and I find it strange he said they were staying somewhere else and not on the mountain. I guess Juan has them scouring further afield for vampires, and Colton has been using it to look out for me in case we crossed paths.

Please tell me you have the sub pack with you. I have at least a pack of nineteen coming. This might be a fight.

I add in an afterthought. A sudden fear he might come alone, eating at me.

What the hell did you do? Who are they? Not that it matters right now because I'll rip them a new one and, yes, the sub pack and then some. You've missed so much, Lorey. I have so much to fill you in on.

Likewise.

I sigh internally and mouth it to myself. I dread it, even more, knowing that I also have to add my lineage to the list of things Colton should know about. That nausea chokes me again, and I try to push it down and concentrate on the act of breathing in and out.

I can't get into it right now. Honestly, it's better I show you when we meet to see for yourself, and you can tell me then. For now, I need to unlink. This is hard, Colton, and we have a tough road to navigate out of this damn forest. I'll link you when we hit Route 10. Please, understand. It's just easier to explain everything when I see you. You'll understand why.

I'm being a coward. I know if we stay linked while passing the miles to meet, I might tell him stupid things and work myself into a mess of tears and love confessions. Tell the idiot how much I miss and love him still, despite what he's done and the fact it can never go anywhere. Or I might tell him about his mother and have to deal with the fallout of Colton's self-imploding, and I am not strong enough for that or for keeping linked to him when I want to curl up and cry. It's too raw having him back in my head like we've never been apart, and I'm so not equipped to deal with my feelings on top of his shining through. It's a see-saw ride, and I have a lot to process.

Promise me you'll re-link the second you hit the route. I hate this not being able to reach you bullshit; it shouldn't be this way. I don't care what or who he is. I fucking love you, and nothing changes that.

That part shocks me, especially the hostile way he rasps it at me like it's a threat and not a love declaration. Jealousy well and truly piquing in a way he can't control, and it ignites mine, along with the urge to snap 'So much so that you marked Carmen, huh?' back at him. It chokes me up, and I unlink him without responding, cutting him off before I lose my shit at him and compromise our run to safety. That inner rage ignites every time I think of the four days after leaving and that undeniable sign that he betrayed me. He betrayed us. It's not something I can forget or ever forgive.

It has the desired effect of pulling my head out of my wallowing, lovesick ass. Instead of sentimental, weak longings, I now want to rip his head off for being a possessive shithead who thinks he still has a right to me, for swearing at me about this when he should be groveling.

"Ugh. He has a goddamn cheek, telling me HE is not mad at ME!!" I let rip, startling the poor doctor, and the fright almost makes him swerve us into a bush. "You know what, he should be more concerned with how mad I am at *him* and afraid because I'm the one who will rip him a new something when I see him! He should be the one getting sworn at and shielding off hostility, not me!!"

Doc flattens a palm to his chest as though trying to calm the heart failure I inflicted, and he casts me a concerned smile. A flicker of confusion crossing his features.

"Good conversation, I take it?"

He gets a thunderous darkening scowl aimed his way. I look unimpressed and breathe in quick, raspy breaths as my temper rages a little higher. I think it's an aftereffect of holding my anxiety in while linking, and now the dam breaks.

"He loves me, PAH! And he doesn't care who I'm with. As if he has any say in that respect when he pushed me out and made me leave, and then before even a week had passed, he had some skanky *puta* in his bed and completed the marking that should have been with me! Ugh! Is he conveniently forgetting all of that? Is he that dense and that much of a condescending hypocrite?" I'm venting, so wound up with our interaction and triggered over the stupidest part of it. Hating on him as an emotional response and oozing fury, I wriggle about in my seat manically, waving my hands around and kicking the dash.

"Skanky what, now?" He rubs his head, eyes darting between me and the road, and tries hard to make sense of my ranting.

"You know what? If I didn't need that jerk for Sierra's sake, he could go kiss my ass and get used to the fact that I'm dust in his future. Not a chance of ever making me come back, and you know what he had the nerve to say? Do you?" I shout it at him, getting a wide-eyed shake of the head and half-shrugged response.

"I wouldn't like to hazard a guess, but I'm presuming something that hit a nerve or ten." It's a sarcastic yet wary reply with a feeble smile.

"He said, 'I hate this not being able to reach you bullshit, and it shouldn't be this way.'" I mimic Cole's slightly accented dialect in a mocking male tone, bouncing my shoulders as I say it in a macho way, and kick the dash in fury when I let it out, hurting my toes inside my boot, which only makes me madder. "He is the goddamn reason I left! Oh, my God. Why the hell did I think that running straight back to that complete dumbass was the best plan? I should have known he would only piss me off completely."

"Don't kill me for the suggestion, but maybe because he is the best option, and you two clearly have a few issues that need to be resolved. He may be marked elsewhere, but it sounds like his heart is still fully invested here, and your overdramatic response screams you love him still." Doc points at my chest, meaning my heart, and I shake my hands out in frustration. I want to show him what overdramatic looks like as the urge to air punch him out of the truck hits me for that less than helpful observation.

"Colton's heart has never been the problem. It's his big, stupid, inflated head, that big dumb brain that sits in there, taking up space and telling him to do the right thing for everyone else in the pack, except him—and me. That's the only issue we have, and it's an unresolvable one."

361

Reverting to juvenile insults because Colton makes me feel wacko sometimes. Like back after the imprinting when he left me alone for two weeks and then just showed up in my head like some swooning Romeo and screwed me all up. Why didn't he let me die that night?

"Correct me if I'm wrong, but surely marking another would completely dissipate your link and his feelings for you?" He's trying to tug me back to a sense of calm with a bit of question time, but I'm not biting. Too self-absorbed in my rampage of hating on Colton because I have needed to do this for weeks.

"We imprinted. No one knows. And in the entire history of fated mates, no one has ever rejected the bond and not marked— just that dipshit, Colton. So I don't know if it's meant to dissolve the link or whatever, but it didn't. Clearly!" I spit it out, turning away and banging my forehead off the side window to calm down.

"Then maybe ..."

"Don't, okay. I know what I felt, and I don't want to talk about him anymore until I have to see his stupid face. Can we just drive and not talk? Please." I bite my tongue, so many more words poised and ready to spew out, but this is getting me nowhere fast.

"That's fine by me, my dear. This is a difficult path to navigate, and I should probably concentrate on that," he replies, probably relieved to have an excuse not to engage with the hormonal psycho making this time worse than it needs to be. I suddenly get hit with a wave of remorse at taking it out on him. "Fine. Suits me fine." I lower my tone and try for softer, but I sound like a sulking child and shut myself up. I slump back against my headrest, exhaling heavily and staring out the window, pulling my legs up to curl under me on the oversized seat. Bubbling and boiling up inside and counting down the minutes to see that asshat, listing all the things in my head that I deserve to punch him in the groin for.

It's the only way to pass the time, as I'm not ready to simmer and douse these flames I have burning for that jerk. I compile a list with all the bones I have to pick. I am starting with a major one!

Betraying me with that skanky *puta* while claiming he loves me.

362

You're Safe

"Alora, I believe that might be our escort. This is Route 10." Doc nudges me lightly, snapping me out of my long weird daydream in which I bludgeoned Carmen to death with Colton's running shoes before handing them back to him and walking off into the sunset with a flip of my finger. I sit upright, startled by reality. My heart misses a beat, and full-on nerves smack me in the stomach.

There's a convoy of headlights heading our way in the now pitch-dark, long road, stretching ahead, dazzling us slightly as they approach, along what seems to be a long empty highway lined with dense trees on either side of us. I hadn't even noticed the change in terrain when we got off the dirt track and got onto an actual road. My insides tighten, tense, and painfully pray that it is who it is.

I lift the veil and link him in case we're not where they are yet, and this is someone I should worry about. I don't see any other vehicles on the road.

Colton, please tell me that's you, the convoy heading towards the military truck on Route 10?

I hold my breath, pausing as nervous energy overtakes and straining to see beyond the blinding lights, but it's too dark to make out if the trucks are Santo. All I can tell is there is a succession of them as they weave slightly, and headlights shine brightly on the route ahead.

Pullover. It's us. You're safe.

That husky, warm flow of assurance as I hear him inside my mind, and I relax a little, letting out the breath I was holding in anticipation. He sounds weird, tense, and maybe a little annoyed, probably from obsessing over my 'boyfriend' in the last half hour or however long we've been driving. I've been silently staring out the window, lost in my head, and Doc just kept plowing on heading north. No concept of time.

Shouldn't we just follow you?

I query, confused that he should want us to stop and not keep moving with the possibility of a pack on our tail. I don't understand why he would expect us to.

PULLOVER!

It's a sharp command, not a request. No hint of politeness or trying to explain. In that bossy, arrogant, snarly, I am pissed tone that verges on his Alpha gift, I wonder what the hell is eating him. All because I questioned him from seemingly calm and logical to an idiot in a millisecond. Maybe he is like his father after all, and that gives me the unyielding urge to tell him where to get off. It brings back my rage from earlier, and I spin my head to the doctor with an attitude.

"Our Lord and commander says stop." I sound like a petulant child, eye-rolling as I flick my hand at the oncoming vehicles and Doc raises a brow and then frowns instead. "He obviously has some reason to make us pull over, and he doesn't sound like he's in the mood to argue about it."

"Better not disobey an irate Alpha in the making. If he's anything like his mother, I would say it's better to accept a request and question later." It's an almost submissive stance, but Doc looks tired and weary, and maybe he needs a commander right now more than I do. He pulls us over to the side of the highway and brings us to an immediate stop, waiting and watching as the distant vehicles close the gap between us, and the tension becomes unbearable.

"I'll quickly check on Sierra, make sure she's still tubed, and everything is plugged in." He moves first, gets up, and shifts into the back of the truck, exhaling and stretching with relief when he gets to the standing room part of the back. I watch him for a second, but my anxiety, as I can feel Colton getting closer, almost makes me combust.

"I need air." I point out, opening my door and hopping out before I scream. I'm overcome with the sudden heavy nervous tension of seeing him again and the rising flames of temper and accusation because he's being a jerk about it, and I hate him. It's hard to put the Carmen thing aside when I'm going to come face to face with the cheating ass once more.

I expected maybe some sort of sweet directions, not bitchy commands, and aggression from him. My own turbulent emotions are strangling me, and I suddenly have this newfound energy buzzing through my limbs. I can't sit at peace, and his getting closer is like waiting on a tornado hitting your house and knowing there'll be carnage. I have no chance. Colton is the tornado and my heart is my home.

As the first of the vehicles pulls up along the side of ours and disappears behind the bulk of our truck, I lose my nerve completely, turn, and walk to the rear of ours into the darkness, around the back to catch my breath and take a few seconds to recenter myself. I need some Dutch courage and some mood leveling before that moment of reunion with him. I inhale and blow it out heavily, hearing doors opening and slamming and footsteps, and I know I should just do it. Bite the bullet, walk right out to him. I move from behind the truck, walking along and turning up the side to head towards Doc's door. Head in chaos, eyes on the ground as my sight adjusts to nocturnal vision, and I watch where I'm stepping.

I walk smack bang with a certain amount of force into the black-dressed, enormous figure, cutting down from this side, and yelp with the collision. Knocked back momentarily, not hurt, but definitely winded. My heart skipping a beat, instantly making my legs go weak and my insides lurch in surprise.

"Lorey?" Colton's tone drops completely, a breathy whisper as I jump back and stare wide-eyed and lost for words. We just sort of stand and look at each other for a heavy and lengthy, loaded second, so much translating at the moment, and then he lurches

365

forward, partially shadowed out, so I can't make out his face perfectly. He grabs me by the wrist and yanks me to him forcefully.

I don't have time to react, or recoil, because all I get is a flash of glowing amber eyes appearing on that darkened face. Then I'm wrapped in strong arms and molded to a hard, hot body that makes me feel small and precious—wrapped up tight, unable to resist the way he lassos me. He knocks the wind out of me with the intensity of his embrace, hugging me in entirely and burying his face in the crook of my neck, snugly united and highlighting how perfectly we fit together. He squeezes almost all the air from me with the force of his hug, not a single part of me that's not pressed to him. His breath tickles and tingles my skin as it makes its way under the neckline of my sweater, and I'm dazed by the speed with which he absorbed me into his body.

I'm not going to lie and say it didn't make me momentarily forget everything except how he feels, how good he smells, and how right his touch is. Heartbreakingly so. I melt, my head getting hazy with this need to let him hold me, and I have to swallow back the overwhelming surge of emotion that has my heart rate hitching and my breathing getting shallow. Biting back instant tears, I taste my weakness shining through, urging me to wrap myself up and tell him how much I missed him.

He squeezes me half to death. Arms tightly wound around my upper body and waist. A hand comes around my neck, under my hair, to hold me in place. Pushing his face against mine, so we're cheek to cheek, his nose grazes my shoulder, and I hear and feel him inhale and release with the same relief I did. That intense contentment of finally finding home and sinking into it deliciously. Savoring these few seconds of finally getting what you've been craving for, needing, for weeks.

I almost cave, my limbs aching to curl around him to get lost in everything good about him. So caught in the heady sensation of being back in his arms as he wraps me up, like a mouse caught in a snake's death grip, with no hope of escape. I almost fade out into nothing but feelings of tingles, warm inner waves and butterflies, and a sense of belonging when something mentally slaps me in the face and reminds me what a shithead he is. Carmen's smug face in my mind's eye and the pain I felt four days after leaving him.

I shove him back with a little more power than I'm used to, a gush or surge of that misty energy conjuring from the intense anger that comes shooting out at speed and hitting him right in the abdomen with enough force I send him reeling back. His arms are impulsively splaying out to stop himself, and he manages to stay upright, even though it's obvious I threw him off. That look of utter shock that I just overpowered him and almost landed him on his ass, and my surge of aggression, when he thought snuggling was on the cards.

I don't forget the betraying asshole has a mate out there who wouldn't be too pleased to see how he's behaving with another femme even if I was his fated mate once upon a time.

"Don't touch me! Who the hell do you think you are, huh? That you can just yell at me, make demands, and then come walking on over here and grab me like that? Like you don't have a shitload of apologizing to do." Its fury building from inside me, aching to be released, and his simmering to low glow eyes fire right back up, like two very terrifying orange beacons in the pitch black. I can almost feel mine glowing in response, and it feels good to let my inner wolf peek again.

"Are you kidding me right now? Do you know how much shit I've been through for weeks trying to find you, and *this* is the thanks I get? You asked me to come! I'm beyond happy to see you. Excuse me for wanting to react and touch you when you're all I have thought about for weeks." My anger seems to feed his, and instead of love confessions and apologies, I'm getting asshole Colton. Sometimes I forget he's a Santo, and then he swoops right back in and reminds me what arrogant douchebags that whole bloodline is.

"I didn't ask you to look for me all those weeks, so don't even start with that bullshit. And you ... YOU are the reason I left, so no, I owe you no thanks and give no shits about whatever you've suffered in the meantime. You don't get to touch me anymore. Now shut up and let me pass. I have to tell him you're here. He's probably hiding in the back already, wondering what is going on." I attempt to get by him to head for the front of the truck, but he steps right at me, blocking me, so I bang into his torso and step back. Full-on aggression mode is switched on, and he's towering over me menacingly.

"Him? About HIM! Whoever he is, whatever the fuck he is to you, I'm going to fuck him up!" It's a vicious, jealous outburst, fueled with a sudden searing rage that even I can feel flowing from him as he springs back to me, almost shadowing me. He gets that close, bringing his nose down to mine, eyes burning bright, and I slap him in the abdomen.

"No, you fucking won't. Stop being an idiot. Just shut up and get out of the way." I push him again, and this time, he doesn't budge. His apparent mood is worse than mine, and he sticks his ground and stays as intimidating as ever, right in my face. That low growl of the wolf coming through at me.

"You're *mine!* Not anyone else's, and if I have to take down an asshole who thinks he changes that, I will. We are not done, you and I. He is about to learn that. I'm not even playing, Lorey. I will kill that motherfucker where he stands." I've never seen Colton like this. I can almost taste the fury pulsing from every pore as he loses a small ounce of control and his teeth peek. I'm only making him worse, and this is not the best version to introduce to the doctor or his mom. Even I feel a little tiny ounce of fear at this version, and I think maybe I pushed him a little too far with this whole other man thing. I need to calm things down and not bite, even though his statement makes me want to rip his throat out. This isn't helping any of us.

"I'm not yours, so you have no right to make any kind of threats. Not anymore. Just stop, okay. It's not like that. You need to calm down and not scare him. He's human, and he's not the reason I asked you to meet me." I reel in some of my anger, my voice softening as best as possible with this constant internal pain, reminding me never to let my stupid heart soften for him again.

I catch the hemline of Colton's black hoody, yanking him with me instead of still trying to get past him and change tactics. I turn and head to the truck's rear, pulling him when he stubbornly holds

368

still, fighting me for a moment, and then he relents and follows. The aggression and pain oozing from him have me all kinds of uptight, but I bang on the truck's back door to let Doc know I'm back here, and I hear the lock slide open.

Colton bristles instantly. I almost feel him ready to pounce in fight mode as we're about to come face to face with a guy he deems a threat to our bond, as ridiculous as he's being, and the door opens. I, too, brace myself if I might have to intervene and defend Doc from an angry wolf attack. I am fully prepared to take Colton on to save Doc's life; after all, I owe him.

Having heard our conversation, Doc sticks his head out warily, and his white pallor makes him almost glow in the darkness, a worried expression all over his face. He opens it wide enough to pop head and shoulders out, and Colton goes from a poised, lethal killing machine stance to a sudden 'what the hell' expression in seconds. He looks from him to me and back again as all manner of confusing emotions flicker across his face.

"Doctor, umm?" He seems to be dragging his memory as he says it, staring at Doc like he can't quite believe what he's seeing and trying to remember that mouthful of a name. That hostile, jealous need to maim him dies instantly as he realizes there is no way in hell I'm looking to mate with someone older than my parents. I feel it wash away, and the surge of relief that bubbles over affects me too, taking the edge off my anger and realizing half the time I don't even know whose mood is whose as we feed each other and react. My aggression slides away like I got hosed down with a cool jet in a heatwave.

"Ah, dear boy, you remember me. Look at you all grown up and rather hunky. You are very tall for a Santo. Wow, you certainly beefed up somewhat, did you not? Look at those shoulders. I bet you can bench press ten of Alora on a bad day. Such a specimen!" The doctor and his usual inappropriate babbling to diffuse an otherwise awkward situation, and I shove Colton aside and yank the door the rest of the way. Impatient to rip this BandAid off completely and show him why we brought him here.

"Excuse me," I say to Doc politely, suggesting he let me by and stop shielding the truck's contents. He shuffles aside as I climb up, getting halfway up the high step when Colton lays his hands on my waist, gripping me lightly, and pushes me up the last distance. It both riles me that he thinks I need his help like some feeble girl who didn't survive alone for weeks in the wilderness, and yet makes my heartache that he still, even mad and confused, wants to take care of me.

God, I hate him sometimes.

"Colton, come," I command, knowing the inside of the truck is pitch black in this darkness, and he has no idea who lies inside until he gets up and his nocturnal vision kicks in. I doubt he would recognize her scent as it's been so long, and she smells almost human due to not turning for nearly a decade.

He doesn't question, he just hops up effortlessly behind me and follows me so close his body touches me from behind, and I know it's deliberate. I can feel it in him, the longing and ache to get close to me again, almost as much as it's growing in me to be touched by him. I am aware of his proximity, like a throbbing pulse in the air, making me hyper-sensitive to his energy. I shake it off, knowing he's looking down at me and not ahead. I can feel his breath on my neck as he very clearly stakes his claim on me. Personal space is not in his vocabulary at this moment in time.

He is all in wolf mode in his head and acting like a male hitting the haze. Possessively close, practically bearing down on me as the femme he clearly wants to bone. It's a little unnerving that he is being so weird, but I get it—I left him. I knew where I was and was in control of my being gone, so I never had that frantic pain of loss. I always knew where he was and how to reach him and could have if I needed and wanted to, but he had none of that.

He just had silence. No idea where in the world I went and did not know if I was okay, so I guess it's why he seems a little stirred up and wolf crazy. His bond instinct to protect me must have made him insane these past few weeks, and until now, I never really thought of it. How that must have made him feel and the powerless nature of it. Especially if he could feel my fear, panic, and sadness in everything I have been through. His wolf is taking over, and his instinct to stay on my ass and convince me I need him stuck to me. That primal, aggressive urge to stick to his mate and kill anything that comes near her.

Usually, the human in us counterbalances it a lot better than he is, but I guess I can let it slide while he's caught in our first moments of reunion. My scent alone must be affecting him on all kinds of unbearable levels because he is getting under my skin and making me crazy. It's taking all my willpower not to turn and wrap myself around him.

I walk a few steps to put distance between us unsuccessfully as he bumps me the whole way in an almost claustrophobic manner. I stop when I know we're fully inside and then reach, feeling his face above mine with his taller height, having him towering behind me. I cup his chin just behind me, stretching my arm slightly and lifting it so he looks directly at the corner where Sierra is lying. His senses are all on me, so he hasn't even clicked she's here. That there's anyone else in here with us.

There's a moment of pause. I sense the heart stop and inhale. His shift from 'I need you' possessive, over hormonal crazy to 'what's going on?' confusion and the 'is that?' shock as everything about him changes. I feel everything that he exudes, and it makes my own emotions fade in comparison.

Colton steps around me instantly, freeing me from his presence as his attention is swept out from under him and darts to the bed in the dark. Swift and direct as he sees precisely who it is in the dim light. Doc is shuffling around and clicks something that illuminates the back of the truck with built-in low lights, and I focus on Colton sliding to his mom's side, scooping up her hand carefully, and almost gasping in shock. He leans in, making her look so small compared to him, and gently strokes his thumb across her pale hand. All the tenderness of a sweet child, infatuated with the mom he's been pining for years.

"Mom? Is that really you? Can you hear me?" He sounds like a lost little boy, so young and vulnerable, with an aching rawness to his tone, and, for a moment, I forget my anger, and nothing but compassion for him fills my heart. I can feel how this has ripped his heart open, and his pulse is racing so speedily that mine matches it. Colton regresses ten years, and he's just a boy finding the mom he's needed for so long, so much more than anyone could ever have known.

"She's sedated. Doc needs to wake her, but she doesn't know what's happening. Colton, you need to know ... there's nothing wrong with her mind." I point out, coming level with him and resting my hand on his arm as he stares at her, eyes fixed on her face. His breathing is shallow, and the confusion and pain are evident under that furrowed brow and glowing amber eyes. He can't contain his emotion, so his wolf is showing. He swallows hard, reaches out, and lifts a strand of her hair before brushing it back gently, so carefully like she's fine china, so fixated on her like this is some dream he doesn't want to wake from.

"How ... where?" His voice breaks, a harsh croak, and Doc keeps his distance to let me be the one to explain. It's not easy to tell a guy that the father he's loved all this time is why his mother was imprisoned and put in a coma. I don't even know how or where to begin, and I hesitate, looking at Doc and mildly panic-stricken for a moment when it comes to me. Doc shrugs and nods as though encouraging me. I think he's a little intimidated by Colton, to be fair. I mean, he did threaten to kill him three minutes ago.

I don't need to tell him. I need to show him. It's the only way I know-how.

"It's a long story. I think maybe it's better to do it this way. So you can see for yourself," I whisper, reaching up and laying my fingertips on his temple and waiting for his permission, tensing as my touch seems so light and hesitant on him, that familiarity dragging me to draw closer. Colton nods, oblivious to me while his attention is on her, knowing I mean, projecting my memories. I can't blame him; he's searched for her for so long, so no wonder she's all he sees.

I close my eyes and push them his way, rifling through and trying to find a starting point as I drag them to the forefront. I decide on one, right from my decision to turn east and follow that path, to finding the facility, then being caught. Deacon, the doctor, the cell, and finding Sierra, right until we got out, and I linked Colton. I show him every second on that timeline, even how they kept her and where hoping it all filters in while he's so distracted.

I need to give him all of it, even the parts I'm afraid of him knowing. I don't have the words to tell him about his father, and I don't have the strength to tell him about my family. Or that we're both hybrids.

Colton stands stock-still as it all plays in, and he relives what I did in the past couple of days, seeing, hearing, and learning everything I did. Feeling what I did and experiencing everything he must have felt from afar. In microseconds, the way transference works. Even the part I was most afraid of telling him—that I'm a half-breed vampire.

I feel him close me out as soon as the images of the last memory fade away like a shutter coming down as he disconnects from me. That wall of emotion blanks and pushes me away. It's not something most wolves can do, especially to an imprinted bond, but Colton does it right now and shields me from everything he's feeling in the moment and shuts me out. It's an Alpha gift to protect loved ones from pain and horror.

It shocks me and hurts me a little, but I don't think he's doing it to punish me. I think he's doing it because he knows his emotions are completely overwhelming and doesn't want to make me feel them. He's protecting me and pulling back, so he doesn't share what he's experiencing. He stands, lets go of his mom's hand, and looks over my head at the doc with a glazed, distant expression and not what I expected. A look of determination as that leader takes over, and he stands that little bit taller, moving in to take charge.

"How long do you need before you can wake her?" There's a coldness to his tone, a lack of feeling, and I wonder if he has withdrawn even from his emotions because it was too much for him, or if he is just really, really pissed. I honestly cannot tell, but there is a brewing storm in the air around him, even if he is shielding me. I guess finding out everything in your life was a lie, and the villain in your story is your father, has to hurt as much as when I learned about what he did to my family.

"A couple of days to bring her round fully, but she may take weeks to come to and recover enough to turn properly; there is no telling. She's been asleep for a very long time, and I don't know what kind of harm that has caused her." He looks helpless, and I can tell he also doesn't know how to react to Colton being so ... unemotional. It's like he didn't just find his long-lost mother sedated in the back of a truck, and he's absently directing some lost tourist where to go next.

"I'll drive. You stay back here with my mom. The manor is another thirty minutes away, minimum, and we need to get going before that asshole Deacon, and his failure sub pack show up. I don't want to be spilling blood in human territory." That growl, a hint of anger, and I guess I feel a little smug about that. Colton might rip that jerk a new one after all. I hope Deacon does show up because I know my Santo will kick that Santo's ass into next week, and I don't mind letting him have that one. Watching will be as much joy as doing it.

He doesn't even look at me, just nods at Doc to bolt the doors and then walks forward to the cab and climbs into the driver's seat, smoothly and fluidly, like he's driven military medical trucks his whole life and doesn't even blink an eye at it. Stopping and staring out the window at the assembled vehicles out there, I know he's linking the pack to tell them to move. He's issuing orders, and I follow and climb into the passenger seat, a little afloat with the sudden disconnect and unsure how to behave. This version is a Colton I don't know, and even I feel like I should do what he says.

I screw my eyes up at the trucks, counting maybe five, and way too many for the sub pack unless they're spread thinly among them, but I can't make out who's driving. The headlights are screwing with my vision, and I can't see anything but light glare when I try to look past them. I wonder if Meadow can see me, and I long for nothing more right now than to hug her. She would get a hug; Colton can go to hell, well, maybe not right now, as he seems like he could probably use one.

As soon as we hear the door lock slide and click into place, he glances back to make sure Doc has pulled down one of the folding seats and strapped himself in before moving us on. The fleet of vehicles roar into life, and two stay back to let us pass and follow. We're flanked, and Colton just focuses on driving. He positions us right in the middle of the other cars as though they're escorting some president. Precious cargo that needs their protection.

I guess we are. The Luna is as important as the Alpha in a pack. She's our Queen.

The need to have him say something overpowers my need to be mad at him, and I reach out and place my hand on his bicep gently.

"Are you okay?" I sound like that feeble girl from so long ago that imprinted on him and not the person I've grown into these past weeks. When faced with this guy, it seems I become a submissive, lovesick fool, and I silently hate myself for it. Colton seems different now, though, as I sit and evaluate his profile in the backlights shining at us from the black four by four in front.

He looks like Colton, still a cute boy with prominent dimples whenever he moves his face, which could melt any grown-ass woman's panties. He is still a handsome, dreamy, pretty boy face, with that air of cheeky confidence, yet he seems older. More mature, maybe slight aging that has him seemingly less carefree, high school jock, and somehow more severe and capable in a way he wasn't before. There's been a shift, and some of his youthful light has gone out. There's a sense of darkness around him that was never there and without tapping into his feelings, I don't know what it is. It's more than just learning about his mother; it was there when he walked into me outside the truck. Colton's carrying a weight and I want to know what it is.

"I don't want to talk about this right now. I need to ... just let me be, Lorey. Just for a minute." A petulant shrug of his arm, so I stop touching him, and it's like I've been scolded. An unexpected rebuff from the guy who just minutes ago hugged the life out of me with sheer need, and now I'm not allowed to touch him. I shouldn't be upset. He's hurt, he's processing, and he's in his head, and it's pretty hypocritical for me to be mad about that. I didn't want him touching me, and that hasn't changed.

I try to link him, thinking maybe talking that way will help soothe him, away from the doc's ears, and he might be more open to being less cagey with his feelings, but he has the door closed, and I can't get through at all. He's locked me out in every way, and I don't even know if this is normal behavior for him when he's nursing pain or if this is because he remembers I'm not his mate and he should only share that space with her.

Fuck you, Carmen. Fuck you, Colton.

I hate that he can make me feel this way, a new storm swishing inside me, and I have to stop myself from glaring at him. A fresh surge of conflicting pain, and I resist the urge to slap him. I sit back in my chair and pull my legs under me, hauling my body in tight to self-soothe, calm the torrent of crazy, and try not to stare at him. It's hard when he's right there yet feels a thousand miles away, and my own emotions are in an uproar. I can't even pick a side and stick to it.

I'm so confused by my idiot thoughts and responses. I want to be mad at him and hate him; I have every right, but when he's near, I can't stop this overwhelming pain and heartbreak he causes me, although right now, I've added compassion and empathy to that mix, and I'm dying inside for him. Even while cursing him. I want to ease his pain, and as stupid as it seems, I'm devastated he's closing me out like it has nothing to do with me.

"Where are we going?" I utter it his way, unable to not say something to him, even though he said he doesn't want to talk. Colton exhales with a sigh that signals he's not really into answering, but compelled to do so. I can't sit in painful silence feeling like this.

"To the manor I inherited from my mom. It's someplace my father had no control over. It's where we've been staying these past weeks. Lorey, I told you, so much has changed." Colton's eyes flick my way. He frowns at me, sighs again, and then looks back at the road but doesn't elaborate. I get he's currently working through some of his own shit in his mind, but an explanation would be nice. This minimal chat bullshit isn't working for me.

"Such as?" I push, locking my eyes on him with a flash of stubbornness, and I can't miss the way his whole body tenses up. The exhale, his frustrated grip on the steering wheel because it's obvious I'm not going to shut up and leave him alone, and that has him rolling his shoulders to relieve tension while he concludes that answering me is inevitable.

"The pack is divided. Half are here with me, the other at the mountain. There was a fight when I challenged my father for leadership, and it got real messy. With more attacks in the West, the people were turning, and he was becoming a dictator, forcing the people under his command and treating them like they were all his prisoners. I had to do something, and he didn't like it. He lost! I'm the rightful Alpha of the Santo pack now, but instead of stepping down gracefully as the laws dictate, he ordered those loyal to him to take out me and mine." It's an exasperated tone, explaining something he doesn't want to, and it revs up that aura of closed-off hostility around him. I gawp at him in wide-eyed shock, heart thundering crazily, trying to pull those words together. It hits me that while I was having my existential crisis, so was he.

"I don't know what to say." I stammer, side-swept with that revelation of events that I honestly never saw coming at all. That explains that cloak of darkness around Colton. Since I left, his entire world turned upside down, and his father already gave him reason to hate him, making my enlightening news less unbelievable. My memories only added fuel to his fire.

"There's nothing to say. My father tried to kill me. You were the catalyst. I guess it was you leaving me and realizing I was an idiot and lost the only thing that should have mattered. I failed you, and then a shit storm blew up around me with another vamp attack, and life imploded. My father's men are at war with his people and still under threat of new vamp attacks. We're scattered across the north, and I have a sizeable chunk at my mom's estate, hiding out and scared shitless." There's a calm sort of acceptance in his tone, as though he's not okay, but this is his reality, and he's dealing with it the only way he knows how.

"Oh, my God." I feel sick as bile rises in my throat, the levity of the situation finally coming through to me. Everything is in an uproar, and he's been in the middle of an actual war. I was an idiot to think that he'd been sitting twiddling his thumbs at the packhouse while I've been gone.

"It's not the same size as the packhouse by a long shot, it's a homestead, but it has some land. It's isolated from humans, surrounded by forests, and for now, we're managing to defend it pretty well. I'm more focused on keeping my people safe and giving them a place to rebuild before I go chasing vampires and starting fights like my father seems to be doing. It's all he cares about, and now knowing what you showed me ... it makes perfect fucking sense. The war was his glory days; he was a commander with an army who jumped to his orders, lording over a united race. I wouldn't put it past him to somehow deliver a means to the vampires to rile it up again." The anger simmers in his tone, and it's evident that Colton has been going through it as I have.

"Do you think we were meant to die in the orphanage attack? Was it him?" I touch on the memory Colton would have seen of Doc and me theorizing this exact question, but Colton shakes his head and glances my way with complete cynicism.

"No, he didn't seem to know that was coming, and from what you've shown me, your death is hers." He nods at the rearview, so I glance back at his mother. "Her death is his. He wouldn't have wanted it. And until I challenged him, he was still reeling me along like he thought I would somehow support him in his madness. He didn't want me dead; he wanted me bound to his 'loyal' so I would follow him into war." That edge of something else clawing in, like maybe anger at not seeing it before.

So, Juan wasn't behind the orphanage, but he created the tech to disable us. He sold it out there, not caring who got hold of it, because he wanted the vampires to think they had a weapon to restart a war. He had to know that once they got it, they would have the confidence to come at the wolves again, so he waited.

The vampires thought they had a foolproof plan. They aren't as strong as us, but with something like the isolation box, they would be stronger and have a shot at taking us down this time. This means Juan has to know how to combat it and disable the effects of the box. He would never let them have something that would give them their victory, of course not; he'll have a master plan that he's going to sit on until this thing is in full throes. He has to keep his weapon hidden and let this brew long enough to give the packs a need to unite before he brings out whatever that is and proves victorious once again.

Juan craved the union of all the packs, not just the north, and he knew the only way to force that kind of need was to push us back into war. He supplied the possibility and then sat back and waited, his arrogance telling him he would be the one chosen to lead them all. And now he has the answer to their weapon, forcing the packs to select him. It's his leverage. The wolves from every land will want the weapon to counteract theirs. It shows how insane he is to believe he would reign and lead when, the first time, my mother pushed him off that pedestal. So easy to knock down and replace. Did that teach him nothing?

And then, when he had the steps in place to ignite a second chance at gaining a crown, the Fates intervened instead, and nothing has been a coincidence since. Turning and imprinting me only weeks before the vampire's first attack—solidifying a white wolf in the midst, hoping to restore the balance because they knew what was coming. Tying me to a Santo. It all makes sense; every single piece of the puzzle fits. They always meant for me to end up in Colton's arms in the middle of it all. I'm the Fates trying to reclaim a prophecy that Juan keeps trying to destroy.

I turn my attention back to what he said, dragging my brain from that to this. Head a tangled mess of emotions, but the logic of the bigger picture is sliding neatly into place. I pick up on something he said.

"What do you mean bound to his 'loyal'?" I don't even know how he could do that.

"Carmen. She's the daughter of his Beta. He's always tried to push me to stick with only the wolves he approved of. He hated that my sub pack was never the children of his subs. He just had to accept it, but Carmen, I realize he kept pushing femmes at me from certain houses, and he only wanted me to mark and settle down once you posed a threat."

And we come straight to the one thing that chokes me up and makes me hate him again. He says it so matter of fact, like he didn't just stab me in the chest with a dull object and twist it for good measure. He just admitted it. That he's bound to Carmen and his father wanted it that way. He maybe didn't say it outright, but he said enough for me to interpret it that way. I fall silent and turn away as tears prick my eyes and make me feel stupid. Crushing that pathetic, ever hopeful, annoying shining light that pops up no matter what I tell it.

I might be the Fates trying to set the scales right, but Colton is not part of that plan because no way in hell would they allow him to be such a dumbass and do such a hurtful and stupid thing if he was my forever. How could he be if they let him mark her and break me all over again? You don't come back from a betrayal of the mate bond, not like this.

"So, your father's raging a war with not only vamps, whom he set in motion, but his pack, even though his intention was to lord over you all? And half of you now live in the manor that belonged to your mom, a half-witch? A manor you knew you had but didn't need. All while I was off finding your mom, who holds the key to us having some sort of powerful gifts to put things right?" I digress, trying to put everything in order and avoid mentioning what a douchebag, selfish, hurtful, cheating dickhead he is.

"Yeah, sounds about right. My mom's family is mostly gone. Not that I ever knew them, and I only knew I inherited this manor because she left it to me as a gift on my sixteenth birthday with a femme she trusted. It sat empty. She never lived there, so we had some cleaning up to do. Generally, though, I'm guessing she really is a witch, as it was completely untouched, and no one seemed to be able to get in until I tried the door. It was weird but ... a goddamn witch! The strangest part is that I don't feel shocked. It's like I knew, but I didn't. I can't explain it." He's slowly coming back to that swoon-worthy high school jock as he talks, hints of regular Colton shining through, but it doesn't dampen my hurt feelings.

I allow my eyes to stray back to him, holding my outward cool and trying not to let all I'm thinking spew out at him while focusing on the crucial issues in this conversation and not on him and me. I'm trying to absorb his words and that other slight issue that has been getting to me.

"At least it's not a vampire. Can't say that was welcome news," I answer sarcastically, a little more edge to my tone than I intended, watching that slight change to his expression and completely unable to read it. He half frowns, his jaw tensing a touch, but he doesn't have any kind of overdramatic response—no instant hatred or recoiling in disgust.

"It is what it is. It doesn't change who you are. It's just something to figure out, I guess." He doesn't look my way, and I can tell he's not as okay with it as he's making out, but he's also not freaking out and calling me a monster, either. I expected a more significant reaction, to be honest, and this seems anticlimactic. I probably took it worse than he is.

"The sub pack won't accept me back when they find out." I point out as if that was ever in my master plan, but I guess it partly is. I mean, everything is upside down, and my plan to leave and run just brought me back to where I started, among the people I left behind—no idea what the future holds anymore, especially if the wolves are warring too. The pack seems like my destiny, even if he is not.

"Why not? You think they'll care? You're Alora, and I'm Cole to them. They won't give a shit if we're half-breeds. That's not how they are; it's how my father is. And we're not the only hybrids hidden in the Santo pack. Nor the subs. Secrets are rife in my father's kingdom because he's an asshole, and it took me way too many years to realize that and see through him." He grips the wheel, that growl again in the undertone as his own words touch a nerve, and I can tell the whole father thing is getting to him way more than anything else. Maybe finding out about his mom was the final straw.

381

I grasp at that tidbit of information though, shocked, instantly grabbing at the file marked Colton's memories but know I won't even know what to look for in the nineteen years' worth of them, and instead start pulling names out of boxes to figure out which subs are also half breeds.

"Who? What secrets?" I blurt out, overwhelmed by too many scenarios and thoughts. The downside to having a head full of someone else's memories is that they are too vast sometimes to know you possess an answer without guiding you to the right visual. I probably have so many things in my head about him I haven't even opened and explored. I never stopped on any conversations about hybrids in the pack.

Colton sighs, tapping the steering wheel as he guides us onwards and shrugs. Like this isn't news to him and acting like it's nothing in the grand scheme of things. To him, maybe, but I spent my life being told I was an impure reject only to find out the Santos have been interwoven with that all along.

What the hell?

"The twins are hybrids. Angelics, actually. Then there's Meadow; her mother was a shifter, not Lycan, still a wolf, but different. She's fierce because she's multi-gifted like you are, and my father made sure no one knew his son was pack-bonded with impure breeds. He couldn't do anything about them, as they are all Santo by blood, and he'll never shame his bloodline or admit that most of the pack comes from interbred unions. There are hundreds of supernatural species, wolves are highly sexed horn dogs, and they will fuck anything." It's delivered with a callous smirk and a hint of pride at his species being hoes. Only a man would be proud of that.

"Eww, Colton!" I slap his arm, stinging my fingers as I do, disgusted and a little offended by that last sentence. It's hardly admirable in a species that also likes to mate for life when they pick the right one.

"It's true and the biggest secret of all. The haze doesn't just make us want to bone each other; it's a free-for-all and has been for centuries. I'm pretty sure my father isn't even a hundred percent

Lycan. He can't trace his roots any more than anyone else, and the history books are a complete fabrication, with every Alpha removing any part they deem shameful. They're bullshit ... like him removing prophecies. I would put money on the fact that the Santo wolves, being all shades, are a massive nod to us being a mixed species. The original Lycans were always brown. Brown with amber eyes. Most of the Santos are gray."

"Why am I only finding this out now? How long have you known all of this?" I blanch as my head spins, and it's like I'm relearning the entire history of everything I've ever known. All while he's over there like Mr. Cool taking it in his stride. Barely even a blink that our entire existence is based on horse shit. Nausea envelops me, and I get a little lightheaded with the number of explosions going off in my brain.

"Not long. The Shaman he's with us now and no longer bound to his Alpha Juan because I'm the rightful leader, and he doesn't have to obey my father anymore. He can now unleash all he knows without fear of the Fates punishing him for betrayal. He's a wealth of knowledge. Like what having red eyes in white wolves means, and why you had extra strong powers." He raises a knowing brow at me, and even that clicks into place.

"You knew?" That statement makes my head spin and I honestly can't even with him right now. My stomach is all in knots, my palms sweaty, and I think my lungs were on the verge of packing in with the fear of his reaction, but he already fucking knew! I gasp at him, sitting tall and leaning at him in utter disbelief.

"I've known for a couple of weeks. It all slotted into place when I found out, and now I know why you found it hard to home in on your abilities and why they weren't run-of-the-mill wolf gifts. You might say I've had time to get used to it."

I slump back, rubbing my temples with my fingers as everything blurs slightly and the lack of oxygen from gasping hits me between the eyes. I feel woozy.

"What else did he tell you?" I breathe out, feeling surreal now.

"Nothing that important in our current situation. Just general history of our people and the fact you're not the first like you.

383

Neither was your mother. He knew nothing of my mom's whereabouts, breed, or my father's actions before he came to the Santo house seven years ago. The Shaman previous to him died, and he came to us from my family's origin in Colombia. He never really fell for my father's bullshit and has always kept his peace and distance from the pack elders and the sub packs loyal to my father."

It all explains why, after imprinting, he was the one to intervene in the room, and Colton always said he trusted him. Now I know why, and it clicks together, another puzzle piece falling into place. Another random tidbit from our combined past that had more meaning than either of us comprehended at the time.

"Everything is crazy, yet all seem to tie together. Even us." I drop my hands on my lap, still leaning my head against the rest and suddenly so very exhausted with thinking, feeling, talking. Everything is taking its toll, coming to a massive head, and draining what little energy I have left inside me. I'm heavy and weighted down in so many ways, all while his presence is screwing me up, and I want to curl up and shut it all off for a bit.

"I knew. About us ... the whole witch thing. Something in me; it wasn't a surprise when we imprinted. It's like I always knew, yet somehow my brain didn't know-how. Maybe I have her visions, and somehow, when she bound me, I lost their memory. I can't grasp it, but it's like all of this was always out of reach of my fingertips, but I knew it was there. When it happened, it was like déjà vu in a sense." Colton casts me an apologetic look, and I get that hint of regret, slowly filtering my way as if he's lifting the wall between us a bit at a time, yet it's too late. A dimple appears with a boyish smile that does nothing to lift my growing black cloud.

I just glare at him, trying to make sense of it but at the same time, hating on him all the more with what he just admitted to me. If he knew somehow, why did he let me go? Why did he reject me?

"Then you're an even bigger idiot," I snap, emotionally spent, which adds another layer of fatigue to what I can't handle—turning my head and staring out the window, tensing up and bristling with that same pain again and fighting my stupid tears. I'm getting so fed up with feeling like shit when it comes to him. And he sits and admits that he maybe knew I should have been more important to him all along. Screw him. It crushes me, and I no longer want to talk and figure any of this out. I want him to leave me alone.

"I learn from my mistakes. I'm here, aren't I?" I can feel his eyes on me, but I refuse to look. Heart struck with a clawing, slicing agony.

"You can't undo what's done. Just drop it, okay. Now isn't the time to talk about us. We need to get your mom someplace to wake her up, see what she has to say about all of this, and how we unbind these gifts that are somehow going to do something in this shit storm." My voice is low and husky. I sound upset, yet probably tired, and I can feel him eating away at me with his eyes as he tries to read me.

"I can't believe I ever doubted you wouldn't be the Luna we all needed. I was wrong to doubt you, to doubt us. I am sorry that I wasn't what you needed. I can't tell you how much I regret everything, baby." There is genuine sorrow, and it's just another nail in his coffin.

"Don't, okay. It's been a long freaking day, and I'm exhausted. I want to close my eyes and think about all of this later. I feel like my head will explode, and we're not even getting the whole picture yet. I've been running for so long, and I think my body is finally giving up on me." It's a hint, turning fully away from him as I try to get comfy on the worst seats ever invented as we bump along a relatively smooth road. Colton looks at me; a long pause of seconds relents, exhaling heavily. He knows defeat when he senses it.

"Try to sleep. The manor is a while away, and it's not like I'm about to let you out of my sight anytime soon. We have time to talk. I think I also need some headspace to figure some stuff out. I can't believe my mom is lying behind me. This is all so surreal." There's a lightness to what he says, and I blank it.

I curl up against the window fully, not like I needed his permission, but I'm grateful he'll leave me be. He still thinks that I belong to him, even though he has an actual mate somewhere out there, most likely in this manor, and he needs to remember that. I'm not his, he's not mine, and when Sierra wakes up and unbinds me, we need to figure out how to keep our distance and navigate this if we're all going to get through it.

Colton's story and mine will head in different directions when Sierra tells us what to do. We both need to accept that and deal with it.

HOMESTEAD

The warm sensation sliding around me, and the sudden weightlessness I experience wakes me up before his
voice does. A feeling of floating as everything comes back to me, and my brain re-engages with my limbs as warm hands and body transfer heat to mine.

"Baby, we're here. Wake up." Colton's honey tone slides over me as his scent submerges me in a comfortable, firm hold, submerged in his delicious scent that makes me giddy, and I blink my eyes open to find myself in his arms while being scooped out of the truck as he stands by my door. The night is cloaking around us, but the illumination in front of me makes my eyes blurry as I try to adjust and screw them shut quickly. Taking a moment to savor that in-between awake and dreaming state. He has me in his arms, pressing me to him, one under my legs and one around my back while my face is in against the crook of his throat, nestling me in as the cool air brings me round fully.

I impulsively slide my hands up his expanse of hard chest, searching for a place to anchor myself, aiming to slide around his neck when sense fully awakens me, and I realize this is probably not wise when my heart is so bruised. Getting tangled up with Colton is not what I need. It's far too easy to accept his touch and willingness to add intimacy to the mix, but I have to be stronger than him.

"I can walk. Put me down." I croak hoarsely, my sleep-addled tone heavy, and wriggle to free my legs. Resisting even if it's feeble, and thankfully he isn't fighting me.

After a moment of hesitation, Colton relents, sliding my feet to the ground carefully, but he keeps me anchored to him with the arm around my waist and tugs me front on. Bodily closes the gap between us and lifts his other hand to stroke my cheek as he leans in to bridge the height difference. Rendering me momentarily senseless, as that burning connection makes my knees buckle almost wholly. He cups my face and pulls me in, bringing his forehead down to mine, and pushes us together intimately. Our breaths mingle in the cool air, and I'm overly aware of how dangerously close this is. A little inch more, and we'll kiss. Caught tired, slow in reaction speed, and somehow feeling vulnerable at waking up to his touch.

"When my mom's settled in the infirmary, we need to talk. We need to figure this out and fix us. I missed you more than you'll ever know, Lorey. I'm never letting you go again." His eyes stray to my lips, and that crazy, overwhelming urge to lean in and take what he's pondering doing almost kills me. My lips part slightly as the tug of desire pulses through me with hunger, and I'm powerless to pull back when caught in his breath this way.

His touch goosebumps my skin all over, the low intensity of his voice drawing me in as if no one else exists around us, and I almost weaken to the point of melting into him. My pelvis and between my thighs heat to molten lava at this kind of contact with him, and I almost have to press my knees together to gain some control. The haze is approaching, and I guess it's already screwing with my libido, or maybe it's always just him, and I'm still a weak fool for this man. More so when caught off guard and too tired to think straight. So easy when this feels so right, but I catch myself and finally muster the strength to pull back, covering his hand with mine and sliding it from my face.

"Colton ..." I start to rebuff him, but he doesn't let me loose as easily as he put me down.

"We can't ignore how we feel about each other. That we're meant to be." It's a hint of desperation in his ravaged tone, mirroring my urges, his jaw tensing and squaring off, which only makes those irresistible dimples prominent. Those lowering brows bring out the cute-boy face—leaning closer and making it harder to breathe when my senses are filled with him. It sparks that self-defense mechanism in me, though, that urge to run far away before he cripples me again, and I slide my hands between us and push him away with enough force to get him to release me.

"Why not? You did!" I bite, stepping back coldly, as his hold drops and the sweep of hurt and regret is evident on that flawless face. It tugs at me, slicing my heart with a sharp stab, but I don't weaken, pushing my pain and agony away and refusing to break. He can go to hell if he thinks he can be mated elsewhere but still have a side chick, so he doesn't have to live with the mistake. I won't be some dirty secret that has to steal moments with him, and share him with her, just because he didn't manage to break our bond by taking another. I'm not doing this, no matter how much I yearn for him or still love him. I have more respect for myself than that, and I won't be one of those wolves who disgrace themselves by committing adultery with a mated, even if we were destined.

He broke this, not me. He made his choice, no matter what his reasons were. It can't be undone.

"You're angry, hurt, and upset ... all valid, and I understand why. If you need time to forgive me, Fine. But I'm not going anywhere. I'm not giving up. I need you, and I'll earn your forgiveness, no matter what it takes." Colton is back in serious, soft-faced, high school, hot boy mode, and I shake it off.

I ignore him, trying to blot out words that wound me to the core and turn to walk away, but he catches me by the wrist and stops me in my tracks—tugging me back slightly and igniting further fury. Burning, searing touch that was invented to torture me by being both the best feeling in the world and the worst. That bubbling temper dominates the pit of my stomach, but before I can turn to tell him to back off, my thoughts are interrupted by a high voltage distraction.

"*Chica*!!" Meadow comes bounding from nowhere, darting at me like a lioness pouncing its prey, like a freight train and a tornado all in one, and sweeps between us, hauling me off my feet in a bear hug that momentarily dazes me and spins me around with alarming strength for a girl shorter than me. "*Dios mío, niña, te extrañé mucho.*"

She's strong and persistent in her very aggressive affection. She smothers me in Latino love, squeezes me so my ribs almost crack under the strain, and then dumps me on my feet to grab me by the face with an insane grip. She kisses me all over my cheeks, nose, and forehead like an overbearing momma, and it's a furiously fast barrage that doesn't give me a second to counteract. I can only screw my eyes shut, pucker up my face to protect my poor features, and accept this ambush while trying to unhook her fingers around my cheeks before she leaves bruises.

"Mead ... ddd ... ooww." I try to wriggle free of those clawlike hands, and the lipstick smeared attack on my face, giggling wildly at the ridiculousness, but she's relentless. Finally, once I'm sure every inch of my face is in matching rouge red from her lips, she lets me loose.

"Oh, my God, my baby girl, she's come to me, and now I can die happy knowing my *Hermana* is home." She's being overdramatic, her accent heavier than usual with the surge of emotion she's spewing. She's still holding me in her arms, but I have to say the feeling is mutual. I've never been so happy to see another femme in my life. I throw myself at her for a second hug, this time one I can take part in, and she squeezes me once more so I get to wrap my arms around her properly.

I can tell Colton has moved away as his invasive presence releases the stranglehold on my heart and a glance tells me they're at the rear, removing his mother's bed as members of the pack move in to help. There's a lot of chatter as people figure out who's coming out of the truck, and I can feel the whispers spreading through the pack as the atmosphere is charged with shock and excitement. I can see some pulling out the machines and cabinet and putting ramps in place. A hive of activity over there, with Doc directing with that unique accent of his above the drone, issuing orders to his new mass of helpers.

"Let me look at you." Meadow drags my attention back to her and pushes me back to arm's length, and even though it's dark out here, lights from the vast, towering house standing tall in front of us illuminates this area enough that we can see each other with clarity. That was the light that hurt my eyes when I woke up.

"You look so good, so healthy. Your hair has grown, you're losing your puppy face, and ... oh, God! What are you wearing?" Meadow's face and tone altogether drop as her eyes run up and down my attire, and she visibly gawps. The look of sheer disgust which envelops her expression makes me laugh.

"Escape clothes!" I shrug under her scrutiny, amused by how she's now holding the arm of my sweater between two nails like it's a dirty rag, and lets go before rubbing her fingertips as if to expel the grime. I'm not dirty, but her reaction is priceless as she shakes her head at me.

"Why do you keep letting that boy pick your clothes, huh? It's not a good look. Colton has no taste for female things. I mean, he dated Carmen for two years, which says it all, *Chica*." She bobs her head from side to side, waving a pointy red nail in the air, and I let out an involuntary snort-laugh. She's so 'hood sometimes; I love her to bits.

"He didn't. Dress me, I mean. He found me like this. It's all I had to hand." I look down, pulling at the gray sweats a little as I take in my baggy outfit and oversized boots, but it's not as bad as she's making out.

"We need to remedy that. Once we get our Luna inside and comfortable, you and I need to burn these. Maybe bury them and perform some kind of last rites." She tugs at the hemline of my sweater and then runs a set of talons through my hair to push it off my face and draws me back to her. "You do look different, though ... like you only left for a few weeks, but you've grown in years. You look beautiful and less tortured. My baby's growing up so fast." It's an insightful perspective, but she's right. These past weeks, I felt like I've matured and grown as a person in subtle ways. Eating less, exercising more, I probably look slimmer. And I knew I had shed puppy fat while being out there in the wild.

I'm no longer in that frame of mind that I'm some feeble no one that isn't important. I know I'm the center of something, and this is where I need to be for now. I'm not sure about being less tortured given my current situation: cheating mate, relearning my past, and finding out my entire pack was murdered. I would say I'm just handling it better than I would have a few weeks ago. I feel mentally stronger.

"Why, thank you, although I'm tired. I need sleep. I must look a wreck, but you're right. We need to get Sierra inside." I nod to where they all seem to have everything under control. Catching sight of the bed coming into view and Colton stuck to his mom's side, her hand in his once more, even though she is still dead to the world. He's looking at her with so much adoration and fixated that it makes me feel wholly broken as I watch him. A longing for that without complication, without this mess between us. To have him look at me the way he's looking at her, that unconditional love that's so hard to find.

We move out of the way as they swing past, and I flatten against the truck as the entire entourage gets by us and follows close behind, meadow sliding her hand in mine and guiding me with her to tag on at the end when they get past.

"Ahh, Alora." A voice comes from my side, and then I'm divebombed by an enthusiastic male who footballer-style wrestles me into a hug before I'm hit from behind by another. Equal stealth and strength, and I almost fall over with the weight of two heavy boys hugging the life out of me. Unable to breathe and unsure if this is an attack, I crumple almost to my knees.

Domi and Remi nearly choke me to death, ruffling my hair, picking me up between them before I get ground into the mud, and I get a kiss on each side of my face in unison. Sloppy, wet, a bit eww, but overall, it's kind of sweet.

"Our little sister came home. Our puppy!" They both state in synchronized perfection, sounding like a melody in their singsong playfulness. I get yanked from side to side, set on my feet, and then let go just as Cesar appears in front of me, Meadow moving aside with a look of joy on her face and smiling like a proud mother.

"Don't you ever do that again, Missy! Do you know how worried your pack has been?" Cesar swoops between the twins, his accent as equally heavy as his mate's and a stern, paternal tone to match that serious frown he is giving me. He gives me a less ferocious cuddle, a quick squeeze, and a kiss on the cheek before he pulls back and the rest of the sub pack seems to appear around me.

Mateo, Radar, Jesús all crowd in at me, and I guess they were part of our escort to get us here. All of them take it in turns to lean in and welcome me back with a quick embrace and a peck on the cheek, a few words of welcome until I'm blushing and awkward with all this attention.

"We missed you. Don't run like that again. We're your pack, man. We were all crazy worried." It's Jesús, and he bops me on the head with a soft fist and shakes his head at me, a real frown on his face that shows his genuine emotion.

"Yeah, kid, little pups like you shouldn't be out there alone!" Cesar reiterates his earlier statement.

"Colton has been unbearable, dude. You, girl, are getting chained to him, so we don't have to endure that again." Mateo pushes the twins aside and clears a path in front of me as he tries to move us along, and Meadow ducks into the center beside me, catching my arm in hers and starts walking me in behind the boys as they turn and begin leading the way. Some turn to walk backward as they interact and throw me smiles and genuine looks of relief that I'm home. I can feel it all around me that it's real and honest. My adopted pack's genuine relief and love swell my heart so much it hurts. None of them are faking it at all, and I don't question where that particular femme of Colton's is because, right now, I don't want to know, and I don't care.

"You missed a war. Colton put his daddy on his ass. It was epic." Jesús seems a little too gleeful over that fact, skipping sideways in front of me somewhat boyishly, and Mateo shoves him in the shoulder playfully, out of the way. A warning tone to his words.

"Shut up. Colton hears you talking like that, he'll put *you* on your ass. You know how sensitive he is about all this right now."

"Yeah, pipe down, bro; he's only a few feet ahead. Have some respect." Radar, the voice of reason, leans in; he pats me on the arm in afterthought, with a nod, and a wink, to say, hey. That always terrifying white eye, blank, dead, but his good one is kind of shiny and happy, and it makes him a little less scary to look at. The scar isn't as much of a visual draw as when I first met him, and he steps in, speaking a little lower, nearer my ear.

"Welcome back ... and thank you. For finding her. She's been missed for so long; some of us were losing hope." There's a strange tone in what he says, a distant look in his eye, and as he talks, his gaze wanders to the bed ahead of us. He shoots off instantly to catch something one of the trolley pushers drops. Scooping it up before it hits the ground and merging into that hobble of people to replace it on the bed.

"Radar always had a thing for Sierra. You've no idea how much this means to him for her to be home." Meadow whispers in my ear, hushed, so the rest don't catch on. Like it's some unknown secret, and I quizzically glance her way.

"What? Isn't he too young? Aren't they like son and mother age?" I flash a look at him again in the crowd, then back to her in confusion, but she shakes her head.

"Radar is our *Papi*. Every pack has a mature mentor. He's older than all of us, mid-thirties. He went to war as part of Luna's guard. He got that scar on his face by protecting her with his life, and it almost ended him. Goddamn silver and wolfsbane, I shudder to think. He's always been a slave to Sierra and never mated because his heart lies with her, devoted and loyal. It's kinda sad to be that crushed on someone; even in their absence, you still pine for them." Meadow is hushed, but the torn tone of genuine empathy drags through her voice, a hint of actual pain for her packmate.

"They had an affair?" I gasp, my head spinning at that point alone, and I can't help but stare back at Radar in the people before us, seeing him in a whole new light. He's not exactly ugly or unattractive. That scar is a major, but he has a nice face despite it, and a robust and tall build, like Colton. I guess the white eye makes him a little badass in that rugged, hero-type way.

"No, you know the laws on adultery with a mate bonded wolf. Radar is straight down the line, not a rule breaker. He never told her, so she never knew; he never even dared to look her in the face all those years because he was completely submissive in the hierarchy to her. It's forbidden for the guards to look upon the Alpha's mate and make eye contact. The Luna had many guards, and he just blended in, I guess. He was the only one of her guard to make it back alive, though, probably because he was so badly wounded and recovering that he was taken down and missed the last battle they ever fought. The Luna's guards were all massacred in that last fight. Then everyone came home, but she had gone before he recovered enough to regain his duties." Meadow shrugs, retelling what she knows, and I inhale heavily as pieces click in place, and it leaves a bitter taste in my mouth.

Juan probably had them all slain too, because they would have been loyal to their charge. Their Queen. She was their focus, not Juan, and Radar escaped only down to being almost dead. This means he missed what happened with my mother and knows nothing of what Juan did. He would be dead too if he'd been there, which removes any doubt that he was ever involved. He didn't even get the chance to save her from being sent away. I think if he had been, he would have died to rescue her all over again.

However, the adultery thing highlights how much Colton doesn't respect or care about me if he expects me to throw aside the laws and have an affair with him, anyway. He's an asshole of the highest order if he thinks that's a solution to him marking that puta. We all know the shame it carries, and I could be completely exiled from this pack if we went through with it. His Alpha role would dissolve, and he too could be dethroned to live in shame. He can't have his cake and eat it.

I blink in Radar's direction, trying so hard to get my head around this new information as we sweep into the brightly lit grand foyer of a massive entranceway of this so-called homestead. It's amazing and huge. Prehistoric and the décor is old-world witch, but I don't doubt it can house a vast amount. I mean, the manor Colton grew up in was more of a castle and housed hundreds; this is small in comparison, but still a freaking castle in its own right.

The hubbub of the crowded hall and the wave of bodies moving around and up and down the stairs as the word spreads their long-lost Luna is back makes this place feel pretty overwhelming. However, it's not enough to distract me from watching Radar follow the group. Stopping when they get so far as Colton and Doc wheel Sierra's bed towards a narrow hall to the left.

"I should go with them." I nod after them as more of the group of helpers drop off, leaving a bare minimal body count to turn her bed into a door. Mainly Colton, the doc, and a couple of femmes who are helping with the cabinet and her machines.

"Yeah, you should. We're all going to go back out on patrol of the borders to watch for your tail; we have to keep this place safe. Tell Colton to link me when he wants me back to take care of you and find you some decent clothes. I'm sure right now Sierra is his priority." She clasps my hand tightly, squeezes it, and leans in to kiss me on the forehead before nodding towards the door that Colton and his skeleton crew went through.

"Meadow ... I'm so glad to be back," I say honestly, an afterthought, as she moves away, warmed by the tearful smile she gives me and that little rub of my shoulder to say it's all going to be okay. Despite everything, even finding out that I could survive out there alone, I have missed her and being around people. Being in a warm and safe place, I don't have to hunt for my meals anymore. It reminds me of what a pack can be like. I can do it alone. I just prefer this, not out there. Being here reinforces it. I don't want to go back out and disappear anymore. Everything's different, and I don't want to leave again.

"We are all happy to see you back. I made a mistake in letting you leave. Colton is still trying to forgive me. Don't do it again." She laughs, but there's a serious edge to her tone and a look that hints at an actual warning.

"I'm not planning on it. All of this is bigger than us now. Priorities have changed." I point out, and she exhales with another nod.

"Good, because he'll strap your ass to him and put guard duty on you twenty-four-seven if he even gets a hint you might take off again. That boy is not playing no more, *Chica*!" That head wobble and finger point always make me smile at her, but I 'hmm' then gesture I should go. I don't care right now what Colton thinks or wants. I need to see what's going on and then sit. I only dozed in the truck for a short time, and I'm physically exhausted and could do with a moment to get used to this buzzing house. After weeks of nature and solitude, this human chaos is a bit much to get my head around. This whole thing is mentally overwhelming, and sleep is all I want, even though I'm not going to get it for a while.

I head after Colton, trace their steps down a hallway, and turn right through the door they went to, which takes me along a short hall, through two double doors into a proper infirmary. It's already like a mini-hospital wing, which is weird given our kind's ability to heal, so I guess this is from when the witch side of Colton's family stayed here. It's white, large, yet crowded with cabinets full of potion bottles on every wall. Some of it looks dated, but mostly there are modern additions, obviously brought by Colton's medics who are hurriedly wading in and helping move Sierra to a central bed that's more substantial than the one she's on.

Wolf packs do have medical staff and doctors. We sometimes need them, especially in the younger ages when we have not yet turned, and we catch diseases or get injured. We're vulnerable in youth, much like mortals are. It's irresponsible for a pack not to have the means to protect all in our group.

They switch over her machines to full-size ones, change her tubes, and hang up her saline bag on a trolley to the side. Some of the wolves already in here file out, gazing longingly her way and nodding at Colton as they leave. I know the link between pack members is generally the preferred mode of communication, but it sucks that, to me, it's a silent wall. I watch in envy as so much translates between them, but I hear nothing.

I miss pack linking and the sense of unity it gives you as a whole; it reminds me I'm never really going to be part of this pack. Colton could initiate me in now he's Alpha and has that power, and I could maybe link that way, but once his mate gets a whiff I'm here, I don't doubt world war three will erupt. She'll never let him put me in the pack to have more of a bond with him.

I don't know where she is, but she has to be around here somewhere. After all, she is his Luna now. Mates never stray far apart, and as the Luna, her job is to care for the vulnerable in this massive palace. She probably got left behind here when he came for me because he knew she would aggravate the situation and make things worse. Not that it needs much help.

Doc moves in to talk with a woman in a white coat I recognize from the Santo medical center in the valley. She has two nurses flanking her as they busily squirrel around, put trolleys away, and sort out the haywire mess of machines they've taken from Sierra. Tidying up and making her ready for her new stay here. I stand back to watch as they settle her, and the transition is complete.

Colton pulls over a high stool to the head of her bed and perches down beside her, oblivious to me over here, leaning in and saying something softly as he strokes her hair back, fully locked on her face as everyone else seems engrossed on the care plan they're discussing. I can hear Doc listing medications and withdrawal key points, step-by-step what they need to do over the next few hours, but all my attention is on that solitary, strong, broad figure with his back to me and that longing pulling me to comfort him.

Despite everything going on, we both have so much chaos in our heads and a shared pain from finding out things that turned everything upside down. Now isn't the time to hold that against him while all this is going on. Neither of us was prepared or mature enough to deal with the tsunami of shit we've endured these past weeks, and I'm weary as it's all caught up with me. I don't want to carry the feelings of hurt and hate on top of that, too; not right now.

We have to figure this out, wait on Sierra to see if she has an answer, and focus on the fact that Deacon and his crew will follow us. Soon as they wake up and realize what's happened, I'm sure they will notify Juan, and there will be a mad scramble to get here before she can tell everyone the truth.

I can be mad at Colton, hurt by him, but he's my Alpha right now, and I need to look to him for leadership and keeping us all safe. If all I do is argue and carry a grudge, I'll make it harder for myself. The pack, this house, this place, it's where I'm meant to be through this, and I need to put this shit aside and stop thinking about myself for a little while. About how what he did broke my heart when the priority is everyone else and Sierra right now.

"This is not the little sub pack and hide out I imagined it would be." Doc infiltrates my thoughts, appearing beside me with that soothing English dialect that's becoming like a warm hug, and I have to smile at that.

"Me either. I knew nothing of what's happened since I left. It's crazy." I shrug, eyeing up the room with a sigh.

"Yes, Colton gave me a condensed version as we wheeled Sierra in. He looks as tired as I feel, and we're both sagging over here, probably just as eager for a bed as the other to lie down for a little while, but both of us have to be here. Although, I'm rather glad that we ended up in a place that ensures I have time to wake her safely. I don't need to rush and risk her body going into shock. This was definitely your Fates guiding the way and providing us with ample shelter for a very difficult task."

"How long do you think that will take?" I ask genuinely, eager to see Colton finally get to reunite with her after all these years. Eyes fall on that beautiful man as he tends to his mom lovingly.

"We've come up with a plan to slow down and stop the sedation meds over forty-eight hours, to let her brain come out of the coma of its own accord. We'll monitor her, keep her stabilized, and adjust as she progresses. She might have a few days of a vegetative state where it seems like we've lost her—that's normal. Eight years is a long time to live in a dream world, and the mind is a complex piece of hardware that sometimes requires a reset period. We'll just take this as it comes and hope she'll be one of the rare cases of long-term coma patients to come out and be able to interact within mere days." He nods, a look of relative confidence on that lowered brow.

"She's a wolf. I say stack your bets on the positive side." I perk him up with a cheeky smile, and it gets a little one in return.

"Quite!"

"I don't know where we go from here." I point out, nodding at Colton across the room, not meaning just him and me, trying to hide the longing that crosses my face, and Doc nudges me with his shoulder.

"I'm a believer that a good cup of tea and a long chat usually resolve many of life's issues. Problems that seem overwhelming are sometimes just smoke and mirrors, and getting it all out is sometimes the only way forward." He raises those bushy, gray brows with a knowing expression, and I nudge him back.

"Like confessing all to a strange girl who fell into your medical facility?" I smirk.

"Exactly. Sometimes you have to throw away your entire life's work, put your trust in a higher power, no matter how many signs are killing your hopes, and know they won't steer you wrong if you just stop fighting it." His eyes stray to Colton, which has the annoying effect of dragging my vision back to him. That strong, upright figure, looking a little too inviting while framed by the light from the lamp over Sierra's bed. Always so unruffled, even in the face of a storm. He's solid, calm, and takes it all in his stride.

"Good advice, Doc. Not so easy to follow, but yeah ... I guess." I exhale heavily, feeling hopeless when he's over there, looking like everything I need to cure me of my eternal agony. "We'll figure this out together, young lady. After all, you are our savior." He throws his arm around me awkwardly, squeezes me, and then drops it just as quickly as though he crossed some boundary that threw him well outside of his comfort zone. I get the overwhelming surge of flustered, eccentric cringing at his public display of affection and let out an involuntary giggle.

"I guess I better go white flag the Alpha until we can see where all this is going. Might make life easier if I give him a few days' grace." I shrug it out, knowing that Colton probably could use less stress until Sierra wakes up.

"He's young, headstrong, stubborn like his mother, and still finding his feet in his new role. Go easy on him. He has the world on his shoulders, and he needs a little help in holding it up. His head is not quite where it should be." He glances at him and then off to the femme medic across the other side, who waves him to her.

I nod, taking the hint, and push off to walk toward Colton, leaving Doc to wander back to the femme in the corner, pouring over some clipboard as she jots things down.

I take a leveling breath, push all my riots of feelings into one tiny box, and sit on them for now. Determined to be civil and not let everything ooze out of me while he needs a friend. I approach him from behind, and like in the truck, he's so zoned in on his mom that he doesn't acknowledge me coming close until I get right up beside him and lean in to look at her. Eyeing her up now that she's settled in here, and it's odd, but I swear she has more color to her pallor and her hair looks a little shinier. It's almost like she knows she isn't alone anymore, that she's surrounded by her people and their love, even if it sounds ridiculous.

Seeing them together like this highlights how much he looks like her now he's an adult. He always had her strong DNA with the same profile, small nose, and perfect bone structure of two very beautiful people. The dark hair, and straight brows, although Sierra is noticeably pale compared to Colton's tan, he has all year round. She is lithe and feminine in her build, though, and Colton, well, he's your typical muscular, tall, and built Alpha type. He has more muscles than brains sometimes, and he has a nice ass.

A nurse pushes a stool up behind me with a smile and nod, and I take it gratefully, sitting beside Colton and trying hard not to reach out to touch him. He looks so lost in the moment, eyes fixated on her. So many thoughts must be running through his head. It's like watching a pained child trying to figure something out, and that maternal instinct in me revs up a thousand watts and makes sitting here unbearable.

"I can't believe she's really here ... that's she's real. The times I have dreamed of seeing her again." He whispers it, that sexy voice low and rough, alerting me that he's aware I'm beside him after all, and I relax into the seat, propping my feet up on the bar and leaning towards him slightly. I am suddenly consumed with fierce protectiveness over him when he seems this vulnerable.

"I'm just glad that we got her here. That you came when I found her." What else can I say? Nothing I can add right now will ease the tension as we wait, and he knows everything I do about all of this.

"How could he do this to her? How could he not love her the way he was supposed to?" His eyes run back to her face, once again strokes her hair, and he's so lost in his feelings that he overlooks my sarcastic eyebrow lift and tilted chin gesture I give him.

That's an excellent question, Colton. You might know, given you clearly have the same flaws! Why couldn't you?

I shake it out of my head before he senses my attitude, scolding myself for such an impulsive response, but still, he is dense sometimes. I know this projecting crap will only make me mad, and I don't bite or say it out loud, but goddamn it, Colton. Really?

I know he doesn't need this right now, so I sigh it away, breathe slowly, count to ten, sit a little taller, and focus on what he needs instead. Reminding myself that this is bigger than us, I have to be less irate.

"He betrayed the mate bond; he doesn't deserve her." I point out flatly, then curse myself under my breath for still pushing it out there, even if I didn't mean to. It's like everything we are saying is so damned obvious, yet Colton doesn't even click. He doesn't move or react, just that same silent, fixed stare as he watches her breathe, eyes on her closed lids, and sits. I feel like screaming and hitting him over the head with the nearest hard object, but instead, I stare at the ceiling for a minute and let it pass. Sooo slowly.

"I should have found her a long time ago, before any of this. I should have looked harder, but I was young and stupid, and I believed my father when he said it was for the best."

Oh, for the love of God! I mean, when you decide to avoid a topic and they just keep pushing it between us like some sort of annoying sign, it grates a tiny bit. I give up, eye-roll upwards at the Fates, and mentally ask them if this is deliberate.

That heartbreak and rawness in his croaking tone, though, finally tell me how much his father's betrayal is screwing him up, and I focus all my energy on that and not the universe trying to make me smother him with his hoody. I instinctively wrap my arm around his, hoping contact will keep me from heinous beatings, and lean my head on his shoulder, trying to blank them out. He's still trying to shield me but, this close, he's failing to do it fully, and I can feel it inside me. I want to ease his pain as it flows through me and circles around my own heart and stomach.

It's heavy, deep, and consuming, and I forget everything about being upset or angry with him. I slide my flattened palm along his arm instinctively, cover the back of the hand he has laid on his mom's, and entwine my fingers in his so we hold hands on top of hers. Colton turns his head with my contact and rests his chin and mouth on top of my hair, pushing in against me, so we're half cuddling but not really, just touching, leaning together, and for once, I don't push him away or feel the need to jump out of proximity. We both exhale simultaneously, a heavy releasing of tension, hurt, and energy, as we sag together, and everything pauses for a second. That calm silence his touch always brings me.

I can feel him feeding off me, soothing him slightly with my touch as an imprinted mate should, and I close my eyes and enjoy the stolen moment I'm allowing myself. I can push everything aside and pretend that it's okay to be what he needs when it's about her when the topic isn't us, and markings, and anything other than being a support for someone who needs it.

"I don't know how to lead, Lorey. These people, this pack. I'm just a kid. I'm not ready." The devastation and self-doubt rip through me as it emanates from him, and I look up from my nestled position, shifting to see his face without breaking away. Hating that he feels so out of whack, and the classic, confident rock I've come to depend on is wavering.

"You're a born leader. Maybe it seems hard right now, and things aren't clear, but you are the best for your people, Colton. Look around. They're here with you. You did this. Safe, protected, you stood up and made a stand for them against someone you love. You put them first, always. The good of the pack it's always your primary focus, even when other things get in the way. How can you doubt that? It's what makes you the strongest kind of leader!" I praise him with honesty, heartfelt, and hushed, as I whisper the words he needs to remember. How he can doubt himself this way is beyond me. Everything I know about him makes it obvious; he was always going to be the best kind of Alpha. He is!

"Maybe I just want to be a selfish kid. Who took the girl he wanted and walked away, and screw all this. I should have left with you. Belonged with you wherever you went." He sounds defeated, and I know this isn't him. This is a tired and uncertain guy who has had a lot thrown at him. In one day, his ex-mate resurfaces, dragging his long-lost mom along, and he finds out his father kept her prisoner after murdering his people and destroying the life he thought he knew.

It hurts to hear him say it, feel it. The regret of what happened with us, even while I'm trying to ignore it. The tears bite at my eyes, and a lump forms in my throat that almost chokes me, inflicting a unique body and brain ache that's hard to shake off.

"Maybe you should have, but you would never have forgiven yourself. You made the choices you made for the pack's good, even if it hurt us. If you left them, he would never have relinquished control, and they would suffer still. The Fates had a plan, and maybe leaving with me would have changed my path and never led me to her. And what about her? You've waited for her for ten years; she needs you. They all do. I finally see how this is so much bigger than us, Colton. Why it had to be that we couldn't be together. It was by design, and we did what we were meant to, even you when you rejected me." I nod at Sierra, my voice strained with my undercurrents of agonizing emotions, knowing that all of this is his pain talking and the desire to run away from everything hurting him. A typical fight-or-flight response and I felt the same when I learned about all of it. I still feel this way. To run and bury my head and wish it'd been different. It's fear, overwhelming, but it's pointless, and running won't fix any. Juan has to pay. The balance has to be restored, and Sierra needs her son. Colton needs to lead.

Colton sighs slides his arms under me fully, picks me up, surprising me with the sudden maneuver, and drags me to his lap where he wraps around me. He buries his head under my chin, against my chest, so I have no other option than to hold him, taking from me what he needs, even if he should have asked first. I relent and wrap him up in a hug, be the strength he's lacking while doubt and heartbreak consume him. It's awful, and yet the best thing, to allow myself to be this way for a while, even if it confuses my heart.

"The people, the war, the future—it's all interwoven. Us, your mom, your dad, we can't run away from this even if we wanted to. We're part of it, even in our mistakes and heartbreak. The Fates know what they're doing, and for whatever reason they did this to us, it'll make sense in time." I run my fingers through his thick, short hair, stroking it back and soothing him against me. Caring for him, giving him what I can as it stirs up all kinds of longings and warm sensations in the pit of my stomach, being connected to him like this.

"I denied the Fates, Lorey. Maybe I was meant to find her with you, by your side. Maybe I screwed everything up by rejecting you." He squeezes me harder, pulling me closer, so I end up almost entirely entangled in his body. It starts to feel inappropriate and way too intimate as I naturally fit up against him in the hollow of his lap. Especially with my ass nestling in his groin, I'm fully aware he's carrying a pretty healthy package because it's now somehow worked its way into a position where it's wedged in between my ass cheeks and distracts from the heavy feelings of this scenario. Distraction at its finest, a pretty sizeable one at that, and I try to focus back on what I'm meant to, but it's not easy.

My eyes scan the room for signs of Carmen crashing in here because of my guilty libido as my nether regions tingle. I'm heating up with being this close, skin sizzling, and stomach flipping over at something so innocent. I don't seem to control it now when all I can focus on is the fact I can feel it through his pants and mine, and it's impressive.

It's not like I haven't seen it when he's turned from wolf to human again. It's just that when he's standing up, and there's a lot of abs, pecs, and muscles all leveling out the eye candy, you don't size up what you don't want to get caught looking at. I looked that one time accidentally, and it was memorable.

I wriggle to get his 'situation' from under me, not that it's reacting much. It's that I'm painfully aware of it through thin sweats, and once your head goes somewhere like that, it's hard to get it back out of the gutter. I've been having lucid pornographic dreams about him these past weeks while out there alone, but the reality feels a lot more ... substantial and within grasp. Swallowing hard, trying to bring my mind and hearing back, but failing badly.

I blush crazily, aware I'm being a freak. Heat spreading up from my boobs, neck, and cheeks makes me sweat instantly and overheat so that I must be visibly turning rosy. Scared to put my hand anywhere, and flinch anytime I feel an ounce of movement under me while trying to avoid looking down or directly at him, and subtly attempting an escape from impalement without drawing attention to it. Becoming that awkward, sex-starved teen virgin you read about in young adult romance books.

"I don't think they ever intended you to be with me. This is where you're needed. They wouldn't give you a role if they didn't think you could do it." My words are rushed, babbling mainly, cheeks flushing, and breathless. Focusing on sliding sideways like some sad little untouched having a freak-out because he has a penis, and I just realized I'm sitting on it. Distracted from the gravity of what we're talking about because Colton is making me ... hot.

That's the word! Really, really hot. Squirmy. My whole body is pulsating with need now that it's caught on to what's happening. I think I'm experiencing my first full-on hormonal breakdown, full haze mode, and craving things I shouldn't.

My wiggling seems to change the atmosphere a little, and the way he frowns at me as he sits up and glances down at my weird moving in his lap says it all. I react by looking much like a rabbit caught in the headlights, widening my eyes in embarrassment, and try to smile, albeit weirdly, at him to distract him from the fact I'm trying to dislodge my butt from his manhood. I feel like an idiot and slide straight back into his groin with a minor bump that extracts a twinge of movement that makes me gasp lightly. I ignite a semi now that he's aware of where my thoughts are and my grinding on it unintentionally.

Oh, my God. I didn't mean to, and now, it's like the elephant in the room, and I spaz out mentally. Freak out fully. Completely flustered, flushed face, I know I'm probably crimson from chin to roots, and my movements are clumsy. It feels bigger like this, and it intimidates me a lot more now I can feel it getting hard and probing my ass way more.

I get a hint of dimple as a slight knowing smile moves in, a raised brow, and his whole aura changes from down and depressed to 'well, hello, are you doing what I think you're doing?'. That cheeky twinkle in his eye is unmistakable; my hormones give his hormones the come on. I see the slide of Latino Lothario as Colton's whole aura changes to wolf mode, and his eyes begin to glow. His prey caught in his sights, and I become hyper-aware that every cell in my body heightens to crazy levels. His wolf rattles mine, and I can't stop how she peeks out, knowing my eyes glow in response to his primal signals as she delicately uncurls. I'm suddenly super aware of every part of his anatomy and tingling with apprehension as our bodies tune into each other in the first stages of going into heat. This is new for me, and the timing couldn't be any worse.

He slides his hand under my hair to catch me in his hold, locking his eyes on mine as his pupils dilate, and things get real heavy, real fast, so my lungs stop functioning. He lifts my chin and brings his face to mine, so our noses graze. The contact ignites a fire inside me, and I groan softly, so quiet no one in the room hears it but him, and I forget there are other people in here. Colton is in horny mode, his erection growing under me, making this worse, and I think he even forgets we're sitting beside his mom. I almost self-combust as though he zaps me with a taser when he grips me a little harder and moves in with intention.

"I don't believe *never* was in the plan. You're here now. They brought you back to me." His voice tickles my mouth as he runs the tip of his tongue across his bottom lip and sucks it in, sexy as hell. It's so soft it's barely audible. I pant in response as one of his hands slides under my ass and cups a cheek with a slight squeeze. My underwear gets clammy, my heart rate almost explodes, and I press my thighs together to combat the aching sensations down there while I bite on my lip to control the desire to do that to him. My head gets foggy, and all I can do is lean in like I'm starving and crave to have that tongue in my mouth. The memory of his kiss fueling me with abandon. My nails rake across his chest as I slide my hands up in readiness to curl around his neck—instincts taking over as my wolf dominates with her unyielding need.

He tilts down softly, and I know what's coming, the slow move in, the way he lifts me to him by the ass as he grazes his nose against mine, and as much as I start to get drawn in, aching for him to do it, something tugs me mentally, clawing slowly at the back of my mind. I'm almost drooling as I relent and close my eyes, my heart pounding through my chest, and I want his hands to slide up my shirt and feel me out. Yet, I can't.

Sense claws at me as he gets so insanely close. His lip softly slides against mine, igniting a desire and passion unmatched, and it takes every ounce of willpower and strength in me to close my mouth, breathing so heavily I might pass out and inhale through my nose like I badly need oxygen. It's excruciating and takes everything I have in me to lean back and break the headiness of being caught up in his scent, his touch, and his power over me, which inevitably leads to more. Our mixed emotions of intense desire and need for sex are pulsating between us, and I honestly don't know where I find the strength to break it.

I lift my hand and stop him midway, with a hand over his soft lips, and close my eyes tight while I try to regain some control and attempt to rationalize. Breathing in and out and slowly counting to ten while praying my body calms down and saves me from my weakness. Colton pauses, sensing my change, and has the decency to sit still and not push me. I swear, if he did, I would lose and probably traumatize Doc with a vulgar display of porn in the infirmary. I thank the stars Colton doesn't force my hand, even though his need is almost overpowering me.

I turned this year so this will be my first heat, and God, it's going to kill me if this is anything to go by. We clearly have the attraction, and every day the haze gets closer, my body will betray me like this. Maybe this is that creeping in, or perhaps it's just the downside to imprinting so that when we get too intimate, the need to screw gets right in there. Whatever it is, it's a reminder to stay away from him like this from now on. Close contact is a no. We can't fight it.

"Don't. Some things I can't forgive. You're just making this messy." I shove him back forcefully, my voice shaking and not able to breathe properly. It's a whispering tone as I slide off his lap, standing on Jell-O legs and lightheadedness. I avoid his eyes, but Colton isn't about to give up.

He catches me by the waist and pulls me to him, so I collide into his now standing frame and almost crumble. Maybe it's a last-ditch attempt to play on what's already ignited between us and throwing caution to the wind, but I'm getting stronger by the second now I haven't got him all around me, hemming me in.

"Are you really going to stay mad at me for eternity and deny this between us? Come on, baby. I get that you're angry, but really? Never? When it feels like this. When we both want it this much." He leans in, aiming to carry on his smooth seduction, nuzzling into me as though this is merely me being stubborn, and this is all a game. Pulling me up against him and wrapping me in tight as he tries for a second attempt at a kiss, but it riles my temper, and I snap - from lust-crazed to pissed in zero point five seconds.

"Colton, stop it, let me go." I fight him, but he has octopus arms and gets me tangled up with him no matter how I try to escape.

"No can do. It's not in me to let you go again. You've got me crazy right now." He makes a joke of it, pinning my arms around me, swiftly leans in to peck me on the lips, and gets himself a knee to the groin. I'm not playing. I know I started this, but I'm stopping it now, and he needs to accept it and fuck off.

However, Colton is faster than me, blocks my assault, and gives me that cheeky, dimpled grin that infuriates me—making light of the heaviness between us and pushing my mood off like water off a duck's back.

"Nice try. Good to see your time without me brought out the fierce. I like a bit of rough in a girl." He slowly unwinds me, chuckling at my furious glare, then leans in, cups my face, and steals a quick lip to lip kiss before I slap him hard in the abdomen for doing it against my will. Crossing the line, even if a second ago, I was begging for it.

He makes an 'oof' noise, clutches it, then throws up defensive palms and laughs at me. He's not deterred or mad; he sees that little thing between us as a ray of hope that he might get his way if he plays his cards right and might even take advantage of getting up close again. My hackles rise, and I go into defensive mode, eyes glowing with a warning that he needs to back off. Insides calming from what that was and instead igniting in a fury, ready to claw him half to death.

"Okay, I surrender, red eyes. I get it. You need more time, and I need to up my apology game. Maybe calm my testosterone while I'm at it." That smug, cute-boy face and the bro mannerisms as he adjusts his black sweats and rolls his shoulder to relieve some of his sexual tension.

"You need to go choke." I snap at him sulkily, pushing past him in barging for the direction of the door, irritated by him, at him, at me. So annoyed that he took liberties when I was showing weakness and pissed me off all the more.

"It's not a preference, but I'm into trying it if it gets you hot." He adds with a raised brow, that complete inappropriate sexual innuendo getting another slap in response as I spin on him, instinct making me lash out to maim the asshole. He cowers away playfully, laughing harder at me and clutching his side as though hilarity is painful. Utterly entertained and amused, not fazed by my anger one bit. Not taking this seriously at all and not injured by my feeble aims. This guy who was literally seconds away from betraying his new mate bond and cheating on his Luna.

JERK!!

He backs away with a raised set of hands, that goofy smile of adoration, looking at me in that wicked, devilish way that makes my blood boil—all happy, teenage asshat who sees nothing wrong with what just happened.

"Honestly, you just ... arghh," I half growl at him, self-combusting with sheer frustration and pent-up rage. I am no longer willing to play this weird whatever it is, lose my cool, and be as immature as him. I turn again, go to storm out of the infirmary, fueled with hot anger and returned hatred. Seeing Doc and the medic glancing my way as I stomp my hardest towards the door, glad they didn't see us getting hot and heavy and throwing daggers back at the room I'm leaving.

I walk smack, bang into an incoming figure in the doorway and almost trip over them, muffling a shocked yelp as they right me on my feet with a mumbled apology and then look past me directly.

"Alpha, we have incoming." It's a low, tense sentence, and my heart stops beating. It shuts me up, and I mentally try to calculate if it's been long enough for Deacon and his pack to get here. It's only been a couple of hours; surely it can't be. My blood runs cold, cooling my jets, and dispersing my tantrum as seriousness makes me turn to look back at Colton standing in the room by the bed.

Colton mentioned attacks. Maybe it's Juan and his men, or maybe it's vampires. I feel instantly sick, my insides turning to dust, but Colton springs into action, the ever-ready warrior, the smile fading and the carefree dropping around his feet. He seems to grow taller, more robust, his eyes turning to soft glowing amber as his expression calms completely. A born leader pushing everything else aside when faced with an actual threat.

"It's showtime!" He sounds out confidently, those eyes burning brighter as he bristles up and gets ready to go out there and take down whatever threat is coming for his people.

DEACON

I flash a wary look at the doc in the corner, who turns a shade paler, his brow furrowing, etching his features into that of worry, and he casts an evasive look back at me. He darts a glance at Colton, then back again to me, suddenly sheepish.

"It can't be Deacon, right? It's too early!" I point out while asking him to confirm, to calm the sudden whirlwind of nerves, hating the apprehension I can feel from him, but he swallows loudly.

"I may have exaggerated our head start somewhat, a teensy little bit. I didn't want to alarm you and give you a reason to doubt coming with me, dear girl. If you knew they were hot on our heels, so to speak, you would have queried the plan. I had faith the Fates would intervene if we just got out. I had to keep the sedation low, so I didn't kill my human staff in the process, and sadly that meant the wolves recovered quickly." He's apprehensive about admitting to a lie, recoiling slightly, and I give him a deflated smile, translating that it's okay and it doesn't make much difference now because it is what it is.

"Damn right, it's Deacon. Meadow and the pack are tracing them down the north road, following them. They'll be here in a couple of minutes." Colton growls and sweeps past me, determination oozing from him and that growing hostility coming off like dense smoke. He's moving into battle mode in his head, and I can't do much except follow him out of the infirmary. I should be out there for this entourage to arrive. After all, it's because of me

412

and Sierra they are even coming. "You should stay here." Colton flashes me a moody look, fierce, overbearing protectiveness shining through, and gets my 'hell no' glare of warning flashed right back.

I'm not about to sit in the corner and be cotton-wrapped because Colton thinks he needs to take care of a feeble petite femme. This femme took down a bear; she will not be intimidated by that idiot Deacon.

"That son of a bitch darted me in the back. I'm not missing him crawling up and realizing this is a Santo domain! I want to experience that epiphany and watch him grovel." It's through gritted teeth as my aggression flares, thinking about that smug asshole's face and the longing to kick him in the balls when I was in the facility. That slight simmer of rage ignites, and my skin tingles in anticipation, revving up my anger for that slimy weasel.

"You stay on my ass. Stay close where I can intervene should I need to." Colton drops that overbearing, no-nonsense command, and turns away, obviously picking up on my stubborn tone and knowing arguing with me is futile. He still has to be in charge of my safety, though.

He leads the way immediately, straight out into the hallway, through the foyer, and out the open main door at hyper-speed. Other wolves either get out of the way or turn and follow their leader as I assume he links and issues orders.

He's eager to get out front and await our guests. His wolf is peeking in the glowing eyes and that snarl in his tone, but he keeps it in check and stays primarily human. Rolling his shoulders and leaning forward slightly so that stance of psycho comes through prominently when we come to a halt at the gravel driveway that spans the whole front width of the homestead.

Wolves tend to hunch forward and look at you with a tilted chin. It's usually because we prefer to go to all fours as wolves, even though we can walk upright, and Colton seems caught between the two. Stance and lowered head as his eyes glow viciously and his words take on that dominant growl in the undertones. He isn't planning on turning, but he intends to intimidate the shit out of Deacon. I can sense his actions and read him way better than I used to. I wonder if our wolves are synching a little because of the closeness of how we got in the infirmary, or maybe I'm just getting better at dissecting the mood and picking out who belongs to who.

He leads us out across the cleared sweeping gravel drive. All the vehicles are gone, and I can see how massive the forefront of the homestead's entry is. Without the wolves flanking and taking us in without seeing it, I can appreciate the wide, vast space, treelined with dense forest, and only one narrow opening coming northbound. Colton was right about this being smaller than the manor at the mountain, but it's still pretty impressive.

The headlights flash in the far distance through that gap in the trees, and I realize it's because the road is straight and long, and standing here, we can see it for a couple of miles. Being dark means seeing the flickering lights moving in on us, like incoming orbs bouncing around on uneven gravel terrain.

"Two trucks. Radar can pick out heat signatures of twelve wolves between the two," Colton murmurs at me as if Radar being able to do that isn't a surprise, and now his name makes perfect sense. He can see body heat through objects and infrared sight.

Something slight catches my eye, distracting me from this wonder, just past him as I look his way. Adjusting my nocturnal vision, I realize Santo wolves move in from the tree line stealthily and stand out around us in the shadows. Watching, waiting, prepping to be there should their Alpha need them, I again hate that I'm not linked in and hearing the communications between them all. Obviously, by the silent way they get in position and nod at one another, there's a line of chatter getting them where needed. They're preparing for battle because they don't know how things will play out.

"Doc said there were nineteen wolves at the facility, so I'm guessing he left a few behind to keep the humans in check," I add as an afterthought, sticking close to him as a few warm bodies close up behind us, wolves I don't know well, but we're being flanked by more than a dozen anyway. I wonder where the sub-pack is.

Colton paces, side to side. Adrenaline and hostility are so high he's even affecting me, and my body vibrates lightly. Watching the oncoming truck bristling with fierceness, all I can do is watch and wait with bated breath. Nervousness hitching up because I don't know how this will go, and even though we outnumber them, I'm still not a wolf who's ever had to battle another wolf like this. Colton doesn't count that one time he triggered me, and I can't even remember it happening. Even while still crazily angry at Deacon, I feel nauseous and start wringing my hands together to calm my stupid nerves.

Colton walks six feet to the left, turns, and walks it back again, like a caged animal, and I can taste his impatience in wanting to deal with this. He's stiff and solid, ready to pounce, and I can taste the nearness of his wolf as he's on the edge of turning. It's like a high-level energy feeding mine, and my inner wolf wriggles around with a need to show face.

He's in full-blown aggression mode, his Alpha scent getting so heady that my wolf snarls in response, and I have to take a deep breath and count to ten to keep her tamed. He's riling the pack, and the murmur of restless snarls around me tells me they're all poised and ready to fight, feeding on their leader's need to attack. The psychic bond of a pack, so that when their Alpha hits a battle, they all rev up and flock to him, ready to die for the good of the pack. It's becoming unbearable and invasive, as it shrouds like dark smog around us, and I can hardly breathe with the impending pressure.

I touch him on the shoulder to break his intense focus on the incoming as he paces past me for the tenth time and he pauses, spinning his head to me away from the road. His reaction is like I jolted him with a Taser because he was caught up in his instincts and senses.

"Deacon's a coward and no match for us. Be still. You're making the pack restless and bloodthirsty." I try to soothe him with a slight squeeze. Colton inhales slowly but reaches out and runs his thumb over my bottom lip gently, igniting a crazy number of butterflies in my stomach with the simplest of touches as he focuses those glowing eyes on mine.

"He laid his hands on you. Kept my mom prisoner. I don't care if he refuses to fight or runs; I'll take him down." The vicious, lethal, protective side is coming out, and I can only give him a soft look. I can't argue when he's fueled by instinct and rage. I can only let him be and let him handle this his way.

"Many of these wolves have never known battle. Think of the vulnerable among us. We want them to feel safe here, not traumatized by a war on the doorstep. Be a leader. Put vengeance aside for the good of those. There are children here." I remind him gently, and it has the same effect as a calming wave washing over him. It's enough to level down the rage, and he exhales heavily to release some of his tension, knowing I'm right. He nods, releasing me and turning away to watch the road once more, but I can already tell he's reeled in so much of his testosterone already. My words are having an effect.

The wolf hierarchy is not that complex, and wolves have certain traits you just have to accept. One is that a male is deathly aggressive, possessive, and protective of his mate, even if they're imprinted, but she isn't technically his. The need is the same. To be honest, Colton's an Alpha, which means his protective instincts are enhanced naturally, at about five hundred percent higher than most. The good of the entire pack, putting his people above all else, is a born Alpha trait, and it's crazily hitched up to about a thousand times more intense once a dominant takes on his role as leader. So, that fuels Colton. I can see it in him, making him antsy, interwoven with turmoil and rage. I'm not just his fated mate; in his head, I'm part of his pack too, and Deacon disrespected me. He also disrespected the Luna. Colton's loyalty to his mom is as strong as his love for her, for me. As Alpha, he wants to reset the balance, to deal with the insult and offense dealt this way.

The headlights pull my eyes from Colton to them as they flash violently, swinging around into the car park as they trundle in and catch us all standing here waiting. The low humming of two big green military trucks that I recognize from the bay. Both have tented backs and seem so much bigger out here in the dark.

416

The first truck veers left, skids to a halt, obviously not expecting the welcoming party out front, and maneuvers an emergency divert. The second one slams on the breaks immediately, sliding on the gravel an extra few feet, and stops dead in the entranceway, blocking it off in a mist of scrambled dust.

There's a moment of pause as no one moves, and the sound of the humming trucks is the only noise ringing heavily through the eerie quiet. The distant whoop, whoop of wolves coming from behind alert the presence of our sub pack returning behind them, and they seem to be in joyful spirits at trapping these bugs in their web from all sides. It's as though everyone holds their breath and waits for someone else to make the first move, and Colton becomes stealthily still, wholly trained on the first truck as he homes in on the driver's seat through the side mirror.

His low growl vibrates through my stomach.

It's Deacon. I can smell him.

He surprises me with the low, husky hostility in our link, and I blink, stomach-turning itself in knots as I realize what he just said. I'm trying to ignore the tone of a killer in his undercurrent because I know Colton is a seasoned warrior, and I'm about to see it for a second time.

How do you know what Deacon smells like?

I blanch, looking from Colton to the truck and trying to figure out how we would know that unless he knew him. He couldn't have gotten the scent from my projected memories. Deacon is a Santo, but if he's been at the facility for years, I assumed Colton would have been a boy and not known him. Deacon is older by maybe ten years, and I don't recall pulling him from any of his memories, but I haven't looked.

That asshole and his pack snuck off into God knows where after his father died, but I know him. He tried to take me down in front of his pack when I was a kid to exert his dominance and humiliate me. I handed him his ass. I hate that motherfucker with a passion. Knowing that it's his pack that held my mom and now comes after you both, I swear I will rip him limb from limb.

417

I swallow hard, eyes widening, and gulp back a slight tremor of 'oh shit' now that I realize this is more than Colton being pissed on behalf of his mother and me and Colton thinking about diffusing things. It's also about already hating the idiot who followed us here. His rage revs up and surges through me, and I know I need to settle him once more.

We have young here; we have pregnant women and elderly wolves. We have families, and a hundred windows face this way. We need to shield them from the horrors and instill that this place is a sanctuary. I have to calm Colton and push this fight outside our boundaries, away from watching eyes. I don't want him to rile the extended pack and rip a dozen wolves to shreds here like this, even if it is Deacon.

Someone opens the truck door and slides out, dressed in dark clothes, and I recognize the tall, cocky swagger right away. That air of asshole he wears so well. Deacon looks around, noting all the wolves scattered in a circle surrounding him, and then locks eyes on Colton as he seeks out who he should interact with and seems to sag visibly. He obviously remembers Colton well.

It's in his body language and the death of confidence. He hesitates and then walks toward us with his hands raised as a sign of submission. Colton stands taller, lifting his head, and seems to grow a few inches as he locks him with a penetrating glare. Colton moves in front of me instinctively, sidestepping and pushing me back with a hand slid across my abdomen firmly. I can tell it's a protective move, instinctual, and I can't be mad about it when it's a purely automatic response to an incoming threat.

Deacon's pack slides out of the two trucks, looks around them, and stands back in their vehicles' circle. I can see the hesitant and questioning looks they throw between one another as they recognize certain members, and it's obvious they didn't know they'd followed my tracks to a Santo lair. They stay put and look towards Deacon for direction, showing zero signs of hostility now they see us.

"I'm only doing what I'm told, Colton. I didn't come here to fight. I didn't even know you'd broken off and had a Santo sect here. I just need to take my patient and my prisoner back. Your father was very clear about that." Deacon isn't so smug now; I can taste his nervousness and smell his fear in the air as he closes the gap and comes within four feet. I'm sure the second he realized he was rolling into Santo space, he shit his pants and had a moment of 'what the fuck is going on?'. I move around Colton a little to aim a nasty glare at Deacon's smug head and catch his eye flicker as he notices me and looks back at my Alpha.

Colton snorts in response to what he said. His body bristling with a pulsing desire to rip at Deacon, and I impulsively lay a hand flat on his back, a reminder to stay calm. I can feel it oozing my way, his emotions enraging mine, and that insane desire to turn and bite the asshole in the face. I have to inhale deeply, breathe, and count to ten to make it pass, willing Colton to draw some of this settling energy from me.

"Prisoner? Patient? Do you mean *my* mom and *my* femme? Pretty sure you can't be talking about walking in here uninvited and thinking I will stand back and let you touch either of them." Colton steps to him and closes the gap completely, aggression pulsating, and stands nose to nose with Deacon. He's taller than him by only an inch, but he seems more dominant as Deacon hesitates but stands his ground. After all, he is a pack leader, and his own are watching him closely, so he needs to curb the weakness to keep face. Colton is growling, so low it's reverberating through me, and my wolf is getting all kinds of excited. I try extra hard to pat her down and tell her off.

It's the weirdest thing, but seeing and feeling him this way makes me crazy hot, and I curse my damn hormones and that damned haze moving in on me. My wolf wants to play with him in many dirty ways, she's just torn between ripping Deacon's head off or stripping Colton naked for his show of fierceness, and I have to work twice as hard to restrain those urges. She's all swooning and needy at a time when she needs to shut up and be still.

"Your father won't care. I'm just doing what I'm told. He won't like this one bit. Just take it up with him when we leave and deal with him yourself." Deacon doesn't seem to get the memo, and it dawns on me that much like I didn't know, he doesn't either. Colton is his rightful Alpha, and just by questioning him, he's breaking all kinds of rules and respect.

He's oblivious to the pack split, and to him, this is Colton setting off on his own to start a separate sect while still under his father's order. It happens when males who are next in line become impatient for dominance; they can set up camp somewhere else with those willing to follow. Big packs like the Santos dominate entire regions because of previous generations splitting and setting up across the land to ensure challenges and disputes don't arise when young males get too big for their boots. There's always only one head Alpha, though, and Deacon assumes it's still Juan.

"My father is not the Alpha anymore! I am! Now back the fuck up and listen to me because this is how it's going to go." Colton snaps at him, making Deacon flinch with the intense crazy that came through with that response, and he wilts slightly. Colton was right. Deacon is a coward, and when he doesn't have a dart gun and a facility keeping wolf gifts at bay, or thick Plexiglas prisons, he's just a weak omega who is the lowest of our pack.

"Juan is my Alpha. I don't know what makes you think otherwise, and for all I know, you could be lying." Deacon truly is an idiot of epic proportions, and, much to my surprise, Colton doesn't punch him in the face but laughs instead. There is a deranged, yet somehow boyish, noise, and he raises his head and looks at the trucks behind Deacon's head.

"Do you hear that, Meds? I must be lying!" Colton's eyes are on the vehicles, and I squint to see where he can see her. I can't. I can smell the sub pack on the wind, blowing this way gently, but there's nothing but shadows and darkness beyond the lit area we're standing in.

"I guess we witnessed a mirage then, huh?" Meadow appears on the roof of the first truck, coming out of the shadows and strutting across the thick solid canvas of the covering like a supermodel. Hand on her hip as she glares this way, and the sub pack emerges creepily too. Some around the sides of the trucks, pouring in like beetles and scaring Deacon's pack half to death with their sudden appearance. Cesar appears behind Meadow, while Mateo appears on the roof of the other one. Ninja stealth and almost magical appearances. They know how to spread out and look like there are more of them. They have a force that's hard to miss.

"Let me have this one; he's cute, and I want to play with him!" Jesús slides up behind one of the men, slightly further out from the rest. He jumps a mile high, growls at Jesús, and then runs to his pack to avoid the taunting smirk and kissing motions. The twins chuckle as they round on them, making more sexy winks and kissing motions, cooing naughtily. They're humiliating them while standing casually. Languishing like they're hanging out in a field waiting for a sports tournament to begin—no hint of fear, wariness, or even rage. Just taunting confidence of a pack that knows, as a unit, they're fierce.

"I don't think you're his type. He likes the soft, submissive femmes so that he can feel all man about it." Radar pokes fun at the member trying to cower behind his pack, and Colton grins at the hilarity of his very intimidating fellows. Obviously, he's used to this kind of response when they encounter an enemy, and he doesn't seem fazed by it. It now makes sense who was whooping and making a noise upon arriving as though heading to a party. They're comical in a terrifying, psychotic way, and you can tell every one of them has tasted blood on a battlefield. You only get that kind of bold scariness from experience.

The jokes and presence of his subs seem to have calmed Colton down considerably, and I can sense the waves of fury ebbing away as he realizes this pack isn't worth it. Not one of them is trying to enforce a fight, and Deacon seems to be trying to diffuse rather than entice despite his eyes faintly glowing. They're what I thought when I met them, omega cowards, and they're not even worthy enough to fight them.

"You don't want to battle; that's fine by me. My people don't need bloodshed on their doorstep. We have children here, but you're not leaving with either of these women without going through me, so maybe you should turn around, tuck your tail back up your ass where it belongs, and tell my daddy I said to go fuck himself. That I know everything. He'll know what you mean. Maybe on the drive back to the mountain, you and your crew should evaluate which side of the Santo pack you're going to run with from here on in because the future doesn't look pretty if it's his." Snarling in his face, returning to intimidation and no hint of hesitation or nervousness. Colton is about an inch away from pissing on Deacon and marking his territory. His overwhelming hostility has the other wolf crumbling.

Colton doesn't sound like Colton. He sounds like a man, not a boy. I'm seeing him in a new light, a confident leader who is highly accomplished at handling people like Deacon. I've never had to come head-to-head with fierce Colton or seen his natural aggression beyond the orphanage, and I wonder what his taking his father down looked like. I can't lie; my inner wolf likes it, and I'm almost drooling over him at the moment. My insides all churned up, and I have to step back and take a few deep breaths to calm the raging hormones once more. The Fates picked the right male to match me to. I couldn't want him more than at this moment. His dominance turns me on.

"I ... umm. He'll kill us if we don't take ... umm... I don't know what went down, but I'll have to see for myself what Juan says about this." Deacon is at a loss for words, and I can feel every ounce of his bravado slipping away. He visibly swallows as he realizes he just questioned his possible leader, and I swear he almost sits on the ground the way his legs seem to twitch momentarily.

"I'll kill you if you touch her. So, there's that." Colton reiterates with a head nod and shrugs. I shake my head at Deacon, disgusted with the weakness I see before me and smothered in confidence as my temper ignites.

"Not so tough when you don't have me disabled and stuck alone in a glass room, are you?" I snarl, moving out entirely behind Colton, half expecting him to hush me and send me back, but he doesn't. He turns to me slightly, catches my eyes with his glowing amber ones, and then slides aside to encourage me to come closer. I guess because he knows Deacon is no real threat to me. He relaxes a little, and like a wild wolf would encourage his mate to take part in a hunt or teach her, he urges me to him. He just let his subs berate theirs, so I guess it's my turn. My wolf ignites at the invitation, eyes burning in my skull, and I know they must be glowing as red as Colton's are amber with the tension in the air.

"What the fuck?" Deacon almost trips backward as he scrambles a step away and locks an alarmed pair of human eyes on mine. Shocked at what he sees.

"Miss those pretties, huh? I guess probably because you were busy shooting her in the back!" Colton teases cruelly, pulling me with a hand on my upper arm and sliding me in front, so I'm between him and Deacon. Getting me close even though he wants me to stand up to this asshat, but he needs to know he's also keeping me safe.

"What the hell is wrong with her eyes?" Deacon can't conceal his fear, and this time he trips trying to get away and lands on his ass. He is scrambling as he thuds with a soft noise and tries to reel backward away from me.

"Nothing. I think they're sexy. However, it does mean you had a lucky escape. Had my *Princesa* here not been more concerned about getting the fuck away from you, she could have taken down your entire team with minimal effort. Maybe I should let her rebalance the scales if you think you can take her." Colton slides his hand up my back and moves in next to me, so we're hip to hip, lazily lassoing his arm around my shoulders, so it hangs casually, and adopts that teenage boy pose of a guy taking the piss out of someone he deems inferior. Deacon hesitates. I can see the questions forming in his head as he looks from Colton to me and back and scrambles to his feet, backing away. It's obvious he's rattled, and he keeps gawping at me and then back at his pack as though they're linking. I see the unease as they look at one another and shrink closer to the vehicles, our sub pack moving in and not giving them an inch.

"Why don't we make it fun? If he can take you, his pack gets to leave. If he can't, well … we kill them." Colton turns to me with a dark expression, a wry smile, his words making the blood in my veins run cold, but his mind-link kicks in immediately.

I won't ever let anyone hurt you; he'll not take that offer, so relax. He's about ready to run. I'm not going to kill anyone. I'm just messing with him, baby, because it's fun.

Colton is doing what a mate should do. Teach, guide, and instill confidence in his femme, and I can feel him encouraging me to take back my power from Deacon. It ignites a fire in me that pulses through my bones, muscles, and nerve endings, and I can almost taste that thin veil coming at me without trying. Maybe it's the inner rage I felt from the second this asshole pulled up, or perhaps it's having Colton by my side coaxing me, encouraging softly, being what I need, yet knowing it can never be that's churning me up and empowering me insanely.

"I'm not in the mood for shredding my clothes, so how about ... if he can get to his truck before I get to him, I forget all about it. He can go, and we're done." I raise a brow, sarcasm oozing from every pore, and Colton smiles, looking at our prey. He knows I will make Deacon run back to his truck like a coward and humiliate him in front of everyone without even attempting to follow. I understand why his subs like teasing and tormenting; it gives me a real power kick.

"I'm not against you shooting him in the back, baby. An eye for an eye." He leans in and kisses me on the temple, lingering a moment as Deacon continues glancing from him to me and back again. Deacon pales visibly and starts to stammer and stutter. Raising his hands and looks about poised to go running away, tripping over his own feet and falling epically to his knees in front of everyone. Colton breaks into a laugh and completely ruins it. That proper hearty break of mood, as he lets out that youthful, entertained, sweet melody of husky beauty.

"I'm sorry, I can't ... it's too funny. Fuck off, Deacon. None of you are welcome here. This is where my mom and my femme stay, and if we see you here again, I'll happily rip your throat out. Take that as a friendly warning and tell my father whatever the fuck you want. Just leave!" Colton doesn't waste for an answer; he slides his arm from me and turns, pushing his hand into mine to get me to follow him back to the manor and leave this idiot to get chased out by the subs. Colton is doing what I asked and ensuring we do not expose the vulnerable to gruesome violence. He's leaving before he does something stupid to these idiots.

I'm slower to turn and catch Deacon's eyes ignite from the corner of my eye. His left-hand claws up with sharp knife-like talons as he lets that part of him turn before he lurches to his feet, extending his hand, and aims right for the back of Colton's skull. Right at a wolf's skull, it's a death stroke with enough force, and I impulsively yell out.

I throw my hand out to stop him, aiming right for that son of a bitch in an impulsive reaction, with my palm stretched towards him. To shield my love, to save him from harm. Pure instinct is taking over with the way my heart leaps into my mouth, and my whole body pauses in shock and disbelief, my veins running cold.

I need to protect my fated mate at all costs, and I don't think or hesitate. Colton is my soul mate and half of me, and I won't let that piece of shit Deacon take a stab at his back and end him in such a cowardly way.

Much like watching a wet baseball thrown hard, losing its water content and spewing traces in the air as it hurls at speed, I send something like a transparent orb at him from my splayed hand. It travels fast and straight, slowing down time and space, so I see it happening almost in slow motion. It hits him right in the chest with so much force it makes an echoing thud that reverberates around the clearing. It has a similar effect to that of the bear, only with less velocity and rage behind it, more shock, more focus, and a reaction more than anything. Deacon goes from jumping towards Colton with intent to being rammed harshly in the chest by my orb and thrown a few feet behind him into the side of the vehicle. He comes to a shuddering halt as his body slams it and dents it like I just canon-balled it with a steel boulder.

He stops dead, groaning in pain, the air silencing around us as he slides down the side of the truck, winded, gasping for air, and in utter shock as his pack cowers around, watching this show of force.

425

The air sizzles around us as everyone who just witnessed it stares in utter disbelief—shocked.

"Well, that's a gift." Meadow's voice floats my way, breaking the silence and the tension as I inhale and look around to see most eyes are on me. It's only now I realize she's only seven feet away to my left; she must have leaped to come to the defense of Colton too, and her eyes are glowing amber, ready to take down that son of a bitch had he struck her Alpha.

Deacon's pack wastes no time running, dragging Deacon with them back into the two trucks and speedily getting off the ground. Soon as they do, the trucks rev into life and back out at speed, gravel spraying all around us in dramatic fashion at their fast and furious exit while Colton turns to me and catches me off guard.

He picks me up, hauling me up in a sweep of weightlessness, grinning at me proudly, and hooks my legs around my waist as he does so, pulling me down and kissing me right on the lips as he yanks my body into his. I have no time to react, pulled in and held tight as his warm lips press to mine and take my breath away completely. I hate that his kiss is still familiar, ignites feelings inside, inviting, like finding my way home, and I have to stop myself from leaning in and letting him continue.

"That's my girl. Warrior queen protecting her man. Thank you, baby." He moves his face back, so we're no longer close enough to do it again, causing a little wave of disappointment that I chastise myself for. My cheeks flushed with heat and embarrassment that he kissed me in front of everyone. So breathless from his unexpected attention and aware that every wolf out here is looking at us. I shouldn't untangle and get him to put me down while his pack watches us. It'll make it uncomfortable for him.

It's disrespectful to humiliate the Alpha. Instead, I slide my hands around his neck to steady myself in this pretty weird position I find myself in, aware this is inappropriate for a marked wolf, yet I allow him to carry me like this. I am aware I still don't see any sign of Carmen, and I'm sure I would have heard her if she had seen this. No way she wouldn't be screeching me to deafness if she's around. His hands are now under my ass to keep me lifted as he turns me around to the approaching sub pack like this is perfectly natural for him to carry me this way. They swarm in around us.

"What was that exactly?" Cesar comes out first as Colton bounces me a little and smiles boyishly. He's overcome with weird, joyful energy and a strong sense of pride that suffocates me as his emotions drown mine out.

"That was Lorey and part of what she is capable of doing. Telekinesis possibly. I think she might be an Empath, too. Christ, that was impressive as fuck." He spins me, and I get a little jiggle before he slides me down to the ground onto my feet and tugs me in against him, lassoed by that arm once more and held lazily. I don't know how to feel about it, as everything rushed me at once, and it was impulsive. The reaction, seeing what I did again, and then this. I have to stop and let my brain catch up to his words.

"What?" I turn to him and gawp, eyes widening at him—so many questions about where he just pulled that from.

"The Shaman knows a lot about this shit, and it's common in vampires, apparently. Absorption is her wolf, and this it's the other half. Alora is a hybrid of the two. I am too; only my mom's a witch." Colton's voice drops as he says it, and I swear, the entire area falls deathly silent, unbearably so, as the entire sub pack and those beyond who heard him stare at us with open mouths of disbelief. He just outed us for the whole pack to hear, and those who didn't will know soon enough as gossip spreads through the link. Colton clearly doesn't want secrets the way his father did for years.

"Like us?" Remi finally butts in, breaking the tension, and I stand stock still, my heart beating through my chest at the fact he's going to tell them everything now. I was so not prepared for this. My body turns icy cold as fear overtakes me, my lungs almost shrivel up, and I sag a little to cower in his arms as they all move in on us; a sea of faces, endless questioning looks. Colton seems completely serious, but I can feel his hesitation in what he's doing. That ingrained fear his family bonded pack will reject us and send us into exile, or worse. A pack has a right to kill intruders or any they deem a threat, and I guess I'm definitely in that category.

"Kind of. I think you need to let me bond project to see what Alora and I know." Colton looks around them, and I hold my breath. Waiting, poised, but none of the sub-pack seems to have any dramatic reaction. There's confusion, a couple of questioning glances between them, but overall, they just nod. I didn't know packs could project to one another as a group, but it makes sense. If you make a chain and pass memory to memory. I just thought it was something only imprinted or mated could do.

Meadow turns and stares out at the wolves in the clearing. I can tell she's linking. Within seconds, they all turn tail and head back to wherever they came from, clearing the area and giving us space and quiet. They heard, and I don't doubt they will get answers after the sub pack gets them. Our secrets, who we are, Juan's complete lie in life, are about to become public knowledge, and I couldn't be any more terrified. No more secrets within this pack, no more hiding what I am. What we are.

Meadow steps up first and lifts Colton's hand to her temple, adding mine to the other side of her face, and smiles encouragingly. So much faith and love in that one slight nod.

"We're your pack; show us the truth. It won't change a thing about what we are to you."

REMEMBER

We're sitting in a study with a large double bed in the corner that looks entirely out of place in an alcove, as though it's a new addition, with the sub pack eerily quiet as they all absorb everything we showed them outside. Sat in slightly dazed moods as we all digest the truth of our collective memories.

It's a small room with a bay window, an oversized couch, and an armchair cozily nestled in front of a rustic fireplace. A sizeable handmade desk sits off to the side, just in the nook of the window space, facing inward with a worn chair tucked behind. There's an entire wall lined with dark stained bookcases, crammed full of old leather-bound journals of varying shades of tan, brown, and black, with no titles on display, and I wonder what exactly is contained within the aged pages for them to bear no mark. There are oddities and bottles of all kinds nestled among them, and facing that wall are three ample cupboards in matching deep wood that narrows the space considerably. There isn't much floor to move around, yet it has a snug quality rather than crowded.

The décor of dark fall hues, golds, oranges, russet, and browns, rich in color, only makes the room close in on us more. Especially with the heavy drapes at the window in dark red velvet, blocking out what should be light, but it's almost the middle of the night already, so there's a wall of black in the windowpane. The lamps are dim, almost candle flickering in intensity, dotted sporadically around small side tables and shelves, and add to an eerie atmosphere as the pack all sit around nestled together. Some of them are perched on the arms of chairs, lounging, while Colton stands by the fireplace, and I'm lying down on the bed, out of the way to get some rest. The bed's modern. I can tell by its comfort and the crisp, new bedding that it was put in here recently.

My body is weary and heavy, and it feels good to know what a comfy, safe bed feels like again. It's been so long since I was in a room by choice, surrounded by people I care about in a safe space, and I can spread out and not have to be on high alert. Weeks of living with tension and heightened senses are all coming to an end, and I realize how exhausted I am. It feels beyond amazing to not have one eye behind me and one eye on my surroundings, worrying about my next meal or where to set up a good camp.

Colton moved us in here once they'd seen everything they needed to see in our shared memories, and it was apparent they needed a little privacy to talk this out and calm down. We were making a spectacle out front, and even though other pack members dispersed, we caught many gazing at windows.

The reactions varied, and I think they're all still reeling in shock and sadness at finding out they were raised with so many lies for so many years. The man they trusted proved himself to be the villain in our own story. Despite it not being their family or their parents, I can imagine it's still their pack, blood, and alpha. It has to cut deep. The Santo pack has always been a proud close-knit unit, even for its massive size. It's how it's lasted the test of generations.

Meadow sobbed, hugged me like she would crack every bone in my body, and went into a Spanish rant that involved a lot of cussing for a solid ten minutes while she stomped around, throwing her hands in the air dramatically and pointing at the sky. I think she was telling the Fates off for allowing all of this, but as Spanish is a language I never picked up, I've no idea. She was animated and filled with fury, yet deep sadness, as she stopped to catch her breath and cry some more.

Cesar quietly stared at me for the most extended moment until I felt almost uncomfortable, a thoughtful face etched with concern before apologizing to me wholeheartedly about everything his 'blood' has done to me for most of my life. Right before moving in

430

and giving me a tight embrace that genuinely felt good. It was solid and real, and I could feel his genuine remorse for being part of the bond that took away all of mine. Cesar is a paternal role in the subs, and for the first time, I felt like one of his pups.

The twins sat on the ground, overcome, and shook their heads in disbelief. Lost, yet somehow enlightened simultaneously, and kept staring at each other, clearly mind-linking to question every detail. They seemed to be the slowest at figuring out how it all pieced together, then just sat and looked bewildered. Blank expressions, except for wide eyes and a downturn of their mouths. Sadness was evident in their aura.

Radar lost his shit completely, and I flinched when he growled out loud, cursed Juan's name, and stormed off mid-rant; semi turned into a wolf because he couldn't control it and gave us space. His words mumbled, yet I heard the name Sierra and how Juan kept her a prisoner of her own mind all these years and denied Radar his right to protect his Luna. Radar seemed the one with the most fury, but I guess given how he feels about Sierra, then it makes sense he would react aggressively. He returned after Meadow was done cursing the Fates and stood silent and broody while occasionally staring at the ground in deep thought. His mind was in turmoil.

Mateo, as always, the calm within the group, kept questioning Colton, saying things like 'I just can't ...' and then turning over every detail as though he needed confirmation. Emotionally, he seemed in disbelief, his manner calm, yet that look of heartbreak in his eyes at the fact their Alpha lied to them all. He stayed close to Colton, providing a sense of stable quiet when the others were in disarray.

Jesús vented loudly, at nothing, at everything, wandering in circles and talking to himself while kicking gravel across the drive with force. He would come back to the circle every so often, rub my head, and say, '*Lo Siento mucho, niña.*'

I think it means sorry, but I'm unsure, and I didn't want to ask while everyone was visibly shaken. Jesús has something of the dramatic about him, and his energy was bristling the air anytime he paced close. That need to hurt something for hurting his pack. It was overly protective, and I could almost taste his desire for revenge against Juan.

Colton and I stood side by side, and he took my hand, waiting for them to have some time to let it absorb. I stood blank-faced and numb, fatigue controlling my body. The only thing I could focus on was Colton's warm skin against mine and how it was so heartbreakingly right. His touch, as always, killed me softly.

Now we're all inside, nursing mugs of coffee, except me, as I declined and wanted to lie horizontally while they all bashed it out between them. I need a little quiet and calm to let everything that has happened in the last two days settle and wash over me. It feels like my head has been bombarded and knocked to hell, and somehow, I'm mentally bruised and in need of soft, soothing silence. It's quiet now, and they are all stuck in their minds, with the occasional infrequent sentence thrown out there, but mostly nods. I think this may take more than a few short hours for them to grasp the enormity of the situation and the past. We still don't know what else Sierra will add to the pot if anything.

It feels good to be back among them, though. The familiarity, the safety, and even though I was only part of their pack for a short time, I feel like I'm home and back within the arms of my family. Something I've wanted and ached for the last ten years of my life and never thought would exist within the Santo pack. Especially after finding out all of this about Juan. Carmen is still not here, and I'm starting to wonder if her absence has to do with the war on the mountain.

Colton said her father was Juan's Beta, so he would forbid her from coming here and maybe even held her hostage to make sure she didn't shame her family by following 'the traitor.' I can't imagine that would have gone down well with Juan if his second in command's blood had followed his son off the mountain. Juan already believes he's more powerful than a mate bond. That would explain Colton's desire to start something with me, as though he didn't already have himself a femme tucked away. He thinks his mate is unreachable, unattainable from circumstance, and a lost cause that he chose under pressure, and he believes he can ignore the bond and start afresh with me. Because our emotional bond was never severed, and his feelings didn't change as he hoped.

It's not happening. The very thought of it chokes me to the core and makes my heart constrict and pulse painfully. That uncomfortable heaviness in my gut reminds me I can never forget that he gave up on us and did what hurt me the most. I can't move past the betrayal of what he did, and I definitely cannot become some tarnished femme willing to have someone else's mate just because she can't physically be here. It makes me sick to my stomach that he would even ask that of me. Love means nothing when you are mate bonded to another. It's against the rules, the pack laws, and my moral code. I deserve more.

"So, what now? Alora is in danger if Juan now knows she's here. He may try to pull together enough wolves to attack the homestead!" Mateo breaks the silence, bringing all eyes to him as he nestles in the armchair. His words get me out of my thoughts, and I sit up on one elbow to look at him. My gut swirled a little, and anxiety set in that my being here might just endanger everyone I love. More so than already, and I can't predict if that's true.

"No. My mom life-linked to her. If anything happens to Alora, then my mom dies too, and as she's still bonded to my dad, it'll be his end. He's crazy but not stupid. He'd never jeopardize his own life. He won't attack because we outnumber him in terms of warriors, and he already lost at the mountain. There's no point in trying to get them back now. He knows we have the truth, and soon we'll spread it among our pack to let it free. Containing it won't be his goal anymore, as he can't turn back time. The only threat now is Alora rising to fulfill the prophecy that he can't do a damn thing about. We protect her. We keep her close within our circle, the same as the rest of us. We shield her and my mom. They're the two most important people in this, and to me." Colton turns and leans against the mantle and exhales heavily. Fatigue is showing on his face. His pallor is pale with dark smudges under his lower lids, his body sagging instead of the usually confident, strong, and tall posture. He catches my eye across the room over the heads of those on the couch and gives me that soft smile that makes my heart giddy and my insides erupt in fluttering butterflies. I look away quickly, my face flushing with the stupid reaction, and lie back down to avoid his eyes on me. I don't want to constantly feel his pull, sending my body into crazy spins and tingles. I want to sleep and not feel and not be torn every second with this gnawing ache for him.

"Right now, all we have is time to kill. It'll be a couple of days before we know how much recovery Sierra will need. It may be weeks before either of you is unbound. For now, we need to spread this among the pack and let them decide whose side they are on. Hybrids have always been a secret, and now their leaders are mixes of the enemies they hold within them. The pack needs to know everything, and after, those who are still here, and choose to stay, can never hold it against any of us again—we are who we are." Meadow gets up and stands beside Colton, turning to the rest of the pack and drawing my eye back across the room at them from my horizontal position. What she says makes perfect sense, yet it's utterly terrifying.

Outing everything to the rest of the pack. Telling them what I am, what he is, what they are, and opening all out and laying it bare for them to choose which side they want to follow. We may lose everyone. There has never been an outpouring of such honesty among this pack for decades under Juan's rule. Some may not want to accept the truth.

"We give them a choice, and until my mom wakes up, to decide. Stay and accept Alora and me or go back to the mountain to my dad, whom they might deem their true Alpha if they think I'm impure. From now on, no more secrets. We let the Shaman teach what he knows to be true in the school hall, and whoever wants to know can join in." Colton's voice is hoarse, with a husky undertone of fatigue, and he rubs his hand over the back of his neck, rolling his shoulders before exhaling heavily. A sign he's stressing about this choice, but he knows it's inevitable. His intentions are the right thing, but there's apprehension in him and fear the pack will up and leave when they see what he is. What I am.

434

"Let's get to it at first light. We can split up and project in small groups at a time. Let them pass it on. Won't take long to cover the entire pack and spread the memories. That gives us the whole day to get through them, but we should all sleep right now. We've had a long night, and the new patrols are doing the walks already. We need rest." Meadow claps her hands to get everyone up. The heavy mood and simmering anger at the lies they were drip-fed their whole lives hang like smog in the air. It's so thick and dense you could cut it with a knife.

The subs are angry, hurt, and confused, but one thing is clear, it didn't change the loyalty or love within any of them, and through all the emotions swirling in this room, one stands out the strongest. The unity and devotion they have for one another. The sense of solidarity that shows every one of them is one hundred percent behind Colton with whatever he wants to do. That's a real pack, that's the bond of family, and I know I'm not officially one of them, but they make me feel as though I am. They're my pack. No matter what happens with Colton, they're not going to lose me a second time. I need these people.

One by one, they stand and shuffle out of the room, some of them stopping to fist bump Colton in that same bro way they have with one another and then wave my way. I sit up properly, pulling myself to the edge of the bed to stand and find out where I should go, but Colton's voice in my head stills me.

Stay put. You look beat and need the rest. This room is fine, and no one will come in here without my say-so.

His voice inside my head is always that aching wave of intimacy yet sorrow, and all I can do is nod his way and avoid direct eye contact. I'm too exhausted for any more emotional head mess, and I can still feel his lips lingering on mine from his kiss earlier, tingling softly, reminding me that for him, I'm stupidly weak, especially when I'm this tired.

I flop back down, glad I don't have to find the energy to go anywhere, but at the same time, I feel a little disorientated at the thought of staying here by myself. I've been alone for weeks, knowing only solitude, sounds of nature, and the wilds. Now, here

I am, thrust back into civilization and tossed around for the last twenty-four hours in bizarre and noisy chaos, and I haven't had a moment to re-acclimatize or even catch my breath. It's all a chaotic mess of craziness, and now, with the opportunity to lie back and let it sink in, it seems terrifying. I depend on their company to keep me sane and stop my mind wandering, and I'm not sure I want to be alone anymore. I think I had my fill of it in the forests. I stop him from leaving as I'm reminded of the never-ending loneliness I experienced.

"Where will you be?" I sound as desperate as I feel, blurting out a delaying tactic, and I scold myself for the neediness. Having no answers and direction other than just waiting is like pulling the rug out from under you. It doesn't feel very good, and he's been the constant and stable, wise words in all of this. Right from day one, and at the moment, I need it. I guess I feel out of whack and set adrift now all my plans were upended, and life got utterly side-tracked.

"Across the hall in the infirmary with my mom. You can have this room until we figure things out. If you need me, link me, and I'll come back." He throws me that sexy, genuine smile, his voice low and fading because he, too, is exhausted.

"This is your room?" I blanch, wondering why the Alpha of the pack isn't upstairs in a grand suite as is standard within a pack manor. Now I also feel guilty that I'm taking his bed when he needs it and also a little worried that he's setting me up in his room because he might think he can wear me down and start something in time.

"Yeah, space is at a premium. With many families needing bigger rooms, it wouldn't have been right to monopolize one when I can put a bed in here and double up the communal and my room. It's not like I sleep in here much. Plus, with all the building work outback as they construct small homes, we'll soon move a lot of the pack out into the forest we're clearing behind us. This is all temporary while getting this place ready to be our permanent home. You need it more than I do." It all sounds so plausible and logical, and I can't help gazing at who he's become, somehow seeing him in a new light.

In just a few weeks, he's grown so much, and the needs of his people have taken the forefront of his priorities, as they should. There's a new level of seriousness and command to him, a hint of maturity beyond his years, and all it does is weigh me down heavily. Liking this about him, but that just makes it hurt more. Colton is everything I would ever want in a mate, and it just kills me, ripping my insides apart, that he gave up on me.

I glance at the window as though trying to see out into the darkness at the building work being carried out, but really, it's an excuse to break away from the way his eyes are holding me hostage, and I'm suddenly on the verge of stupid tears. The burning intensity of them is pooling in my eyes, and I have to swallow hard and blink them away to regain control. That same lingering need coming from him gnaws at my soul constantly, and I lose my courage, sounding feeble as I utter a few words breathlessly.

"I could use something to sleep in." I hesitate, knowing it's a lie and I could just strip off, but something in me doesn't want him to leave yet, even if it's just prolonging the agony and making me feel worse. Since I came back, we haven't separated properly for any length of time, and now I'm experiencing some crazy anxiety about him leaving when I feel like there's still so much left unsaid, unresolved. He's the anchor in my boat, and I'm on a stormy sea. I need to break this dependency on him if I'm to survive here from now on.

The whole Carmen thing, saying he still wants us, kissing me outside, Sierra, the Doctor ... the future. It's too big for me to handle or think about, and my brain is scared that letting him leave will open a dam in my brain that I have no energy to deal with. He already has me teetering on an emotional breakdown with tears threatening to spill out.

"The middle cupboard has everything you need. I wasn't about to leave any part of you behind because I wouldn't rest until we found you. Sweet dreams, baby." What he says confuses me enough to distract me completely, screwing my face up in confusion as he walks out the door. Too focused on discovering and already climbing off the bed to open the oversized wooden cabinet to see what he meant.

Much to my shock, every item I left in my room at the packhouse is in here, folded neatly, stacked up, and waiting for me to reclaim it. From clothing to shoes to my boxes of sentimental items and keepsakes. All has its place and fits neatly, taking over an entire cupboard in Colton's room.

My hands tremble as I reach out and touch the first of my sweaters, my legs turning to Jell-O, and a wave of lightheadedness because of my extreme reaction to something so basic. A lump forms in my throat that almost chokes me, and tears sting my eyes with venom, and I know I won't be able to hold them back for long. My emotions suddenly become nosedive, and I cough on a sob trying to escape my throat.

I don't know why this gets to me so badly, but it does. He took care of my things, hoping he would bring me back here one day. The fact he took the time to pack up everything that was mine so carefully and brought it when they all left the packhouse together. They must have had limited time to pack, considering they were going under hostile terms and had to get out, yet he made sure he left nothing of mine in that place. It's all here. Every single thing that I never knew I missed until now. All clean pressed and set in here with almost military precision.

I try not to ponder on it, push it out of my head, and focus on a task of doing instead of thinking. It's all I can do if I don't want to succumb to these overwhelming feelings and all the questions about Carmen. Doubting myself and what I felt in the forest, but there's nothing else to explain what that was. It had to be him marking her or betraying our bond in another way. Nothing can compare to the level of pain, heartbreak, and betrayal I felt, and I should remind myself of that and not get lost in him as he tries to win me around. I need to stay true to the fact and ignore how much I still love him. How every sense, and fiber in my soul, aches to be reunited with him in even the most minor ways.

I inhale heavily to self-calm and level myself out, shake my head and give myself an internal rattle to snap out of this. I haul out the oversized nightshirt that Meadow gifted me, my all-time favorite, and underwear, and quickly strip, loving the feel of soft, delicate lingerie and a basic cozy and loose T-shirt printed with delicate pastel florals over gray sweats any day. It's the little things that can restore you in weird ways.

I yank out my toiletries bag and find my hairbrush, facial wipes, and self-grooming products I left behind, as they were too heavy to carry, and start to put myself to rights. There's a mirror over the mantle, and it's only now I can see how grubby and worn I am. I look like a hobo who hasn't seen water in weeks, and my hair is a dull brown because it's so dirty.

Meadow was right, though; I do look different. My hair is longer, my face slimmer, and I have aged a little in my time in the wilds. My green eyes seem brighter. The color is more intense. My skin tanned gently from being outside all the time, and I have a natural rosy glow to my cheeks, nose, and forehead that has brought out a few light freckles. I seem taller, but I think I stand differently now. Upright, almost proud, and the small amount of growth my hair has had, makes all the difference. Even dirty, the layers are softer and hang around my face and past my shoulders in a much more flattering style than how the orphanage used to cut it. I like this look, and I might just let it grow out fully.

I clean my skin, brush out my hair as best I can, and find all manner of debris and twigs in the knots. I feel grubby now I have clean pastel clothes against my skin and try to make myself presentable while contemplating linking Colton to ask if he has a bathtub nearby. Although it's late and I'm tired, maybe I should just clean up, sleep, and worry about bathing in the morning.

It feels good to cleanse some of the grime off with wipes, and I look around for a means to brush my teeth, as that in itself will make a massive difference to how gross I feel. I wander around looking for a water jug or something I could use and stumble upon a door I previously missed because it's stained the exact color of the surrounding wood. There is a small door in the corner, next to the desk, tucked in and narrow, to the right of the last cupboard, and almost entirely concealed. I open it hoping to find something useful. It slides open behind the wardrobe to reveal a tiny bathroom, to my delight.

A shower looks newly installed with an array of toiletries in a basket sitting within, some towels hanging at the side, and a fluffy mat on the floor that hints this is where he gets ready most days. The air smells faintly of sealant and paint as though this was a recent conversion, and I guess that makes sense if Colton had this room repurposed. He can get up, shower, and get ready here without going to find an available bathroom. There's a small washbasin and toilet fitted into the space snugly, but not so much that it's crammed. I strip back off without hesitation, the urge to jump right in with the desire and need to be clean and hygienic once more overtaking tiredness.

Outside living is great when you're outside, but it makes you feel yuck once you're back among people and cleanliness. As I slide under hot water from powerful jets, this right now is as close to heaven as I've been in a while. I close my eyes, tilt my face up at the jet, and let it wash over, cascading all my worries and aches away with the goodness only a hot shower can bring.

Hot water, soap, and shampoo. It all feels fantastic to be back in civilization with real home comforts. No more river washes or using stones to scrub my clothes, and plain water to brush my teeth that always had a faint trace of fishiness. I can lie to myself every day and say that I was doing great out there and would happily have existed that way for eternity, but one shower unravels all of it. The bed is calling to me, soft sheets and springy mattress, and being able to walk barefoot on smooth carpeted surfaces and not having to choke half to death on fire smoke to get any kind of light in the darkness. I was never built to live truly off-grid and isolated, and being back here highlights all of it.

I spend a good forty-five minutes scrubbing every inch of my body and lathering up the shower products deliciously. They smell like Colton, but I don't mind it at all. It's comforting, familiar, much like his presence always is. He always smells good; citrus-fresh, with subtle undertones of musk. An enticing, heady scent that ignites so many memories of being close to him at just smelling his products. On me, it's maybe a little masculine, but it's better than woodland damp and stale river water. It makes me feel human again, although it kills any urge to sleep and revives my energy levels, which maybe I shouldn't have done.

I brush my teeth when I get out, oddly obsessed with peppermint toothpaste now I get to use it again and redo my teeth four times just because I can. Running my tongue over shiny, smooth enamel and the breathy fresh taste when I inhale. I brush out my damp hair after I rub it almost dry with the soft towels hanging nearby and cover my body from head to foot in the lotion from my bag that smells like tropical fruit, trying to smell female again. It does a great job blending with Colton's scents, and I end up sort of pineapple scented and smelling somewhat edible. I quickly redress in my underwear and nightshirt and revel in how good clean feels. There's no comparison to this kind of sensation.

I feel a thousand times better and hurry back to my cupboard to find thick fluffy bed socks for my now soft and supple feet and climb on the bed to braid the front of my hair to keep it off my face. The layers are long enough now, and always falling in front of my eyes, so I French braid across the front and down one side of my face with a little rubber band from my bag.

I hop up to admire myself in the mirror once more, and the difference it makes is impressive. Radiant and squeaky clean; my skin flawless in its sun-kissed beauty and glowing. My hair is lighter and shinier now I've stripped the filth out, and the natural highlights of my blonde are softly shining through. The style frames my face and draws attention to my now slimmer cheekbones and long neck.

I look less like a child and way more woman, and I can't help the little confidence boost it gives me. My green eyes shine brightly back at me, despite hints of dark circles under my eyes, but overall, I look pretty. I never used to think I was anything of the sort, but now I see it. I'm finally seeing what Colton sees, and it's not a girl anymore or a shy feeble little no one who used to cower away from all Santos. I now stand tall, with my chin tilted up, and there's more

441

presence in my posture than before. A look in my eyes says 'fierce' because I've lived through some amount of shit so far already, and no one will push me back in the shadows. I have fuller lips, a defined bone structure, and a better length of hair that suits my face shape. I could give Carmen a run for her money looking like this, and honestly, side by side, I'd put my bets on me. It's weird to appreciate myself this way, finally.

I scan the room, aware that now I have this boost, I no longer want to lie on the bed, and the wildfire in me is up and revving inside. I don't want to lie down until my hair dries anyway, and I now have the urge to check on Sierra and see how she's settled. Colton looked tired, so maybe I should offer to swap. Sit by his mom while he sleeps in here and gets some much-needed rest. We are sharing, sort of, so maybe we could alternate, and when one uses it, the other stays with Sierra until we figure something else out.

I'm sure the only thing to sleep on in there is a couch unless they have more beds on wheels to give him, and I make up my mind that it's the only thing to do. He's essential to the pack, and I'm not really, not right now anyway. He should rest well, in an actual bed, in his own room, and I think I want to sit by Sierra for a little while, surrounded by noise and movement, like I was in the forest, until I feel calmer about being back among everyday life. I need a transition period.

I check myself over once more as my nightshirt slides off one shoulder, exposing soft, peachy skin, and try to figure out if this is modest enough attire to walk around the homestead. I'm covered, and the shirt is almost to my knees and not thin enough to see through. It's baggy and pretty shapeless, but it does cling to my breasts as it keeps sliding down off my left shoulder so that I don't look frumpy in it. There's a peek of shadow from my navy underwear, but it's a shirt overall. I don't need to get dressed. Not really.

With my mind made up, I pad out into the hall, clicking the door closed quietly behind me, and realize how quiet this place is at this hour. It must be after midnight for sure, but I can't be certain and tiptoe down the dimly lit hall towards the door we took Sierra through earlier so as not to make any noise and disturb people who may be close by.

I know where the infirmary is, and I don't hesitate to click open the door and slide into the extra hallway that shields the infirmary from people walking in, the airy box area painted white with gray vinyl floor. I make my way through that second door to the double doors with windows, and through the glass, I can see Colton sitting by her side, reading a book to her. His back to me and tilted down towards her at his side. I can make out his profile and the book perched on the side of her bed.

Doc is asleep on a bed in the corner, looking utterly comatose with a blanket thrown over him, and the femme medic is standing off to one side at a counter and doing something. I guess she's on night duty while Doc sleeps. There's no one else there, and the lights are low, so the only brightness comes from the medic at her workstation. The rest is dim, even where Colton sits, and I can barely make out the low hum of his voice as he talks to her.

I click the door open as quietly as I can and move in quickly and silently, but he seems to know and immediately looks my way, catching my eye and then sliding his vision up and down me with an appreciative half-smile as he does.

You look knockout and much like the old you. Although, why aren't you in bed?

He mind-links me, and, despite myself, I blush and make my way to him to stand beside him at the bed. Trying to ignore the rise in heart rate and how overly aware I seem to be now that I'm back beside him, wearing noticeably thinner clothing, so his body heat warms me by being close.

I couldn't sleep and figured you might want the bed, and I could stay with her.

Colton shifts in his seat and turns so he faces my way and hauls over another stool next to him and pats it for me to sit.

"I don't want to leave her just yet. Sit with me; keep me company." He locks a look on my face; that half-smile melts me with those overly cute dimples that set my belly alight. I slide onto the seat immediately, too swayed by that face and hating myself for

443

the obedience, knowing it's probably stupid to cozy up beside him in the middle of the night, given the last time we got so close in here. Still, something inside me is urging me to stay with him. The desire is more potent than my will, and even though I try to sit away slightly, once he turns back to his mom, his shoulder and arm fit snugly against me and make me tremble with the effects of his touch. That awareness zooming back in, and every inch of my skin tingles in recognition of his body heat, betraying me.

"What are you reading her?" I ask, focusing on something else and pushing him out of my mind, ignoring my traitorous body, and trying so desperately to breathe normally as my breaths get shallow. I hush my voice so as not to disturb the sleeping doc, and it covers how breathless I've become while this close to him in such an intimate setting.

"Lady Chatterley. When I was young, it was her favorite book, she always read it in the garden while she watched me play, so I figured maybe she might like it. The doc says she might be able to hear us, so I don't know ... maybe it's stupid." Colton reverts to that boy once more, the one I met and knew all these years, and it tugs at my heartstrings so deeply I just have to touch him.

"It's not stupid. It's sweet and shows her you love her. If she is aware, then it's probably nice to hear your voice and a story instead of noise and chaos and feeling ignored. I can't imagine what she's gone through." The tugging of my heart pushes me to lean against him and lay my head on his shoulder impulsively, seeking to be soothed. Fitting like he was made to have me curl up beside him, and he readjusts his position, so I slot right in at him, resting his cheek against the top of my head. Much like me, it seems anytime I'm close or touch him, he also has to respond to the pull and always touches me back. I hate that even when we're no longer allowed or able to be together, our need to be this way overpowers everything else. It stirs up so much ache inside me and brings that awful choking sensation back to my throat.

I'm torn in my sadness for Sierra and driven by the force of his pull whenever he's close. I know I'm betraying myself by initiating the touch, and I'm trying hard to fight it. Colton is too easy and too inviting, like a safe harbor that calls to me to shelter from the cruel world, especially when I'm feeling vulnerable, and tonight, this was probably a bad idea. I've had no real sleep, my emotions are all over the place, and I'm too tired to fight any of it.

"Maybe we can stay here like this until she wakes up, and I can stop thinking or feeling and just take a minute." Colton's voice is as soft as mine, hushed, and his breath tickles my forehead as he utters the words. Igniting goosebumps and all sorts of crazy feelings and thoughts at his suggestion. To sit here with him like this for two days and ignore everything, pretend for a little while that this is all we need to care about. Cuddling up doesn't sound wholly awful. It sounds like stealing a few last moments before reality sets in, and I can't say I'm against it. Pretending for a little while that we're okay and there's nothing wrong with his touch.

Colton takes my silence as an agreement and reaches out and flips over the page of the book as though he intends to start reading to her again. It pushes me to curl up against him all the more, settling in to listen and mentally chastising myself to pretend this is a frozen moment. Where nothing matters except listening to him read and watching her sleep.

"My two favorite girls. What more could I want?" Colton slides his arm from between us and instead lassoes it around me and pulls me in against his chest, fully igniting that sense of safety and security. I melt and give up completely, sinking into his embrace and blotting out all the noise coming from my brain, all the words of warning and refusals. I want to be held by him and cherish this moment if I need to get through the rest of my life watching him bonded to someone else.

His hand on the book slides away, and he places it on Sierra's forehead instead, gently stroking her hair back and then resting lightly on her hairline as he leans in to see the words on the pages. I pull my feet up on the bar of the stool and drop my knees against his, drawing warmth in every area of my body now, sliding one arm behind him and making the most of allowing myself to be immersed in his body. I reach out gently and touch Sierra's hand as instinct takes over; the need to let her know I'm here too is all-consuming for some unknown reason. The sudden compulsion to connect to her somehow complete this little circle we have going on.

"She's so very beautiful. You look like your ...."

My words die on my lips as my fingers slide over hers, and I capture her hand in mine. A warming sensation travels from my fingertips, and something crazy happens to me. My mind jolts with the force of an electric zap that yanks me closer to the bed, and I almost tumble out of Colton's arms, but he catches me, hauling me tight to him.

I gasp out loud as my brain somehow loses control of all its faculties, my vision whites out, blinding me insanely, so that I grab hold of his leg with my one free hand to steady myself and lose all ability to hear, feel, or see. The only sensation I'm aware of is the burning connection from Sierra's hand to mine and the same burn coming through Colton's arm around my waist. The touch connects the three of us, consuming me until I can't fight it.

I entirely blank out, losing all sense of everything. I can't open my eyes or feel my limbs like I'm a mass of unconnected thoughts with no physical form. It all slips away like trying to hold water with your fingertips, her, her, the room, and all I can do is ride with it.

I try to take a breath, but even that seems futile as I'm nothing, lingering in airless space, finding myself in darkness so eerie, yet familiar, as sounds and smells filter through and bring brief moments of time to the surface. It's distant at first, as though traveling along a tunnel and they're at the other end battling through a fog. They're not the infirmary; they're something else that tugs at my memory bank and draws me back in time as I fall into a memory I never knew I had.

The smells of summer pushes me into a brighter place, and I blink and slowly open my eyes, suddenly aware of touch and sensation as I regain complete control of my limbs, but there's no one here with me. Colton isn't here. I can't feel or sense him, and I seem to be in another space entirely. In a room, lying down, one that haunts me from the past. I lift my hand to touch my face and gauge the reality of what I'm seeing, and I'm startled to see it's so

446

tiny and childlike. I blink some more to clear the fogginess so I can look again.

Everything comes into focus slowly; it fades back in, and I know immediately where I am. The small makeshift attic room, hastily painted pink by the family that took on a child whose own had gone to battle. I'm back in the temporary space of my guardian family, back when my parents went to war. The cozy bed, the painted dressers, and my ragdoll, Annie, sits on the side of my bed, watching me in my slumber. It brings back so many mixed emotions and memories, but none I can ever recall like this. This seems new, yet everything is here and precisely as I remember.

It's dull, nighttime, although it's not complete darkness, so it must be summer, and I know I'm supposed to be asleep, but something stirred me from my dreams of my mother and father running through our meadow in a game of tag. My senses alert me to the window in the far corner, and I watch in terrified silence; a vulnerable child. Something begins to climb through with precise movements and silent intent. My heart hitches, racing and pulsing so profoundly I feel it may rip from my chest. Frozen in terror, unable to cry out for fear that the monster climbing in may see me if I make a noise.

The dark, shadowy figure, wearing a large, heavy, black cloak with the hood pulled up to mask their identity, slides up the unlocked panel of glass and slowly and carefully climbs inside, pulling their heavy robes with them, and almost soundlessly lands on the space in front of my window. I resist the urge to pull the covers over my head, my blood running cold with the terror of what is here, panic enveloping me as I try to call out for my caregiver in youthful hysteria.

"Don't be afraid, little one. Hush now!" The female voice comes from under the hood, silencing me mid-scream with its familiarity and a raised palm. I'm startled into silence because I know her. I recognize her smell, sound, and presence as it calms me, and she turns towards me entirely. All I can see are two electric blue, glowing orbs from the dark shadow of her hood as she looks directly at me. Her eyes are mesmerizing, and I've never seen such a color before.

"You know me, Alora. I'm here to protect you. I'm Luna Sierra Santo. I come as a friend of your mother's. Be still now. I have much to do."

A MEMORY LOST

I lie still, watching her, frozen, breath raspy to match my elevated heart rate, but my fears calm and fade as she slides down her hood with a slow, even slide and illuminates the room with a magical blue glow of both her hands. Like a mesmerizing smoky orb around each that follows and traces with every movement. Hypnotic in nature.

Despite looking exotic, Sierra Santo is a beautiful woman with almost milky skin. Her dark hair frames a delicate bone structure, and her eyes, although electrifying blue right now, are almond-shaped under straight, thick dark brows, so perfectly symmetrical. She has pouty lips and an ever-present youthful charm that completely warms her to you. A face that says, 'You can trust me' to match the surrounding atmosphere of serene she always carries.

I sit up, gasping in wonderment at the light show and reaching out to touch what I can see as she moves in and sits on the side of my bed with grace. She lets my hand wander into hers, seeking and investigating, before firmly surrounding my small hand in her fingers and encompassing me with the warmth. I expected the blue air to be cold, but it's almost like being submerged in a hot bubble bath, and I giggle at the tickle.

"Don't be afraid, Alora ... it's magic. Special, gentle, and yet so very ethereal and kind. Would you like to do some magic with me while I tell you a story?" Her eyes are still that dazzling brightest azure, and I look from her hands to her eyes in awe at the vibrancy of this mystical light she can produce. My curiosity is killing the last

449

of my fears, and I nod with the enthusiasm of a child who wants to discover more. Naïve courage because of my innocence.

Of course, I shouldn't be afraid. This is Luna Santo, and I know her. She comes to the library to read us stories and plays with us sometimes. Well, she did before all the grownups left to fight a battle. Like my mommy and daddy have, my big brother Jasper and my grandparents. And most of the rest of the Whyte pack.

I'm staying with Mommy's friend while they're gone, Aisha Munro, one of our pack, which is big and round because she says she's having puppies. Sierra has a son around my age, but I don't like boys, and I don't like playing with Santos. They're always so pushy and aggressive when we do, and I prefer my friends from the Whyte pack. We're softer; we play less rough games than fighting and hunting. They're just stupid boys.

"How can a wolf do magic?" I ask, blinking trustingly and adjusting to see her in this dimness, leaning up against my headboard and shuffling my butt so I can sit properly. With blue as our light source, everything it touches between us is shaded in cold hues, which add even more magic to the atmosphere, and I smile as I watch it envelop my hand and spread up my arm. It feels strange but good, like soft, gentle air being blown across the surface of my skin, only warm.

"Well, that's a story and one I would like to tell you. Remember how we used to read at the library when you all lay on the floor and closed your eyes so you could get lost in the pictures your mind created? If you like, we can do that now so you can listen and empty your mind from any distractions. I need you to focus on my words and not my light." Her voice is so soothing, low, yet pretty. It has a husky depth that is a little lower than most femmes, but it's melodic. I've always liked Sierra's voice; it has a calming quality, like a warm wave washing over you on a cool day.

"Yes! I love your stories." I reply in unleashed excitement, hurrying to lie back down in my bed and eager to hear this one. I bounce and shuffle while still holding her hand and wriggle myself down like a squirming caterpillar into my sheets once more, pushing my head back against my pillow, sinking in. I don't care why she's come in through my window and not the door. Or why she came in the night. I want to be a good girl and listen to her magical adventure story. The one in which a wolf learns magic. That's crazy, and even I know wolves can do no such thing!

My mommy used to read me stories in bed, and maybe because she can't be here right now, Sierra came to do it instead. She's a Queen, so she can go home when she chooses, but Mommy is a warrior, and she has to stay away and protect us from the evil men who came to the mountain to hurt the wolves. Mommy is strong, fast, and a good fighter for being a farmer wolf, so she said it was important that she go with them to chase the darkness away.

Sierra tucks me in neatly, pulling my blanket up to my chest, but keeps my one hand in hers snugly and tightens the grip she has on me. She slides back a little and lays my wrist on her knee, which splays open my palm to disengage hers, so she can touch my hand without holding it properly, and with gentle strokes, begins to circle in the center in a rhythmic motion. The sensation sends shivers and goosebumps across my skin, but it brings back the sleepiness and has the same effect as rocking me back to sleep.

"I learned to do magic as a tiny child, about the same age you are now. It wasn't easy, but when you discover a gift inside you that aches to be set free, nothing can hold it down forever. Open your mouth, Alora; I have a sweet-tasting berry that will help you sleep when I'm done telling my tale." Her voice is calm, as though she's telling me secrets, and I obediently open my mouth as she pops a small, round, semi-soft object in my mouth, and I automatically begin to chew. The juice explodes with the first squish between my teeth like a delicious fruit bomb of sticky sweet nectar, leaving a beautiful taste of raspberries, strawberries, and other wild berries that seem to mingle in my mouth and coat my tongue as though I just drank a whole glass of squeezed berry juice.

"What was that? Can I have another?" I ask while opening one eye to look her way. It was so tasty I could eat a whole bowl of whatever that was. She's leaning over my hand, looking at me, and shakes her head with a soft smile on her pretty face.

"Hush now and listen. Close your eyes. One is more than enough, for you see, one little berry has the power to make tonight fade away further than a forgotten dream, where no one will know where to look to find it. It's a very special berry, only found in crevices of magical places, in whimsical woods, and with my help, it has a little added spice." Sierra picks up a strand of my hair and twirls it with her free hand, never breaking contact with the first, and I settle back down into my dark blankness as I shut my eyes to focus only on her voice once more.

The night air is still and quiet, and for once, I can't even hear the owls in the trees or the leaves rustling in the wind outside my window. There are no other noises around us, not even the ones of the house creaking or the Munro's coughing in their sleep, which is a little odd, but maybe I usually sleep through the night and don't know the world sometimes falls silent.

"My story may not make sense, sweet child, but one day it will, and when you remember it, remember this night and this moment, and all will fall into place. You'll know why I came." Sierra Santo brushes a hand across my forehead gently, an affectionate yet straightforward touch of a mother, and I nod, not willing to interrupt her anymore, so eager for this story to begin even if I don't grasp what she means. I love tales about witches, magic, and brave heroes, and I hope this will be a good one. I can already tell as she's playing with my hair like we've started a great adventure.

I feel her sag against my thigh and sigh before her voice fills the air, still hushed yet clear and true.

"Once upon a time, a special girl called Danya lived near some breathtaking mountains in a land filled with immortals. She was only small, barely a girl.

She was unusual, though, as, before her, no other of her kind had been borne that had ever survived beyond the womb. They say the Fates blessed her very creation with a purpose in mind. That she was of two breeds united, who had lived on the land side by side for centuries; her mother, a light walking wolf, fell in love with a dark creature who could never face the sun, a vampire.

452

By their union, they created a child of two worlds who could walk in either sun or moon and harness the best of both. You see, these two breeds were once allies, co-existing together. One in the night, and one in the light, protecting the lairs of each, so other immortals and human hunters would never hurt them at their weakest.

But a terrible king pulled them apart in the worst of ways. He believed the breeds uniting, creating a new kind, would overpower all the immortals, outbreeding his wolves and this girl, with her unique gifts, and could show them the way. She was not just any hybrid child, she had powers unlike any we had seen before, and she wanted only unity among her people. That was her fated purpose."

I gasp a little and cover my mouth right away so as not to disturb her, and utter only a breathless 'WOW' as I become immersed in this tale. My little heart picking up speed with the wonder of it. Sierra smiles softly and continues.

"The Alpha king was enraged with the girl's audacity, that she should one day rise and derail him, taking his wolf kingdom away. So, he did what he thought would save his rule, and he slaughtered the girl Danya when she was merely a child. Her mother, too, who tried to protect her, was slain in a pool of blood. The King was a liar.

He blamed the dark creatures for the deaths of their own and ignited anger in the wolf packs to seek vengeance for the bloodshed of an innocent, while he denied the act himself."

"He killed the little girl and her mommy?" I blurt out in outrage, unable to contain my angry shock, inhaling hard, and opening an eye to blink at Sierra. Sierra gently moves her hand over my face and closes my eyes once more with her delicate fingertips, pushing me back to quiet, and continues. I try to keep my eyes closed this time, the excitement bubbling within my veins.

"Now, the nightwalker, he was not just any creature ... he was what they call an original, much like the Alpha of the wolves. An ancient. Beings that were the first of our kind and created many purebloods.

453

Danya's mother had lain with the King of Vampires, probably why her child took hold and came to fruition, as ancients are the purest of our kind. His broken heart and need to avenge his love and child drove him to sheer madness, and he swore to avenge her death by slaying all wolves he deemed responsible for their demise.

The Kings met in battle, and what were once allies and peaceful unions became bloodshed and death. It spilled onto every land until it forced both to find refuge in parts of the world where the other did not stray. In the years following, those born of mixed breed, who came after, where unions were made in secret from those who didn't want the wars, were hunted down and slaughtered by both kinds for treason. Unions between the two breeds were forbidden. So those born of light and dark fled and hid and always kept their secret about who they were, in any way they could. Danya was not the last."

I sigh heavily, letting out a slight noise, but Sierra is making sure I keep my eyes closed, and I picture such a pretty girl with white hair, saddened with little pangs in my heart that they ended her in such a cruel way. I wonder if a wolf can be both, like me, and one of those creatures Mommy is fighting. I wonder if this story could be a little bit true. It would be sad if all these wars were because a bad man killed a little girl. All because he was afraid she would take his crown away. What a silly man.

"Stories told are a funny thing, as they change and grow, and details are forgotten or exaggerated, and soon that story of years gone by gets lost among the wolves, and visionaries too afraid to correct the tellers.

We witches became the enemy because we held truth and sight, as Alphas removed traces from our history and beheaded witches who spoke out. The wars raged on, decade after decade, for hundreds of years, until no wolf or vampire knew why we came to hate one another with such passion. The witches still whispered the secrets, though.

All was to be forever that way, quiet secrets, until a visionary, a seer, saw something that changed everything, and she sacrificed her life by spreading a prophecy to any who listened. Neither side trusts the motives of the witches, but we have always been the peacekeepers and the healers among you all. Our hearts were open to love all kinds, and we only wished to serve the needs and cure the sick, but this hatred had pushed some of my kind into terrible darkness who use their gifts for bad. And we no longer tried to right the wrongs of your people."

Sierra again lifts her hands from my eyes, although I keep them closed, ready and waiting for her words, and she returns to twirling my hair.

"This Seer, she saw an end to it all, in the form of a white wolf with a vampire's blood running through her veins. A direct descendent of both bloodlines, both ancients. The prophecy was clear that only a femme could carry the gifts needed. She would rise and lead her people ... not in war, hate, and death.

No, that was never the prophecy, but she was to unite and repair the bonds between the two because a warrior she may be, but her truest gift will be the love she has inside her, and her power will reset the balance. She will not wipe out the vampires; she will find something among them that will show her how to fix the rift. They possess something she needs from them. She's a healing balm." Sierra sighs heavily, fatigue in her voice, and a sense of hopelessness dulls her tone.

"A new King was rising among the people and his bloodline. The king of old was not willing to relinquish his throne, either. That same power madness infected his mind, and he purged the lands of any white wolves he came across on his battlefield. Not that there were many, as the flaws in our kind make their birth almost impossible. He broke the laws and killed his own, and to hide his secrets, he killed all that were linked to them and removed any trace from the packs. You see, losing our kind in battle raises no questions, and he knew he could never let a white wolf rise. Such is his need for that power; he married a witch-wolf and hid her identity because he thought she would make him rise as the chosen one."

I wonder if our Alpha Santo is that king. If Sierra is the magical witch in the story. Maybe she means Juan Santo is the evil king.

How silly. Juan isn't a bad man. He's the one Mommy went to war with. He is our people's king now.

"There was one who shone bright and started to lead a better way. Turn the battles in our favor, but she was letting the vampires live and showing mercy all too often. She believed she could end things if she could meet with the Coven King of Darkness and put an end to it all. She said she had a way. A future with peace.

The Alpha king was furious, but the witch Luna had affection for the white wolf, and she begged him to leave her be. The king knew the white wolf was too strong for him and that his witch mate would try to intervene. So, while he pretended to allow her to travel alone to find this leader of the vampires for a solution to the fights, he struck down her family, and her mate, putting an end to her own life, too.

He used the link between bonded mates to his advantage. He thought he had ground the prophecy to dust once and for all, with no more traces of white among our kind. There was devastation in the air and a broken witch-wolf in heartbreak.

The king, however, was reminded of a child who had stayed behind and had not yet come to turn and show her true colors. A femme child with the possibility of her hybrid mother's gifts. But you see, the king's mate ... she *is* a witch, bound by a bond to him, yet she does not support his actions.

That wolf was her sister in friendship, maybe not in birth, but she adored her as though she was blood and what he did broke her heart. The betrayal of his people, the murder of his own, the betrayal of his bond to her in hurting her closest. That witch, she knew he, would come after the rest of the white wolf's pack and end any chance of another rising ever again.

She chose her people over her bond, her love of the white wolf's child, and it brought me to you." Sierra stops stroking my face, and her words make me jump. So caught in the wonder of her tale that it's a surprise for her to say that.

"Why me? What am I to do?" I try not to open my eyes, as she said not to, and screw them shut as hard as I can while holding myself still. My little heartbeat rising again with awe and excitement for this fantastic story.

"You are the last white femme, Alora, so I could not stay behind and let you die. I had to come and protect you with the gifts I've hidden for so many years. Don't be afraid. One day, when this comes back, you will know what to do.

My son, Colton, is a good, sweet boy, but I must leave him for a little while, even though it kills me. You'll be what he needs when the time comes, and the Fates will draw you to him. I've seen it; the Fates have deemed it so. Saw the pairing of my child and my Marina's as a resolution to the binds we find ourselves in. Our children will be the unity our three kinds need, and together they will rebalance what nature intended for our people.

The berry I gave you will make you sleep, and all that you know from the moment you woke at my appearance until you wake in the morning will be gone. Until such a time when we three touch and I can lift the binds I'm about to place on you.

If something happens and I can no longer be found or help undo this, your mate bond to my son, the finalizing of the union, will restore this memory and the gifts I'm about to bind. It will break the spell, and you'll shine, sweet girl, with my son by your side. My aura shimmers around and through you, weaving its path as I have given you my words, and our souls have become so wholly entwined within my magic. Look now."

I flutter my eyes open with her permission, a little slow at first, and can see what she means with a quiet inhale of surprise. I'm completely enveloped in a blue glow, all around me and somehow inside me, and I lift my one free hand to see there is not a single piece of me that is not illuminated as it pulsates from every pore. Making traces in the air with my small movements.

Sierra takes both of my hands in hers, holding my entire tiny fist inside her palms and firmly squeezing until I can't free myself. Her eyes glow brighter, the room becoming light with the power of the glow we are emitting, and her face transfixes me as she locks her eyes on mine.

"I'm binding my life to thee, willingly our souls entwine.

My air is yours, our hearts beat in rhyme, and together we are one 'til the end of time.

By blood, we may not be linked, but in love and bond, by magic synced.

We now are forever to die as one.

For you, my child, this spell will be done.

I bind thee gifts until a time predicted when the world and all within shall be shifted.

When love breaks the ties I place upon thee, your mind and power shall be set free.

We shall meet again, in a time and place that the Fates decree."

Sierra utters these words, almost like a song, as everything between us pulses, and hums, with a static that electrifies the room, and we glow to an insane level of brightness. I screw my eyes shut; body energized and almost fit to bursting with the sudden rush of adrenaline rushing through me.

I feel like I'm standing in a wind tunnel, yet nothing moves, and almost as quickly, it stops dead and drops back to a dim glow as only Sierra's hands remain blue, and those two piercing eyes return to their natural dark brown color. I blink my eyes at the sudden darkness of the room, adjusting as it all comes back into focus, and look at her in question. Her eyes are full of tears; little rivulets stain her pale cheeks as they roll down, and she smiles at me softly.

"He's coming, and soon this family will die, too. They're killing what is left of the Whyte pack as we speak, and they'll tell those of the mountain they chased vampires into our lands and couldn't get to them in time. As I have become, you'll be a thorn in his side, and he'll have no choice but to put you somewhere in the hope you'll be forgotten. My fate will be whatever he decides, but I doubt it'll be here with my people.

If you die, I die, and, in turn, he dies too. That will be my homage to your mother, so her death was not in vain.

Sleep now, sweet girl ... before the horrors come to this room. I don't want that memory for you of this innocent family's demise, and I will stay here until he knows he can't touch you. For now, for eternity, if he wishes to live.

My sleeping berry is potent. You will know of nothing more, my angel, only peaceful slumber. For tomorrow, they will break your heart and tell you of the saddest moment you'll have to live through for the next ten years. I'm not a warrior; I'm a healer, or else I would have done more for her, for all of you, and I'm so sorry. I truly am.

My son, though, has so much fire within him, just waiting to be unleashed. He will be a great warrior one day, your protector, your love, but you will show him the way. I had to bind his witch gifts as a baby for fear others would see it in him or that Juan would see him as a threat, but he possesses sight and abilities he knows nothing of yet. I bound him, and like yours, his gifts will unbind when he marks you as his mate; or I'm returned to you both to do it myself. Whichever comes first... You two are our future, Alora." Sierra strokes my face one more time. The sleepiness becoming overwhelming, and although the words she says alarm me and pushes fear into my heart and a pain so deep because she said my mother is dead, the effects of that berry are pulling me into darkness. I can't fight them. Tears bite my eyes, and I make a painful sound in response, yet it falls almost like a breath and fades away as I succumb to its power.

"I want my Mom." It's a whisper as I try my hardest to fight the effects, but my eyes drift closed, and Sierra's voice is all that gets through, her tone low, husky, and torn as she cries through her words.

"I'm so sorry. I really am. I want her to come back too. You are all I have left of her. I only wish I could stand in her place and shelter you now, but he won't let me be with you. Our time will come; I will see you again. Sweet, sweet, Alora." She sobs a little under her breath and then swallows it down and pushes herself back to calm. "I'll sing to you, the wolf song. Such a pretty lullaby that will help you go to sleep. Your mother said she used to sing it when she nursed, and it was always Colton's favorite melody to fall asleep to ... shh now."

Sierra gently starts to sing, her voice wavering with emotion but still lovely and quiet, almost a whisper so as not to disturb anyone else. The words of the Nordic song of old that we sing at the Awakening ceremonies, according to my mom, because I'm not allowed to go just yet. They're for the grown-up wolves who have something special beginning, and I hope one day that will be me, too.

The notes and melody fill the air like a beautiful ghostly echo, calling on our ancestors to help pave my path to slumber, and I black out entirely as voices invade the room where I lie.

YOU ARE MINE

I gasp, inhaling a deep, almost vicious breath as reality crashes back in on me, shuddering my brain around my head, and I'm startled awake, back where I began, in the infirmary and gripping onto Colton's leg for dear life. So disoriented as my vision returns to normal. I can hardly breathe for a moment and have to drag air into my lungs while I get my bearings and shake my head to clear my blurry vision.

"What the hell?" It's an automatic response as I try to catch my breath, and Colton's arm around my waist loosens as he lets me go a little. I guess he was holding me up, and I flop as I'm released, using my hands on my knees to bend forward and finally pull myself together. It all starts to fade, and the noises and smells of reality bring me back to clarity.

"That was a memory; I saw it too." Colton's voice is gravelly, as though he's just as shaken as me, and I untangle myself from him and stand up. My body is spiking with unwanted tingles and feelings I can't contain as many things rush through my head. I guess we somehow mind-linked when all three of us connected, and he got the memory, too, seeing what I saw. My emotions are all over the place, as though I just experienced something traumatic, and he gets up to follow me around the bed, sensing I'm not emotionally calm.

"Are you okay?" He can sense my weirdness, and I wrap my arms around myself to shut out the cold, clawing feelings rising to strangle me. Knocked sideways mentally, just needing a moment to claw my mind back together and figure out why my heart is

461

pounding through my chest. I feel sick and agitated. It's more than the memory invading my brain; it's what Sierra's words told me.

"All I remembered before that was being asleep in that room and then waking up in a new place with other kids in the orphanage. There was nothing in between, and now I know why. He must have taken me there, and I forgot it all when I slept. They told me the Munro family was gone, but I never really understood what they meant by that. Not until later, when I was told the vampires came. Just a kid, and then they told me my family was dead, and I never stopped to question anything beyond that." My voice cracks and my throat is aching with the effort as it drives home that now, I fully understand they were killed because of my mother's and my gifts.

All of them! My mother, family, Munros, and the whole pack died because of us and what we are. The vampires were never the monsters in our midst. We were. The wolves and those of us who would slaughter women and children in the name of power.

We created wars to cover our sins and let hatred rage for centuries without learning from our mistakes. It makes my skin crawl to know the vampires were the innocents in all of this; they are just avenging their lost loves. They were fighting the Juans of the world for what he had done, and now, I'm on the side they are, trying to find reason in the death of everyone I cared about.

"She really is a witch. I mean, I know I saw what the doc' said and all of this, but seeing it. It's a whole other thing." Colton pulls me back to him with his voice. He sounds distant, and his tone is low as he turns his head to her. That spike of emotion hits me hard in the stomach once more. Tears threatening, and the sudden rage shooting up through my stomach and chest. A pang of anger aimed his way. I remember her words and what she said, and not for the first time, anger so intense for Colton that I could hate him.

"Why didn't you just do it when you were supposed to? We could have avoided all this! It would have been done, and we would have remembered. Our gifts restored and taken another path! Why didn't you just mark me when you had the fucking chance? You're an asshole! You could have stopped so much of this bullshit by doing what I needed!" It's a sob, the dam breaking and my pain showing, set loose amid the fury as tears hit my cheeks.

I spin away from him, aware the medic in the far corner is trying to pretend she isn't here, and I'm going to wake Doc up. I don't want people watching us or hearing us fight. I want them to leave me alone while I go somewhere and cry this out, hate on him, and mourn the path we never took. So much hurt that could have been avoided. The Fates didn't separate us to lead me somewhere else; they were backtracking to fix his wrong decision and circle us back around together to fix this. He just kept, and keeps on, screwing it up.

"Hey? Lorey? What the ...?" Colton seems surprised by my reaction, staring at me as I walk off. As I stalk out of the room away from him, he doesn't hesitate and follows me. Close on my heel as I push through the doors into the middle hallway, where he catches my wrist and tries to tug me back. I shrug him off, pull my hand away and keep going. My head is bubbling with the facts staring me in the face, my heart twisting with the reminder he destroyed everything between us.

"Leave me alone. You ruined it all!" I'm crying, broken and tear sodden with the out-pour, wracking pain in my chest that makes it difficult to breathe as though an elephant is sitting on my ribs, but he does not relent and sticks to my ass trying to catch my hands.

"Baby, come on. Can we at least talk about this ... about that? I know I fucked up, but this isn't ruined. Just give me the chance to do something about it." There's panic in his tone, an attempt at gentle and soothing, with a lot of confusion about my change of feelings. In no mood for him anymore, and I want to lie down and let all this wash away on a sea of heartbroken tears. I storm down the hallway to the room I'll be sleeping in and push the door open, slamming my palm on the wood, swinging it open at speed, so it crashes against the wall behind and exposes the room.

Colton doesn't give up; he's hot on my heel, relentless in his pursuit, and almost suffocating me with his proximity. This time he catches my upper arm, grasps tight, yanking me to a stop as I proceed inside, and spins me to him, so I have no choice but to face him. I tense, my body turning stiff in defense, and my eyes glow red in readiness to battle myself free.

"Talk to me!" He snaps the order at me, but it only riles that inner fierce that hates when he tries to command me to do anything.

"Stop it. Let me go. I don't want to talk to you. It's pointless, and it's done. You were an idiot. You broke me, broke us, and now my memory tells me all you had to do was mark me, and it would have changed everything! Why did you have to screw it up? Why did you have to choose her over me?" I slap at his fingers on my arm and shove at his chest, trying to have him release me, but Colton is as stubborn as I am and only tightens that grip and stands steady, turning around halfway to push the door closed behind us and conceal us in here. His face shows hints of anger in that furrowed brow, and one dimple is prominent as a scowl slowly appears. His eyes amber to match my fierce glow.

"Okay, first, marking you would have changed everything, yes, and I regret it; I fucking do, Lorey. More than you will ever know, but we would never have found her. You had to run. I see that now, to find her, and maybe any other way we wouldn't have. My mom would still be hidden because of that choice.

Second, how can I fix the damage if you won't give me a chance to try? I am not the one fighting this, and I'm not the one refusing to try. You were never the second choice for me. I love you, and we're here together.

The problem was, I didn't want anyone else and didn't have *any* fucking choice." His tone is tinged with anger, yet also not. He's mad that I'm resisting and making this physical; pissed at me for what he thinks is me being overdramatic, but he's trying to get through to me and communicate with that subtle hint of control and softness, but it just breaks me even more. Sagging as tears pour down my face, I keep tugging at his fingers like a spoiled child to be set free. Unable to do much more as energy drains from me. I'm exhausted, and this isn't helping.

"How can you fix it? You marked her! You betrayed the bond, and you're linked to another forever. I won't be your whore, and the memory said marking—not screwing. Let. Me. Go!" I tug one last time, glaring his way through watery eyes. He finally releases me with a sharp inhale and stares at me like I have two heads as I jump back out of his reach. My entire body wracked with the pain I've been carrying all this time, my throat aching with finally saying it out loud and how much agony those words inflicted on my soul.

"I did what now?" On the other hand, Colton seems a bit shocked and dumbfounded, and his tone drops a level or two, his hard eyes homed in on mine. His pulsating temper subdues to a low thrum, and genuine confusion replaces the shock on his face with a deepening of his brows as he narrows his eyes on me, and that dimple disappears again as his mouth straightens out.

"I felt it, so don't try to deny it. I know what you did." I snap at him, consumed with grief, and turn away, unwilling to let him manipulate me with fast words and untruths. Wiping my face with the back of my hand and pull myself together, trying so hard to find my inner rage again over this damn stupid weakness at what he's done to us.

"We're linked, you and I. Meaning you feel things like me marking someone else. Which you couldn't have because it didn't happen! Is this why you are so fucking mad at me? You have this crazy notion in your head I marked Carmen?" The bitter way he says it, the tinge of anger, and the less than friendly deliverance, only fuel the tornado in me I was trying to calm, and I spin back on him, eyes glowing painfully as my inner wolf jumps out to battle for me.

"Don't you dare! I did feel it … the pain and betrayal. About four days after I left, so don't stand there and fucking lie to me about what you did! I'm not stupid." I yell it at him, temper hitching, and equally riled as I stand up to him, but he doesn't back down. Colton can be scary as hell when riled, and he seems to stand taller and bristles at my verbal attack. His eyes, much like mine, increase in a glow of an equally pissed wolf, and he reaches down to the hem of his T-shirt and yanks it up over his head in one swift, hasty motion and throws it on the bed, exposing that tanned, muscular physique. He spreads his arms out wide and looks me dead in the eye before turning slowly and giving me a full three-sixty of his naked torso.

"Show me. Because marking is a two-way thing and something I wouldn't be able to hide! Look *real* hard, Lorey, because, I swear, I haven't fucking marked anyone." He bites it at me as he comes back to face me, and the blood drains from my body, leaving me cold inside as I take in his tanned skin, free of any mark.

It's hard to stay on this idea about marking when there is nothing on the flawless physique except inky tattoos of his pack tribal on one shoulder and a lot of carved, toned muscle. My anger simmers. But she isn't about to back down because I know what I felt in the woods. That kind of pain and betrayal didn't happen for nothing, so he had to have done something.

"Fine ... Okay, so maybe it wasn't that, but what I felt was real. You obviously just screwed her then. Either way, this will never happen; the bond is marred and damaged, and you did this to us." I cross my arms across my chest, my fight dying because I was so sure, yet I'm wrong. My heart is pounding like a war drum within, and my body is beginning to tremble with the excessive amount of pain and energy coursing through me. Colton looks like he might explode; standing menacingly close, a new rage ignited in that angular face as he tenses his jaw and grits his teeth.

"I did NOT fuck her!! What is wrong with you? All this cryptic bullshit since I came for you. The refusal to let me touch you, all this. You think I cheated on you? That's what all of this is about? Because ... you felt it?

No, Lorey, what you felt around four days after the mess hall conversation was me finding you gone. Me coming back from four days of recon with Mateo to find not only the girl I decided to fight for had gone, and that completely destroyed me, but my Beta, my best friend, kept it from me! Stopping me from being able to find you and betraying my trust in the worst way.

Meadow broke my heart with a betrayal. You broke it by leaving. I came back for you and to tell my father I would go and take you with me if he stood in my way. She knew that your leaving would break me, and it did. I wasn't ever going to mark Carmen.

YOU are my mate and have been since the second we imprinted, no matter what I said or how I seemed. I always wanted you. I'm devoted to you, crazy about you, and I won't be happy until I'm marked to you! You're my soul mate, and I need you. Why the hell would I fuck that up any more than I already did?"

I stand in stunned silence. Colton is breathless with the deliverance of an angry, then almost soothing to calm splurge of words. His whole demeanor softened as he reached the end, and his eyes returned to chocolate brown as he let go of the rage and tried to drive the point home that I was wrong.

He stands now, looking at me with a slightly furrowed brow over that cute-boy expression of 'forgive me,' and I can't move. My stomach twisted in pain and caught in a world of confusion as his words reverberate through my mind and heart, and I see-saw a bunch of emotions all at once. The elation that, in one rant, he wiped away all doubt and confusion about why he's been trying so hard to get us to connect romantically; the sweep of mad at myself that I left when I did and could have been with him all along. He's right about Sierra, though. I wouldn't have found her otherwise, and maybe the Fates always intended it this way after all.

I feel so stupid, guilty, and ashamed, and I regret it took until now to know this. I look down at the floor, unable to look him in the eye while shame washes through me and my stupid pride takes a dent.

He didn't break the bond; he didn't betray me, and in fact, he came home willing to fight for me, only to find I'd gone, and it was too late. I'm mad at myself for the weeks of shutting him out when, with just one link, he would have told me to come home or come for me. Weeks of heartbreak and loneliness when he was always there waiting for me, looking for me, and not about to give up on us. He meant it ... he really didn't, and I've held him at arm's length because I believed the pain and betrayal was something else.

"Why didn't you just ask me when I came for you? This could have been over then." Colton steps toward me. His voice is now low and level, with regret seeping in. A soft little movement closer towards me to tighten the gap and surround me with his smell and presence. I stay still, eyes dropping to my feet in apology and mental fatigue. Finally, able to let go of some of this anger and pain, and it leaves a gaping heaviness within me because I've been carrying it for weeks. It was all so unnecessary.

"I didn't think I needed to. I felt something; we're linked. I figured you knew that I knew." I sound feeble and small, tears clogging my voice as he moves closer. Colton slides his strong, warm hands up my arms until they rest on my shoulders, and he exhales heavily as he pulls me the last few inches towards him, so we are only millimeters apart. His touch and heat soothing me with his gentleness.

"I had no idea you even thought it, or I would have told you, Lorey. I didn't know this was in your head and assumed you would have known I didn't mark her. I figured you were mad about how it ended and that I made you feel like leaving was the only option.

I'm sorry, baby, for everything, but I swear on my pack, on my life, on us, that I have done nothing to betray the bond. I've stayed true to you. I'll project every memory you don't have of our time apart and prove it." His soft voice falls over me like a warming balm, and I break down into stupid little sobs and thrust myself at him to be held. I'm the one who needs forgiveness, so easy to break when I now know he did nothing to make me hate him.

Colton doesn't hesitate, wraps me up in his arms tight, and presses me to his chest. A full-body hug, safe and secure as all the pain and heartbreak subside, and I cry for everything I went through these past weeks. Hating him, needing him, being broken-hearted over him. It all seems so foolish and nothing now. I'm wrapped up tight against him with his breath on top of my hair, sweeping it away. The boy who was my rock, and my words of wisdom, right back here, where I need him, and he does what Colton does best. He holds me up and soothes away my anxiety and tears.

"I'm sorry ..." It's a muffled, pathetic noise against his solid, smooth chest. His skin on mine is like coming home to the best place in the world and being enveloped in warm, cozy safety.

"No, baby. I am, for everything. This is my fault. I failed to do what I was meant to. I failed to nurture and protect my mate and didn't even figure out how much pain you were in over a stupid misunderstanding. Forgive me, *Princesa.* Give me another chance to prove I can be what you need. What you deserve." Colton leans back, sliding his hand between us to separate us a little, guides his fingers under my chin, and tilts my face up to him to look me in the eye. The watery mess of a girl having an emotional breakdown, and he wipes my jawline with his thumb to catch some drops waiting to fall. Taking care of me the way he always does makes it hurt with more intensity. I've been so stupid.

"For someone so strong, you sure like to cry a lot." It's a smile with humor that shines back in his eyes, and those dimples make an appearance, melting me a little more. It makes me snort a small chuckle through my tears, and I wipe my nose on the back of my hand, lightening my mood with a smile.

"That's because my mate's an asshole, and he inflicts it." I point out sarcastically, still trying to dry my face as he helps by lifting his shirt and using it to dab my eyes. Colton leans in, and head bops me on the forehead with his softly and sighs at me, his dimples back on show, hinting at a subtle smile.

"Mate, huh? Thought that was never happening again?" A naughty gleam, a cheeky grin spreading across his face, and, despite how much I love him, I have the urge to knee him in the balls for joking at a time like this.

"Don't push your luck. I have plenty to be still mad about." I shove him back by placing two hands on his chest, finding a little of that strength he goes on about, and pull myself together once more, swallowing the sobs and sniffing away the mess. Colton lets go of my face, catches me by the hips with fast reflexes, and hauls me back, so we bump groins, and he nestles me against him.

"Yeah, but ... I know how to fix it. I have a tried and tested method that always works on you." That sly gleam, and before I can open my mouth to question that response with a 'what?', he swoops in faster than the speed of light and kisses me hard on the lips, locking his mouth to mine, fastening us together passionately. I'm too stunned to react at first as his warm, soft lips fit perfectly to the curves and grooves of mine, warming my skin and silencing my upset entirely. But almost like he hits a button, the fire inside me ignites, and I open my lips a little to let him in.

Colton kisses me softly at first, teasing me with the tip of his tongue, and I respond and find a rhythm in the deliciousness of kissing him again. So many feelings are brimming to the surface, and sweet pains at knowing his touch like this once more. We always worked this way, and I let it develop into French kissing, with tongues entwining, lips pressed tight, and our faces connected. I slide my arms around his neck and pull him as close to me as I can. Absorbed in him with no more mental voice trying to drag me away. I wanted him, always. I loved him, even when he broke me, and this is what I've longed for.

Colton slides one hand over my ass, cups it smoothly, and lifts me to him with that aggression of a horny wolf while his other arm snakes across my upper back and his hand find the base of my neck. Holding me tight as he slides it under my hair and cocoons me within his hold. He presses us together, so my curves fit his hard angles, and I'm left feeling small and fragile within his muscular frame. Wrapped up tight like he'll always protect me from all the dangers in the world. My feet are free of the floor as he lifts me high; I lift them behind me and let him hold me fully.

Nothing will stop it this time, as the fire builds between us, and this pulsing need almost winds me with the ferocity with which it consumes me. Colton subdues my fierce, with his special way of caressing my tongue so my toes curl before pulling out and sucking my bottom lip in such a way it almost makes my panties selfcombust. My body is throbbing with need and desire, and I turn up the heat on his kiss, nibbling his bottom lip ravenously and reveling in how he matches the desire.

Lust spreads through my loins so that I'm wrapping myself around him in any way humanly possible. My fingers in his hair are gripping tight, pulling my knees up, so he slides me around his waist and bounces me higher in his grip. Tilting his head back to keep kissing me, I bring my chin down to stay glued to him as I'm now higher than he is. My gentle turns savage, and this all-consuming

470

ache to be satisfied cries out for him, igniting the passion of my wolf as she gets a little crazy and savage.

We lose the softness of the make-out session and turn almost feral in desire. Grips tighten, kisses turn from romantic to aggressive, consuming us both as we continue. Colton runs his fingers through my hair and tugs my head back so he can access my neck with dominance. Tracing his tongue and teeth down my throat before allowing me to pull back down to be rewarded with another taste of him. This overwhelming energy inside me takes over, and somehow being wrapped up this way is not enough, even though Colton has lifted my feet from the floor and has me suspended in mid-air, straddling him. I want to explore his naked torso with my tongue, to feel every part of his skin on mine, and we have clothes in the way.

I break free, dropping my legs down again, push his face sideways with my hand on his jaw, and lean down to kiss his neck, licking over the pulse in his jugular, tracing from jawline to Adam's apple as he slowly puts me back on my feet. His skin is slightly salty yet delicious, with that unique smell and taste that is only his, and it pushes the need higher inside me. Blood hitting boiling point, and all I want is to experience his mouth on every inch of my skin. Body heating from inside, and my core is pulsating with a strong need to feel him inside me. I want to be joined to him in intimate ways that are only meant for us. I want to taste his blood and mark my mate.

As soon as my feet hit the floor, I shove him backward with newfound strength, away from me with a giggle. Biting on my bottom lip to curb this insane horniness threatening to consume me. He hits the bed and topples over with a manly chuckle. Colton smiles, rights himself to a sitting position, and props one hand behind him so he can lean back and watch me. His eyes devour me, glowing amber with ignited passion, and I can almost feel his heart pounding in time with mine.

"I want you so badly; I can't take it." He utters in a husky tone that's almost inaudible, but it fuels me onwards. I climb on top of him and start untying the cord of his dark sweatpants at the waist.

Confident that he's mine to do what I want with, do as I please, nestling over him so my hands are between my legs to access him.

Colton sits up so he can use both arms, slides his hands up my throat, and circles around my jaw, burying his fingers in my hair before tugging me down and kissing me until he has me breathless. Leaving me to pull his sweatpants loose while he focuses on teasing my tongue with his once more. I close my eyes and savor the way he feels. Nothing matters anymore, all the weeks, the tears, and the fights of the past. All that matters now is how good this feels and how every one of my senses is screaming at me to make him mine.

Once I'm done untying him, I let my hands roam over his chest and abs, appreciating every solid form of hot, smooth sexiness, up and down, until I slide over those shoulders and feel every inch open wide to me. Enjoying the fact I get to explore without boundaries and that I have the right to do it, as he has with me.

He's a perfect specimen, and just his body alone makes me hot and willing to lie back and have his puppies. I want him; my inner thighs are throbbing and damp, and I'm aching for him to put his hands anywhere he pleases, much like I'm doing, but I feel like he's being respectful and cautious about how far he can go. He isn't sure if this leads to sex or just a heavy petting session, and I can feel his hesitation flowing my way.

"Are you going to do this or keep me waiting?" I break from his lips, teasing him, inviting him to take this further, and smile naughtily, so he doesn't misunderstand. His eyes lock on mine, and he matches my seductive smile.

"Oh, baby, you're not getting out of this room until I've done everything I've been thinking of doing to you for the past weeks. Do you know how badly I've wanted this, how many dreams I've had about being able to do this to you? I swear you've been the star of so many pornographic wet dreams." Colton doesn't give me a second to answer that as he catches me in another kiss, catching hold of me, and flips us over with a quick, expert move, so I end up flat on the bed. He crawls on top of me and holds himself off my body with strong arms. I guess the hot dreams were not a one-way thing then. Colton better buckle down and hurry up if those are anything like reality.

He doesn't break the kiss he has me caught in, and I seek out the smooth, hard muscle with my palms and feel my way over him. Colton leans on one elbow to keep himself propped up, and his other hand slides down my thigh until he finds the hem of my nightshirt. He slides a hot, flat palm under the edge, tracing up the curve of my hip and abdomen before smoothing to my right breast and cupping it firmly. Squeezing and caressing my nipple through the thin lace of my bra until he has me arching and wriggling under him in a frenzy of 'take me now.'

It feels unlike anything I've ever known; his touch searing my skin while touching me in places no one else has, but it throbs and aches in such a good way I want him all over me in every private place I have. I never knew a touch could ignite fire and longing with this much intensity, but his does.

There's a mix of apprehension and nerves in the pit of my stomach as we get hotter and heavier, despite wanting it more than air, and Colton lowers his pelvis between my thighs and gently grinds against me, igniting a craving with the goodness of his attention. I moan and bite his bottom lip, gripping his shoulder as I lift my hips to him and push him to do it harder as the sensation arouses me thoroughly, and I swear, I've never been so ready to lose my virginity as I am at this moment. This dry humping thing he has going on is enough to push me over the edge, and I'm almost insane with the craving to get him inside me. If all of this is anything like the end result, I have no desire to keep waiting. Only the niggles and worries in the back of my mind are stopping me from pulling my clothes off and prompting him to go faster.

I've heard it can hurt; there were horror stories from other girls in the home, even those who paired up and marked. They said the first time is not always a pleasant thing, that it can be sore, dry, and awkward, especially if your mate's a virgin. I try to push it out of my head, unable to see how something that feels this insanely good can end up being awful. Colton is not a virgin, even I know that, and judging by his kissing skills, he knows something about a femme's body and how to pleasure her.

I cling to him, wrapping my legs around his waist, and slide one hand between us to rub over the erection I can feel bulging through his sweatpants. Trying to make him want to push us ahead with more haste and smile when Colton groans under his breath at my contact. Both hit fever pitch excitement levels, but he flips from over me, surprising me with the sudden departure that makes me go from insanely heated to instantly cold with the loss of his body heat.

"What are you doing?" I gasp in alarm, shock, and outrage all simultaneously. Blurting it at him and throwing him a confused glare.

"I'm going to end up pounding you into the bed and getting you pregnant the first time if I don't go get something. Trust me, I'm coming right back. Don't you dare move a muscle. The infirmary has some; stay right here, exactly like this." Colton leans up, takes hold of my knees, and pushes them slightly apart with a wink and a smile of cheekiness before swooping down and kissing me on the lips quickly. It elicits a giggle from me that he's both crude and cute at the same time. As soon as he darts out of the room, I flop back on the bed, exhaling heavily, trying to calm my racing heart and draw in some much-needed air.

He has me all kinds of crazy riled up, pulse all over the place, and lungs laboring with his attentions. I lay a hand on my pulsating belly to calm some of this crazy fire burning inside me before I self-combust and pass out. I wave my free hand over my face to cool the intense burning flush on my cheeks and forehead. I thank the Fates I had the foresight to shower earlier.

I have an insatiable yearning, and I can't lie still; my energy levels are boosted, and I'm suddenly antsy. I sit up and shuffle off the bed to pull my nightdress off, but he's back in a flash as I get to my feet. He obviously hyper-sped there and back, equally desperate to do this, and startles me with his return.

"Hey! That's not how I left you!" He comes up behind me and runs a hand up my abdomen, across my breast to give it another gentle squeeze from behind, and kisses me in the crook of my neck, under my jaw. Igniting tingles and butterflies in my belly all over again.

"I was going to take this off." I tug at my shirt to show him and yelp when Colton spins me, almost knocking me over, but instead catches me in his arm. He holds up a pack of condoms, shakes them at me with a mischievous glint in his eye that gets me blushing and looking away in a flash of embarrassment, and throws them on the bed before kissing me lightly on the lips again. His kiss is addictive, and I could have him do it to me every second of every day.

"Allow me." He leans in and yanks the hem of my shirt in one fluid movement as my arms come up automatically, and he swipes the nightdress up and over my head and tosses it aside like it's nothing but a flimsy obstacle. He takes a second to skim my body with his eyes before latching onto my mouth again and kissing me as vehemently as the first reunion, pushing me back into that feverish mode of needing him. Colton's hands are hot and strong. They skim my body, seeking my curves, before sliding behind me as he unclips my bra in a smooth, swift maneuver. Pulling us apart so he can untangle me from it, exposing and releasing my breasts, and throwing it aside. I don't feel any shyness, so invested in my need to be naked with him and allowing him to take a moment to caress them before he slides his hands down my waist.

The hiatus has allowed some of my nerves to kick in, and I swallow down subtle fear, my body trembling as he slides my lace panties down over my hips slowly, sexily, completely undressing me.

"You're beautiful in every way, my perfect girl. I couldn't want you more than I do right now." Colton whispers huskily, right into my ear when he straightens back up and brings us back together, sucking my ear lobe, so my knees almost give way with the erotic sensation. His breath fanning my cheek and shoulder and igniting goosebumps all over.

"I love you." I have to say it to him because it's how I feel as I'm consumed by every nerve ending exploding deliciously, an undying need for him. Forgiveness, letting go of the past, all mixed up with desire, passion, and so many emotions that the words tug at my throat, forming a lump, but it's not sadness. It's complete adoration and incomparable happiness that he will finally be everything I wanted. Everything I need.

Colton pulls back to rest his nose against mine gently, stroking my hair back from my face, and smiles at me in that knee-weakening, full-on dimples way. Slowing down the tempo and breathing out slowly with me as his touch softens.

"I want to hear that multiple times a day for the rest of my life. I swear I'm crazy in love with you, and I'll never let you down again. You're my priority. The Luna the people need; the Luna I need. I'll never doubt us or put you second again. I needed to lose you to realize how stupid that was, how fucked up my priorities were. Your mate should always come first. You will always come first." Colton kisses me on the forehead, a light grazing tenderness that makes me feel delicate and unique, igniting the butterflies inside me and the softer side that is not consumed by lust.

"Unless you turn into a power-crazed psychopath!" I point out in quiet humor and get a flash of that gorgeous smile for my efforts, even if it was a tongue-in-cheek remark that might upset him. A lightening of the intense moment.

"In that case, I give you permission to taser my ass and keep me shackled to the bed for your pleasure. I would happily live like that for as many years as it took to cure me of my crazy." He swoops down, catching my lips while simultaneously scooping me up under the butt and lifting me to him, so I end up straddling him around the waist once more, catching his shoulders with my hands to stop myself from falling backward. He carries me back to the bed this way, never breaking the kiss, and I wrap my arms around his neck, fully entwining him, never wanting to let go ever again. So many times, I almost had him, and he slipped through my fingers, but not this time. He's my captive, and I will fight tooth and nail to keep him here.

Those weeks of being apart, the heartache and pain from being imprinted on him, yet always turned away, all fall around us to dust like they don't matter anymore. His touch is a balm that heals so many wounds, pushes so many painful emotions entirely out of me, and the confidence in knowing he will never reject me again gives me new life. He's in control here and no sign of doing anything except marking me and finalizing the union with sex. He's mine, finally. And nothing is going to come between us or stop us this time around.

Colton gently drops me on the bed and steps back while he strips off his pants and boxers, kicking off his socks and shoes while I pull my socks off and throw them past him. Two completely naked people with glowing eyes as our wolves peak and urge us to unite them, too. We take a silent, almost synchronized second to admire the beauty in each other, in all our glory, both liking what we see.

The way he looks at me, eating me with his eyes and devouring every inch, makes me feel sexy and desirable, and that tingle of need flushes over me once more, dampening the nerves and hesitations, and I reach for him. Colton takes my hand and climbs on the bed, pushing me back against the pillow, and nestles over me more gently than before. He strokes my hair back and fully lays his body into mine, all curves and angles matching, and he slides between my thighs to find a comfortable position.

"Are you nervous?" he asks, losing that wildfire in his eyes and toning down to a simmer as he picks up on my underlying anxiety. Lifting his hand and stroking a thumb across my bottom lip as gentle as a fluttering butterfly. The calm in him pushes through his crazy hormones, and it does so much to help me simmer.

"A little," I admit, not liking that this softness quietens the flames of passion and brings the fear to the forefront a little. I think I would prefer getting lost in the haze instinct and having him just do it when I'm wound up and crazy for him, even if it hurts that way. Get it over and done with, so I can then know what the after feels like and experience future times, as it's meant to get better the more you do it. My stomach lurches with a bout of nerves, and I swallow down the apprehension.

477

"I'll try not to hurt you. We can go slow, be gentle. Marking doesn't have to be crazy and aggressive or bouncing around the furniture. Your first time should be special. Besides, if I don't calm down, I may only last like five seconds, max." Colton's heart is beating as fast as mine. Still, as he utters soothing words, I can feel him physically leveling out, his passion and desire simmering because he's pulling the emotion through instead of the lust, and it's dampening both of us as we feed on each other.

"I don't think I want to anticipate. I'm ready to just do it," I whisper, my innocence showing, and he laughs softly. Bringing that hand and smoothing it down my cheek, the obvious adoration in how he looks at me.

"You clearly don't know what foreplay is or, you know, the joy of working up to it." He grins and kisses me quickly. I blush at that, and he leans in and kisses me a little more intensely, grinding his erection against my intimate places, skin on skin, and I gasp in ecstasy at the unique pleasure waves it causes to ripple through my stomach and up my legs.

"See, sex is about more than just getting it in there. Trust me. I'm not about to make *our* first time together uncomfortable because you aren't ready." Colton strokes his fingers down my throat and across my breast and ignites that same pleasure, caressing my skin so it almost burns with his touch, and those warming, churning feelings between my legs stir up again to fever pitch. They never lay low for long, even when he's taking a breather. Just one touch, and he stokes the fire right back up to where it needs to be, and I stop worrying about going slow.

He moves down my body and kisses my throat, then slides down and licks my nipple before teasing it between his teeth and I arch, bent almost double, as I lift my spine off the bed and moan like crazy with the contact. Colton doesn't relent. He works down my body, kissing, licking, and caressing, and carefully slides his hand between my thighs, waiting on my refusal sounds before he gently rubs across my aching core, his fingers trailing between the folds smoothing dampness across from within me.

I almost spasm with the mind-blowing sensation it elicits. That simple caress down there almost sends me over the edge, and I grab his hair and bury my fingers into the longer length on top to grip onto him as he moves further down. Colton takes it as a sign that I like it and carries on with a second caress, this time circling at the front and almost making me squeal—it feels so good.

I close my eyes and give way to the sensation as Colton gently eases my legs apart at the knees for better access and lifts one of them to open me fully to him. I tense in anticipation, waiting on the piercing pain, and I've worked myself up to believe it'll happen as they told me it would. Sharp agony and dry, uncomfortable, grating thrusting, but I groan in pleasure when a hot, smooth tongue probes me instead. I wasn't expecting him to put his mouth down there, and despite the surprise, I almost melt to goo because it's, honest to God, the best feeling in the world.

"Oh, God." The sensation is nothing like I imagined, not even close. Colton sucking and licking down there. Warm and wet, yet unbelievably good. Something that should feel icky, or weird, or even unbearably embarrassing, instead is making my toes curl and gasp for more. Clutching at him to urge him to do it harder. The pleasure runs up my limbs, warms my stomach, and the motion of what he's doing has me writhing about the bed in seconds, making noises like a dying animal, and all I can do is grip onto his hair and try not to implode completely.

Colton doesn't stop what he's doing, and something firmer, longer, and stiffer gently slides inside me a little way, and I almost experience my first inner explosion. I think it's the beginning of an orgasm, but because no one has ever touched me down there, and this is my first sexual experience, I have no idea what it should feel like, so I can only assume. I start panting and let go of him to grab the bedsheets as I focus on doing nothing but succumbing to how amazing this feels, lifting my hips in time to the way he's probing me. If I knew sex was like this, I probably wouldn't have been so subtle with Colton these past weeks. I would have just pushed him up against a wall and groped him.

"Good, huh?" His smug tone comes at me, but I can't answer, only breathe in short raspy gasps as waves of growing heat and tingles start in my toes and work their way up my limbs and into my pelvis, making me tremble uncontrollably. He continues to slide what feels like a finger gently in and out of me, only a little way. His tongue is back on the frontal portion as he sucks and licks my clitoris. I groan heavily in response to his question, pulling my knees up as my body can't stay still from the extreme ecstasy coursing through me.

"Oh, God, oh, God. Mark me. I swear if you don't get up and do this, I might eat you." It's a crazy, breathless whine as the need consumes me, and something big builds up in my stomach with nerve endings that feel like they're climbing. Even though what he's doing feels divine, and I'm so close to some weird precipice, I want to feel him instead of his hand. If that can send me into a spiraling mess of goo, then I want the real thing and experience what that can do.

Screw foreplay. Mark me already.

MARKED

Colton laughs at me, but my insane need must be waving at him and overwhelming him, too, as he only stops to put on the condom and gets on top of me right away, with no hesitation. Abandoning this slow and steady for instant gratification.

"So maybe next time foreplay will be lengthier. You're wet enough already that it shouldn't hurt much, so maybe we should just get this done, and then the second time, we can go slower ... enjoy it without the tension." He braces himself over me, leaning in to nuzzle his nose against mine. I open my eyes and stare straight into glowing amber eyes. The most gorgeous male I have ever known, nestling his body back onto mine. He doesn't say anything, just a kiss on the end of my nose as he catches me unaware with a little smooth slide of his pelvis and completely enters me. It doesn't give me time to tense up or expect it, just boom, he's inside me, and I'm thankful it's how he did it.

I gasp, as first the pleasure of him doing it expands and stretches me out in ways I never knew could be so amazing within my body, but then that sharp stab of pain as he completely buries himself inside me, which almost knocks my breath away as I wince and shudder underneath him. A slicing, almost snapping of something that pangs through my abdomen, no more severe than a horrible one-second period cramp, but enough to knock the wind out of my sails and the blood to drain from my face. My moan turns to yelp as my body stiffens, and I instantly go rigid in his arms, afraid to move or breathe. He pauses for a second before pulling out of me slightly and slowly and resting over me, coming to a complete stop. His eyes on mine intensely.

"You okay?" He leans in and kisses me tenderly on the mouth, seeking me out to make sure I am as I wriggle my body and try to recover quickly from that burning sensation traveling up and across my stomach. I only end up moving myself down so that he slides back to where he was, but a soothing warmth replaces the pain as he fills me again, and I moan under my breath at the reigniting pleasure.

"Don't stop." I breathe the words at him, clinging to his arms, closing my eyes tight, and gripping his biceps with fervor. He lowers his head and traces his tongue across my throat, distracting me for a second, igniting tiny sparks and goosebumps across my skin before moving his hips and pushing into me once more.

It's the most pleasurable pain I've ever known. Stingy, a little tender, yet it fades with every stroke he makes, pushing in and out until he finds a slow rhythm, and I adjust to better move with him. It's uncomfortable with the first few, but as I seem to self-lubricate once more and his body grinds into mine, bringing us together properly, it changes to that waving sensual deliciousness that I felt when he used his hand.

There is a tiny ache deep inside me that is being massaged by Colton, sliding in and out in slow, even thrusts. My gasps turn to moans once more, the warmth soothing away the worst of the pain and the slight burning inside dampening. He kisses me, caresses my face with one hand, tracing my cheek and eyebrow, and showers me with nibbles and small kisses across my jaw and mouth as he increases with speed and has me moaning, groaning, and arching under him. Over and over, growing faster together, as the minutes' tick by, and he intensifies what it does to me as he gets a little more aggressive with his thrusts.

He strains over me, careful not to crush me under him, and it leaves him free to move, focusing all his attention on the noises I'm making and adjusting to what he deems is something I like. The subtle changes in angle, rhythm, and ferocity, as he feels me out, listens, and responds to my body, intending to make me enjoy this.

He's attentive, and I thank the Fates they gave me a lover who knows what they're doing. I get that he probably wants to change position, but this works for me, and I'm not at that stage of complete immersion where I want to start experimenting. This is overwhelming enough and feels good as is, and I don't want to move in case it hurts again.

Sex is unique in a surprising way. There is nothing to compare to what it feels like, but I guess this could be horrendous poorly done. With Colton, it's mind-blowing, pure ecstasy, even with the first hurdle of pain, as he dominates my body and I become this heavy lump of uselessness wrapped around him. Completely surrendering to what he's doing to me, and can only make noises and take shallow breaths as the feeling builds up inside me to levels that blot out any ability to think beyond sensation.

"Marking hurts. I can't do anything about that, but it should take the edge off if I get you close enough to climax." Colton's voice comes through, right in my ear, low and breathy, husky, and so sexy in its hoarseness as he also revels in the pleasure of being inside me. Mid-thrust, mid-groan, but I'm so lost in darkness inside my body, overwhelmed by this growing mass of goodness as it crawls up my limbs and devours my skin and body slowly.

A hot wave of tingles and pleasure creeps up and wraps around me until it reaches my stomach and ties it in knots. My breathing is rapid; my moans are voiceless, breathless pants now. As it grows to an overwhelming crescendo, threatening to pull my mind and vision into this wave of something building, Colton leans down and, without prior warning, sinks his teeth into the soft curve above my breast, inflicting a piercing, stabbing agony that is a hundred times worse than breaking my hymen. In both pain and ecstasy, I cry out as his plan comes to fruition and everything inside me explodes magnificently, with an overwhelming orgasm.

The bite mark is numbed out as I lose control of my body completely. My first real climax devours me whole, and it's more powerful than I could ever have predicted. An explosion of stars blinds me and sparkles across my entire vision as I spasm and lose control of my limbs, my body pulsing and twitching with extreme mind-throbbing pleasure, and I cry out again.

For my first ever, it's probably the best thing I've ever felt in my life. It's like sneezing really hard, only a hundred times better, and it affects every nerve ending, leaving you wholly sated. It lasts only seconds, but those few delicious, long-drawn-out moments of complete loss of control are pure bliss as I soak Colton between my thighs. They leave me with residue tingling across my skin, inside my stomach and pelvis, which has me stretching out like a satisfied cat and enjoying the waves that fade out slowly with whimpers of approval.

As soon as the waves subside, I slump into a useless mass, and I come back to reality, completely aware that Colton is no longer inside me or biting me. I blink my eyes open to look at him. My skin flushed, and a little embarrassed that I had just had an all-out spasm attack and cried like he was killing me. There's no pain in my chest or between my legs, yet I don't want to look and see some deep bloody mess down there. Although it doesn't feel wet, there's literally no trace of blood on Colton's face from what I can see.

"Look at you." He grins at me, prodding me very lightly in the cheek where I can feel a buildup of heat and assume I'm rosy. I must look like I fell asleep and was woken suddenly, as my eyes are heavy and almost unfocused. I guess I look like you're supposed to after a mind-blowing orgasm, and he seems pretty proud of himself. The aftereffects are as good as during, and my body is weightless and relaxed, like a thousand years of stress and tension were lifted off in one amazing explosion. I could fly if I weren't wedged under him, and he looks equally relaxed and happy with himself.

"You feel up to it being my turn? All you have to do is complete the union, but you need to be on top." He points out, a hint of tiredness in his voice. I reach up and stroke my fingers across his jawline, loving the feel of subtle stubble as it grazes my delicate skin. I couldn't love this face anymore if I tried right now. He just blew my mind.

I blink at him, then down between us as I think about it, and as good as what I just experienced was, I honestly don't think I can do round two just yet. My body has gone on vacation, and my legs are like Jell-O. I'm not even sure I have the full use of them anymore. My lady parts are throbbing now the pleasure has stopped, and it hurts down there like something got snapped or grazed inside. Slightly burning. I feel tender and maybe not quite ready to put his manhood back in there, for tonight anyway.

"We might have to do some recovery time." I point out. The horror of a rematch must be evident on my face, but he only shakes his head at me, a smile breaking across that cute-boy expression, and my favorite dimples shine down at me.

"Trust me, as much as I hate to admit that our first time lasted under six minutes, which is pretty embarrassing, I already came. Due to lack of action, way too much build-up, and the excitement at finally being able to touch you. We don't need to go for round two yet. I climaxed, and it's very sensitive down there, so we both need some downtime before I make up for this sad attempt and give you a decent second go at it. You just need to get up and mark me to finish this.... You're mine forever, and ever, and ever, and ever ..." Colton buries his face in my neck and starts nibbling me playfully, torturing me with his entire body weight on top of me and pulling a fit of giggles out of me until I fight him off and bat him away.

Sore all over from his nips and grazing kisses and from that five o'clock shadow scratching me and blushing my skin. The fatigue I see in him is drifting my way.

"How am I supposed to get up if you don't get off of me?" I retort, too busy trying to calm the laughing fit he caused me and speaking and breathing simultaneously. Colton rolls off me to let me go, sighs heavily in a sound that is very much satisfaction, and splays out on the bed with his head tilted up at me.

"You just had to ask, *Princesa.*" He lies back, kicking out the sheets from under him as he does so, and pushes them down the bed. I sit up and yank my side back to aid him in his endeavors and get under them so he can pull them over him, and then I slide up onto him. I carefully crawl up, no shyness about being this way, and straddle his hips, so I don't sit on his now soft, flaccid manhood. I'm sure he wouldn't appreciate me squashing it when it's sensitive.

I cringe as my body connects with his, nestling down, tender underneath even though our union was brief, and I catch the look of guilt sweeping over his face before he smooths it out to conceal it. His hand comes up to trace where he marked me, and, finding the courage to look for the first time, I pay real attention to where it is. I'm shocked that there is no pain or throbbing, and I hadn't acknowledged it because it's already healed. There is no blood, no gash, but a perfect bite mark of dark scars that is smooth to the touch, almost like a tattoo in subtle hues. I stroke over it, eyes widening in wonder, and throw him a quizzical glance. I didn't turn, so I don't understand how it's healed.

"Marking isn't the same as inflicting a wound. It heals almost as you're doing it; it makes it permanent somehow so that when we turn, it never goes away—it's magical. I guess having sex while doing it makes a difference." Colton smiles at me, answering the unspoken question, and I nestle over him properly. Taking my time to find a less 'ouchy' position before relaxing slowly and tracing my fingers across his chest, trying to pick my spot to put my mark.

"Maybe I won't bother ... think I might have changed my mind." With a serious look on my face, I joke and sit back to put my hands on my hips instead. I'm feeling playful now I'm in control and calling the shots up here. Colton rolls his eyes and presses his pointer finger on my nose, like I'm a juvenile, before nestling both his hands around my hips.

"You won't be wanting sex from me again then, huh? I'm not that kind of guy anymore; no mark equals no mating. Even when the haze comes." He shrugs playfully, and I shake my head at him and make a 'hmm' noise as though I'm considering it. I like the teasing, it's cute, and I like Colton's playful, cheeky face even more now that I have no more doubts about us.

To be honest, the first time was maybe quick, and I'm suffering a little from it, but I definitely want to do that again and explore how much better it can be. I always heard the first time is nothing compared to when you master it and do it a few times, which means

I am in for a lifetime of amazing sex because Colton has skills. I don't want to miss out on that, and besides, I can't have this sexpot unmarked when the haze moves in. Femmes might kidnap him from me and hold him hostage until they get their fill. I need to mark my man.

"Such threats should be punished, Mr. Santo. I might just go to sleep." I smile as wickedly as I can at him and cast him a raised eyebrow smirk. Warm and cozy in the security that this is real, and he's mine.

"Go ahead. I'm kinda beat. I could use the sleep." He folds his arms behind his head casually, as though he doesn't care, and closes his eyes. It riles me enough to slap him on his pecs with impulsive anger. Sudden fury that he might not be joking causes an internal minor temper tantrum.

"Hey!" It's absolute outrage, but that chuckle he expels is an instant dampening tool. Colton opens his eyes and grins at me, chasing away any doubt that he was not playing, and he strokes his thumbs over my thighs. Cooling my fire and bringing me back to heel with a taming touch.

"Stop messing and make me your bitch already. You know I love you, and this ... it's holding up everything else. Mark me, woman, before I smother you against me and make you do it." There's a tone of seriousness in that, even if it is in good humor, and I know I'm only delaying because I'm nervous about this final step. It's been a lot, and I'm finally going to do it. Not just mark him but unbind something I've been trying to master for weeks, and that's terrifying to me.

When I bite him and taste his blood, it will finalize everything. I'll not only get the last memories we have of being apart of a fresh imprinting but a chance to harness the powers I possess entirely. I'll be Luna, just like that, from one bite, whether I'm ready or not. Whether I'm going to be a good Luna or not. It's a big step, and I am not prepared for any of it, but I need to take a leap of faith.

Fear won't make this easier. It will only make me work myself up into complete anxiety and make him think I have changed my mind. I lean down, inhale slowly to calm the inner trepidation, close my eyes, elongate my wolf teeth and sink into his chest, in a similar area to where he marked me.

There's a moment of complete abhorrence as I bite the soft, salty flesh of the man I adore, hating that I'm inflicting pain and wounding him. The taste of his blood almost makes me gag as it fills my mouth, choking me with its consistency and metallic saltiness. My fangs sink into tissue that's both warm and smooth as a hot liquid, thick and disgusting, hits my tongue. It's awful, but I'm almost wholly distracted a moment later when I am yanked away from what I'm doing as my mind fills with thoughts, feelings, memories, images, and whizzing moments of time all spinning around my head. Just like the first time we ever imprinted, only with less ferocity, less shock at the assault; it's a do-over, only with more potency in other ways.

I lose all sense of space and time as it happens, and I'm not even aware I've pulled my teeth out of him until his hand catches me by the wrist and then the other to steady me, so I don't fall. I'm breathless and feel like I've just been hit by a train for the second time in my life. The dizziness sends me reeling sideways, unable to hold myself taut. The room spins and slumps as Colton steadies me and gently helps me lie on the bed as reality comes back before he pulls me in against him and wraps me in his arms.

I take a moment to recover and come back to the land of the living, where my focus clears from hazy darkness, back to reality. Unlike the first time we imprinted, this time has a wave of surreal and dreamlike that lingers, and the taste of his blood trickles down my throat, warming me, filling me up with insane emotions before finally fading away to a gentle stroke down my legs. It's almost like a mental orgasm with less severity, and I blink my eyes open to find Colton pushed up against me, doing the same thing. Nose to nose, we open our eyes almost in unison before he breaks into a smile and kills the eerie silence.

"That was ... interesting. I feel drugged." His voice is low and husky, and he looks utterly exhausted now. Dark shadows under his eyes, which are a little lackluster in color, even in this dim lighting. It's mirrored in me, and my body has given up any hope of getting back out of bed anytime soon.

That's precisely what it feels like. As though we've been inhaling potent vapors that render you completely relaxed and giddily happy so that you lie around chilling like hippy stoners. Satisfied in every way, and you want to lie here and revel in it. I feel light and free, yet delirious in happiness, as though there are no worries left inside my brain. It's like a chemical high, and it leaves you temporarily content with everything in life.

"Me too." I sigh, fully sated and curling up in his tight embrace as he slides his arms around me firmly and pulls my body to fit his from toes to nose. His skin on mine, close contact in the best way, sharing air, which feels completely natural and so right. Like I was always meant to be wrapped up with him. There is nowhere else in the world I would rather be than here, and I want to stay this way forever. Heart healed, soul complete, and now I can sleep safe and secure beside him and never know that kind of loneliness again.

Colton reaches down and pulls the sheets over us, up to my shoulder, and reaches up over his head to press something attached to the headboard. All the lights in the room go off in unison, every single lamp, and dim glow, leaving us illuminated by the moon coming in through the window behind him as the curtains sit open. The darkness makes this seem more intimate somehow, and I lay my head against his chest, inhaling his unique smell, making me feel complete. Content. Home.

"So much for reading to your mom." I point out with a soft, almost inaudible tone, smiling as his arm comes back around me. He nuzzles his chin on top of my head as he gets comfy and yawns, stifling it with a fist over his mouth. I can feel genuine fatigue coming from him and how desperately he needs to sleep.

This was a big thing between us, and even though we should mark the occasion by staying up and talking about what this was, how momentous it was for both of us, I want to experience sleeping in his arms and waking up to him in the morning to start our lives as mates.

"I'm sure she'll forgive me, considering I not only marked my mate but restored the powers we lost. That deserves sleep, in a bed, with my new Luna in my arms." He yawns again, straining his voice, and then buries his face back in my hair with a deep exhale.

"My powers!" I squeak and shoot up to a sitting position, forgetting all about being too tired to move, extending my hands and staring at them as though they will suddenly look completely different, and I would somehow know. I didn't feel anything that was explicitly power-related, but then again, what would that even feel like?

I blink at them, turning them over in the dark until I catch Colton looking at me oddly. Focused entirely on my face with that hint of amused adoration I sometimes notice in him. Colton seems happy, which makes me all bubbly and gooey inside because I know I did that for him.

"What is it you expect to see?" He laughs at me and sits up to prop against the headboard to watch me, giving in to the fact I'm not about to let him sleep, and I shrug.

"I don't know, maybe glowing, or something like ..." I casually flick my hand towards the cabinet across the other side of the room, not sure what I'm doing, and then shriek in utter surprise when the contents on the top swipe off to the floor in a clattering heap that almost makes me have a heart attack. I gasp in shock, staring at the mess and then my hands, before turning to him like a kid who found a dollar in the street.

"Like that?" Colton looks impressed and not the slightest bit mad I sent a whole array of bottles and whatever onto the floor, making a substantial unsightly mess. I gawp at it and gently push the same motion at the already broken remains. Willing myself to do it again and squeal when they spread across the floor by about a foot as though an invisible brush swept them away. It's almost like breathing. I can willfully extend my touch and move things in ways I could never dream of before, and it excites me on a whole other level. My insides are bubbling like a mini volcano, and I jiggle on the bed, unable to contain my glee. The vapor energy, or whatever it is, is clear now, and I can't see it the way I did in the forest because I'm no longer battling the spell trying to bind it.

"It's your turn!" I bounce at him, grab his hand in excitement, and yank him a little, dying to see he's now unleashed whatever it is. Maybe he might have Sierra's blue glow, which would be totally cool, and perhaps a bit of a turn-on, but Colton shakes his head at me. Despite my juvenile attempts to haul him up with zero success.

"I don't even know what gifts I should have, so maybe that can await my mother waking up. Baby, it's late. Can we please sleep before I pass out and wake up in a tornado because you get carried away with being able to move things with your mind?" Colton tugs me back to him, despite my slight protest, and I fall against his chest and nestle in the crook of his arm. Relenting when his warm touch reminds me of how good it is to be held by him, and I exhale noisily. Huffing because I just found I have a new toy, and 'daddy' Colton is telling me to put it away and go to bed.

"We still have so much to figure out and do. We have all the time in the world and a minimum of two days before my mom might wake up. Can we concentrate on us, and this, for now, and sleep? God, I need sleep. In case I didn't mention, I haven't slept all that much since you left, and when I did, I dreamed about you and woke up feeling like shit. One good night with you in my bed might be the difference between a good day tomorrow and me strangling you to death for keeping me awake till stupid o'clock." He mockingly catches me by the throat, gently squeezes while smiling at me, and gets a scowl in response to the pretend threat, his eyes half-open. He looks exhausted.

"Nice. So romantic and loving. Is this what marking you brings out?" I point out with sass and get mauled with kisses scattered across my eyes and forehead for the effort. He drags me into the sheets, hauling us down to lie flat, and brings me back to my previous snuggled-up position in his arms, where he has my nose against his, except this time in a vice grip, so I can't go anywhere.

"My Luna, you're mine. We have so much shit still to get through and deal with. Let's just sleep on it and see what tomorrow brings. You aren't just Alora Dennison of the long-forgotten Whyte pack anymore. You're Luna Alora Santo, my mate, my heart, my soul, and we have an entire pack relying on us to get through whatever storm is coming our way. We will need to answer so many questions over the next few days. We also need to present you to your pack. You're one of us now." That voice of reason and a reminder that this little bubble of ours exists only in this room. There is a bigger world out there and issues we have yet to face.

"You're right. It's easy to forget the threats when it seems so safe in here with you. Your mom, the attacks, the future. It's all still so unclear, except for this one thing. We're never going to be torn apart again. I love you." I relinquish the fight and slide my arms around him as best I can while lying on my side. Curling up against him, skin to skin, and close my eyes to absorb how good he feels. No awkwardness, no strange residual embarrassment from having sex for the first time. Just this connection and a sense of home that he gives me make me feel like everything will be okay as long as he is by my side. We can face whatever is coming together with the pack and with whatever gifts we just released.

"I love you more. You're home, and I intend to keep you by my side forevermore." Colton kisses me on the forehead before snuggling in close, and the heavy exhale signals he's done with talking and looking to sleep with his mate in his arms.

For the first time, on the first day of our future lives, truly together.

For more info on L.T.Marshall books, please visit
www.LTMarshall.com

Made in the USA
Columbia, SC
03 September 2024

41525846R20300